Devil's Dilemma

Sirena Robinson

Supposed Crimes LLC • Matthews, North Carolina

Published in the United States.
Supposed Crimes LLC
Matthews, North Carolina

Second Edition

ISBN: 978-1-938108-56-3

www.supposedcrimes.com

This book is typeset in Goudy Old Style,
licensed by Ascender Corporation.

Books in This Series

Acknowledgements

To my wonderful betas who have worked on this novel: Adrian, Amy, Di: it couldn't have gotten here without you. Thank you so much for the ideas, the support, and sticking it out with me. A huge thank you to my parents, husband, and sister for their support through this as well. Tierra, without you annoying me to read every word I ever wrote, I probably wouldn't have ever been brave enough to let anyone else see it.

Prologue

"Do Mom and Dad know you're here?" A girl with striking green eyes and dark hair sat up, rubbing her eyes sleepily. She turned on her bedside lamp, offering a blinding smile to the man who stood near her window.

"Your parents were called away. They asked me to check on you. They'll be back before sunrise."

"Are they okay?"

The man in the white suit smiled reassuringly. "Don't worry. They'll be just fine, and home soon." He crossed the room and laid a hand on her head. "You should go back to sleep. I'll watch over you until they return."

Just as he was about to disappear, the child cleared her throat. "Uncle Gabe?"

Gabriel stopped and looked down at the child. "Yes, Amaya?"

"Will you stay and tell me a story? Just until I go back to sleep?"

"How old are you now?"

"Nine and three-quarters."

Amused, Gabriel perched on the side of the bed. "Well, I suppose little girls aren't too old for stories until they're ten human years. You've a few months left."

Amaya lifted the blankets and shifted over so that she was snug against the wall. "I want to hear about the meeting."

"I've told you that story a thousand times before." Gabriel humored the child by shifting to lean against the wall, his body completely on the bed, draping the blanket over his legs. He felt as out of place as he looked: an Angel in a frilly pink bedroom, with a slight child in purple pajamas curled up against his side.

"It's my favorite."

Sighing, he nodded. "As you wish. Now, how is it that you humans begin your stories?"

Amaya giggled, familiar with the exchange. "Once upon a time, silly."

"Right. Once upon a time, there was nothing but empty space. No planets, no people, no animals, nothing. And God was lonely by himself. So He created Heaven. And to keep Him company, He created Angels. Because the Angels needed something to care for, and because God craved more, He created Earth and humans. Angels were in charge of taking care of the people, and people were supposed to worship God. But eventually, one of the Angels, God's most precious Angel, decided he wanted to be in charge instead of God." Gabriel paused. "This is the scary part, remember?"

Amaya sighed. "I'm not seven anymore. I can handle it."

"Okay. Lucifer, the special Angel, tried to convince the other Angels to join with him and fight against God. And many of them did. They fought brutally. Many Angels died on both sides, and at the end, God was forced to create a special place for all of the Angels that betrayed him. So He created Hell. It was horrible, hot, ugly, and a place that no one was ever meant to go. Lucifer became the King of Hell—much the same way that God was the King of Heaven. They each had Angels, but God wouldn't let the others be called Angels. So they became Devils. They were evil, and received pleasure from causing others pain. But this fight left one thing undecided. Do you know what that is?"

"The people."

"Right. Both God and Lucifer wanted the people. When God made Earth, He never thought that they would go anywhere but Heaven. Lucifer wanted to get a chance to get some of them to Hell, so that his Devils could hurt them forever. This hurt God's heart because He knew that the only way to avoid an ongoing war, was to come up with a compromise. So He held a meeting. He met with Lucifer, one Angel, and one Devil. Do you know what they met about?"

"To decide how the world would end!"

Amused by her excitement, Gabriel nodded. "Yes. So eventually, after several hundred human years, they decided on a system. One person would be born, sometime, and would have a choice to make. Heaven or Hell. For twenty-nine years, this person would be shielded by a Veil placed on her by the Devil and Angel in charge. The Devil would get ten events to wipe out the natural inclination of humans to follow God. It would make her a blank slate. After twenty-nine years, both sides would be able to make their case. Then, on her thirtieth birthday, she would have to make her choice. This choice would have a great price. Do you know what that was?"

"Her life." Amaya's eyes got wide. "Why did she have to die?"

"Because this was not a choice that could be made lightly. By requiring her blood, both sides ensured that she would take it seriously and be sure about her decision."

"What happened if she decided not to pick?"

"That's the part that's in the Bible. The Apocalypse. Jesus, the Son of God, would come back and would take home everyone who had already given their soul to Him. Then, Lucifer would get seven years to convince humans to come to him. Anyone who refused to go with Lucifer after the seven years would be taken to Heaven and humans would cease to exist on Earth. A lot of people would die bloody, horrible deaths, and there would be a lot of suffering. This was to ensure that she would pick. Failing to would put the blood of millions on her hands. But both sides wanted her to Choose."

"Why is it so important?"

"Because it ensured that Earth would continue. If she Chose God, Devils would be stuck in Hell for a million years, and Angels would have free reign over Earth. After the million years were up, everything would go back to the way it was before, with both sides competing for souls. If she Chose Lucifer, it would be the opposite."

"What if she died before her birthday?"

"The Apocalypse. That was one of the rules. Neither side was allowed to kill her or the End of Days would start immediately. So no one wanted that. They both wanted her to pick. Not only would it delay the Apocalypse, but it would give one side a million years without interference from the other. In addition, if Heaven won, there would never be an End. People would go on forever. If Hell won, at some random point, after the million years ended, the Apocalypse would still happen, and the world would still end but only God would know when, and it would give Lucifer seven more years to make a play for souls."

"How would they know who gets to pick?"

"It was decided that it would be a birth out of death. No one would know what that meant until it happened, but everyone thought that it meant the Chosen would be born after her mother was already dead. She would be ripped from the womb, not born, and she would live a life of pain and suffering. All of those things: the events, the absence of God, the inability of the Angel to interfere until the twenty-ninth year, the pain and suffering—it gave an advantage to Lucifer. But God was confident that His creation would still pick Him."

"Has it happened yet?"

Gabriel stood, tucked Amaya into her bed, and pulled the chain to turn off the lamp. "I've told you a thousand times, my darling girl. It happened three years before you were born."

"You've never told me what happened," Amaya complained, pouting. "I want to know who she picked, and who the Angel and Devil were. You always promise to tell me, and you never do."

"One day you'll be old enough, and you will know the whole story." He bent and pressed a gentle kiss to her forehead. "But for now, it is time for little girls that are nine-and-three-quarters years old to go back to sleep. Your mother will have my hide if you're tired in the morning for school."

"Can't you please just tell me who she picked?"

The Angel smiled patiently and placed a hand on her forehead to nudge her into sleep. "That, my child, is a story for another night."

Chapter One

December 25th, 1999 - New York City
"BRAXTON'S ASLEEP, finally. He kept begging me to put his new bicycle together."

Miranda Winslow looked up at her husband from where she was picking up ripped wrapping paper. "I thought it would take longer than that. He was wound up from all those presents."

"And I'm going to spend all night putting things together." Allen knelt next to his wife and began picking up boxes and pieces of tape that were stuck to the carpet. "You've got to start getting pre-assembled toys. I am not good with screwdrivers."

"I know. That's what makes it so much fun. You can wield a scalpel like Picasso does a paintbrush, but you can't figure out which end of a screwdriver goes in the screw." She sighed, heaving herself to her feet, and took the trash bag he held out. "I wish you didn't have to work on New Year's though."

"Just be grateful I didn't have to work Christmas. And I'll be off by midafternoon New Years' Eve. It'll be fine."

"If you say so." Miranda walked into the kitchen to set about pouring herself a cup of tea. "It was good seeing you home all day. It's been a long time since you had some time off."

"That's typical residency. I'll be an attending in another two years, Miranda. Next year I'm up for Chief Resident, and the schedule will be even worse, especially considering that I'm doing emergency medicine. I'm not going into dermatology or a nine-to-five specialty."

Miranda put her hands on her hips and glared at her husband. "Allen, give it a rest. I married you straight out of college. I put up with thirty-hour intern shifts, days on end when I didn't see you, when you slept at the hospital for weeks at a time. I gave birth while you were in a final. I have been handling this as long as you have. I know how to be a doctor's wife. Now, give me a little credit."

Grinning, Allen crossed the room and slid his arms around her. "I'll give you all the credit in the world, Mandy. You're the love of my life." He bent and scooped her up into his arms. "What d'ya say we go upstairs and work on giving Brax a brother or sister?"

Miranda looped her arms around his neck. "I say it sounds like a plan."

Allen had gotten to the second step when the doorbell rang. Before he could set her down, it rang again, followed immediately by persistent pounding. Brows knit in concern, he placed Miranda on the landing, hurried through the house to the front door and opened it without looking through the peephole. Had he looked to see who it was first, he never would have answered.

"Dad."

Robert Winslow pushed past his son into the house, closed the door, and turned the lock. "I need to talk to you."

Allen crossed his arms and blocked his father from going further into the house. "There are such things called telephones. I told you the last time that I didn't want to come here anymore. I don't want Braxton around this type of life."

"This is important." He shoved past his son and paused to kiss Miranda on the cheek. "Nice to see you again, Miranda. I don't suppose you have any coffee on, do you?"

Annoyed, but always a gracious hostess, Miranda moved back toward the kitchen. "I'll put a pot on. Can I get you something to eat? We have leftover turkey that I can warm up."

"Thanks, but no. I grabbed a burger at a truck stop a hundred miles ago." Robert went into the living room, sat down on the couch, and gestured to the chair. "Well, sit down, Allen. We need to talk."

Clenching his teeth, Allen sat. "Dad, I told you, this is not the life I want. It isn't what Miranda wants, and it's not what we want for our son."

"I love how you assume I'm here about hunting. Did it ever occur to you that I just missed my son?"

"Aren't you here about hunting?"

Robert balked for a second, then nodded. "Yes. I am. But you still shouldn't assume things. I need your help."

"Forget it."

"No. This you'll want to hear. This is important. I've been hearing rumblings. There are rumors going around that the Chosen will be born soon."

"Where did you hear this?"

"Some crackpot psychic. But it's enough to have the demons sitting up and taking notice. They killed her when she wouldn't give them any more information. Apparently, some higher-ups in the demon food chain are taking the rumors seriously. They think the Chosen will come within the next few years—if he isn't already here."

"You're sure?"

"As sure as I can be. I mean, there's no being exact. It's supposed to be a big mystery, but there haven't been rumors like this in centuries."

"Okay, so let's say it is true. What does it matter? There's nothing we can do to stop it. There's no way to even find out when or where or who. It's supposed to be a complete surprise, Dad, you know that."

"I want you to come with me, catch a high ranking demon, and torture it until it spills whatever information it has. I know it won't be anything that we can completely rely on, but it might be a starting point. If the Chosen is coming, we need to get to him before the demons do."

"And how do you suggest we do that?"

Before Robert could answer, they all jumped at the sound of a slamming door and turned to see Braxton run down the stairs and launch himself at Miranda, tears streaming down his face. Experienced with the bad dreams of small children, Miranda scooped him up and went straight for the rocking chair in the corner of the living room. Allen glared at his father—the message clear: do not say anything in front of the kid.

"Tell Mommy about it, baby. What happened in your dream?"

"I saw an Angel and a mean woman who killed two people. She made them crazy. And there was a baby. It was screaming, but no one would make it stop. The woman laughed and laughed, and there was a body with blood all over it."

Robert and Allen exchanged a panicked look, both of them realizing that Braxton was not describing a dream. Robert stooped next to the rocking chair. "Braxton, can you look at me?"

Slowly, Braxton lifted his head, his hands clenched in his mother's hair. "Who are you?"

"I'm Daddy's father. I need you to tell me something about your dream. Can you do that?"

Tearfully, Braxton nodded. "I'll try."

"Can you tell me their names? The Angel and the woman. Did you hear their names?"

Braxton closed his eyes, thinking back over the dream. He'd been lying next to the vent, trying to hear what Mommy and Daddy were talking about, and then he must have fallen asleep. He remembered standing in a hospital, watching a man and woman come in bleeding. Doctors had been rushing around, trying to save them. There was a baby screaming, and the woman with black hair and a red dress had been happy that the two people had died. She had called him Gabriel, and they had talked about a veil. Was someone getting married? The Angel had told him his name was Gabriel. But what was the woman's name?

"It started with an A. And Gabriel. The Angel was Gabriel."

Allen rubbed his hands over his face. "Miranda, take Braxton upstairs."

Knowing something was going on, but understanding that her four-year-old didn't need to hear the conversation, Miranda nodded. "I'll be back as soon as he's asleep."

"Salt the windows and put a protection bag under his mattress."

Miranda looked startled when Robert spoke, and her eyes flew to her husband, seeking reassurance that nothing was wrong. But Allen nodded reluctantly. "Do it."

Robert waited until Miranda was safely out of earshot before speaking. "That settles it. The Devil was Alaria. Alaria and Gabriel are the ones in charge of the Choosing. And your son just saw it."

"He's never had a vision before, Dad. Never."

"My grandfather had visions. He could see the future sometimes. Really important events. He saw his own death, and the death of my father. Dad couldn't, neither could I. And I don't remember you ever having any. You were a Healer, I'm a pure Hunter. Dad wasn't a true Warrior, but he wanted to be one more than anything else in the world. It's possible that Braxton is a Seer."

"Braxton is going to be a normal child. I am not telling him about this life. I am not telling him about what you do."

"It's in his blood. And he obviously just had a vision about the birth of the Chosen. I just wish he was older so that we could get a better sense about when it was going to happen. It could be tomorrow, or fifty years in the future."

"Or it could have already happened."

"Don't be idealistic. If it has already happened, it was very recently. The Choosing certainly hasn't taken place or there would be no more demons on Earth. If he were near the age of the Veil coming off, there would be much more activity."

"This is not the life for him."

"That should be his choice to make. And it is our job to keep him safe. If the demons find out that he can see the Chosen, they'll hunt him until the ends of the Earth. He must be kept safe. He must play some role in the Choosing."

"No." Allen stood up and strode purposefully toward the door. "He is my son. This is my family. Miranda and I decided long ago that we wanted nothing to do with the Warriors. You're not going to come in here and convince my son that you're some sort of superhero. I want you to leave now, Dad. I'll keep my family safe. You don't have to worry about that. And as far as I am concerned, it was nothing more than a bad dream, and if you ever tell him any different, I'll see that we move so far away that you'll never in a thousand years lay eyes on any of us again. Have I made myself clear?"

Robert walked to the door as well. "I only want to help you, to help Braxton. But I'll go. He's your son, not mine. And when you get him killed by trying to keep the wool pulled over his eyes, it's me you'll come to for vengeance." He placed his hands on Allen's shoulders. "That was a vision, son. Not a dream. And when he figures out what is going on, he will want the answers that I can give him."

"I'll give him answers to any questions that he has. Your life is not our life, Dad. It's not the life for my son." Without any gentleness, Allen placed his hand on Robert's shoulder and very sternly pushed him through the doorway.

"He's important, Allen. If he can see the Chosen, he might be the key to finding him. We need to encourage him to explore his ability. We need to find out if there is any way to induce the visions, to make them happen. Once he's older, he could be the greatest weapon that our side has against the demons in the race to locate the Chosen after the lifting of the Veil."

"No."

Without waiting for Robert to say another word, Allen closed the door in his face and turned the handle lock and the deadbolt. Then he did what he hadn't done in years. He went to the pantry and found a container of salt and spent the next twenty minutes lining the tops of every door and window in the house. By the time he was done, Miranda had come back downstairs.

"What's going on, Allen?"

"Nothing. Visions run in my family. Unless we tell him differently, he'll think they're nothing but dreams."

"Your father said he saw the Chosen."

"No. Braxton didn't see the Chosen. He's a normal little boy, Miranda. He's going to have nothing to do with this. None of us are." He went to Miranda and wrapped his arms around her, offering comfort with his warmth. "Don't worry about it."

"You had me salt upstairs. That's not nothing."

"Because there's no telling what could be following my father. He always brings trouble, and it isn't much of a stretch to think he brought the supernatural kind, too."

"Do we have something to worry about?"

"No. We both grew up with Warriors. We can handle anything that comes at us. I don't think anything will, but it's fine. There's nothing to worry about. I promise."

Chapter Two

December 31st, 1999 - New York City
DIONNE JAVENSEN looked down in dismay at the ratty, stained clothes she had stolen from the Goodwill store down the street. She huddled in a corner of the tiny apartment she and her boyfriend were squatting in, wrapped in a threadbare blanket as a barrier to the cold, and perched on the only piece of furniture they had: a dingy mattress thrown on the floor, bare of sheets and pillows. Her stomach rumbled, reminding her that she hadn't eaten, and she hoped that Jack would bring food home along with the drugs.

Food had become more and more important to her lately. She'd found herself ravenous, even when she was high, when normally the last thing on her mind was what to put in her mouth. She glared at her stomach when it growled and scowled at her belly, unaware at how it protruded from her thin, frail frame almost comically and announcing to the world what was happening to her.

When the next hit was the most important goal, it was hard to drum up the interest in spending money on birth control pills or condoms. So they didn't. And over their three-year relationship, Dionne had suffered several miscarriages. But something was different about this one. It was stronger. And by the time Dionne had realized, not only that she was pregnant, but that she wasn't going to miscarry, it had been too late for an abortion, even if she had had interest in finding the money to pay for it—which honestly, she hadn't.

So they'd lain on their mattress, flying free on a high of heroin, and they had developed a plan. She would deliver the creature, and they would tie it in a bag and dump it in the river. By the time the body was found in the spring, there wouldn't be enough of it left to identify. They'd be free of it.

That was until it started moving, and kicking, and constantly reminding her of its presence. It took what little food she ate and interrupted both her highs and her sleep with the constant movements. Over the past several months, Dionne had begun to regard her baby as inhuman, an evil thing that stole everything from her. And the longer the pregnancy went, the more drugs she took—still hoping against hope that the thing would die on its own. Finally, sick of hearing her complain about the evil creature residing in her uterus, Jack had come up with a solution. Cut it out.

In the grasp of an unbelievably powerful high, it seemed like the perfect solution. After it was gone they would be free. Free to go back to sweaty sex and nights uninterrupted by the kicking of the thing. Their minds made up, Jack had left the apartment to steal a knife from the grocery store down the street, and she had set about preparing their next hit, using the last of the drugs they had in the apartment. Knowing that Jack was coming back with more to get them through the night, she used more than she normally would have.

Dionne carefully poured bottled water into a metal spoon. She placed the spoon over the flickering flame from the candle burning in front of her. Making sure not to spill the water as it heated, she reached into a baggie and pulled out two syringes and a small packet of a dark brown substance. It was a shame they couldn't afford the good stuff, but anything would do in a pinch. Sticking a finger into the water to test the temperature, she smiled and crumbled the tan substance into the spoon. Careful, don't want to spill any. Too expensive to waste like that. She used the tip of the syringe to mix the heroin into the water until it dissolved completely. She used her teeth to pull the depressor out of each syringe and carefully poured a dose into each, tapping to make sure there's no air. Getting air in a vein hurts. Definitely don't want to do that again.

Dionne looked up when Jack entered the room, a wicked looking butcher knife in his hand. Instead of fear, relief washed over her. She took a deep breath, her fingers tingling and a knot of anticipation forming in her stomach. Running her hands over her protruding belly in what should have been a loving motion, she smiled, stretching her skin over the sharp bones in her face. In mere minutes, it would be over. Soon the creature living inside her would be dead, and she could move on with her life. After it was over, she'd make sure to go downtown and get condoms at the free clinic, too. She had no desire to go through this ever again.

Anxious to get her fix, she handed Jack his needle, waiting impatiently while he prepped a vein and injected the liquid. Within seconds, he was swept away on his trip, and he grinned maniacally as he picked up the knife. Following his example, she quickly injected the drug, choosing to main-vein it, inserting the needle into the big vein in her forearm, hoping for an even more intense trip. She closed her eyes, waiting for euphoria to sweep her away and for the world to spin away. The drugs hit and she let herself float away on a wave of bliss. Pleasure radiated out from the injection site until her whole body tingled. Slowly, she opened her eyes, wanting desperately to see the bright colors and lights that always manifested when she was high. Instead of the beauty—she saw demons.

The black figures floated around the room, their red eyes glowing menacingly as they mocked her. Then the floor opened up, and she saw into Hell. She saw the Lake of Fire with bodies chained to the bottom, their eyes wide and unseeing, their mouths open in a perpetual scream that was neither heard nor acknowledged. A red sky was dotted with black clouds, and in the distance, she saw a castle made out of onyx that managed to look both frightening and beautiful at the same time. As Jack approached her with the knife, she realized that the demons wanted her to kill the child. Something about that realization broke through the drug-induced haze, and she threw up her arms, intending to stop him from cutting her.

Jack was bigger, and he was stronger. No matter how hard she struggled, he was determined to do what they had agreed to do. He slashed, cutting through the flesh on her arms, holding them out of the way and plunging the knife into her over and over, spraying her blood on the floor, on the walls, on his own face. Gasping for breath, writhing in pain, using her last bits of life, she screamed like the Devil himself was chasing her, as if the fate of the whole world depended upon her getting the attention of someone who would stop Jack from continuing his demonic mission.

Dr. Allen Winslow rubbed his eyes tiredly. He'd been on his ER shift for nearly twenty-four hours and was half an hour away from being able to go home to kiss his wife and son goodnight before collapsing for several hours of much needed sleep. Then, he would get up and celebrate New Year's with a four-year-old who was just starting to notice when his Daddy wasn't home on time. He'd been scheduled to get off at noon, but a last minute cancellation by his replacement had required him, as the low man on the totem pole, to put in a double shift on New Year's Eve.

Allen checked his watch out of sheer boredom and smiled when he saw the position of the hands. Eleven-thirty-five. Only twenty-five minutes until he could leave, and the ER was nearly silent. The few patients that had come through the doors in the past twelve hours had been either released or sent up to various wards for continued treatment. They were running a skeleton crew with only two doctors and five nurses, which was less than half of the staff normally on the floor, even at eleven-thirty at night. If only it could stay quiet for thirty more minutes, the senior resident on the night shift would arrive, and Allen could go home.

As it always did, fate seemed to have another ending in mind. At eleven-forty-five, the call came in that there was an ambulance en route with a stabbing victim. The paramedics were doing CPR with little response, the second victim was undeniably dead, and the one barely hanging on seemed to be nine months pregnant. When he heard the description of the patient, Allen's head snapped up. Obstetrics was as understaffed as the emergency room due to the holiday, and he knew the resident on duty was performing an emergency C-section and hysterectomy that had come in through the ER two hours earlier. Knowing they were likely facing what would be a futile situation, he rubbed his face wearily and turned to the rest of the staff.

"Kathy, go upstairs and get an infant intubation kit and a baby warmer. We have a full term stabbing victim coming in, and OB's busy. We're probably going to have to deliver down here. Mika, I need a surgical tray set up in trauma room one. Jake, come with me to the ambulance bay."

The two doctors rushed to the ambulance bay just as sirens sounded at the end of the street. Within seconds, paramedics were unloading two gurneys. One, a man, was staring through dead eyes, with not even a whisper of a breath gurgling through the blood starting to congeal around the jagged wound on his throat. Jake, the intern, automatically took charge of that patient, going into a trauma room to go through the useless motions of trying to bring a dead man back to life.

The other patient, a woman, was still alive. Her chest and legs were riddled with stab wounds, and she was losing more blood than Allen had known could possibly be contained in the human body. Her eyes were wide and glassy, nearly unresponsive, and her breath was gurgling, bubbles of blood coming out of her mouth as the paramedics held a mask over her face to force oxygen into her lungs. There were claw marks on her protruding stomach that looked as if someone had tried to rip the baby from her womb.

"I'm Dr. Winslow. You're at Mercy Hospital in Brooklyn. Do you know your name?" When there was no response, he looked to one of the paramedics. "Do we know who she is?"

"ID says Dionne Javensen. Twenty-seven. Found drug paraphernalia at the scene, along with alcohol and used syringes. The other guy, Jack Samson, was high as a kite and slit his own throat when we tried to take her. She's been unresponsive the whole way here. She had a heartbeat on the scene, and we've been able to keep it going with compressions. Temp one-oh-three. Eyes sluggish, but responsive. We counted thirty stab wounds, primarily to the chest and legs, none on the abdomen. Fetal heart rate is one hundred, and the fetus is in distress."

Allen took over pumping the air mask as they raced through the sliding doors and into the bright lights of the emergency room. They turned a corner sharply, barely managing to avoid tipping the gurney. The door to one of the treatment rooms slid open with a quiet whisper, allowing them access. Blood splattered the floor and the pristine white sheets of the hospital bed as they rolled the gurney next to it. Next door, they could hear the intern declaring a time of death on the man. He exchanged a dark look with Kathy and then turned to the rest of his team.

"Prepare for an emergency C-section. Get the crash cart, charge to three-sixty. Let's see if we can get her back into a rhythm. Round of epi and atropine. Move her on my count. One, two, lift!"

Allen took the paddles from the nurse and pressed them to the naked chest of Dionne Javensen. He forced hundreds of volts of electricity through her body and watched it jump on the table. The monitor beeped twice and then went flat. He waited fifteen seconds to see if that would change, and then nodded to Kathy.

"Another round. We'll try this one more time."

Again, they went through the motions, and again, the line fell flat. Kathy shook her head. "A-fib. We're getting no cardiac activity, Doctor."

"Okay, open up the trauma surgery tray. Resume CPR. Clamp to Kathy. Nine-blade to me."

A young nurse, her scrubs splashed with blood, paled as she reached for the scalpel. "Dr. Winslow, shouldn't we get her up to OB?"

"No time. They have one resident who's in surgery right now. This woman is dead. We have less than five minutes to get this baby out. Call the NICU and notify them that we probably have a critical baby coming up."

With that, Allen gripped the scalpel and made a deep incision in the woman's abdomen. Working quickly, he and Kathy pulled apart the skin, slicing through the seven layers of tissue before reaching the uterus, exposing the swollen organ. He carefully made a cut, and pulled a tiny infant from the womb. Within seconds they clamped the umbilical cord and cut it, separating the infant from its dead mother. The baby wasn't breathing, and he hastily dried it, trying to provide enough stimulation to induce a cry, a breath—anything. He carried the baby to the warming tray, suctioned out the nose and mouth, and began vigorously massaging the chest.

"Come on, baby, breathe. Prep the paddles, charge to fifteen." He took the smaller paddles normally reserved for direct placement onto a heart. "Clear."

The baby's body leaped, and then with a weak cry, she began to breathe. Allen bundled her in a blanket and placed an oxygen mask on her face. Kathy, always a step ahead, had already placed an IV and started a drip before he could even ask her to. They took the time to exchange one jubilant look at having saved a life together before the harsh reality came crashing back down on them.

"Get this baby upstairs. Time of death on Dionne Javensen—eleven-fifty-seven p.m., December 31st, 1999. Time of birth for baby Javensen—twelve midnight, January 1st, 2000."

That was how, in a brief moment between morning and night, between one day and the next, between years, centuries, millennia, Griffin Elizabeth Javensen was born. In that brief moment, when time stood still, as death gave way to life, and child was ripped from mother, she took her first breath. With that breath, she was Chosen.

In the moment that she was Chosen, two figures appeared in the emergency room, seen by no one, the presence of each a surprise to the other. They looked at each other with thinly veiled hostility, then, almost in sync, turned to observe the scene that was playing out in front of them.

"I'm surprised to see you here, Angel."

"Did you think I would miss the birth and the placing of the Veil? Why would I trust a demon to protect the child from any interference for the next thirty years?"

"Human years are supremely insignificant, Gabriel. To us, I need only protect her for a heartbeat. And it would serve you well to remember that I was once an Angel, too."

Gabriel, in his white suit, with his blond hair perfectly slicked back from his perfect face, scowled, his expression leaving no doubt at his displeasure. "That's true. Until you betrayed our Father and chose to follow the Fallen One. You've been a consistent pain, Alaria. I would never dream of allowing you to handle something so important on your own. How long have you known tonight was the night? I just received notice moments ago."

"As did I. I arrived just as they brought in the mother. She died."

"Obviously, her soul is yours—as is the soul of the father."

"We did quite a number on them. If I'd known they were the parents, I'd have done better."

"Which is precisely the reason Lucifer and Father decided that neither of us was allowed to know in advance. I don't have to remind you to follow the rules, do I?"

Irritated, the woman sighed. "I'm not going to risk having this taken away from me. This is my chance to get the seat to the left of my master. I'm not going to let anything stand in the way of that. No, I'm not going to break the rules. We'll place the Veil to guard her from both demonic and angelic interference, and then I'll begin my events. Unless I kill her, you'll have no reason to interfere until we lift the Veil in twenty-nine years."

Looking mildly amused, Gabriel offered a tight smile. "I won't interfere, but I do plan to exercise my right to be present for your events. Like it or not, we're going to be seeing each other regularly for the next three decades."

Alaria, resplendent in black and red leather, shrugged her shoulders. "Unfortunate as that may be, I suppose I'll have to come to terms with it. I plan to make my events count, Gabriel. By the time I'm through with her, she won't believe in God or Angels, or anything but Satan. When she chooses Lucifer over a God that has continually forsaken her, my brethren will rule the Earth, and you and yours will be banished to the pearly gates, unable to guard a single one from whatever we decide to do to them."

"It's a risk we're all taking, Alaria. We're confident that the innate goodness of humans will win out in the end. This is about the humans deciding whether or not the apocalypse happens and which side they want. She is randomly chosen as a representative for the entire human race. You're given your events to wipe her clean—to make her neutral. Not to ensure your victory."

"In this case, it's the same thing. Let's get this over with. Are you ready to place the Veil?"

Together, Angel and Devil raised their hands and created a smoky screen of silver silk. It drifted through the emergency room, swirling around the various nurses and staff standing between it and its goal. When it found the infant, weakly crying in the incubator as the nurse waited for the elevator, it enveloped her within it, dissolving into her skin until nothing was left. Their job done, the two turned back to each other. Gabriel smiled, his lips pressing together in a thin line, making him look at once annoyed and grimly satisfied.

"It is done. Can I assume that you're not using any of your events tonight?"

Alaria pondered that for a long moment and then shook her head. "She's too young. There's no point in starting before she's old enough to understand what's happening." She smiled sharply. "No, she's safe for tonight." Her eyes narrowed and she glared at the Angel. "What have you planned, Gabriel?"

"I'm just wondering if there's a reason for the infant to be disabled. If that somehow factors into your plan."

"I need her healthy. The birth is not supposed to provide me a vegetable to play with." She shrugged carelessly. "Do what you will."

"I trust you'll give me advance notice of your events before they occur so that I may be present?"

"Not a chance in Hell, but I'm sure you'll find out somehow. You always do."

With that, Alaria disappeared in a cloud of black smoke and blue flame. Shaking his head at the dramatics, Gabriel crossed the hospital with nothing more than a thought and looked over the shoulder of one of the doctors working on the infant. He slowly stretched out a hand and laid it on her small, red forehead.

"Here is your miracle, my child. Be healed. And always remember that God has not forsaken you. He awaits you on the other side of your challenge. Choose well, and do not forget who made you."

The hair rising on the back of his neck, he turned slowly and saw a small boy standing in the middle of the mayhem, people walking right by him without seeing him. Interested and grateful Alaria hadn't realized he was there, Gabriel walked over. The little boy looked up at him, his face wrinkled with barely restrained tears.

"I want to go home to my Mommy and Daddy. I don't want to be here. That lady is mean."

"That lady is a Devil, child. I don't know why you are here or how you can see this, but you must do exactly as I say. I am an Angel. My name is Gabriel. If you ever come somewhere like this again, you must immediately close your eyes and think about home. You cannot be here, Braxton. It is too dangerous. You are important. I don't yet know how, but I am sure that you are. I want you to practice right now. Close your eyes and think about your bed. Now, try to go there."

It took a couple tries, but soon, Braxton was gone, and Gabriel was left standing by himself to ponder the most recent development. The appearance of the boy had been unexpected, and piqued his interest. It was something he intended to look into, and keep to himself.

Could the night get any longer? It was four A.M., and instead of being in bed next to Miranda, Allen was walking into the waiting room to tell two middle-aged people that not only had their daughter been stabbed to death, they had a grandchild that would most likely be severely brain-damaged from the drugs their daughter had taken throughout her pregnancy. Oh, and by the way, that her boyfriend had tried to carve the baby out of her abdomen with a butcher knife before slitting his own throat.

"Mr. and Mrs. Javensen?" A couple looked up at the question, and Allen turned in their direction. As he walked, he took in their appearance. Both were in their early fifties and looked tired. The man was wearing an untucked shirt and mismatched socks. He had deep lines etched in his face and eyes that were both filled with apprehension and resignation. His wife was younger by a year or two and sat straight, clasping and unclasping her hands nervously. She was a slight woman and was dwarfed next to her husband. When she looked up at him, instead of apprehension, he saw hope. A hope he was about to dash to pieces. Resignation in his own eyes, he extended his hand to each of them in turn. "My name is Dr. Winslow. I treated your daughter when she was brought in tonight. Would you come with me to my office, please?"

Robert Javensen shook his head, his eyes shining with tears, and his face set in a mask of resignation. "Did she OD? Is it finally over?"

Sighing, Allen nodded. "Drugs were involved, yes, but that's not the extent of it. I really think this would be better done in private, sir. Please, come back to my office."

The woman, a slight brunette in jeans and a flowered blouse, her hair in a messy bun, and her face devoid of makeup and streaked with tears, shook her head. "No. We've been waiting for this call for ten years, Dr. Winslow. We lost our daughter a long time ago. For years, we put her in rehab, paid for her to get clean, to get an apartment, helped her get jobs only to have her go back, to have her rob us blind, spend every penny she made on drugs, to show up to family functions high. Nothing we could do helped her. I'm sorry, but no, Dr. Winslow. We will not come back to your office. Just tell us if she's dead or not, and let us go home and go to bed. Tomorrow, I expect we'll either be making arrangements for another stint in rehab or for a funeral. Just please tell me which one." Margaret Javensen put her face in her hands, the action of a woman who had simply had too much and who had been pushed just a little too far.

Nodding, Allen sat down on the coffee table and reached out to cover Margaret's hands with his own. "Your daughter was brought in a few hours ago with severe stab wounds. She did not have a pulse or a blood pressure. She wasn't breathing on her own. She also appeared to be about thirty-four weeks pregnant. We did everything we could, but the blood loss was too great and the wounds too severe. We shocked her heart, performed CPR, and administered the maximum amount of medication, but it didn't work. We performed an emergency C-section, and the baby was born not breathing. We shocked her and were able to restore the heartbeat to a regular rhythm. The infant is breathing on her own and is upstairs in our Neonatal Intensive Care Unit. Would you like me to take you to her?"

Margaret stared at him blankly. She blinked several times, struggling to make sense of what she had just been told and trying to realign her reality to make room for a new being. "She was pregnant? She did drugs. She drank. The baby can't be healthy. How is it even alive?"

"It's too soon to know that. In the interest of being completely honest, there is a strong likelihood that there will be some level of brain damage. There may be physical disabilities or mental impairments. With the amount of heroin in Dionne's system—if she sustained that amount of use throughout the pregnancy, it's improbable that the infant will ever be normal."

Margaret sighed deeply and wiped tears away from her eyes. "I'm fifty years old, Dr. Winslow. You expect me to take on a special needs baby?"

Robert shook his head before Allen could answer and reached for his wife's hand, holding it between both of his. "We simply can't go through that again. What we went through with Dionne—it nearly destroyed us.

We're good people, but there's only so much you can ask of us. What papers do we need to sign to give her up?"

"Mr. Javensen, I understand that you're tired and that you've been to Hell and back. This baby should be dead, but she's fighting. There's no guarantee that she'll be impaired. It's a likelihood, yes, but her even being alive is a miracle. She needs her family. What happened to Dionne was not your fault. Sometimes a child just chooses the wrong path. Before you give up your grandchild, I have to ask you, if Dionne hadn't died tonight, would you have left her here, or would you have tried again?"

Margaret straightened; her face defiant; incredulous that anyone would even question her dedication to her child. "She was our daughter. No matter what she was, we loved her, and we always did everything that we could to help her get better. We have always tried to save her."

"Then take my advice. Do the same thing for your granddaughter. Try to save her."

Chapter Three

April 21st, 2004 - New York City
Griffin was lying on her bed, a coloring book open and crayons on the bed in front of her with the blue one, her favorite, clutched in her little hand. Mommy's birthday was tomorrow, and she had decided to make a card with rainbows and teddy bears on it. It had to be a surprise, so she had stayed awake until she heard Mommy and Daddy go to bed. After hearing their door shut, she had turned on the princess lamp next to her bed and gotten out her crayons and a coloring book. She'd carefully studied each page until she'd found one that had been perfect. It had even said "Happy Birthday" across the top of it. Griffin had labored over writing "I Love You, Mommy" in very wobbly handwriting underneath the bears that decorated the page.

Her task nearly done, she didn't notice when her eyes started drifting shut. She blinked and jerked once, then gave into sleep and sank to the bed. Her eyes drifted closed and the crayon rolled from between her fingers and slid onto the floor. Just as effortlessly, Griffin slid into sleep and into the dream.

She rode on a dragon. The dragon was beautiful, with blue and purple scales that breathed green fire and sailed through black clouds amid a red sky. It was so incredible that it surpassed any fairy tales that she had ever heard of, and it immediately captured her attention. She stretched out over the neck of the majestic creature, holding on tightly, and leaned over as far as she could, her eyes voraciously taking in everything.

Then, without warning, she fell, careening through the clouds, the only breath she could manage coming in a piercing scream. Her arms and legs flailed as she tried to fight the effects of gravity. Then the fall slowed, and she was placed gently on the ground.

Tears of terror rolled down her face, and Griffin clutched her teddy bear tightly to her chest and turned in a circle, her footie pajamas protecting her sensitive feet from the cracked, hot ground. Scared and confused, she began walking toward the shores of a big lake, thinking that if it was anything like the beach, there would be people down there who might be able to tell her how to get home or who would call Mommy and Daddy to come and get her.

The closer she got to the water, the worse it smelled—like the eggs in the fridge that one time that they had gone away for a week and the electricity had gone off. The whole house had smelled bad for hours. Daddy had turned green when he'd opened up the fridge. Steam rose from the black water, and as she got closer, she realized that it was boiling.

Knowing better than to touch the roiling water, she tiptoed to the edge and peered in. Dead, staring eyes and silent, screaming faces peered back at her. She screamed, jumping back from the edge of the lake, and ran away. There were people—thousands of people—chained in the lake, boiling, unable to speak or see.

"It's horrible, isn't it?"

Griffin turned at the sound of another voice and found herself looking at a woman who had to be the most beautiful person she had ever seen. She had long, thick black hair, wore a skin tight red leather shirt that had no straps and had leather cord crisscrossing down her back, tying it tightly. She also wore black leather pants, spike heels, and had her nails painted blood red. Her face was classic curves and lines, and her eyes glittered gold in the hazy red light.

"Who are you? Where am I? Where're Mommy and Daddy? Can you take me home?"

The woman smiled, holding out her hands, palms up to stop the wave of questions. "Whoa, Griffin. One question at a time. My name is Alaria. You're dreaming. I can only talk to you in your dreams, and it's very important that we get to talk. This is the only place I can bring you that's safe enough for us to talk openly. You can go home anytime you want. All you have to do is concentrate on waking up and you will."

"I don't know you."

"No, you don't. But I know you. You're a very special little girl. You're going to do very special things. Will you walk with me?"

Naturally a friendly child, Griffin took the hand Alaria offered. Together, they walked along the bank of the lake toward a sprawling black castle that pierced the sky with its towers. "What very special things?"

"We'll get to that. Tell me, what is it that you want to be, more than anything else in the whole world?"

"A Princess."

"A Princess? Imagine that. Do you see that castle?"

"The black one?"

"That's the one. Well, there's a King who lives in that castle, and he's all alone. He asked me to find him a very special little girl so that he can have a Princess down here to rule with him. Would you like to meet him? I'd bet that he'd like you. And if he does, he could make you a Princess."

"Can Mommy and Daddy come?"

"Not right now. They don't belong here yet. You would have to come alone, and eventually, when you're older, you could rule this whole kingdom. There would be an army at your fingertips. You could destroy everything, do whatever you please."

"I don't want to have an army. I want a unicorn. And a dragon."

Alaria sighed. Griffin wasn't ready. Too young, too optimistic. It was time for the first event. "What if I could bring your Mommy and Daddy here? Then would you agree to be the Princess?"

Griffin thought about that for a minute, then shook her head. "Princesses go to balls and ride in carriages. They don't have armies. I don't want to be your Princess."

"Very well. Wake up, Griffin. Go to your parents. I have a wonderful surprise for you."

Griffin woke up suddenly, back in her bed, her head lying on her coloring book and the pretty blue crayon right next to the bed on the floor. She blinked rapidly, trying to adjust to the light from her lamp. She hopped out of bed, paused to pick up her teddy bear and clutched it tightly to her chest before she stood up. She carefully opened her bedroom door and concentrated on tiptoeing down the hall to the bedroom where Mommy and Daddy slept. If they caught her up, they'd get mad, and then she wouldn't be able to go to the park in the morning. The pretty lady in the dream had told her there was a surprise, and Griffin really liked surprises.

Cautiously, she opened the door and peeked in. She saw them both asleep, and a little braver, pushed the door all the way open. Something was not right. The window was open, and Mommy hated the window open. She said it wasn't safe and always made sure all the windows were locked every night, even though they never opened any of the windows. She padded toward the bed, intending to tell Mommy that the window was open when she saw the dog.

Or, at least, she thought it was a dog. It was huge, taller than she was, with a wrinkled face, long teeth, and a deep growl. Its fur was black and matted, and its nails gleamed like metal in the sliver of moonlight spilling through the curtains. It growled deeply, and then another, even bigger dog, jumped in through the window. They ignored her and circled the bed, the bigger one going to Daddy's side. Then they attacked.

Mommy woke up first. She screamed loudly, thrashing and struggling to get away from the giant black dog. It closed its teeth on her leg, ripping deep furrows in her flesh to expose the muscle and bone underneath. Blood hit the wall with a wet splat and it sprayed across Griffin's face. The sensation of warm, thick blood on her skin was enough to shake her out of her shock.

She pressed herself against the wall, trying to be invisible. Daddy was yelling, crying, begging for her to run, but Griffin couldn't manage to get her feet to move. The dog sank its teeth into his face, tearing his cheek from the rest of his head. It chewed once and swallowed. Griffin threw up.

Mommy's eyes were blank and glassy, and they looked almost like some of the marbles they had played with in the living room floor. Her body jerked and moved as the dog ripped pieces off. Her throat was ripped open and Griffin could see bones, white and stark against the dark blood pooling on the bed. Daddy held out one hand toward Griffin, pointing to the door, his mouth open as he tried to talk. Blood gurgled up from his lips, spilling down his chin and mingling with the blood gushing from his chest.

Griffin was unable to tear her eyes away from what was happening. Blood soaked the sheets, covered the walls, and had splashed on her, soaking through her pajamas. Tears slipped silently down her cheeks, mixing with the blood and dripping off of her chin. Daddy's eyes rolled back in his head and the dog used its massive jaws to rip through his rib cage and expose the barely beating heart. It buried its snout in the chest cavity and opened its mouth to close around his heart again, almost reverently. With a muffled growl, it ripped the still-beating organ from Daddy's chest. It gleamed red and shiny in the moonlight for a moment before the dog swallowed it, and for the first time, Griffin screamed.

She screamed until she couldn't scream anymore. Not hearing her, or not caring about her, the dogs ripped them apart, dining on their flesh, blood gleaming in black fur, shining in the moonlight. Blood dripped from their fangs, soaked into the sheets, ran down the side of the bed and pooled on the floor.

In the corner, two invisible figures watched the scene with almost disinterested objectivity.

Gabriel sighed and crossed his arms. "You should have told me you were doing something tonight. I figured it out when you released the Hell hounds. I wondered if you were going to kill her."

"Why would I do that? By doing it this way, she's traumatized for life, I get a couple of souls to play with, and the hounds get dinner. Everyone wins."

"The dreams aren't part of the deal, Alaria."

"Nor are they forbidden. We two are allowed to have contact with the Chosen. Granted, we all assumed that meant we would observe, and that I would have events, but my job is to make her Choose Hell. What better way to do that than if I can convince her to come to Hell and rule until she turns thirty? At the very least, if she agrees, I arrange a convenient accident that puts her in a coma and take her mind down there."

"You cannot take her physically. Humans cannot survive."

"I know that, Gabriel. I'm not stupid. I'll not take her down there bodily. I can visit any human I wish in their dreams. You can too, if the mood so strikes you."

"You know that I don't, that I trust her nature to win out in the end. I agreed to do this with as little influence from Heaven as possible. The agreement is that I will have contact with her only if she requests it after the Veil has been punctured. You indicated that you would do the same. Leave her alone, but for your events."

"I never actually said it. Be careful with Devils, Angel. We're known to lie."

"As I'm well aware. I can't say I'm surprised, but I am disappointed. Nevertheless, I have complete confidence that she is not going to agree to go to Hell. As she gets older, she'll realize where it is that you're taking her. If she figures out what's going on, Alaria, you're going to be in trouble."

"I'm going to arrange for her to have the worst foster homes imaginable. By the time I take her again, she'll be begging me to make her Princess of Hell."

"We'll see." Gabriel turned back to the grisly scene. "They're certainly taking a while to die."

"Humans can be difficult. He's mine."

"She's mine. It's not over yet though. God will save them up to the last heartbeat. He still has time."

"He's been mine since he came of age, Gabriel. He is not a backslidden human. He never went to God."

Gabriel smiled then, and Alaria scowled. "Just because they chose not to know my Father in life is no indication that they won't come begging for mercy at death. He's mine now." He allowed his wings to spread, impressive and blindingly white. "Now, if you'll excuse me, I have souls to collect."

"You aren't the Angel of Death."

"No, but I'm here. Saves him a trip."

Dr. Allen Winslow was just getting on his shift. He'd been up late with his wife, Miranda, who was incredibly bored on bed rest and couldn't sleep. His son, Braxton, who was eight, was currently obsessed with baseball and had demanded hours of practice with his Dad before bedtime. Staying up until past midnight, when the early shift started at six, made for a very tired doctor hoping to catch a couple more hours in the on-call room.

That, however, was not meant to happen as the first thing he saw when he entered the emergency room was blood everywhere. On the floor, the walls, the curtains. Nurses worked to clean it up, while doctors came out of one of the trauma rooms—gowns splattered with more blood, and their faces tinted slightly green. That told him that the scene he had just missed had been bad.

"Kathy, what's going on?"

Kathy stood from where she'd been scrubbing blood from her shoes. "A couple was brought in. Their four-year-old called 911. She woke up in the middle of the night and went into her parents room to find them being attacked by wild dogs. They were dead before the paramedics got there. She was covered in blood from lying with her Mommy until the paramedics pulled her off. She hasn't stopped crying long enough to let us check her out. The social worker is with her now."

"Wild dogs? In New York?"

"Your guess is as good as mine. They have a townhouse in Brooklyn, and they sleep on the first floor. There was an open window. It's obviously an animal attack. They're torn to shreds, and it's definitely not human teeth marks. The only question is why they didn't attack the little girl, too."

"Maybe they weren't hungry."

Kathy shuddered, undoubtedly thinking about being eaten alive. "I don't even want to think about it. You're good with kids. Do you think you could you try and calm her down? Check her over?"

Allen shrugged. "Sure. I'll give it a try. I make no promises." He took the chart she held out and headed for the exam rooms.

Stopping to pull on a white lab coat and drape his stethoscope around his neck, he entered the examination room. He felt his heart break at the sight of Griffin, dried blood on her face and clothes, a tattered, sad teddy bear clutched in her arms, and dancing pigs covering the footed pajamas that zipped all the way to her throat. He nodded to the social worker, who stared at him for a long moment, and then with a shrug, left the room.

"Hi. My name's Allen. I'm a doctor. Do you mind if I sit next to you here?"

Griffin silently moved over a fraction of an inch, which Allen took as an invitation. He slid onto the exam table next to her. She stared studiously ahead, not looking one way or the other, her fingers turning white from gripping the teddy bear so tightly.

Griffin turned her head slightly to look at him out of the corner of her eye. When she spoke, her voice was little more than a weak whisper. "Mommy and Daddy are dead."

"I know. I'm sorry about that. They were hurt really bad. I don't think anyone could have saved them."

"Not even God?"

Uh oh. Sticky ground there. "Well, God can do anything. Maybe He didn't because He wanted your Mommy and Daddy to come home."

"I need them here!"

"Sweetheart, sometimes God does things that we don't understand. Things that don't feel very good when they happen. Someday, maybe soon, maybe not, you'll understand why this happened."

"The dogs were big. Bigger than me. I tried to scream, but I just stood there. I didn't even try to save them! And now they're dead, just like my real Mommy and Daddy."

Taken off guard, Allen flipped open the chart and scanned it. Griffin Javensen. The baby that he'd delivered by emergency surgery four and a half years earlier. Whose parents had died in a drug-induced rage. Whose grandparents had seriously thought about giving her up for adoption until it became clear that she was truly a miracle baby and had not suffered any long-term side effects from the circumstances surrounding her birth. Now those grandparents were dead.

"Well, I don't know what to tell you, Griffin. What happened was horrible, and I'm very sorry about it, but I promise you, someday, you will understand why. I don't think you'll ever be happy that they're gone, but at some point you'll be at peace with it."

Griffin turned her head then, her eyes much older than they should have been. "Where am I going to go now?"

"I don't know. What I do know is that right now, the most important thing is making sure that you're okay and getting you some clean clothes. Is that okay?"

Griffin studied him seriously. "Mommy always told me not to let strangers touch me, but since she's dead and you're a doctor, I don't think she'd mind. Do you?"

"No, I don't think so. I'll get someone to clean you up. Her name is Kathy, and she's a nurse, which is almost like a doctor. She's a very nice lady who has a daughter about your age. You'll really like her, okay?"

"Okay."

Allen slid off the table and opened the door. "Kathy? Can you clean Griffin up and get her into a gown for me to examine? She's going to be more comfortable with a woman."

Kathy nodded. "Sure. I'll be there in just a minute to clean her up. Everything all right, Allen?"

He closed the door softly behind him to keep Griffin from hearing. "No. We delivered her, New Year's Eve, 1999. That couple that came in, she was full term, he'd tried to cut the baby out, killed himself. That's the baby. Her grandparents took her, and now they were just killed by wild animals."

With that, Allen Winslow went into the on-call room, locked the door, and cried.

Chapter Four

December 31st, 2012 - New York City

GRIFFIN SNUCK OUT the window of the apartment where her foster parents lived, praying that they wouldn't hear her. It was a small apartment, and along with Cate and Phil, there were their twin two-year-olds and two foster brothers. The boys slept on the couch, the twins had the big bedroom, and Griffin slept in what had originally started out as a laundry room. In fact, it still had the washer and dryer in it. Laundry had become her responsibility.

She'd been with Cate and Phil for five years, and even though they were veteran foster parents, they were horrible. They didn't do anything except drink and party. Cate worked, but Phil stayed home all day, and as soon as the three kids were home from school, he put them to work. Or more accurately, he told Cate he made all three of them, but since Adam and Ryan were boys, he liked them better. While Griffin was left to cook and clean, he took the boys fishing, let them try beer, let them date, and was even letting them get their driver's licenses.

But not Griffin. Both of her foster parents hated her. They got her up at the crack of dawn and made sure she had enough work each night to keep her up well past midnight. She took it because she had nowhere else to go. Before she'd ended up in their home, she'd been passed through half a dozen foster homes, never staying anywhere for more than a few months. No one ever wanted her to stay. They never treated her well, and they never loved her. She was smart enough to know that while Cate and Philip were neglectful, there were worse situations to be in. At least they didn't beat her.

In a few hours, she would be turning into a teenager, and that wasn't something she wanted to do sitting in a glorified laundry room in an apartment listening to toddlers wail and Phil and Cate have sex. She wanted to be with her friends. She snuck out the window and dropped lithely onto the ground below, her worn tennis shoes nearly silent on the snowy ground. She made sure to brush her footprints away and then loped down the road and turned into the familiar driveway to Lexie's house.

By the time she finished the two mile walk, she was nearly frozen, her lips tinged blue from the cold, and there was a thin dusting of snow on her hair. Her face lit up with anticipation as she checked the time on her watch. Only an hour left until midnight. She had a feeling this next year was going to change her life.

Lexie opened the door the moment Griffin hit the bell and squealed as she launched herself at her best friend. "You're here! Come on downstairs. Everyone's been here for hours. We're getting ready to play spin the bottle, and Lucas is here!"

Lucas was the tallest and best looking boy in the seventh grade. Griffin had harbored a crush on him for almost the entire year. She desperately wanted him to be her first boyfriend, and the thought of him kissing her, even in a game of spin the bottle, sent butterflies swirling in her stomach.

"Really? I thought his mom said he wasn't allowed out this late."

"He told her he was going to a lock-in at Mark's church. Mark told his mom that he was spending the night with Lucas, and they both came here instead. After the party's done, they'll sneak back in Mark's window and hope they weren't found out."

"Them and me both. Phil and Cate were in their room watching TV and the boys were out for the night, so I should be safe, at least as long as they don't come up with something that they need me to do between now and morning."

"No use worrying about it now. You're here, and I'm going to make sure you have fun. Come downstairs and let's play. My brother is upstairs, and we'll get him to drive you home after this. Say your foster mom forgot or something."

Griffin nodded and followed Lexie down into the basement. The music blared, and bowls of pretzels and chips decorated every available surface. There were open boxes of pizza on the coffee table between the two lumpy, worn-out couches and a cooler full of pop in the corner. Within two minutes of stepping off the staircase, Griffin had a can of root beer and two slices of pizza and was being hurried into a circle to play spin the bottle.

Lexie got an empty beer bottle from upstairs and laid it in the middle. "Okay, everyone, the rules. When you spin, don't do it too hard. If this breaks and we end up with glass everywhere, I'm dead meat. If you're a boy and you land on another boy, you get to go again. Same thing with the girls. Otherwise, it doesn't matter who you land on—kiss 'em. The kiss has to last five seconds, and it has to be mouth to mouth. No skipping your turn, and if you're in the circle, you play. No chickens."

Somehow, Griffin made it all the way around the circle and no one landed on her. Then, for her first turn, she landed on Lexie. Being the adventurous girl that she was, Lexie grinned and leaned over, kissing Griffin solidly on the mouth. The girls both laughed, thinking nothing of it, and the bottle was passed to Lucas for a second time around.

He gripped the bottle tightly and sent it spinning. The rotation seemed to go on forever, and then, it began to slow. Slower, slower still, until finally, it came to a stop, pointing directly at Griffin. Still coming off of the high of her last spin, and eager to make everyone laugh again, she rose up on her knees, waiting for Lucas to do the same thing. But he didn't.

"Gross. I'm not kissing the foster kid. I might catch AIDS or something," he scoffed at her, gaining momentum when his buddies started laughing. "Besides, she doesn't even have boobs yet, and her face looks like a horse. Come 'ere, Lexie, you take her turn."

Griffin felt the room closing in on her. She scrambled to her feet, grabbed her jacket from the back of the couch, and ran up the stairs, hot tears running down her cheeks, which were bright red from humiliation and anger. Lexie waited only a split second before jumping to her feet as well.

"Way to go, Lucas. Could you be a bigger jerk?" She ran after Griffin, bounding up the stairs two at a time. "Griffin! Wait!"

Griffin paused at the front door and looked back. "I'm going home. I should have known better. No one likes the foster kid."

"I like the foster kid, Griffin. You're my best friend."

"You're the only one. It's better if I leave anyway. I don't want to get caught."

"But it's your birthday in twenty minutes. I have a cake and everything. It was supposed to be a surprise. You can wait in my room until I get rid of them, and then we'll have a sleepover."

"I can't. I'm going to go home."

"At least let me get Ben to give you a ride. He's seventeen now, and he hasn't had a wreck yet."

Griffin glanced out into the snow that was coming down harder now than when she'd arrived. "Okay."

"Ben! Come down here!"

Ben, the starting linebacker for the high school football team, loped down the stairs. "What's up?"

"Can you take Griffin home? The boys were jerks and hurt her feelings."

"Lexie!" Griffin's face flushed red from embarrassment. "He doesn't need to know that!"

Lexie looked at Griffin, her eyes wide. "What? He's my brother! He doesn't matter."

"Thanks, kid." Ben grabbed his keys and dangled them in front of Griffin's face. "Let's go, sport. I want to get back before the snow gets too bad."

Warily, Griffin followed Ben to his car and slid in the passenger's side. He crossed in front of the car, climbed in, and started the engine. Griffin twisted around in her seat and waved at Lexie as Ben pulled out of the driveway. Then, she faced forward and put on her seatbelt, ignoring the urge to tell him to do the same.

"Do you know where I live?"

"Griffin, everyone knows where you live. The ghetto."

Unreasonably hurt, she sank down further in her seat, tears welling in her eyes. "It's not my fault that the state put me with them. And you can't catch AIDS from kissing. Besides, I don't have AIDS anyway."

Ben glanced at her, confused. "Who said anything about AIDS?"

"Lucas. He got me on spin the bottle and didn't want to kiss me because he said he'd probably catch AIDS, and that I had a face like a horse."

"Kids can be mean." Ben put on his turn signal, made a right turn, and pulled into a deserted alley where he put the car in park. When he turned to look at her, his eyes were glassed over and had a red tint to them.

"What are we doing here?" She looked around at the alley, taking in the snow accumulating on the ground. Ben reached over and pushed a button on his door. The sound of the locks snapping into place made Griffin jump. Her heart sped up in her chest. She turned her head and took in the red eyes. Something was different.

"It's okay, Griffin." Ben snaked his hand around the back of the seat and rubbed her neck. "I want to get to know you better."

His voice was different. It was rough and gravelly, much deeper than it had been even just minutes earlier. Griffin shifted nervously in her seat.

"Are you okay, Ben? You're freaking me out."

The monster wearing Ben's skin smiled. "Ben's not here right now."

Griffin's heart pounded against her ribs and her throat constricted. "What are you talking about? Just take me home, Ben, please. I want to go home. Now."

"No. I don't think I will."

He lunged across the seat and grabbed her arms, forcing her to kiss him. Griffin screamed into his mouth, the sound muffled by his tongue and teeth. She bit his lips, clawed at his face, bucked her whole body in an effort to escape, but he was much bigger and much stronger. He grabbed her hair, pulled it, and jerked her head back. She sobbed and screamed when his hand closed over a barely developed breast. She choked when he ripped her pants and tore them off of her.

Nothing she did stopped him, or even deterred him. Her teeth sank into his arm and she slammed her forehead into his face. Blood from his nose spurted onto her, but not even that broke through the haze he was in and he still continued to dominate her. Just as the assault progressed from her struggling to him plunging into her, forcing his way into her body, making her wail with pain and anguish, the clock turned to midnight. It was her birthday.

She smelled sweat and the leather of his varsity football jacket. The denim from his jeans scraped her tender skin. His breath was warm and wet on her ear, and his breathing was quick and ragged from the exertion of pumping himself into her.

Her head hit the door handle, and she'd lost one shoe in the struggle. She weakly tried to pull her hands loose from where he held them above her head. She sobbed silently from the pain, the burning sensation between her legs almost too much to bear. Tears choked her as she tried to breathe. She attempted to focus on something, anything other than the pain. The delicate folds of her body stretched and tore, and blood dripped out of her, soaking into the upholstery as he continued his violent assault.

Her head was yanked sideways, and she was forced to endure the pungent smell of Ben's breath as he forced his tongue between her lips. Griffin wondered briefly if biting him would make him stop, but didn't have time to act on the thought before he grunted with release, trembling from his orgasm.

Her thighs were wet and sticky with a mixture of semen and blood. She cried out when she sat up, her body bruised and sore. She stared at

Ben and watched as he sat back in the seat, his half hard penis still hanging outside of his jeans. Their eyes met for a brief second, and then Ben threw his head back, a massive swirl of red and black fog spewing from his mouth. Griffin screamed and threw herself at the door of the car, tumbling out onto the sidewalk. Her jeans were ripped and still around her knees. One foot was bare and the snow was icy and cold on her naked bottom.

Gabriel stood in the deserted street, his face creased with despair, the wrinkle in his nose showing his disgust. Alaria was by his side, her face lit with delight as she watched the scene unfolding. He shook his head slowly. "This is your event? The rape of a child?"

"The point of this, Gabriel, is to make her so miserable in her own life that she jumps at the chance to join me in Hell the next time I offer it."

"The boy? He's possessed then?"

"Not exactly. He's stupid. He offered a Devil his soul for the state championship last year. When I learned of his sister's relationship with the Chosen, I took on the contract. I went to him and offered him a way out. I would destroy the contract for his soul if he allowed a demon to use his body for a couple hours. He'll remember nothing about this when he wakes up tomorrow morning."

"He'll spend the next years of his life in one of their detention facilities."

"Better than an eternity in Hell, I suppose. Don't tell me you care about a boy who sold his soul over a game?"

Gabriel eyed the situation with objective disregard. "He made his bed. It was his choice, and unfortunately for him, the consequences are going to be long-reaching. He should be grateful that they end now. I can't remember another person who sold his soul and ever got it back."

"It's unfortunate that I had to return it, but she is worth it. It's ultimately a small price to pay for the Choosing to come out in my favor."

"It's much too early to tell how it will turn out, Alaria. She's still good. She still prays to God every night. I can hear her." Gabriel shifted his eyes from the alley to study the face of the Devil next to him and watched her for a reaction.

"As do I. You'll notice that her prayers are much more desperate than they used to be. The foster situation is degrading, thanks to yours truly.

When you learn some of the things I have planned for her, you'll be sick to your self-righteous stomach."

"It would not surprise me." He turned back to the scene unfolding and felt his heart twinge in sympathy for the girl, something he hadn't felt for a human in centuries. He'd discovered long ago that people generally got what they deserved. Griffin's only crime had been being born. Born to suffer, born to die, born to Choose. It wasn't a fate he would have wished on his worst enemy, let alone upon an innocent child. Nevertheless, it had to be done, as she had been Chosen by God. He shook his head as Griffin tumbled out onto the pavement. "There. It's done."

Alaria laughed and started to fade. "The show, yes, but this event is far from over. I'll see you in nine months, Gabriel. I have made her pregnant."

Before Gabriel could speak, Alaria disappeared with a thunderous crack. Moments after the Devil had gone, the hair on the back of his neck stood up, alerting him to someone's presence. Concerned, he looked around and turned in a slow circle to view the entire alley. There was no one within his sight, and no sign that anyone had been there. He shook his head to clear it. "Being on Earth is making me paranoid."

That having been said, the Angel, as the Devil had done, began to fade. The only difference was that seconds later, he reappeared.

"What've we got?"

"Thirteen-year-old came in about thirty minutes ago. She walked from one of the boroughs. She's dehydrated, hypothermic, and busted up pretty badly. Says she's in foster care and asked us not to call her foster parents. She says she was raped. The police have been notified, and they're sending someone down. She asked for you specifically."

"It's my last night, Kathy. I don't want to finish up with a teenage rape victim."

"I think you do."

Allen Winslow took the chart she held out and glanced over it. "You're sure?"

"It's her. Griffin Javensen. She remembers you from years ago, says she doesn't want anyone else."

"Does she know who raped her?"

"I don't know, Allen. She won't talk to me. This is the third time this girl has been in with very serious situations. It's like she can't catch a break."

Allen had been a doctor for nearly twenty years. He had a wonderful wife, a son in high school, and a nine-year-old daughter who was determined to play football. He had a good life, and because he had such a good life to go home to, he had always been able to set aside the horrors that he saw on a nearly daily basis. Except for that of a small child, covered in blood, wearing footed pajamas and clutching a teddy bear, who had cried for her dead parents.

And now she was back, the victim of a rape and beating who was juggled through the foster system until she was so disillusioned by it that she didn't even want the people raising her called to be by her side. It was all because of the image of her as a little girl with that damn bear that he couldn't stand the thought of denying her request. Knowing that he was beaten, he glared at Kathy and headed toward the exam room.

"Fine, I'll do it. But this is it. No more hard cases tonight. It's my last shift before the move."

"I still can't believe you're leaving us for small town life. Where is it you're moving to again?"

"Miranda's father left us his ranch outside of Billings. There's an opening for Chief of the ER there. It's less money, but I want Brax and Sam out of the city. Brax has been having a rough time with his grandfather's death."

"I know. We'll miss you. Now, go take care of this girl. Call me in when you're ready to do the rape kit."

Allen nodded as he entered the room and took in the sight awaiting him. Griffin was a tall, slim girl, with blood-matted blonde hair and porcelain skin marred by dark bruises and shallow cuts. Her eyes, which were a clear, rich gold, were dulled by pain and horror. She wore a hospital gown, and he saw ripped clothes, a ratty coat, and worn out shoes laying on the chair in a clear evidence bag.

"I remembered you from last time. You were nice to me." Her lips started to wobble as she tried not to cry. "People really aren't very nice to me, and I thought that, right now, I need to be treated nice. So, I came here, and I asked for you. I really hope that's okay, because I don't know what to do if it's not."

Right then, all annoyance he had felt at being asked to handle the case evaporated, and he was left with an aching sense of sadness. "It's okay.

I'm glad you did. I'm going to take care of you, Griffin, and it will all be fine."

Griffin broke down. She sobbed and dropped her face into her hands, her shoulders shaking uncontrollably—the sound of her heart breaking. Instinctively, Allen gathered her close, tucking her head in his shoulder and soothing her as he would one of his own children. She clung to him, her fingers digging into his shoulders and her tears hot on his skin.

When she was done, he eased her back from him and handed her a tissue to wipe her face. He snagged a stool and sat down so that he was at her level. "Now comes the hard part. When he raped you, unless he used a condom, there's going to be evidence left inside your body. We need to get it. That way we can prove who did it, and he can be punished. He hurt you, and we need to take pictures of the injuries so that the police can show it to a jury. It's going to be hard, but we need to do it. Do you understand?"

Griffin closed her eyes, wishing that she could just make him stop speaking. "Yes. I understand."

"We'll give you pills to keep you from getting pregnant, and we'll give you antibiotics to keep you from catching a sexually transmitted disease. Okay?

"Okay."

"Good." He rolled to the door and pushed it open. "Kathy, we're ready to start in here."

Chapter Five

December 31st, 2012 - New York City
BRAXTON LAY ON his bed, tossing a baseball up in the air and then catching it. He glared at the boxes littering the floor of his room and scowled at the moving truck parked in the driveway. He didn't want to move. He was seventeen, it was his senior year of high school, and he had gotten accepted onto the all-state baseball team. No amount of reasoning could convince his parents that they didn't need to move.

All because his father's father had gone and got himself killed. Not that Braxton saw what that had to do with moving, but apparently he had no say in the matter. Neither did his sister, Sam, who was nine. She was okay for a nine-year-old. They got along well enough most of the time, but now that they were getting their lives uprooted for no good reason, they had joined in rebellion.

Mom kept telling him that his grandfather had been involved in some things that he shouldn't have been involved in, and he owed money to a lot of people who might come after Dad to get it, even though Dad hadn't talked to his father in years. It was too dangerous to take a chance, so they were moving to Philadelphia. Of course, they had told everyone they had inherited some property in Montana, hoping to get everyone who might have been after Robert Winslow onto a false trail if they came looking.

Something about the whole story didn't make sense. Wasn't that what the police were for? Besides, it wasn't like the mob or whoever was going to come after a seventeen-year-old who still had to drive his mother's car, or a nine-year-old whose biggest concern was the next sleepover. Mom and Dad were insistent, and Sam and Braxton had no choice but to go along with the decision they had made.

Annoyed even at the thought of it, Braxton threw the baseball into a box and looked at the clock. Only seven. Five hours until he would be hailed downstairs to watch some stupid ball drop on television with his mother and sister. Not that Dad could be bothered to come home at a decent hour. He was Chief of the Emergency Room. That meant he had to be there longer than anyone else. It sucked. Especially when he had to be home and his mother and sister were watching kid movies.

Yawning, Braxton laid his head on his pillow, glaring at the clock. It would be hours before Dad got home—if he got off when he was scheduled to—which was anything but a certainty. He was tired, and he was mad, and he was hurt. Thinking about all that he was missing, the friends he was leaving, and the baseball team, just made him angrier and more hurt, so he decided to stop thinking about it. He reached for the clock and set his alarm for ten-thirty. A nap would help clear his head, and it would still give him time to suffer through the last half of a movie with Sam and Mom before watching the ball drop and wondering when Dad would be home. A perfect compromise. He'd seem like the perfect son so that Mom would clear him to go to Doug's New Year's Day party the next night, and he wouldn't have to put up with his family.

He drifted off quickly and his mind lulled into a dream. There was a flash and a loud noise, and then he was standing in a deserted alley, watching a car roll to a stop. He looked around, saw a man and a woman speaking in low voices several yards away. Within seconds, a girl's screams filled the air.

Braxton lunged forward, intending to help the girl, but he found that he could not move. It was as if his feet were rooted to the sidewalk and he was incapable of moving forward. He tried to yell, but his voice wouldn't work, either. He heard the woman standing on the street start laughing, and the man shook his head sadly. Blood sprayed the inside of the car's windshield, but still neither of them made a move toward it, and no one passed by on the street to help.

After several gut wrenching minutes, it was over, and a young girl—probably a couple years older than Sam—stumbled out onto the street. Her face was bloody, her clothes were ripped, and she was holding her pants up with one hand. One of her shoes was missing. Tears rolled down her face, and she screamed for help over and over again until Braxton's heart wrenched in sympathy. He continued to try to move, to go to her and tell her that he would help, but he couldn't manage to take even a single step. He knew he should leave, but he couldn't help it—he had to watch her to see if she was okay.

He'd been having these dreams since he was a little boy. Sometimes they seemed so real that he wasn't sure he was even asleep, but more often than not, they were like this. He would witness some horrible event, unable to move, to speak, to help. Normally, he would do what the strange man had told him to do. He would close his eyes and think of his bed, and momentarily, he would wake up there, with only blurry memories of what he had seen.

Tonight, he didn't want to leave. He wanted to help. He was a man; it was his job to protect women, not to hurt them. He wanted to go find the man who had so obviously beaten and raped this little girl and pummel him.

Movement caught his attention, and he saw the man and woman disappear. Then, seconds later, the man reappeared and walked over to Braxton. Nervous, Braxton closed his eyes and tried to think of his bed. Not since the first time had someone known that he was there when he'd appeared.

"It won't work. Not with me."

Braxton opened his eyes and glared at the man defiantly. "Who are you and what do you want with me?"

"My name is Gabriel. I'm an Angel of the Lord, and we have met before, Braxton Winslow. I told you the last time that you are not supposed to be here and that you are to try to go back home as soon as you appear."

"That man raped her."

"He did, yes. But it has little to nothing to do with you."

"You didn't do anything to stop it. If you're an Angel, shouldn't you try to stop it?"

"It had to happen. As horrific as it was, she had to go through this. There was no other choice."

"Why?"

"Because it is God's will. Braxton, sometimes God allows people to go through bad events in order to use them for His higher purpose. That girl has a higher purpose, and what happened tonight will help her to achieve that."

"The woman was a demon, wasn't she?"

"Yes, she was. How did you know?"

Braxton shrugged. "Seemed to make sense. You're an Angel, she could see you and talk to you, and she didn't seem to like you all that much. So, I thought she was a demon."

"When there's an Angel present, there is often also a demon. They are our counterparts."

"What does God want with that girl? Is she going to be okay?"

"She'll be fine. She's on her way to the hospital now."

"Is this the future?"

"I don't know. For you, probably. I don't know how far into the future, because I have no sense of the human perception of the passage of time. Most Seers see only the future. In rare cases, you may see the past or the present, but most often, you're seeing the volatile future. Because it might change."

"What I just saw might not happen?"

"No. Here, this is real. This will happen. For you, the time or place may vary, but events dictated by God always occur. The only question is when and where, sometimes who. Braxton, there is much going on in the world that you do not understand. Humans are not meant to understand. And there is very little that I can tell you, even less that I have an inclination to tell you. I have not been told that you are important. I may never be. God may have His own plan for you that does not involve Angels. But I need to make you understand one important thing. Coming here is dangerous. If the demons see you, if they sense that you are here, they will come after you. Seers are rare, and they can be used as instruments of good. If you are seen here, you will be in danger. It is imperative that if you wake up in one of these dreams, that you immediately return to your bed."

"This can't possibly be real. I know about Angels and demons, but Seers and murder? That's not anything like what they teach in church."

"The church gets more wrong than it gets right, Braxton. Go home. Help your mother and your sister."

Braxton woke up with a jerk in his bed, his heart pounding and sweat drenching his brow. He sat up and wiped his forehead, breathing rapidly to catch his breath. Automatically, his eyes slid toward the clock. Ten. He'd been asleep for three hours. It had only seemed like minutes.

Man, what a trip. He'd always had very vivid, very real dreams, but occasionally, he had one that felt more like reality. During those times, he always returned to his bed. He'd done some research and discovered it was known as lucid dreaming. It was when someone fell asleep and, for some reason, their mind didn't progress all the way into deep sleep. The subconscious formed the dream, but the person was aware enough to interact with the scene independently. Like having conversations with characters from the dream.

From what he had read, Braxton had ascertained that he was pretty normal. Occasionally, he had dreams that seemed like reality, and his mind had concocted a story to go along with them. It was easier for his unconscious mind to think that he was seeing the future or having a vision than to admit that he wasn't truly asleep. The books told him that most people, at some point or another, had one or two. He could clearly remember five, each one different, with different people, save for the rape victim, whom he had seen once before. If he had to guess, he would say that his mind had created the girl to deal with some of his own issues, and waking up inside had disrupted the process.

Satisfied with his own logic, Braxton climbed out of bed and kicked a box across the room. No need to guess what his issues were. He didn't want to move. Simple as that. He scowled at his empty dresser and stalked to the door, needing to escape his bedroom. He jerked the door open and found his sister standing on the other side, her hand poised to knock.

"What's up?"

"Mom wanted me to come and get you. She said there's enough time before midnight to watch another movie, and you get to pick."

"You mean you'll actually watch something other than Beauty and the Beast?"

Sam grinned. "You can only take so much, Brax. I've reached my limit. Four movies is enough."

Braxton reached out and ruffled his sister's hair, tousling her dark brown waves. "Well, I'll go pick something bloody then. Purge your system."

Samantha, who refused to go by anything but Sam, was very tall, and her body bordered on too skinny. She was nine and hadn't yet discovered that she was a girl. She spent most of her time playing sports and wearing jeans that Braxton had outgrown. "Works for me."

Before they could do more than walk several steps down the hallway, the doorbell rang. Instantly suspicious, Braxton moved to the top of the stairs. "Stay here. I'm going to go check it out. No one should be here this late."

Apprehensive, Sam moved back toward Braxton's bedroom. "You don't think it's the people after Grandpa, do you?"

"I wouldn't think so. I think Mom and Dad are out of their minds with that, but better safe than sorry. Go into my room, lock the door, and don't come out until I yell for you."

Braxton stooped to pick up the baseball bat he'd dropped at the top of the stairs on his way home from batting practice and crept slowly down the stairs. He heard his mother open the door, heard her surprised yell, and then a man's voice.

"Hello, Miranda."

Miranda backed up, moving quickly into the living room. "Robert, we thought you were dead. Your hunting partner called us and told us that you were dead."

"He was mistaken. Where're Allen and the kids?"

"Out. Allen took them out for dinner."

Robert, his skin alarmingly gray and pasty, grinned. "You're lying. Yell for the kids, Miranda. Tell them to come downstairs. I think it's time that they met their grandfather. I called the hospital before I came here. Allen's in surgery right now."

"Look, Braxton's at a party with some friends. Allen dropped him off on his way to work, and Sam's spending the night next door. Her best friend Leslie lives there and they're having makeovers. Leslie's mom is a hairdresser."

Robert considered that for a long moment, then nodded. "Okay. Well then, we're just going to sit down and wait for Braxton to come home. I don't need to see Samantha. She isn't important."

Miranda's fingers skated over the desk in the corner of the living room as she backed up, searching for a weapon, and desperate to get Robert into the middle of the room. She found a letter opener and tucked it into the waistband of her jeans, underneath her shirt.

"You aren't Robert. I'm not stupid. I know what possession looks like."

The demon wearing Robert's body smiled, and his eyes turned gray. "It was worth a try."

"How did you get in there? He had anti-possession tattoos."

"Those tattoos only work while they're still attached to the body." He pulled up his sleeve, revealing a chunk of skin and flesh that was missing. "I used my last skin suit to cut it off of him. Robert was quite the Warrior. I wondered what it would be like to wear him around for a while, have some fun. So, I possessed a waitress at a truck stop where he was eating. He spotted me immediately, but I'd already drugged his coffee. He passed out, and I took him and cut his protection off. Then, I let him escape."

"Why? Why not just kill him?"

"Because that would be boring. I like to keep things interesting. I knew that Robert would lead me straight to other Warriors. And I liked wearing that waitress for a while. I wasn't quite ready to give her up. So, I let him run. He did exactly what I knew he would and went for some buddy of his. I arranged an attack on the two of them and just as Robert was about to die, I dumped the waitress and jumped into him. I had to wait until he was almost dead so he wouldn't be able to fight me out. Some Warriors can do that, you know. Annoying habit." He shook his head and looked at Miranda with disgust. "Anyway, I didn't want the other Warrior to know immediately, and I needed some time to get at his memories, so I let the idiot bury me. I hang out in the coffin for a couple days, then popped out, found the other Warrior, slit his throat and came looking for Braxton. Robert has some interesting theories about Braxton."

"Robert was a crazy old man. He met Braxton once when he was four. He knows nothing about our family."

"Well, he seemed to think that your little boy has some visions that may give him some inside information about the Chosen."

"It's bullshit. He had one dream when he was four about an Angel. He was asleep with his ear to the vent, listening to his father and grandfather argue. Big surprise there." Miranda scowled, her back hitting the fireplace mantle. "You've obviously never been around a toddler."

"But you still salted his windows and put herbs under his pillow."

"A precaution. Allen and I both grew up with Warriors, as you very well know. Robert was a very suspicious person. He didn't think that anything was a coincidence. There is nothing going on with Braxton. He's a normal teenager."

Braxton crept down the stairs, his baseball bat clutched in his hand. He was as quiet as possible and snuck around the corner into the living room. He knew that his mother had to see him—he was just hoping that she didn't alert the intruder to his presence.

He'd heard most of the conversation, but he wasn't quite sure what to make of it. Demons and the Chosen? Possessing dead bodies? It was more than he wanted to process—more than he could process—when his mother was so obviously in danger, and the man in their living room was quite obviously deranged.

"Who are you? You're going to kill me, so I might as well get to know your name."

"My name is not important. I'm just a normal demon. I was set free from the pit a thousand years ago, so I've become quite strong under the tutelage of Lilith."

"Ariander." Miranda clenched her eyes shut. She had heard stories of this particular demon all her life. He'd been amongst the first to be released from the Lake of Fire, and he had been taken under the wing of Lilith, who was arguably the most powerful Devil in all of history. He was known for his thirst for blood and his ability to possess even those who had anti-possession charms. It wasn't much of a stretch to think he'd figured out how to inhabit a dead body for a short time.

Rumor had it that as a human he had been a serial rapist who preyed on young girls in pre-Viking Ireland. He'd been rumored to be responsible for over five hundred rapes, out of which he had sired more than seventy children, all of whom had grown up to be just as despicable as their father. He'd been killed by one of his victims, who had clawed his eyes out of his head while he had raped her. He'd bled to death, the girl had ended up pregnant, and rather than carry his spawn to term, she had tossed herself off the Cliffs of Mohr and into the ocean, dashing herself to pieces on the sharp rocks below.

"So you know of me? I'm touched." He took another step forward and glanced toward the couch. "Let's sit down and wait for your son, Miranda. There's no reason this can't be pleasant until he arrives. After all, I don't want to kill you yet. I want to tie Braxton up and make him watch while I fuck your brains out. I'll make you watch while I tear him apart piece by piece. Then I'll slit your throat and drink your blood. Doesn't that sound nice?"

Miranda felt her stomach clench, and it was all she could do not to gag. She had to get him into the center of the room, into the Devil's trap that she'd had painted on the subfloor beneath the carpet when they'd moved in. She'd had one done in every room and had made sure Allen didn't have a clue. Her upbringing as a Warrior was hard to let go of, and she'd felt better with the traps.

Braxton was getting closer, and so far, he wasn't making any noise that would alert the demon to his presence. She knew it was only a matter of time before he was seen, but she hoped that she could use Braxton to get Ariander into the trap. If she could trap him, she could exorcise him.

"You know that my husband will find out what's going on and that he will hunt you to the end of the Earth."

"Dear old Allen is welcome to try. The greatest Warriors have tried to kill me, yet they've never been able to succeed."

"You can't kill a demon, but a good Warrior can send you back to Hell."

"Got to catch me first. I can smell a trap a mile away. Haven't gotten stuck once yet. Lilith taught me to sense them."

Braxton met his mother's eyes at that moment and caught the message when she shifted slightly to look at the center of the room. Ariander didn't seem to notice, and Braxton nodded sharply. He understood. Mom wanted the man pushed there. He tightened his grip on the baseball bat, angled his shoulder down, and charged at the body of his grandfather.

He crashed into the demon with a sickening crunch, and they fell to the floor, nearly to the trap. Without waiting to see what happened, Miranda leaped over the couch and grabbed a silver jewelry box off of the book shelf. She snatched a vial out of it, tossed its contents onto the demon, and watched as he writhed in pain, his flesh sizzling at the presence of Holy Water.

Braxton used that second to roll out of his way, kicked with both feet, and pushed Robert the final inches into the center. Miranda ran to her son, heaved him to his feet, and pushed him behind her. Ariander stood slowly, his mouth curving into a dangerous grin.

"Now I'm really going to have fun. Did you think you'd have a chance against me, boy? A baseball bat and a young body? You don't yet know what fighting is, let alone how to do it."

Miranda smiled then too, hers just as dangerous. "He didn't need to have a chance against you. See, you aren't as smart as you think you are. Most Warriors aren't from Warrior lines. The lines were eliminated over the centuries. The current generation dies out before they can reproduce. So, the knowledge that we had hundreds of years ago became diluted. We had to improvise, had to bring in outsiders. My family is different. My lineage can be traced back to the first Warriors. I know tricks that most Warriors, even the greatest ones, have never even heard of. Try to move, Ariander. I'm willing to bet that you've been caught in your first Devil's trap."

Ariander's eyes widened and he stepped forward. After two steps he hit the edge and was tossed back to the middle. "How?"

"I painted them on the subfloor when we were moving in. They're different than a run of the mill trap. I lined them in liquid silver, which shields them from detection. It's an old Warrior trick that has nearly died out. My grandfather taught it to me when I was a kid." In her element, Miranda turned to Braxton and put a hand on his arm. "You're going to see some things you could never have imagined. I need you to go to the kitchen and get salt. Draw a circle of it on the floor and get you and your sister into it. I don't want you hurt if he manages to get out of there."

"I'll get out of here, you know. And then all you'll have done is sentence your daughter to death as well. Let me out and I'll spare her life."

"No, you won't."

"You're right, I won't. But I won't torture her."

Braxton dashed into the kitchen and grabbed the bag of salt they used on the front walk in the winters from the pantry. He poured it onto the floor in a large circle as his mother began to chant, her voice low and intense.

> "Exorcizamuste, omnisimmundusspiritus, omnissatanicapotestas, omnisincursioinfernalisadversarii, omnislegio, omniscongregatio et sectadiabolica. Ergo, dracomaledicte et omnislegiodiabolica, adjuramustecessadeciperehumanascreaturas, eisqueæternæperditionisvenenumpropinare. Vade, satana, inventor et magister omnisfallaciæ, hostishumanæsalutis. Humiliare sub potentimanu Dei; contremisceeteffuge, invocato a nobissancto et terribili nomine queminferitremunt. Abinsidiisdiaboli, liberanos, Domine."

Looking panicked, the demon charged the edges of the circle, wind whipping up and pouring through the room. Braxton dragged Samantha down the stairs and enveloped her in his arms inside the salt circle. Miranda glanced back, saw that they were there safely, and turned back to her mission, repeating her chant.

The skin began to peel back from the face of the demon. His skin sizzled. "You'll regret this. I'll get out and I'll come back. I'll tear you all limb from limb. Once Lilith finds out what you've done, you'll be the most hunted human on Earth."

Her voice got louder as she continued to chant. Smoke filled the room and wound its way around Ariander and Miranda. Braxton crushed his sister to him, his eyes glued to the scene playing out in front of him.

With a loud explosion and a wall of fire, the body of their grandfather melted to a pile of bubbling muscle and bones within seconds. A red and black swirl erupted from the mouth of the corpse and punched a hole in the floor on its drive downward. Miranda jumped back and rushed across the room to gather her children close. Samantha was trembling from fear, while Braxton looked at the scene in confusion.

"Mom?"

"It's a lot to explain, guys. That was a demon. He was inhabiting your grandfather's body. I used a Latin chant to exorcise him. It's way too much to go into now, but suffice it to say that there are things that exist in this world that most people think exist only in the movies. We decided a long time ago to live a normal life with the two of you. We never thought it would come back to haunt us."

"I want to learn. I want to learn everything."

Miranda studied Braxton for a long moment, recognizing the flame that had ignited behind his eyes. "Yes, I can see that you do. And I think the time has come to teach you. Sam, go call your father home from the hospital. Brax, get a shovel. We're going to have to bury your grandfather."

Unwilling to let the topic go without the answers he wanted, Braxton crossed his arms and glared at his mother. "What did the spell mean?"

Miranda sighed deeply. "It's complicated, but basically it is calling on God to cast out the demon, denouncing Satan, and begging for it to be sent back to Hell. It's flowery and verbose, but it gets the job done well enough. It's an old one. Generally people now exorcise in English, or whatever language they speak. But I've found using the original Latin has a bit more punch to it." She straightened then and went to the kitchen for trash bags. "Now, guys. We don't have all night."

Chapter Six

August 21st, 2013 - Brooklyn, New York
"Are you sure this is what you want to do?"

Griffin glanced up at the adoption counselor. "I'm sure."

"Giving your child up for adoption is a very serious thing, Griffin. We want you to think about it carefully. If you change your mind after the adoptive parents take the baby home, it's going to hurt a lot of people." The woman had a friendly face, wide and chubby, with thin lips and a big smile. She laid brochures on her desk and pushed them toward Griffin. "Why don't you read these, and we'll meet again next week?"

Griffin's head snapped up. "No. I can't wait until next week. My foster parents don't know I'm here, and I don't want them to." She looked down at her bulging belly and noticed, almost idly, that she could no longer see her shoes. She hadn't been able to bend down and reach them for six weeks, but even the day before she thought she'd been able to at least see her toes. "Please, don't make me wait. I don't know if I'll be able to get back."

The adoption counselor's face softened, and she pushed her chair back from the desk. She swiveled to reach a shelf that held binders of paperwork. "There are some forms you need to fill out. Health history, due date, prenatal care—that sort of thing. We'll need you to sign a release allowing us access to your medical records. There's also a waiver in there that you'll need to get the baby's father to sign."

"I can't do that." Panic rose in Griffin's throat at the thought of seeing Ben again. "I can't get him to sign."

"Do you know who the father is?"

"Yes."

"Then he'll need to sign the papers."

Griffin closed her eyes, tears burning the inside of her lids. "Ma'am, you don't understand. I can't get him to sign those papers."

"Miss Javensen, the father of your child has rights. You cannot unilaterally decide to give a child up if there is a parent who wants to take possession. This is not a way to get back at a bad boyfriend."

Anger mixed with the fear, and Griffin's eyes flashed. "He raped me, okay? I can't get him to sign because he's in juvie! And I can't come back next week because my foster parents want the goddamn check this baby will bring!" She stood up, her belly bumping against the desk. "If you can't help me, I'll go, but there's no way I can get him to sign the papers!"

"Sit down." The counselor waited until Griffin dropped back into her chair. "Was he convicted of rape?" She sighed when Griffin shook her head. "What's he in juvenile detention for?"

"He took a deal on assault and battery. He's there until he's twenty-five."

"We can file with the court for an exemption. The difficulty with that is that it takes a while, and you look pretty far along. When is your due date?"

"Three weeks."

"That's not enough time."

Griffin glanced at the name on the desk. Nancy Yeager. "What does that mean?"

Nancy crossed her arms over her chest and leaned back. "It means that you would be sent home with the baby until we could obtain the waiver. Or you could refuse to take the child, and it would be placed into foster care until parental rights could be severed. It could take a few weeks or a few months. There's no way to know until we start. The easiest thing would be for you to get him to sign off on this. I know it's hard, and I know you don't want to, but it would make things much smoother. Once we have his signature, you can start looking at the profiles of potential parents."

Griffin picked up the paper. "I have to get him to sign it?"

"It has to be notarized, but yeah, basically."

"What time do you close?"

"Six."

"I'll be back by then."

Griffin left the office slowly, still not used to the extra weight in her abdomen. She ignored the looks she got in the waiting room, which ranged from open curiosity to mild disgust. Once outside, she waddled to the curb and leaned against the post announcing the bus stop. She studied the map of the route until the bus arrived and then boarded, heaving herself up the steps by pulling on both handles. She carefully counted out change and calculated how much she would need to get home, sighing when she realized she would have to skip lunch to pay the fare to get there and back.

The ride was uncomfortable. The seats were narrow and sticky from humidity. Her stomach barely fit, and the man sitting next to her smelled bad. The stench made bile rise up in the back of her throat. It got so bad that by the time the bus pulled up at her stop, Griffin was glad to get off.

By the time she had walked to the juvenile detention center, sweat rolled down her face, burning her eyes and tasting salty on her tongue. The papers clutched tightly in her hand, she walked up the front door and peered in at the woman in the uniform sitting at the computer.

"Can I help you?"

"I'm here to talk to Ben Grayson."

"Are you family?"

"No."

"The only approved visitors for Mr. Grayson are immediate family members."

Griffin sighed from frustration. "I just need him to sign these papers." She held them up to the glass. "It'll only take five minutes."

"I'm sorry, miss, but rules are rules. I can't let you in."

Before Griffin could open her mouth to argue, a small voice came from behind her. "Griffin?"

Griffin turned and gasped in surprise. "Lexie!" She couldn't stop herself from rushing forward and hugging the slight brunette tightly. "I haven't seen you in months! What happened?"

"My parents didn't want me to stay in that school after what happened with Ben. We moved to Long Island." She looked down suspiciously at Griffin's protruding abdomen. "You're pregnant."

"Yeah." She also looked down. "I need Ben to sign papers releasing his parental rights."

Lexie grabbed Griffin's elbow and pulled her away from the window. "He *raped* you, Griffin. He doesn't have rights!"

"Court could take too long. I want to pick adoptive parents before the baby comes."

"Did you know you were pregnant in court?"

Griffin shook her head and sat down heavily on a bench. "No. They gave me pills in the hospital and did a test a few weeks later. I didn't know."

"The test was negative? How did you find out?"

"I started throwing up a lot. The school nurse took me to the emergency room, and they did an x-ray. They thought it was my pancreas, but it was a baby."

Lexie gasped, her hands flying to her mouth. "Why the hell didn't you have an abortion?"

"I wanted to. But I guess in New York you can't be more than twenty-two weeks along. I was twenty-four when they found the baby." She laughed bitterly. "I started growing the next day, I swear. I can't even see my toes anymore."

"Your foster parents must be pissed!"

"They are. The check they get goes to the doctor and stuff. But they want the baby. They say it's the least I can do. That way they'd get a check for the baby, too. Or I'd get a check and give it to them, I guess."

"They can do that?"

"They say they can."

Lexie shuddered. "What are you going to do?"

"I want to give it up. But I need Ben to sign this paper waiving his rights before they'll let me."

Lexie grabbed the paper from Griffin. "Wait here. I'll get him to sign. My parents want to make me come visit my psycho brother— I'll make something good come out of it!"

Twenty minutes later, Griffin was back on the bus, the signed, notarized papers in her hand. The heat was oppressive, and she could feel sweat dripping down her back and soaking into the elastic band of the damned maternity shorts. She gasped in pain when the bus went over a pothole and felt a sharp pang of pain shoot through her back. Absentmindedly rubbing the spot, she used the other hand to dig through her backpack, trying to find any change she'd missed so that she could get home without having to walk. By the time the bus pulled up to the stop in front of the adoption agency, Griffin's whole belly felt rock hard.

Within thirty minutes, Griffin was walking back out of the adoption agency with several binders crammed into her backpack. Nancy had accepted the papers with a smile of sympathy and handed her half a dozen adoptive parent profiles. Griffin wasn't quite able to work up the courage to ask the counselor for the thirty-five cents she was short on for bus fare.

The walk home was more than five miles, and it was already two-thirty. If she wasn't home by four, Cate and Phil would wonder where she was, and the last thing she wanted was for them to know what she was doing.

She walked as fast as she could, her breath huffing and her chest heaving from exertion. The pain in her back was getting worse and the baby was wriggling like crazy.

She laughed at one particularly hard kick and saw the shape of a foot push against her shirt. The baby had been active since right after she'd discovered she was pregnant. Most of the time, Griffin could convince herself that giving it up was best, and she knew that she wanted her child to have a better life than she did. Sometimes, though, when she was laying in the dark, it was easy to let herself wonder what it would be like to be a mother. To let herself love the baby growing inside of her. She'd found that it would be all too easy to grow attached, so she'd worked hard at thinking about it in abstract terms, as if it was someone else's baby that she was carrying.

Griffin was shaken out of her thoughts when a particularly strong pain hit and her pelvis filled with pressure. Confused and scared, she stopped in the middle of the street, leaning over to brace her hands on her knees. From that vantage point, she saw a dollar lying under one of the blue post office boxes. Her face split into a grin from the elation of not having to walk the rest of the way home. That elation dampened when another pain ripped through her and a gush of blood and fluid poured from between her legs. It splashed the sidewalk, soaked through her clothes and covered her feet.

She wrapped her arms around her stomach, tears filling her eyes. Labor. She stumbled to the blue box, dropped to her knees and craned her arm underneath it to snatch up the wrinkled, damp dollar bill. Clutching it in one hand and digging for fifty more cents with the other, she went as quickly as she could to the nearest bus stop.

The ten-minute wait for the bus was agonizing. She concentrated on breathing, on feeling the air come into her lungs and then rush back out. When the bus turned the corner and pulled into the stop, relief flooded her. She stumbled up the steps as fast as she could manage, nearly falling twice before she collapsed into a seat.

Even more excruciating than the wait for the bus was the ride on the bus. A puddle formed beneath her feet from the amniotic fluid still seeping from between her legs. Every bump sent jolts of pain through her. Her lip was bruised and bloody, bearing the marks of her teeth. She pressed her hands against the bulging mound of her stomach, trying desperately to alleviate the pain.

Finally, after more than an hour on the bus, she stumbled down the steps at the stop nearest to the hospital. Tears streamed down her face, and her knees nearly buckled with every contraction. By the time the lights of the emergency room came into view, she was sobbing from pain and doubled over, walking hunch-backed with her arms wrapped tightly around her stomach.

The doors slid open with a whisper, and Griffin lurched through them. The emergency room was crowded with a menagerie of people with a variety of ailments. She ignored them all, her vision focused on the nurse at the administration desk. She took a deep breath and grabbed onto the desk, her knees weak from the pain of a contraction. The nurse didn't even bother to look up from what she was doing, her eyes focused on the computer screen in front of her.

"Can I help you?"

"I think I'm in labor."

Only slightly more interested, the nurse held out a clipboard. "Fill this out and have a seat. We'll call you back shortly."

Griffin filled out the paperwork as fast as she could. She went to the courtesy phone on the far wall and, fingers shaking, dialed the number of the adoption counselor, who answered on the first ring.

"Nancy Yeager, how may I help you?"

"Ms. Yeager? This is Griffin. I'm in labor. I need you to call the parents for me."

"Which parents did you pick?"

Griffin leaned down and pulled one binder out of her backpack, flipping it open to the cover page. The faces of a middle-aged couple stared back at her. "Alice and Duncan Dawson."

"I'll make the call. What hospital are you at?"

Griffin looked down at the clipboard in her hands and obediently read off the name of the hospital. "St. Ambrose."

"Hold tight and call if you need anything else."

Griffin screamed, her hair wet and sticking to her forehead. She gripped the nurse's hand, her young body straining to give birth years before it should have. The doctor looked up from between Griffin's legs, his eyes conveying his sympathy for the situation the teenager was in.

"The baby's coming, Griffin. I can see the crown of the head. You need to keep pushing on each contraction."

"Are the parents here?" She sank back into the hospital bed, sweat shining on her forehead. A nurse wiped the droplets away and offered her a piece of ice.

"The adoptive parents are in the waiting room, yes." The doctor took his gown from the nurse and slipped his arms into it. "Gloves." He slipped his hands into the latex gloves and tied a mask around his face. "Let's get this baby delivered."

"Go get them. They should be here. It's their baby."

"Are you sure? Griffin, you've been in labor for fifteen hours. It's not their baby until you sign the papers."

Griffin bit back a cry from the contraction. When it was over, exhausted from the exertion of pushing, she glared at the doctor between her legs, struggling to see him over the bulge of her stomach. "I want them here. They should see this."

"Okay. Now, push!"

Griffin bore down, her head thrown back and the veins in her forehead popping out from pain. She gripped the nurse's hand even tighter, gritted her teeth, and strained with every bit of strength she had. She vaguely noticed that the couple adopting the baby entered the room, but her concentration was fully devoted to the task at hand—bringing another life into the world.

She felt the give as the fetus slipped from the birth canal into the awaiting hands of the doctor. The moment of relief was followed by the raspy cry of her baby. It wailed, and she collapsed against the pillows, her hand going limp in that of the nurse's as she cried. It was over.

"It's a boy. Eight pounds, three ounces. Do you want to hold him, Griffin?"

Griffin forced herself to open her eyes and looked at the nurse and shook her head. "No. I don't. Give him to Alice. He's her son."

Alice, tears in her eyes, stretched her arms out toward the infant. "Are you sure, sweetheart? You can hold him. We want you to be able to say goodbye."

"No. He's not mine. Take him. Please, take him out of here."

Even hours later, when she was cleaned up and in a fresh hospital gown with her room filled with flowers that Alice and Duncan had bought at the gift shop, she didn't want to see her child. The nurse brought the bassinet down every couple of hours, but Griffin couldn't bring herself to look at the baby. She hated him. She knew the emotion was irrational, that it wasn't what she should be feeling, but the baby embodied everything that was wrong in her life, everything that had happened to her and everything that she would never get to experience. To her, the baby wasn't a miracle.

She expected that the older couple was enjoying their new baby. Cooing and talking in the nursery; excitedly informing their families that all their dreams had come true. What she hadn't expected was for Alice—pretty, tiny Alice—to knock on her door and ask in that soft, silky voice of hers if she could come in and talk for a few minutes. Griffin noticed immediately that a nurse was behind her, again pushing the bassinet.

"I guess."

Alice chose the chair closest to the bed and perched daintily. "I just wanted to take a few minutes and talk to you. Make sure that this is what you want."

"It's what I want. I'm not going to change my mind and take him back." Griffin sighed, battling over how much to tell Alice. "Look, I hope it doesn't make you want him less, but I was raped. And the emergency pill didn't work. I'm in foster care—my parents are dead. My grandparents, who were raising me, are dead. I don't have anything to give him. I don't want him. I can't keep him, because he reminds me of what happened, of everything that's gone wrong in my life."

Alice's eyes welled with tears as she listened to Griffin speak. "No, I don't want him less." She reached out and gripped Griffin's hand. "I don't know what to say. I understand why you feel like you do. I can't say that I wouldn't feel the same way in your position. But please know that what you've done today is the most selfless thing a woman can do. Today, through your tragedy, you've made our dreams come true. You've created a family." She crossed to the door and paused. "If you want to hold him, we'd like that. To let you say goodbye. At the very least you should see him. He's your son."

Griffin waited until both the nurse and Alice had left the room. She fought the urge for another ten minutes before looking down into the bassinet and the face of the baby she had birthed mere hours earlier. Hesitantly, she reached out with one finger and touched the tiny cheek, amazed at the softness. She felt a pang deep within her and smiled weakly. Her still developing breasts ached as they filled with milk; a cruel reminder of the ordeal she had been through.

Tears blurred her vision. She swung her legs around and placed her feet on the floor, leaning down to rest her head on the side of the bassinet. She inhaled the sweet scent of baby. Her shoulders trembled with silent sobs. The tears that had welled in her eyes spilled over, hot and thick. They ran down her face, dripping off her cheeks and onto the face of her son. She wrapped her arms around the clear plastic crib and laid her head against it. Her breath wrenched its way out of her with a keening wail and she held her breath in a futile effort to stop the tears. Her chest burned from holding in her grief. Expelling it with a great, gasping breath, she broke down, her whole body shaking from the force of her cries.

Outside her doorway, seen by no one, Alaria and Gabriel stood silently, studying the scene unfolding in front of them.

"Each time I watch one of your events, it is more repugnant than the last."

Alaria smiled sharply. "That's the whole point, Gabe." She cocked an eyebrow. "I almost wish the girl would have chosen to keep the whelp. That would have opened up so many other fun avenues. As it is, I won't be able to utilize the child for any more of my events."

"Praise my Father for small favors. I'm forced to watch her endure your torture, Alaria. I would not be so compelled with another innocent child."

"The baby might be, but Griffin won't be innocent for long." Alaria laughed. "You'd be horrified by what's coming up next for her."

Gabriel brushed invisible lint from his suit, uncomfortable with the conversation. "You've used three of your events thus far. One third of the way there and she still cries for God at night."

"And He still ignores her pleas. Eventually she will give up. We both know humans can't endure this kind of torture and still believe in Him."

"Job did."

Alaria wrinkled her nose. "Job was a glutton for punishment." She turned an appraising eye back to Griffin, who still cried. "She's on the verge of giving in— I can sense it."

"Was it really necessary to make her labor so long and difficult? How can that be important to this?"

She smiled brightly and shook her head. "It isn't. It was fun though."

Gabriel sighed deeply. "Devils never cease to disgust me." He turned away from the hospital room. "Have you any other atrocities planned for today?"

"Not today. As you said, I've used three of my events. I have to pace myself so I don't run out. She's safe for another year or two." Alaria smiled at Gabriel and snapped her fingers, disappearing with a loud crack, only her voice lingering. "See you next time."

Gabriel spread his wings in annoyance, their width spanning the entire hallway. When he flicked them closed, he thought he caught sight of a teenage boy, though when he turned there was no one in the hallway. He shook his head to clear it and turned in a circle, trying to catch sight of the human boy again. When there was no trace of him, the Angel smiled.

"At least you've learned to lie low, my boy."

With a quiet whisper of his wings, Gabriel disappeared, leaving Griffin, once again, alone.

Chapter Seven

December 31st, 2015 - New York City

SIXTEEN. SHE'D BE sixteen tomorrow. Only two more years until freedom. Until no one could tell her what to do and when to do it. Until Phil would stop sneaking into her room late at night to watch her sleep.

She'd known when it had begun. Right after she'd come back to their apartment after having the baby. He'd stopped viewing her as a little girl and started viewing her as a woman. He'd taken to slapping her ass when Cate wasn't looking and making comments about her developing anatomy. She tolerated it because she didn't have a choice. Because some part of her believed that she deserved it—that she had somehow asked for it. After all, good people didn't have to go through the things she had to go through. They didn't have to survive the tragedies she had—they didn't have a baby at thirteen.

The dreams weren't helping. Dreams that she was in Hell, that she was burning, with a voice constantly telling her that Hell was her destiny, that God had forsaken her, that there was no choice. She couldn't help but wonder if there was any truth to it. If the God she'd always thought of as merciful and loving had completely forgotten about her. If there was any point in continuing to try and live her life the way her parents had told her to in those few short years before they'd been brutally killed.

She remembered Sunday school lessons vaguely. She remembered a plump woman in a flowered dress telling a class full of children stories from the Bible. That God crafted each person lovingly and deliberately. That He breathed into them a soul. He gave them each a purpose. He was supposed to know the very hairs on her head and the thoughts in her mind. He was supposed to do all of those things and know everything about her. And yet He had failed to do anything to stop the horrible things she'd had to endure. Not once had she felt His hand upon her or His presence surrounding her. He knew her, had made her. And even He didn't love her.

Depressed, Griffin rolled onto her side and looked at the closed door. She wondered briefly if Phil would come in again tonight. If she'd wake up knowing before she opened her eyes that he was there, standing above her. She shivered at the thought and felt flickers of anger form deep within her in response to the fear she felt of Phil.

She needed to take the edge off if she was going to sleep. There was nothing she could do to stop Phil, so there was no reason that she had to stay awake and wait for it, either. She craned her arm under the narrow mattress and wiggled her fingers until she felt the edge of the bag that she kept her drugs in. She pulled it out and went through the almost cathartic process of preparing her hit.

Almost disinterestedly, she turned the syringe in her hand from side to side, studying the contents and considering whether or not she was going to use it. After all, it wasn't as if it would be the first time, and it wasn't likely to be the last.

Apparently, she'd inherited her mother's taste for drugs. She liked the way they made her feel—the way they took her out of reality and into a place that felt unreal. She liked the freedom of not having to worry about things a sixteen-year-old shouldn't have to worry about. Like grocery shopping, and making sure bills got paid, and stocking the fridge with beer so that Cate and Phil wouldn't bitch.

She'd turned to drugs the year before. Started out simple, with a boy who offered her a joint after school. She'd accepted it on a whim and had liked the feeling, but it hadn't been enough. Nothing was enough. She never flew far enough, free enough, to fully escape her life. Each time, with a different drug, she got closer. Heroin, cocaine, meth, ecstasy, oxy. She'd tried them all. But each time, she always went home to the drug that had started it all for her, ended it all for her real mother. She knew, if she kept it up, it would end it all for her as well. Heroin.

Griffin had learned to make it into an injection, found that it was the quickest way to get it into her system, and it made the high the strongest. Resolved that she was going to ring in her birthday in style, she flicked the syringe to check for air and then popped it just underneath her skin. She wasn't ready to main vein it yet. Besides, that was much more dangerous than going just below the first layer of skin.

The drug hit hard and fast, sweeping her away in a high so great that it made her begin to giggle uncontrollably. She lay down on the bed, relaxing into the effects. She felt her muscles relax in incremental degrees. Her head spun with a deliciously light feeling and the room was flooded with colors. She smiled as she floated on the waves of careening pleasure as the drugs coursed through her veins. Then, in an instant, everything changed. Instead of floating, she felt like she was falling. The floor gave way into a black nothingness, and she fell, careening down, down, further and further, until she crashed into hard, dry dirt without a bit of living foliage.

Feeling strangely sober, Griffin climbed to her feet and took in her surroundings. There was something oddly familiar about the red sky dotted with black clouds. Dusting herself off, she headed to the edge of the hill she had landed on and looked over the edge and saw a lake. Rationalizing that if anyone was going to find her they would look near water, she scrambled down the steep hill, scraping her palms on small rocks and holding her breath at times to get a break from the smell of sulfur permeating the air.

Once on the beach, she winced as the hot black sand scalded her feet and moved toward the water, intending to walk along the edge and let the water cool her skin. She stopped and jumped back when she saw that the water boiled violently.

She stood back for a long moment, considering where to go from there. Then, slowly, she crept back toward the water to get a better look at it. High or not, she knew that water did not boil for no good reason. When she reached the water's edge and looked into it, what she saw would be burned into her memory for the rest of her life.

The water, even along the edge, was deep and appeared to simply drop off hundreds of feet. Instead of being blue or green or gray or any other color that water was, it was inky black. The longer Griffin stared, the more she was able to discern some shapes. Then, she saw people rising to the surface, their skin white and pasty, their eyes black and unseeing, their mouths spread open in a perpetual scream. They stretched their fingers toward the surface, reaching for relief from the boiling depths of black water; relief that Griffin somehow knew could never be obtained. Their feet were wrapped in chains that descended into the deep water, presumably anchored to the bottom of the abyss.

The moment she saw them, she knew exactly where she was—in Hell.

"That's right. You are."

Griffin whirled and found a gorgeous woman dressed in red and black leather standing behind her. She glided on spike heels and carried a whip in one hand, looking dangerous and like every man's greatest fantasy all at the same time. "I know you."

"So you do remember. I'm Alaria. Welcome home, Griffin."

"Am I dead?"

"No, you aren't dead. If you were, you'd be in that lake right there instead of standing here talking to me. You're here because I brought you here. Because you're special."

"Special how?"

"Walk with me, and I'll explain." She led Griffin back away from the beach and extended a hand to create a path that was more comfortable on Griffin's bare feet. "A long time ago, my Lord decided that he wanted an heir. He set into motion a series of events that would bring us a very special person that would lead us to victory against Heaven. You are that very special person, and I have brought you here to offer you a seat on the throne next to Satan."

Shocked and nearly speechless, Griffin stopped walking. "You're shitting me."

"I assure you I am completely serious about this. There is nothing that means more to me than ensuring the victory of Hell over the Angels. I know what you've been through, Griffin. I know that God has forsaken you. I know that you feel alone and like no one loves you. Like drugs are your only refuge, the only things that can make you feel good. Well, they aren't."

"I'm not selling my soul to the Devil. I can't—I won't."

"You misunderstand. You would not be selling your soul. You would not go into the pit, ever. You would be brought here for eternity to rule alongside Lucifer, commanding his army and punishing everyone who has hurt you."

"Punish them how?"

Alaria smiled because she knew then that she was closer than she ever had been before to winning the Choosing. Griffin was actually considering the offer. "However you want. There would be no restraints placed upon you—there would be no rules. You would get to do as you pleased. If you wished to torture, you could torture. Conversely, you could reward those who have treated you well. You would control the legions of Hell, Griffin. And all you have to do is agree to it."

"How do you know that God has forsaken me?"

Her voice kind, Alaria put one hand on Griffin's arm. "Because I hear your cries for Him at night when you think no one listens. I hear you. I know your pain as He does not. Has He ever come to you, offering to make it okay? Has He ever sent an Angel to you, to tell you that He feels your pain? Have you ever felt His arms around you, comforting you when you sob? I feel your pain. I feel your loss. I feel those things because you were born to be ours. You were not born of God, Griffin. That does not have to be a bad thing. You can have an existence here that is far superior to the one you have on Earth."

Griffin began walking again, her mind racing with thoughts. She had gone to Sunday school with her parents. She knew about Satan and God, and demons and Angels. She knew about Judgment day and what was supposed to happen. What she didn't know, however, was whether or not it was even possible for a human being to be born not of God. After all, didn't God breathe the soul into the body? If she was forsaken by God, did that mean she didn't have a soul? And if she didn't have a soul, what was the damn point in trying to be anything but what Alaria was encouraging her to be?

"How do I know this isn't a trick?"

Alaria managed to conceal her excitement, but just barely. "Humans generally think that we lie to them, and that we'll do anything to win a soul. Generally that's very true. Demons do lie, and they lie quite often. They're known for their trickery. But I cannot lie to you."

"Aren't you a demon?"

"No. I am a Devil. I am one of the original Fallen that joined with Lucifer in the great battle. I was an Angel, Griffin. I cannot lie to you. Demons are souls that were cast into the pit that have morphed to become much more than their human forms allowed them to be. They have been chosen by the Fallen to serve both in Hell and on Earth. In exchange for being pulled from the pit, they are allowed to play aboveground. Their job is to get souls. And they will do whatever is necessary to do that, because if they fail in their task, they will be cast back in the Lake of Fire and brimstone. You saw it. It doesn't look very pleasant, does it?"

"And if I don't stay here?" Griffin spread her arms to encompass all that she saw. The look on her face showed thinly veiled skepticism. She searched the Devil's face for answers, her eyes moving rapidly back and forth.

"You'll be sent back to Earth, where your life will continue. You're simply asleep right now. You can return to your bed at any time. I cannot say what will happen during your life. It may be worse; it may be better. I cannot tell you the future. But I can tell you this. Your task will never change, and you will always be meant to rule here. I can promise you that God will never bring you into His fold."

"And if I stay? Could I ever leave?"

"No. You would be here permanently." Alaria's heart pounded beneath her breast, excitement oozing out every pore. She had waited for this moment for millennia. She was closer than she'd ever imagined to getting the Chosen to stay with her. "But you could visit Earth. You would be able to walk among the humans, enjoy human interaction and human distractions."

Something felt wrong. Something was not resonating with Griffin. She shook her head. "No. Not yet. I'm not jumping into something without doing research. I can't."

"We won't keep making these offers forever. And you'll end up here eventually, one way or the other. We will rise up and defeat Heaven, and you can either be here with us, leading our army into battle, or you can be a casualty of war."

"Then why offer me the position at all if you'll get me in the end? Wouldn't you get more enjoyment out of watching me burn than having a human as your boss?"

"I'm offering you an escape from a world that has given you nothing but pain. And yet you refuse to take it?"

Griffin's eyes narrowed, her suspicious nature making her exceedingly uncomfortable with the situation. "If this was as simple as you say it is, you wouldn't be so angry about my wanting to do some research about it. I have free will; that's my right as a human. And I'll only accept your offer if I decide it's the best thing for me. I want to go home."

"Home? To a shitty apartment infested with bugs and a foster father that watches you sleep and spies on you in the shower? To a reality where you're well on your way to being an addict like your mother, and where you'll spread your legs for any man who looks at you and says you're pretty? Where you're trying to turn every nice word into the love and attention you should have gotten as a child? That's not a life, Griffin. It's an existence. I can offer you a place where you can flourish. Where you can make men love you; where everything is within your reach."

"And I only have to give up my humanity. That's too high a price for something I'm not sure I'll end up getting."

Griffin concentrated on waking up and was jerking to consciousness in her bedroom, the beeper on the dryer waking her from the deep sleep she'd fallen into. Feeling the effects of the drug she had injected, she put her hand on her forehead and tried to make sense of what had happened. It was only then that she noticed she was on the floor and tried to crawl onto the bed. She slipped twice and had to start over, but finally, she lay on her back, clad in a tank top and a pair of panties, the covers kicked to the bottom to accommodate the suffocating heat coming from the furnace.

She felt his presence a split second before the door opened and scrambled to drag the blanket up over her mostly naked body. She was too late, and he was in the room before she could pretend to be asleep. He wore nothing but boxers, which were tented with a horrendous erection as he shut the door behind him.

"Go away, Phil. I'm obviously not asleep, so you can't stand by my bed and jack off tonight."

Angry at being caught and hornier than he could remember being in his whole life, Phil stalked to the bed and jerked the blanket off of her, taking in her almost skinny frame and small, not yet completely developed breasts. "Maybe I don't want to stand over you and jack off tonight. Maybe I want you to do to me what you do to all those other boys. Maybe it's time for you to earn your keep around here."

Irritated, but not yet scared, Griffin stood up and reached for a pair of sweatpants. "What? Flat on my back? I don't think so. I do enough around here without doing you, too."

"You little bitch. We put food in your belly and clothes on your back. We give you a roof over your head. And all you can do is be ungrateful. You're damn lucky we haven't thrown you out after all you've put us through all these years."

"You mean getting raped? Like that was my fault. And the state puts food in my belly, clothes on my back, and a roof over my head. They would do that whether or not you were here. So if you have a problem with me, send me back. I'm out of here in two years anyway, and you'll lose that monthly check. Now get out of my room before I tell Cate what you've been up to."

"She wouldn't believe you."

"Then I'll report you. CPS takes these things seriously, you know. You'd probably lose your license to be a foster parent." She sneered as she pulled on the pants. "Imagine that, you'd actually have to get a job to afford this dump."

The slap took her off guard, and she automatically put a hand to her face where her cheek turned an angry shade of red. Phil looked shocked that he'd done it, but then smiled as if he realized that he had enjoyed hitting her. She saw his fist clench a split second before he plowed it into her nose. She grunted as blood sprayed, and she heard the telltale crunch of a broken nose.

He tackled her, pummeling her with his fists, dragging her to the ground and kicking her. She screamed and flailed, trying to escape him. She pounded her fists into his chest but wasn't strong enough to break his hold. He knelt and pressed his hips into hers. His erection jutted into her groin. He covered her mouth with his and yanked her hair to force her head back.

Griffin was not going to be raped again. Since the rape, she had slept with several men, but she had always done it on her terms. She had vowed that she would never again be taken advantage of by a man.

She consciously forced herself to stop struggling and began looking around for something that she could use as a weapon. She nearly wretched when his hand slid down her pants and he palmed her. She flailed for the ink pen that was just out of reach. When he shifted to remove his boxers, she lurched up, grabbed the pen, and without thinking, plunged it into his neck.

He screamed and rolled off of her, jerking the pen out and sending blood spurting from the wound. She backed up, pressing her back against the wall and watched as Cate burst into the room and took in the situation just as she did everything else. Quickly, efficiently, and ruthlessly. She took in Phil's gaping boxers, the erection hanging out, Griffin's bloody nose, and the blood pouring from Phil's neck. Then, she did something that Griffin never would have guessed.

"Get out of here. I'll put the police off. Go. Now."

"What? Why? I stabbed him."

"The Johnson speaks for itself, Griffin. I suspected, but I never thought—just get out of here. I won't risk him doing this to our daughters. Go!"

Griffin dragged on clothes and grabbed the backpack she always kept stocked with a change of clothes. Without stopping to analyze it, she grabbed Cate's purse from the counter, took all the cash she saw and then did the same thing with Phil's wallet. Stopping only to pull on her coat, she raced down the street and threw up her arm to hail a cab. When one pulled over to the curb, she leapt in and slammed the door.

"Grand Central Station."

Gabriel turned to Alaria, his brows drawn together in mild confusion. "Why did you do that?"

"I can do more to her out in the world than I can in prison. In prison it's expected—it's anticipated. One moment of kindness from a woman who has put her through years of abuse is not going to erase the progress that was made this night." She smiled and ran her sharp nails down his arm. "She almost agreed to remain in Hell with me."

"Almost doesn't count, Devil. You should have learned that by now. She's human. She'll seek out answers."

"I wouldn't bet on it. She already has a deep mistrust of anything having to do with God. She feels abandoned. Like no one has ever been there for her. Except for me. I offer her a chance to rule, to punish those who have hurt her, to get retribution against everyone who has turned their back on her. When she chooses Hell, she will lead us in a siege on Heaven."

"That is not part of the deal, Alaria. You'd best remember that God has not forsaken her. He is a merciful God, and He aches at watching her in pain. Were it not necessary to decide the End, this would not be occurring."

Alaria laughed bitterly. "Your God is not nearly as merciful as you seem to think that He is. Remember why I was cast down, Brother? Not because I joined Lucifer, but because of what I fought for. He has all the patience in the world for humans and tolerates nothing but the strictest obedience from the creatures He made first."

"We were created to obey. Humans were created to have free will. We were made to be objects to do His bidding. You never understood that. We are agents of God. We're able to know Him in a way that no human will ever be able to comprehend. It is a sacrifice I would gladly make had I been given a choice. To know God as I do, or to be able to stumble about as humans, given only the gift of free will? That's not a choice."

"It's of no importance now. That's thousands of years in the past. In case you're wondering, in six human months, she will be diagnosed with cancer. Leukemia, I think. Something nasty that will make her sick, lose weight, and undergo all of those barbaric human medical treatments. It will last for years I do believe. She'll nearly die. But since I can't kill her,

I'll wait until the time is right, until she is so close to death that she's willing to do anything, and then I will offer to heal her. If she joins me."

"You have to heal her at some point, Alaria." Gabriel crossed his arms over his chest. His eyes were focused on the scene still playing out in front of them. He couldn't help the smile that quirked the corner of his mouth at seeing Cate wielding a pair of scissors at her husband and holding the phone just out of reach.

Alaria nodded slowly. She tapped her fingernails against her leg as she considered her options. "I know. Can't have her committing suicide. Besides, I have some other things in mind for this one. Drug addiction, prostitution, some stints in jail, nothing too long. She's going to beg me to take her by the time I offer her a place in Hell again."

It was at that point that Gabriel knew he would have to intercede. Alaria was flirting with the lines, staying just shy of breaking the rules. The further she pushed, the more likely it seemed as if she was going to get her way. He could not allow that to happen. He would do the same thing that she was doing. Flirt with the lines. He knew it was time to go to Griffin and tell her that she wasn't truly alone.

Chapter Eight

December 31st, 2019 - Philadelphia, Pennsylvania
"I'M SORRY, GRIFFIN. The cancer is back."

Those words had been echoing in Griffin's mind for the six weeks since her oncologist had uttered them. She remembered them every time a nurse inserted an IV to start the chemo treatments. She remembered them every time she found her mailbox filled with hospital bills. She remembered them every time she found herself throwing up what small amount of food she could force herself to eat.

Who the hell gets cancer before they got out of their teenage years? That question haunted her, plagued her thoughts, and made her bitter. She mulled it over, like she had done a thousand times before, as she tried to muster the energy to finish tying her shoes before leaving her apartment.

Her fingers were stiff from the cold as she tried to convince the laces to cooperate. It had been two months since the electricity had gotten shut off, and the only heat she had was what seeped through the paper thin walls from the apartments around her. She supposed she should be grateful it was enough to stop her from freezing to death in her sleep.

But instead of gratitude, she felt anger. It was a bubbling, roiling, bitter anger. She felt it toward God, herself, and the world in general. The good thing about anger was that it gave her energy. She used that to force herself to climb to her feet and pull on her coat. Her fingers slipped the buttons into their holes, and she stopped briefly to look at herself in the mirror.

Her hair had almost all fallen out. Her thick, luxurious curls had fallen away to become stringy, patchy tufts of fuzz. Torn between fury and sadness, she did the only thing she knew to do and covered her almost bald head with a scarf. That unfortunate chore done, she opened the door to exit the apartment. She barely noticed that she still reached to turn off the non-existent lights before closing the door behind her.

The walk to work was cold and miserable, but it wasn't far enough for her to able to justify spending the money on a cab or the bus. Resigned to trudging through the icy December sludge, she did her best to ignore the biting wind ripping through her thin, worn coat as if it wasn't even there.

The restaurant was busy when she arrived, as it was every night. She weaved her way through the crowd as quickly as she could, her anxiety already rising since she was—she looked at her watch—seven minutes late for her shift.

Praying that the manager hadn't seen her slip in late, she punched her time sheet and tied on her apron, stopping once to make sure her pen and order pad was in her pocket. She checked the board in the kitchen to make sure what section she was assigned to and headed out onto the floor.

With a smile plastered onto her face, she approached her first table quickly. "Hello, everyone." She surveyed the four men sitting in the booth. "I'm Griffin, and I'll be your server. Can I start you off with some drinks?"

"We'll need a pitcher of Michelob Ultra and a round of tequila shots." The man speaking glanced down at the menu. "Let's also take the loaded nachos and some onion rings." He nodded as if they were done, then yelled for her when she started to walk away from the table. "And four waters."

"I'll get that right out to you."

Five minutes later, her tray loaded with a pitcher of beer, four empty mugs, four shots, four glasses of water and a basket of fried onions, Griffin headed out of the kitchen and back toward the booth. The muscles in her arms, weak from the chemo and radiation, trembled under the weight of the tray. Her legs burned from the exertion and her stomach was tying itself into knots, the nausea threatening to expel the meager contents of her stomach all over the floor.

She concentrated on her current task, which was getting all the drinks to the table without spilling them. So intent was her concentration that she didn't see the puddle of spilled liquid almost directly in front of the booth. She stepped in it, slid, and pitched forward, a scream bursting from her lips as she tumbled to the floor. Her tray flew out of her hands, soaring through the air and falling to the ground, the glasses crashing. Alcohol and water sprayed all four men in the booth and broken glass rained down on the floor and the table. Adding insult to injury, her stomach chose that moment to rebel, and Griffin vomited.

Other waitresses rushed to help her, pulling her up by her arms. She wiped her mouth and turned to the four men. "I am so sorry. I'll get you a new round. On the house."

The man who had ordered glared at her, still wiping booze from his clothes. He stood up and tiny fragments of glass showered the floor as they fell from his lap and hit the floor with almost metallic noises. "I want to see your manager."

Chad, a skinny man with glasses and a moustache, rushed over when he heard the commotion. He shoved past Griffin roughly as he made his way to the table. "I'm the manager. My sincerest apology for my waitress. It won't happen again, I can promise you that. Your meals will be on the house."

"Dude, there's glass everywhere, we're covered in beer and there's fucking puke on the floor! A free meal isn't going to fix that."

"I understand completely. We'll get you a new table immediately. I can assure you that she will be dealt with." Chad threw a look at Griffin over his shoulder. "She no longer works for this establishment."

Fired. Griffin found that yet another word was added to her mental recitation. She repeated it over and over as she trudged home. She climbed the stairs dejectedly and entered her cold apartment. There was an envelope on the floor just inside the door and she stooped to pick it up. She ripped it open and unfolded the paper. An eviction notice. Great. Just fucking great.

Disgusted, Griffin ripped the paper into shreds and tossed it onto the floor. No matter how hard she worked, she never had enough money. The chemo sucked away her energy and the hospital sucked away her money. There simply was never enough. Electricity, rent, medical bills. She'd made headway when she'd been in remission, then lost it as soon as the cancer had come back.

She walked to the lone nightstand in the one-room apartment and opened it, hoping against hope that it wasn't as empty as she feared it was. Instead of the tiny envelope of white powder she had hoped to find, she found the pathetic remnants of her last paycheck. Heart sinking, she counted out the crumbled bills and coins. Eighty-seven dollars. She owed three hundred on rent. She cast a look at the mini fridge, mentally recounting its contents.

She had to make money and she had to have the drugs. What had started as a recreational escape at fifteen had become the only way that she managed the pain from the cancer. She knew she was addicted, and she knew that purchasing the cocaine stretched her already meager budget beyond its limits.

Griffin flopped back on the mattress that was lying on her floor and stared up at the ceiling. She wanted the drugs, but she also wanted to sleep. She looked at the wind-up clock on the floor next to her and considered her options. Deciding on a compromise of sorts, she set an alarm for midnight and closed her eyes.

Sleep overtook her almost immediately. It was as if she closed her eyes to go to sleep and then opened them in another world. She recognized it instantly: the red dirt and the black sky. She turned in a circle and her eyes settled on the onyx towers of the black castle rising above everything else to pierce the sky.

"It's beautiful, isn't it?"

Griffin turned when she heard a voice behind her and found Alaria standing several yards away. "Beautiful isn't the word I had in mind."

"It's been a while since I've seen you, Griffin. Welcome home."

Griffin laughed. "I'm not home. This is Hell."

"I know where we are. I brought you here."

"Going to try to weave another tale about how special I am and how you need me here?"

Alaria smiled softly. "What makes you think I'm weaving a tale and not just telling you the truth? Have I ever lied to you before?" When only silence met her question, she chuckled. "Why do you distrust me so much, child?"

"Because you're a demon. I'd think that would be self-explanatory."

"Then who do you trust? God?" Alaria shook her head. "How is that relationship going for you? Has it changed in the last four years since I last saw you? Any answered prayers to report? Or is He still maintaining radio silence?"

Griffin glared at the Devil. "It's none of your business."

"You need to learn to be a better liar, child." Alaria snapped her fingers and they were both standing in a ballroom. The walls and floors were made out of onyx; the ceiling was carved from rubies. There were three thrones against one wall. Alaria strode toward them, her spiked heels clicking on the floor. She draped herself across one of the thrones, one leg dangling over the arm. "You could have all this."

"No offense, lady, but I'm not exactly worried about ruling anything."

Alaria smiled knowingly. "I know. Let's see if I can name your top five concerns. Cancer, rent, bills, drugs, and food. Does that cover it?"

"How do you know that?"

"I know everything about you."

Griffin scoffed. "That's just perfect. You know all there is to know about me and I know nothing about you."

"All you need to know is that I can fix everything in your life. I can cure your cancer with a snap of my fingers. I can give you piles of money. Enough for an unlimited supply of that white powder you need so much. Or, if you prefer, I can cure you of that, too."

Griffin crossed her arms. "What's the catch?"

"The same as it's always been."

"Before, you said I'd have to stay here."

"You do. But you could access Earth. Go there for whatever you want, whenever you want. There would be no restrictions. Power, glory, money. You could have whatever your little heart desires. No more cancer, no more addiction. What do you want? Tell me, and I can make it happen."

"If you can do it, why don't you just heal me? Prove it. Heal me and then maybe we can talk about the rest."

"It doesn't work that way. To get the prize, you pay the price."

Alaria knew immediately that she'd chosen the wrong words. Griffin's eyes narrowed and she shook her head vehemently. "I'm not going to pay a price. You need me. Or so you say. If this deal you keep offering is so great, then there wouldn't be a price. What aren't you telling me?"

"It's a figure of speech. My gifts aren't free. I do something for you, you do something for me."

Griffin ran her hands over her stubbly hair. "I don't want to stay in Hell. I don't want to give up life. I want life to get better." She turned in a circle, her arms spread wide to encompass the ballroom. "I don't want this."

"You could die. And if you die, you go to Hell. Would you like me to show you the lake again, just so you remember what it's like? Or maybe you'd like me to give you a taste of it?" Alaria's eyes darkened as she approached Griffin. "You keep taking this for granted. I am not here to amuse you, little girl, and I am not here to bargain. You either take the deal, or you take your chances. This is not a negotiation, and my patience is not infinite."

Her eyes hardening, Griffin shook her head. "I'll pass, thanks."

In her bed, Griffin came awake suddenly, her chest heaving as she sucked in air. Her head was spinning and her whole body ached for a fix. She knew she couldn't put it off any longer before she would start into withdrawal. She climbed to her feet as fast as she could and hurriedly left the apartment, barely taking time to pull on her coat and lock the door behind her.

She walked the thirteen blocks as fast as she could to the corner where her dealer worked. Armando, a slick Italian in a cheap suit and puffy coat, leaned against the wall of a building, smoothly exchanging a packet of white powder for a sheaf of bills. He smiled and walked over when he saw Griffin.

"What can I get you?"

"I don't have money."

"Well then, that's a problem, now isn't it?"

"You know I'm good for it. I'll get you the money as soon as I can."

Armando lifted his eyebrows. "I'm not going to give you a fix, Griffin. If I do it for you, everyone would want the same treatment." He grinned. "You could work it off."

"How?"

"I run a side business." When she looked at him blankly, he sighed. "I deal in pussy, sweetheart. We put a wig on you to hide the bald head and you'd be pretty popular with the boys." He looked her over with an appraising eye. "Nice tits, good ass. I could make a few dollars off you."

Griffin felt sick from the suggestion. She wracked her brain for another solution, but found she couldn't come up with one. She needed money—a lot of it—and fast. Money for rent, for food, for bills. If she was honest, she also needed money for the drugs. She battled down the wave of nausea and took a deep breath.

"What would the deal be?"

"I provide the men, you provide the pussy. They pay me. I give you a cut of the money and a supply of the coke."

"What's the cut?"

"Fifty-fifty. You could make a few hundred a night. I charge two hundred an hour for the girls. You do any on the side, that's your money."

Griffin fought a fierce inner battle. She wavered for several moments, her mind racing. Finally, before she even decided to take the deal, the words were forcing their way past her lips. "I need something for tonight though."

Armando smiled. "Honey, you can work that off right now." He opened the door to the building he'd been leaning against. "I've got a room in the back. I like to test out all the merchandise before I sell it." He slapped her ass as she walked through the door. "Some blow for a blow job. Seems fair to me."

It was all Griffin could do not to throw up again.

Across the parking lot, Gabriel stood watching the sick scene play out. Alaria stood next to him, her foot tapping impatiently on the sidewalk. The Angel made a noise deep in his throat. "That's getting incredibly annoying."

Alaria glared at him. "Far be it from me to inconvenience you, Gabe." She rolled her eyes. "I almost had her tonight. I'll get her yet."

"You're much more confident in yourself than your success thus far would justify." He turned away from the building to face the Devil. "She still prays."

"They're desperate and rare now. It won't be long until she doesn't pray at all. She hasn't done so regularly since my last event." Alaria clapped Gabriel's shoulder happily. "I'm making progress, old friend, and there's not a thing in the world that you can do about it. The old man upstairs decided to make humans born good, so I get ten chances to wipe her clean. I'm doing my job, Gabe. They both agreed to this."

Gabriel's eyes were dark from anger and sadness. "That doesn't mean I agree with Him."

Alaria ignored the twinge she felt. "I'm not talking about that, Gabe. I'm talking about right here and now."

"I've no idea of what you're speaking, Devil."

"We both know that was a loaded statement. You may not have agreed all those years ago, but you certainly didn't fight Him over it."

Gabriel frowned as realization dawned upon him. "You thought I was alluding to the Fall." He laughed bitterly. "I've had millions of human years to get over that, Alaria. I don't need to make veiled references."

Alaria glanced at him out of the corner of her eye. "You're nothing but a blind soldier, doing what you're told."

"Doing the job for which I was created. The one you were created for, in case you've forgotten."

"How could I forget? I was reminded of it every single day I was in your ranks. At least now I have freedom." Alaria turned back to the building. "I'm done discussing the past. I've no interest in watching two humans fuck." She smiled at Gabriel saccharinely, the sweet smile looking terrifyingly evil on her face. "Enjoy the show."

With a loud crack and a spark, Alaria disappeared, leaving Gabriel alone. He stood silently for several minutes, lost in thought. Only when Griffin stumbled out of the building, her scarf nearly displaced from her head and her lips red and swollen, did he snap out of his reverie. The sight of the packet of cocaine in her hand made his chest constrict with dread. Fear licking at him, he allowed himself to fade away, leaving Griffin alone.

Chapter Nine

December 31st, 2021 - Philadelphia, Pennsylvania
GRIFFIN SAT UP and reached for her clothes and pulled the denim skirt and halter top on over her naked body. She grimaced when the room spun as she stood and balanced herself on the hotel room's one dresser. Stumbling slightly from both pain and drugs, she grabbed her purse and stepped into treacherously high heels.

"Leaving already?"

"The deal was for an hour. I gave you ten minutes over."

"You could stay the rest of a second hour."

Griffin scowled at the man sprawled across the bed, a cigarette already lit in his hand and the used condom still hanging half off his dick. She felt nothing but disgust. "No, thanks." She grabbed the wad of cash on the dresser and thumbed through it. "Even if I wanted to, you don't have enough money to buy another hour."

"There's five hundred dollars there! We agreed on two hundred."

"I charge by the act, darlin', or the hour, whichever is higher. You wanted sex and a blowjob. That's four hundred." She counted out five twenty-dollar bills and tossed them back on the dresser. She pulled on her coat, pocketed the money, and opened the door. "It was fun. See ya later."

Griffin strutted through the door, intent on keeping up the appearance of being in control. She descended to the dimly lit parking lot, her heels clicking on the cement sidewalk and then on the grate of the stairs. The sound of traffic was louder outside as cars whizzed by and horns honked from the highway.

As soon as she was out of sight of the room, she dropped onto the stairs and pulled off her shoes. She felt dirty—like a whore. And since she'd just taken four hundred dollars for sex, that was exactly what she was. Sighing, she rubbed her aching feet for several moments and then took a deep breath, trying to work up the energy to walk to her car and go home. Her breath streamed out between her lips; she stood, and with the straps to her heels in one hand, she walked around the motel and into the pool area.

She slipped inside the fence and smiled when the rough concrete gave way to cool grass slightly damp with condensation. A noise above her head caught her attention, and she turned, her mouth creasing into a frown when she saw her john punching quarters into the snack machine on the back wall of the motel. He was only wearing a pair of ratty boxers, and his pale skin was almost fluorescent in the moonlight. The sight of it made her gag.

And wasn't that ironic? Fifteen minutes earlier, she'd been fucking him, and now she wanted to puke at seeing his skinny chest. Griffin sighed deeply and rubbed her hands over her face in frustration.

A sharp crack made Griffin jump, her head snapping up so hard she could feel her brain slosh against her skull. She blinked rapidly, not sure she believed what she was seeing, and took several steps back.

"I'm not asleep."

Alaria smiled. "No, you're not asleep. It's easiest for me to see you when you're asleep, but I can always find you, Griffin. I had a feeling you needed me."

Needed her. Like she was a goddamn guardian Angel. Griffin narrowed her eyes. "You had a feeling?"

Alaria shrugged. "We're connected, you and I. I always know when I'm needed."

Griffin threw out her arms, anger dripping from her words when she spoke. "If you know when you're needed, where the hell were you when I was going through chemo? If you're so fucking powerful, why didn't you heal me? I don't need to be the Queen of Hell! I needed to pay my rent!"

"You found a way."

"Yeah, doing drugs and whoring myself out. That's a great life! Just what I always dreamed of."

Alaria began walking, her spiked heels gliding over instead of sinking into the soft ground. When she noticed Griffin was still firmly rooted to the same spot, she sighed and turned around. "If you have questions, you may ask them. But I prefer to walk and talk."

Confused, Griffin scurried to catch up. "You offered to heal me once. Could you have?"

"I'm a Devil. I sit at the left hand of Lucifer. I could heal you."

"Why didn't you?"

"I don't do anything for free. There's a price for my help. I told you that the last time I came to you." Alaria turned her head, her face conveying sympathy that looked only half genuine. "Griffin, you are meant to be in Hell. You were not born of God. Surely you've realized that your pleas fall on deaf ears. Can you really tell me that you still truly believe that God cares about you?"

Silence was all the answer that Alaria needed. She nodded as if there had never been any doubt.

"I can offer you riches, power—whatever it is that you want. I can heal your body or give you anything your heart desires. The Earth can be your playground."

"Why should I believe you're telling me the truth? Hell is supposed to be a place where people are tortured. Why would you want to make it good for me?"

Alaria chuckled. "You're so disillusioned. Most people are. Hell is different than Earth, different than Heaven. Those of us in power have the ability to make it more, shall we say, palatable. You're important, Griffin. You're destined to lead the armies of Hell against the legions of Heaven and help us finish what we started millennia ago. We don't make these offers lightly, and we won't make them forever. You're special, but you're not irreplaceable."

Griffin's eyes darted back and forth as she studied Alaria's face. She closed her eyes, her mind flitting a mile a minute. She was starting to feel the withdrawal from the cocaine she'd snorted before going into the motel room, and her stomach clenched, her muscles trembling from the desire to have more.

What was the point? She'd spent years struggling. She was a whore, working a dead-end job, with a shithole apartment and a car that wouldn't start half the time. She was desperately addicted to drugs and used them to escape from her reality, and the thought of being with a man made her sick to her stomach. She had no friends, slept on a bare mattress on the floor, had no furniture, and couldn't even afford to keep the electricity on most months.

Going along with Alaria had its advantages, if what she said was true. She would be able to stop selling herself to pay bills and buy groceries. And if there was a catch, so what? It wasn't like she stood a chance of going to Heaven anyway. Even if God hadn't forsaken her at birth, He wouldn't want anything to do with her now.

Seemingly able to read her mind, Alaria spoke, her voice gentle and melodic, flowing over Griffin. "You could punish all the people who have hurt you. That boy, the foster parents, everyone who has slighted you. Fuck the men the way they fuck you. Take control, be in power. There is nothing that would be beyond your reach."

"I don't do it because I like it." For some reason, it was important that Griffin make sure Alaria know that. "I don't like the sex. I don't want to do it. I didn't have insurance, so I had to pay all the bills from the chemo myself."

"I know. They would go away. You wouldn't have to make another payment. You wouldn't have to lay flat on your back for any man ever again. You wouldn't have to suck your dealer's dick to get your fix."

Shame washed over Griffin. Tears pricked the back of her eyelids, and she took a trembling breath. "It's not my fault." Her voice was an even mixture of defense and resignation. Alaria reached out and touched her shoulder gently.

"I know that. I can take it away, Griffin. The addiction, the pain. Say the word and I can take it from you."

Tears beaded on Griffin's eyelashes and slipped silently down her cheeks. "What would happen if I died tomorrow?"

"You would go to Hell—a soul like the rest of them. You can't lead if you're dead."

"Can humans live in Hell?"

"You would be alive. You could have anything at all that you wanted." Alaria's glee was barely restrained. "There's no reason to be afraid, Griffin. All you have to do is let go, and let me take care of everything. Say the word, and all the pain will stop."

Something about Alaria's phrasing set little warning bells off, but it wasn't enough to break through the thick, heavy fog that was making it hard to think straight. She struggled to form coherent thoughts, to process the questions that started to form and then faded away. Alaria was still talking, her words soft and melodic, flowing over her like tenderly lapping waves. It would be so easy to just say yes and float away on the gentle comfort that was washing over her.

Just as she opened her mouth to answer, there was a loud crack and everything disappeared. Alaria was gone, the fog cleared, and she was no longer in the park behind the motel. She turned in a circle, confused by her surroundings. There was a white couch and a white chair along one wall with a fireplace that had a happily crackling fire directly across from it. She heard a flutter of wings and whirled around to find herself facing a man clad in a white suit. He had light blond hair that was flawlessly cut and a face that would make any normal woman swoon.

"This is new."

"I'm not a Devil."

"Then what the hell are you?"

"I am an Angel of the Lord. Gabriel, if you want to get specific about it. Sit down, Griffin. We have much to talk about."

Griffin managed to keep her jaw from dropping, but just barely. "That's impossible."

Gabriel chuckled and bent to pour a glass of tea from a pitcher that hadn't been there a second ago. Once poured, he set the pitcher down on a table that had just appeared a moment earlier. "You regularly consort with demons, and yet you doubt that there are beings that exist on the other side of the spectrum?" He shook his head in mild amusement. "Only in the mind of a human could that make any sense at all."

"Alaria has been visiting me since I was four-years-old. Where have you been the last twenty-two years?"

"Twenty-two human years is like a breath to me, child. And I have been here. Watching over you."

"Well, you're doing a pretty shitty job. In case you haven't noticed, I haven't been doing very well lately."

"Your situation has not escaped my notice. Though, it is because of your thoughts that I had to bring you here tonight. Were you as strong as I had hoped you would be, we would not be having this conversation. Unfortunately, the weakness of humans will never cease to amaze me."

"Weak?" Incensed, Griffin surged to her feet, stalking the room like a caged lioness. "Do you have any idea what my life has been like? What I've gone through? What I have had to do in order to survive? Do you know that I cried for God every night until I was sixteen? That I prayed every day for a guardian Angel to help me. And what did I get? A Devil offering to let me rule Hell. God abandoned me, so I decided to abandon Him, too."

Gabriel set the glass down with a sharp smack, the first cracks appearing in his composure. "Sit down and listen to me. God has not abandoned you, and neither have I. I know it seems like it, and for that I am sorry, but it has to be that way. There is no other choice."

Tears running down her face, Griffin dropped onto the couch. "Why? Why do I have to be alone? Why am I the one who has to go through this?"

"I can't tell you. But you can find out on your own. Griffin, Alaria is a Devil, and despite what she tells you, the only one who cannot lie is Lucifer. She does lie, and has lied, to you. But the one thing she told you that is true is that you are special. Very special, to both sides in this, and your role in the history of humanity is more integral than anyone else who has ever been born. You have a great burden to bear, and I know that it seems right now as if it would be easier to simply give up and do what Alaria wants. But have faith, child. Your reward will be in Heaven, because I swear to you upon the name of my Creator that you are not forsaken. That you are loved by God and by every Angel in existence, and that soon you will understand why you have had to endure this life. You are not doomed to Hell. But if you choose to go there, there you will remain for eternity."

Griffin wiped tears from her eyes and laid her head in her hands. "But why?"

"As I said, I cannot tell you all that you wish to know. To do so would break the rules, and this is far too important to risk losing. In a moment I will replace you into your car, and I want you to do something. In your glove compartment, you will find a key to a post office box. Go there and open it. Inside, you will find enough money to pay off your bills and to seek out your answers. There is a priest at a church in Philadelphia that specializes in biblical philosophy. Find him. He will have the answer that you need."

"How will I find him?"

"Have faith. I cannot tell you who he is, or I would risk divulging too much information. Have faith, Griffin, and it will take you where you need to go."

And just like that, Griffin was back in her car, in the parking lot of the seedy motel where she went to meet Ryan every time he came into town and was looking to get laid. Not believing what she had just seen, she leaned across the seat and opened the glove compartment. Sure enough, just inside there was a shiny silver key with a number written on one side and the name of the post office written on the other. She turned the key over slowly, not daring to believe that it was real.

Griffin looked at the fluorescent green numbers on the clock inside the car. Midnight. Yet another happy fucking birthday. She sighed deeply and turned her mind back to her current situation. It was way too late for the post office to be open, but a lot of them left the lobby unlocked to allow people access to stamp machines and boxes. The post office listed on the key was only two blocks from her apartment. It couldn't hurt to stop by on her way home and see if the Angel was telling the truth.

Her mind made up, she continued to back up and pulled out onto the street. Her mind and heart racing, she barely noticed which turns she made and paid very little attention to traffic on the drive to the post office. If her mind wasn't betraying her, her life was about to change.

Hands shaking, Griffin dropped her keys twice in her hurry to get out of the car and lock her door. Giving up on that, she pocketed the keys and ran up the stairs. The doors were open, and the inside of the post office was dark and slightly creepy. She fished in her purse for the pen light she always carried so that she could see her front door when she got home late, and turned on the slim beam to look around. After determining that no one was skulking in any corners waiting to mug her, she approached the bank of lock boxes with cautious optimism.

She double checked the number on the key and quickly determined that the box she had a key for was one of the larger ones. When she found her number, she checked the key again, and when she saw that it was the right box, she felt a tickle of hope form in the back of her throat. She slid the key into the lock and nearly sobbed when it turned smoothly and the door swung open. When she saw several piles of money, instead of sobbing, she felt the first genuine smile she could remember tug at the corners of her mouth. Her mind racing with possibilities, she looked furtively around the post office and opened her purse to tuck it all away safely, locking the box and zipping the key into her coin purse.

If she was any judge of money, and she knew from years of experience not getting jipped by johns that she was, there was enough money in the box to pay off her medical bills, get the electricity turned back on, repair her car, and go to the grocery store. She was pretty sure that there was even enough to get caught up on back rent and put some back for use later. If she was smart about it, she wouldn't have to exchange sex for money again.

Gabriel hadn't lied. He'd given her enough money to get her back on her feet, and he'd shown her that God really hadn't forgotten about her. But just because he'd provided it didn't mean she couldn't lose it if she wasn't careful. She had to use it wisely and get it somewhere safe where it couldn't be stolen.

Her mind racing with possibilities, she rushed back to her car and locked the doors once she was inside. Then, she did something she didn't think she would ever be able to do. She reached beneath her seat, removed her stash of cocaine, and dumped it out the window. If she wanted to take care of her money, she had to be sober to make sure she didn't blow it.

At the other end of the parking lot, Gabriel watched the scene with a slight smile turning up the corners of his mouth. As Griffin's car disappeared around the corner, Alaria appeared with a loud crack, her face frozen with rage, and her eyes sparking flames. Gabriel lifted one eyebrow at her expression.

"Something wrong, Alaria?"

"You son of a bitch! I had her! She was mine, and you interfered!" Alaria clenched her fist, a whip appearing in it. When she lifted her arm and cracked it at Gabriel, the sound was deafening. Gabriel caught the leather in his hands and used it to yank Alaria to him. Before she could struggle, he grabbed her hair in his other fist and jerked her head back, his blue eyes darkening to nearly black with anger.

"You listen to me, you worthless Devil. The only reason she was about to go with you was because you were using your demon wiles on her. Clouding her mind until she was unable to ask the questions she wanted to ask. Had you not impermissibly stepped over the line, I never would have alerted her to my existence." Gabriel yanked her hair sharply for emphasis. "Let me make myself abundantly clear. Our friendship in the past will not stop me from dragging you before God and demanding you be held accountable to breaching the agreement between our masters. I have allowed you to enter the dream plane, to speak with her outside of your events and to have much more latitude than I would have allowed one of your brethren. My moments of reminiscence and leniency are done, Alaria. If you step one toe out of line from here on out, there will be no more discussions."

Alaria hissed. "You self-righteous bastard. You think I interfered? You just negated my last two events! If anyone should be strung up and quartered, it should be your Angelic ass!"

Gabriel twisted the hair wrapped around his wrist, forcing her head to one side painfully. "Shut up. This is not open for discussion. If you deviate from the agreement by even one degree, I will not rest until you have joined your souls at the bottom of the Lake of Fire."

Her eyes flashing with anger, Alaria glared up at the Angel. "You wouldn't dare. You're too sentimental to let anything happen to me."

He laughed bitterly and shoved her back. "Don't trifle with me, Alaria. You won't survive to regret it."

Before the Devil could respond, Gabriel disappeared in a shimmer, and Alaria was left alone to contemplate her next move.

Chapter Ten

April 15th, 2022 - Philadelphia, Pennsylvania
GRIFFIN STOOD outside the church, her heart pounding. After four months of searching, she had found him: the priest that specialized in biblical philosophy. The one who would be able to tell her why bad things had continually happened to her since birth. The one who could give her all the answers she would need to decide what to do with her life. The one who could tell her if it was even worth it to continue to tell Alaria no.

By the time she'd gotten things straightened out with the money she owed and her bills, it was already February. She had started looking for the priest almost as soon as she had realized Gabriel wasn't a liar, though in February she started devoting most of her time to searching.

Most dioceses hadn't ever heard of a priest who specialized in biblical philosophy, and those who seemed to know what she was talking about didn't want to tell her. Apparently, the parts of the Bible not made public were closely guarded Catholic secrets, and they weren't too excited to share them with a non-practicing Catholic former prostitute. That is, until she had recognized one priest as a client from her previous career and threatened to alert his parishioners to the fact that he wasn't exactly celibate if he didn't tell her. When he'd realized she was serious about making his indiscretions public, he'd scribbled down a name and an address.

The address had led her to St. Sebastian's, a large, ancient building in a neighborhood that screamed old money. She dashed up the stairs, trying to avoid getting wet as much as possible. She'd forgotten her umbrella and the weather had decided to rain all day. Dodging raindrops, she pulled open the heavy, creaky wood door.

An old habit born from childhood had her dipping her fingertips into the bowl of Holy Water at the entrance and drawing the sign of the cross across her chest. Her parents had been devout, and in the four short years that she had known them, they had drilled into her the importance of respecting the house of God. She couldn't remember stepping foot inside a church in more than ten years.

"Hello? Is anyone in here?"

There was an answering noise as a chair scraped across the stone floor, and a door toward the back of the sanctuary opened. A priest, wearing flowing black robes and a baseball cap, walked out. "Welcome to St. Sebastian's. I'm Father Brad Dooley."

Griffin held out a hand. "Griffin Javensen. I was given your name by Darren Roberts at St. Steven's. He said you were the resident expert on biblical philosophy?"

"That's me. Come on back to my office, and we'll talk. Can I get you anything to drink? Coffee, tea, hot chocolate? It looks miserable out there."

"I'd love some coffee, thanks."

"Gives me an excuse to have another cup, so I should be thanking you." He led her into his office, went to a coffee pot and began preparing a new batch. He motioned to an old, sagging couch. "Have a seat. Might as well be comfortable. What sort of philosophy are you interested in?"

Griffin sighed, fighting a brief battle over how much to tell him. Then, with a deep breath, she decided to tell him everything. Gabriel would not have sent her to someone that would not help her. He was an Angel; he wouldn't put her in any danger.

"I'm here because the Archangel Gabriel told me to find you."

Father Dooley's hands stilled, and he slowly turned to look at her, a coffee filter in one hand, spoon filled with grounds in the other. His face, round and plump, showed nothing but pure shock. "Gabriel sent you?"

Griffin nodded so hard her ponytail bounced. "I know it sounds crazy, but he came to me a few months ago and told me that you would have the answers that I need. That you would be able to tell me why Alaria keeps trying to talk me into going to Hell with her."

Dooley pulled off his hat and ran his hand over thinning blond hair. "Alaria? You know about Alaria? She doesn't appear in the Bible."

"I know. I checked. She's been visiting me since I was four. I think she had my parents killed."

He studied her hard for a long moment then turned to finish preparing coffee. That done, he reached for the phone. "This meeting suddenly seems like it's going to take a lot longer than I anticipated, and I'm hungry. Pepperoni okay with you?"

He believed her. Relieved, Griffin sank down onto the couch. "Fine with me."

Twenty minutes later, armed with a slice of pizza and a can of soda, Father Dooley sat down in the chair across from Griffin and crossed one of his legs over the other. She was still staring at her lap, as she'd been doing since he'd picked up the phone to order their food. He cleared his throat, both to get her attention and to end the awkward silence. "So, why do you think Alaria is after you?"

Griffin leaned into the couch cushions, her plate of pizza balanced on her knee and her own can next to her feet on the floor. "Because she is. She first came to me in my dreams when I was four. The same night my parents died. I saw her again when I was sixteen, and that night I had to kill my foster father to keep him from raping me." She paused as she remembered the feeling of the pen sliding into his throat. "Well, I think I killed him. He was still breathing when I left, but I don't know if he could have survived. But that's not important." She laughed nervously, then continued to speak. "On my eighteenth birthday, she offered to heal my cancer if only I would go with her. I told her no, and she came to me again a few months ago when I was a prostitute, on my twenty-second birthday. I was about to take her up on her offer when Gabriel took me to some white room and told me to find you for the answers I need. He said that I shouldn't make the decision before speaking with you."

Dooley's brows creased with concern and he sat his pizza aside to focus on her completely. "Why were you going to go to Hell with Alaria?"

"She told me that I was not born of God, that he had forsaken me, that I was doomed to go to Hell no matter what I did. And with the way my life has been, I was ready to believe her. Until Gabriel came to me."

His eyes alight with wonder and excitement, Dooley picked up another piece of pizza and spoke between bites. "Tell me about your life. Start at the very beginning. What happened when you were born?"

Painstakingly, she detailed to him the circumstances of her birth and the horrors that followed. Father Dooley listened intently to what she said and his eyes never left her face as he drank in what she was telling him. When she finished, he leaned forward and braced his elbows on his knees.

"Seven. That means there are three left."

"Three what?"

"Events. You were right to come to me. I may be the only one on the planet who can help you right now." He went to his bookshelf, pulled out an old, yellowed book, and brushed off the cover. "Before the Earth was created and after the Battle, God and Lucifer had a meeting to iron out the ground rules, so to speak. What each of them could do, what they couldn't do, how the world would end. Because when you make something, you have to know that it will eventually come to an end, and God didn't want to have to fight with Lucifer over the end when it was time. You've probably heard of it: the Apocalypse. "

"Of course. Everyone knows about the Apocalypse. What I don't understand is what it has to do with me." Griffin stood to pace the narrow room and ran her hands through her hair in frustration. "I don't even really know what I'm doing here or what Gabriel and Alaria want with me or what the hell is going on!"

Father Dooley smiled, his eyes kind. "Well, sit down and let me finish telling you." He waited until she dropped back into her seat. "When God and Lucifer met, they decided that the end would not be for sure. Everyone thinks that it is because the world is going to Hell in a hand basket, and the Lord will come back at some undisclosed time and there will be seven years of pain and suffering during Tribulation for those who do not know Him. And to a certain extent, that's true. But we were blessed with free will. We can choose whether to follow Him or not, and it isn't quite fair to be punished if we choose not to. God understood that. So He and Lucifer decided that at some point, a human would be born who would be responsible for deciding the fate of the whole world."

Griffin leaned forward. "One person is supposed to save the world? How can one person do that?"

Dooley took a bite of his pizza and chewed thoughtfully. "God has historically chosen special people to do what seem to be insurmountable tasks. He gives them what they need to succeed. This time, He would ask more from the Chosen than He ever had before out of anyone. The Chosen would live for thirty years—a hard life, filled with pain and loss—and on the dawn of the third decade, he or she would have to Choose. The choice is simple. Good or evil. Heaven or Hell. God or Lucifer. And while the choice seems simple in theory, they built in rules that would ensure that neither side had an advantage. There would be one Devil and one Angel put in charge. The Devil would get ten events to wipe out the natural propensity humans have toward good. The only rule is that neither side could kill the Chosen. If the Chosen dies, then neither side wins, the End begins, and all humans are banished to Heaven or Hell. The Earth would cease to exist.

"If Hell is Chosen, demons will be free to walk the Earth for a thousand millennia, Heaven will not be allowed to interfere, and after the thousand millennia, things will revert to the way they are now, with both sides fighting for dominance. If Heaven is Chosen, the Angels will be able to walk among the humans for a thousand millennia, and the demons will be trapped in Hell. After that, things will go back to the way they are now with Angels and demons both allowed on Earth to compete for souls. And if the Chosen refuses to make a choice, neither side wins and the End is started."

Griffin leaned back and stared at the Priest, her mouth open as she considered what she had just been told. "Why would someone not Choose then?"

"Because you don't just say I choose Heaven. The Choice requires a price. The life of the Chosen, taken with their own hand."

"Suicide? They have to commit suicide?"

Dooley shook his head vehemently. "No. There is a difference between suicide and sacrifice. What is required of the Chosen is a sacrifice."

Her frustration building, Griffin sighed deeply. "Okay. So, I'm going to ask again. What does all this have to do with me?"

Dooley leaned forward, bouncing with excitement. "Don't you see? You're the Chosen."

Griffin's whole world upended. She shook her head in immediate denial, her blood roaring in her ears and her heart pounding. "No. No, that's impossible. I'm just a woman. I'm nothing special. I'm not Chosen. God hates me—He wouldn't pick me for something like this. I'm a drug addict and a whore."

"Griffin, you're none of those things. Part of being the Chosen is having to go through things like that. The Devil made you like that. She manipulated your situation until you had no choice but to do exactly what she wanted you to do. Without her interference, you would not have had the life you have had. None of this is your fault. It was all in an attempt to remove your humanity. And judging from what you've told me and what I know of Alaria, it was a ploy to give you no choice but to accept her offer of placement in Hell so that she would have unfettered access to you to spoil you against God. It's all a trick."

"I have to die? In eight years, I have to die? No, I won't do it. They can't make me accept this." Tears flooded her eyes, and she gasped for breath. "It's not fair. I don't want it."

Father Dooley crossed the room and sat down on the couch next to her. He reached out and took her hand, squeezing it to get her attention. "Unfortunately, there is not a way out of this, Griffin. Most versions of the story of the Chosen say that even if she refuses to Choose, she will die anyway. There is a theory that the lifespan of the Chosen lasts only a few weeks past thirty years. It's a built-in safety device to make sure the Choice occurs. I don't know that for sure, but both sides want this to happen. They both want to win. If you don't Choose, the Apocalypse begins, and most likely, you'll die anyway. It eliminates the selfish aspect of human nature. It ensures that you have to Choose."

"The fate of the whole world is on me? I have to decide for eight billion people? Do you know how crazy this sounds? This is impossible."

"The manuscripts with the legend were found alongside the book of John. John was given this prophecy in a dream, and when he questioned it, he was visited by Michael, the Archangel of War, who told him that it must happen and that he must write it down and include it in his other books. It was found thousands of years ago, though it was hidden and not included in Biblical canon. Only a dozen or so people know that it exists, and no one else is told until one of the current priests dies. This is one of the most heavily guarded secrets in the history of the Catholic Church. Even the Pope doesn't know the story."

"What do I do?"

"Well, that's really up to you. Are you so disillusioned that you're willing to allow Hell to rule the world for a thousand millennia? Or do you still have some small bit of faith in Heaven left?"

"Six months ago, I would have said no." She met his gaze—tears still welled in her eyes. "Six months ago, I would really have had to think about it. I truly believed that I didn't have a soul, that God didn't want me—that I was evil somehow. Now, I feel used. By both sides. And I'm angry. At God for abandoning me for twenty-two years, and at Alaria for tricking me into thinking that she was trying to help me. I'm mad, Father. So mad, I'm half tempted to just not Choose at all. To hold a grudge and say fuck them both. Let them hash it out during the End of Days. But I know I can't do that, because it's not fair to the world. And all in all, not everyone I've met has been awful. My parents, the doctor who treated me after the rape, you. There have been a few people that I've encountered that make me think maybe the world is worth saving after all." She shrugged her shoulders and stared down at her lap. "So, I'll do what I have to do. I'll save the world."

Father Dooley nodded, a small smile turning up the corners of his mouth. "Good. This is going to be hard, Griffin. At times, most times, it may seem that God isn't there, that He doesn't care. But a lot of the story is about how much this hurts God, how He hates seeing the Chosen suffer. It was not a decision made lightly, but in the end, it was the fairest way to go about doing things. Only one person had to suffer, and because of that suffering, the whole world gets to live. I know it sucks that it's you, and you feel like it's personal, but I assure you, the decision was completely random. You were not Chosen because you're soulless or because God hates you."

"So, what do I do now?"

"Now, you live your life. Experience everything you wish you could have experienced. See the world, fall in love, have a baby. You only have eight years to cram a lifetime into. When you turn twenty-nine, the Veil will be lifted. The Veil was placed upon you by Alaria and Gabriel on the night of your birth. It shields you from all Demons and Angels. Neither side can find you until one year before the Choosing. Once the last year is underway, you should prepare for both sides to try to convince you. One will try to scare you into Choosing them, the other will probably try to guilt you into it. Heaven and Hell both have their futures riding on you. They aren't going to want to lose. And if Alaria discovers that you intend to Choose Heaven, she will try to have you killed. But until the Veil is punctured, she can find you only in your dreams. She does not know where on Earth you are. That is an advantage. Alaria generally is not known for walking the Earth. So even if she appears in this world, she cannot stay long. She has to use Hell hounds or Lilith to find you. She will not want to use Lilith."

"Lilith?"

"The first. She was the first Angel to join with Lucifer. Many scholars think she was even more powerful than he was. I'm inclined to agree, since Lucifer is contained to Hell and Lilith managed to break free and is able to walk the Earth as she pleases. She's notoriously cruel and rules over all the Devils. In a word, she's the Queen of Hell."

Griffin rubbed her head. "Let me get this straight. Alaria doesn't know where I am. She can come to me, but only in relation to one of her events and to talk to me at other times she has to visit my dreams, where she arguably has no power over me. She can't find me until my twenty-ninth birthday when this protection comes off. Even if I piss her off, she can't stay on Earth long and would have to use giant dogs or the most powerful Devil out there to find me."

"You've about got it. Once the Veil is off, you'll need to take steps to protect yourself. When she finds out that you're Choosing Heaven, and she will find out, you'll be in great danger." Dooley reached for a pad of paper and picked up a pen. "Here is a number for a friend of mine. He's a Warrior. He'll be able to protect you. Don't use it unless you feel your life is in danger. He's a loner, but he's the best I know."

"A Warrior?"

Father Dooley shook his head, smiling. "Sorry. A Warrior is a human who knows about Demons and Devils. They have devoted their lives to hunting the creatures of Hell and sending them back. They deal with possessions, hounds, demons, Devils, and other supernatural events. Spirits, witches, everything evil. Most Warriors are on the payroll of the Vatican to some extent. Brax does contract work, but mostly runs his own team. Since he's unpredictable and grouchy, it works out well for everyone. But he's the best. If anyone can keep you alive until the Choosing—it's him."

"So, that's it, then? You have seven years before demons are going to start trying to kill you, go have fun?"

"Griffin, you weren't supposed to find out what you are. That's why Gabriel couldn't tell you. If he did, he breaks the rules, and he loses. No Angel wants to be responsible for that. But he sensed that you were on the verge of stepping into the precipice Alaria has prepared for you. So, he has taken steps to make sure that you seek out the information about yourself. They couldn't stop you from figuring it out, but they weren't allowed to tell you. This is uncharted territory."

"I want to read it. The prophecy. I want to read what it says."

"It's in Hebrew. I can give you a translated version."

"That's good enough to start. But I want the original. Do you know where it is?"

"No. I don't. I saw it once when they were training me. I was able to read it and translate it for myself. But then it was taken away, and I was never told where it is kept. And it's just a version of it, Griffin. There are only four people who know what really happened that day, what really will happen. God, Lucifer, Alaria and Gabriel. So unless you can get Gabriel or Alaria to tell you what happened, the best we can do is second-hand interpretation. And I can assure you, not everything that will happen, that has happened, is in that prophecy. It's the basics. What the Chosen decides, what she has to do, when she will decide. The rules of play, if you will. It also makes clear that you will be instructed in the Choosing before it occurs."

"An Angel version of 'I'll tell you later.'"

"Unfortunately, yes. But you aren't alone. I'm here for the duration. If you have questions, if you need help, I am here. I never dreamed I would meet the Chosen, and having you here is an honor beyond which you could even imagine."

Griffin stood, a hardness in her eyes that hadn't been there when she'd entered the church. "I don't want to endanger you, Father. And I've no doubt that you'll be in danger should they find out what you've told me. But just do me a favor, would you?"

"Anything."

"Every once in a while, when you pray, pray for me."

Chapter Eleven

December 31st, 2028 - Philadelphia, Pennsylvania

GRIFFIN PACED. Her eyes never wavered from the clock on the wall above her fireplace. Seventy-five minutes until she turned twenty-nine. Her last seventy-five minutes of freedom. In a little over an hour, the Veil would be lifted, and she would be fair game for every non-human creature in existence. So she paced.

In the past seven years, she had built a life for herself. She'd become the manager of a good restaurant in Philadelphia, gotten her GED, moved into a nice apartment, paid off the rest of her medical bills, and taken three trips overseas. She'd gone twice to the Vatican to try and gain access to the scrolls containing her prophecy and once to Greece, where Father Dooley had gotten wind it was being stored. All three trips had been a waste of time. No one seemed to know where it was, and those she thought might have a clue about its whereabouts were unwilling to give her any information.

She hadn't seen Alaria. Griffin got the feeling that Alaria had used too many of her events during the early years under the assumption that she could convince Griffin to join her in Hell. Her plan had backfired. She had underestimated the strength of the human soul and she had been left with seven years of inactivity. If Father Dooley had been right—and the longer it went the more Griffin believed that he was—Alaria only had three events left. If she had learned anything about Alaria over the years, it was that the Devil liked to make her events count for as much as possible.

That meant she would probably be using one to mark the lifting of the veil. Since Alaria was not allowed to know where she was, Griffin was fairly certain that she was unable to keep a constant eye on her life. Alaria had put her plan into place, and without angelic interference, it would have worked perfectly. Griffin doubted she knew about Gabriel's visit.

In one hour, the Veil would lift, and her period of safety would be over. She would be in her last year of life with only 364 more tomorrows left. Griffin hated knowing the exact day that she was going to die. Even worse was the knowledge that she was going to have to take her own life, to offer herself as a sacrifice to pay for the freedoms the rest of the world constantly took for granted. Even Jesus had only been required to be willing to die. He hadn't had to kill himself. It didn't seem quite fair to her that God expected more out of her than He had His own Son.

Father Dooley assured her that the situations were different. Her fate had been decided before God had sent His Son to Earth; before it had even been fathomable that He would need to do something to account for free will in salvation. After all, He had intended for Adam and Eve to remain in the Garden of Eden, but free will had ended that plan. Because people were taking affirmative steps in the direction of Hell, God had to take an affirmative step to offer them a Heavenly alternative. He had sent His Son to show the world miracles. Griffin's role was much less dramatic. She was a representation of the human race, not their Savior, and her job was to decide as a neutral party which fate the human race desired. Had things gone according to plan, there never would have been a need to select the Chosen.

The only problem was that Alaria had not been able to wipe Griffin clean. She still wasn't quite sure that she could take her own life. She logically knew that it had to be done and that she had no real choice in the matter. If she didn't, she would probably die anyway. That was a big plus in the column that necessitated her doing what fate had dictated she do. If she was going to die anyway, she might as well be able to punish the Devils on her way out. It was a vindictive approach to the matter, but it was the only way she could stomach actually doing what she knew she had to do.

Forty-five minutes and counting. Griffin stalked into her kitchen, seized a beer out of the fridge, and popped the top off with a practiced flick of the wrist. She drained half the bottle in one gulp, sat it on the counter and braced her hands on either side. She couldn't relax, and no amount of alcohol was going to change that.

Suddenly, she was unreasonably sleepy and fought to keep her eyes open. She hadn't been sleepy a moment before though. Suspicious, she picked up the beer bottle and looked in the bottom of it. Nothing caught her attention, so she sniffed it cautiously but detected no strange odor. Another sip betrayed no taste that wasn't supposed to be there. Still unwilling to take a chance, she poured the rest down the sink and turned on the water to rinse the beer down the drain.

A light bulb in the ceiling burst, causing her to jump and knock the coffee pot over. The carafe fell into the sink, the pot itself hit the switch to turn on the garbage disposal, and the glass going down the sink made a horrific noise. Griffin reached over to turn it off but was too late. The garbage disposal exploded with a loud bang and a flash of flame. Griffin was thrown backward. She struck her head on the corner of the stove and fell to the floor unconscious.

"This is your last chance."

Griffin looked around and found herself in the familiar setting of Hell. Standing directly behind her, looking gorgeous as ever in leather and with her black hair flowing down her back, was Alaria. "My last chance for what?"

"To take me up on my offer. Lucifer is running out of patience. This is the last offer that we will make to you. Either come here to rule, or pay the price."

Chuckling, Griffin put her hands on her hips. "This is a departure from your normal tactics. Every other time you've tried to woo me into it before sending me back to some new horror you've cooked up for me to live through."

"I'll woo you once you've agreed. You want sex? I'll get you the hottest sex you can imagine. A thousand men whose only job it is to give you orgasms. Or women, if you'd prefer. Hell, I'll give you orgasms myself. You want money? Name a country, and it will be yours. Power? You'll have more power than you can comprehend. What do you want, Griffin?"

"To live past age thirty."

Alaria's eyes narrowed. "So, you know, then. No matter. That makes my job all the easier. I cannot give you mortal life past your thirtieth birthday. But after the Choosing, you will rule here for eternity. It's either that, or you burn in the pit."

"I believe there's a third option. The expert I consulted seems to think I'm not as damned as you led me to believe."

Alaria waved her hand, dismissing the claim. "Did you know that Angels and Devils have the nifty talent of being able to see into people? We can tell, just by looking, whether you belong to God or to Lucifer. I can tell you that you belong to Lucifer. And if you don't believe me, I'll hail an Angel down here to confirm it. Your soul does not belong to God. It belongs to us. You are meant to be here."

"I don't believe you."

"Why?"

"I've seen the prophecy. I know that you have events to convince me that I'm not good like every other human. Humans don't want to be in Hell, Alaria. You tempt them with sin, but if they knew that doing something would send them to Hell, if they really knew the reality, Lucifer would have no followers. You get people by blurring the lines, by always pushing them one step further. You very nearly had me convinced to come down here."

"What changed your mind?"

"I went to church. The Vatican has interesting things to say about you. About how you're a notorious liar. Apparently, only Lucifer never tells a lie."

Damn human. She knew way too much. "Doesn't change the fact that God abandoned you. If you know all that, then you know that He could have stopped this at any time. That He was the one who put you into this situation in the first place. The merciful and loving God has sent you to DIE."

"No, Lucifer sent me to die the day he took up arms against Heaven."

"Do you know that your death will start the Apocalypse?"

"Yes." Griffin nodded her head. "What does that have to do with anything?"

"Then what's stopping me from ripping your throat out right now and ending this damned world once and for all?"

"Because then you lose."

"The way you're talking, I've lost anyway."

"You can't hurt me here, and we both know that. You can't keep me here, either. If you could, you'd have done it already. And I know, from doing research on you, that you can't exist on Earth for long. Add to that you have no fucking idea where I am, and I'm feeling pretty secure."

Alaria grabbed Griffin's throat and dug her nails into the sensitive skin there. "You're right, I can't kill you, and I can't keep you here. But I can hurt you. And I can confuse you to the point you won't be able to remember how to get out of here."

"You spent my whole life trying to convince me that God didn't want me, that I had no soul—that I was damned to be here for all eternity. And it's all a lie. If I die, if I don't Choose, then yeah, I'll burn. But if I Choose Heaven, I'll get to go there. But let me make myself very clear, Alaria. After what you have put me through, I would rather burn in that pit for all of eternity than ever give you the satisfaction of winning."

Alaria smiled, her eyes hard and dangerous. "You don't realize what you've just done. If you did, you'd have tried to keep your stupid mouth shut. The Veil comes off tonight, Griffin. I can send the legions of Hell after you. I can come after you myself. If you're going to Choose them, my best bet is to kill you. Then we get seven years of pain and suffering. Not as good as a million, but it'll do better than none. By the end of the seven years, I'll have billions of new souls down here to play with. That'll occupy us forever."

"You have to find me first, you demon bitch. And I'm not that easy to find."

Alaria laughed and leaned in to whisper in Griffin's ear. "Your priest doesn't know everything, Griffin. I don't like to walk on Earth, but I can. I can stay as long as I want. I wasn't chained to Hell. Only Lucifer and Azazel are confined. Michael tried to chain us, but without God, he was unable to. That led to a nice battle between him and Lilith. See, before all this happened, they were companions for millennia. Then Lucifer took up arms, and Lilith, being power hungry, saw that Lucifer could have more power than Michael, than Gabriel, than any of the other Angels. So she joined with him. She was the first to cross over the line. Because of that, she was the most powerful. When Lucifer was cast out, Michael and Gabriel were charged with chaining us to Hell. God himself chained Lucifer, but the Archangels had to deal with the rest of us. They weren't strong enough, and Lilith nearly killed them all. She hasn't been back to Hell since. She walks the Earth constantly, sort of flipping off Heaven. The rest of us? Well, we prefer it down here, for the most part. That doesn't mean I can't walk up there, or that I won't, from now until your blood pours out on my hands."

Griffin also leaned forward and put her lips right against the Devil's ear. "I know the truth, Alaria. I've seen the scrolls. I know what a fucking liar you are. You're right, Lilith remains free, but that's because she was stronger than Lucifer. She was a more powerful Angel than he was. Rumor has it that she would have tried to overthrow him had he won. God banished you all to Hell, and the Angels trapped you in here. Over the centuries, you've managed to free demons, and they've gotten humans to agree to host you. Once you have a willing host and you're out, you're free to come and go as you please. But only a handful of you are strong enough to possess a human from down here. After all, proximity is everything. And I know you've never possessed a human."

"That's what you think. Your scrolls don't know everything, and they don't cover, oh, the last two thousand years. I decided when you were born that I might need to go above ground and take care of that little issue."

Alaria threw Griffin to the ground with a flick of her wrist and strode over to stand above her. Griffin tried to get up, but Alaria lifted one foot and placed it on her chest, forcing her back to the ground—unless she wanted to be stabbed by a stiletto heel.

"Let's get this straight. You are telling me that under no circumstances will you Choose Hell. Is that correct?"

"I think that about covers it."

"Okay." Alaria stepped back and started to walk away. "Go home, Griffin, it's time for event number eight."

Griffin woke up, smoke surrounding her. She coughed, rolled onto her side, and tried to sit up but was too dizzy. Panicked, she began to drag herself across the floor, stopping to wipe blood from her eyes. That was when she heard them. Growling was the first sign, and with her heart pounding, she rolled onto her back and saw two giant black dogs hovering in the corner. They were still transparent, but she had a feeling they wouldn't stay that way for long.

Then Alaria appeared. She smiled and threw out her arms as the clock struck midnight. "Demons, Devils, Hounds of Hell, hear my command. The twenty-ninth year has commenced. The Chosen has betrayed us. Heaven cannot be allowed to win. The Chosen must die. With the power given to me by Lucifer, I now charge all of our numbers to find the Chosen, hunt her down, and kill her. With the task I was given at the very beginning, I now do my duty, and pierce the Veil. She is open and vulnerable. Find her, and do your duty!"

Lightning flashed, and Alaria glowed red for a long minute. The room went completely black, and Griffin heard paws on the floor. If the Veil was gone, and Alaria was there, then she had been able to bring the Hell hounds into her apartment. They were going to rip her to pieces.

Finding strength she didn't know she had, Griffin forced herself to her feet and tried to run. She'd only gotten two steps before one of the hounds was upon her. Teeth ripped into her flesh and blood began to flow. Alaria laughed and spread her arms again.

"See this, Gabriel? She'll die tonight, and the End will commence!"

There was a loud explosion, and the front door of Griffin's apartment flew in. A man dressed all in black with shocking blue eyes and blood red wings stood there. He lifted one hand and sent out a bolt of lightning so strong that it incinerated the Hell hounds. Griffin sobbed with relief when they disappeared and began trying to drag herself toward him, leaving a thick trail of blood behind her.

"I warned Gabriel that he was too lenient with you. This is unacceptable."

"Michael. So nice of you to join us for the festivities. Please, step aside and let me finish what I came here to do."

"That's not going to happen, Alaria. I won't let you kill her."

Alaria pursed her lips and tried to look concerned. "But you hate humans. You used to find them insignificant and unimportant."

"This one is different. Generally, men are good for nothing other than mild amusement. I've never seen why my Father found it necessary to make them, but He did, and it is my job to protect them."

"You're the Angel of War, Michael! You love a little bloodshed."

"Wars can be Godly. And while it is true that, as a rule, I enjoy watching humans destroy each other, I do not encourage it when I am not ordered to do so. Wars effect change. If God feels something needs to change and does not want to interfere with free will, I am sent to plant the seeds of war. But this war—it is between us, Alaria. It does not involve the humans. You will not kill her."

"It's one human. One insignificant life. And she's important to me. You would enjoy the Apocalypse. Lots of wars. Step aside and let me start it. Then you'll never have to deal with humans again."

"I'll enjoy the Apocalypse when God is ready for it—after a thousand millennia of angelic rule. I'm sure there will be plenty of wars between now and then."

"There's no guarantee the world will end after the rule."

"And there's nothing saying that it won't. Or maybe we'll do this again. Wouldn't that be fun?" Michael considered that for a moment, and then shrugged his shoulders. "It's of no concern. Go away, Alaria. I'll not let you have her."

"You would take on the legions of Hell over one human? I'm willing to go to battle over this, Michael. Can you say the same?"

Michael looked up to the ceiling, and it suddenly became transparent. Above the apartment building were more Angels than Griffin had ever imagined existed. Alaria paled when she saw them. The Angels faded from sight as the ceiling regained its opacity and became solid again.

"I never come unprepared. When Gabriel came to me tonight and told me that you had taken her to Hell, I knew you had something planned. To borrow a human phrase, I called in the troops." He glanced to the side and nodded. "Right on time, Gabriel. Alaria was just telling us that we were about to battle Hell again."

Alaria sneered, her breath hissing out between her teeth. "This is not over, Michael. The Veil is off, and I'll have her yet." She looked around the room and turned in a circle as she tried to sense where Gabriel was. "Gabriel, you're a fucking coward sending big brother Michael to fight for you! You don't even have the balls to face me yourself. I'll kill you, too!"

Michael smiled, the expression looking anything but friendly. "You're welcome to try. But I promise you, Alaria, if you kill her, this will cease to be between Devils and Angels."

"You wouldn't dare involve them. This is none of their concern."

"It will be if you break the rules. They agreed to the terms, and you were charged with carrying them out. If you don't abide by the rules, I'll see to it that you are chained to the bottom of your own pit for the rest of eternity. I promise you, you will never see the surface of the Lake again."

"You're welcome to try." Alaria studied the situation, then smiled when she heard the telltale rustling of demons entering the room. They formed behind her, some in human form, others in their true, monstrous shapes. Michael reached behind his back and pulled his sword from its sheath.

"If you want a battle, Devil, then a battle you will get. But you are outnumbered a thousand to one."

"I'll take out some of your troops."

"I'll take out all of yours."

Knowing it was true, Alaria took a step back. It was time to reevaluate. She hadn't anticipated Michael's involvement. "Very well. We'll fight another day then." She looked at Griffin, barely conscious and writhing on the floor in pain. "Enjoy your reprieve. The next time I find you, you won't be so lucky."

Alaria disappeared with a loud bang, and slowly, the demons surrounding the apartment dissipated. Once they were all gone, Michael turned to Gabriel, who had glimmered into the room. "I'm going to go take precautions to prevent this from escalating onto Earth. I'd suggest you take care of that human."

"Caucasian female, age twenty-nine. Suffering from various lacerations and puncture wounds along with smoke inhalation and burns over thirty percent of the body. Pressure fifty-three over twenty-nine, breathing shallow and erratic. We've been infusing fluids, but she's losing blood quicker than we can put it in. License says she's B positive."

"Call down to the blood bank for twelve units. We've got to stay ahead of the blood loss. Notify the O.R. that we'll be up—get the burn unit standing by. Get x-ray up here, get a cat scan and have the crash cart standing by. Do we know what happened?"

"Fire started in her apartment, knocked the damn coffee pot into the disposal and made it explode. The puncture wounds look like dog bites. Animal control is searching the area."

Dr. Allen Winslow pushed open the door to the examination room, guiding the gurney to the table. "We'll figure it out later. On my count. One, two, three!" He took the IV bag and hung it on the pole next to the head of the bed. "Give me Fentanyl and sux. We're going to intubate. Jackie, push the meds, get epi and atropine standing by." He cut Griffin's shirt off and held out his hand. "Clamp. We've got to get the bleeders clamped off to get her up to surgery."

"Blood's here."

"Start a second IV and begin transfusing." He glanced at the monitor when it began beeping. "Begin chest compressions. Start a round of meds." He picked up the defibrillator and rubbed the paddles with gel. "Charge to two hundred." When the beep told him the machine was charged, he moved over her prone body. "Clear!"

Chapter Twelve

February 15th, 2029 - Philadelphia, Pennsylvania
GRIFFIN WOKE UP slowly, the pain the first thing she noticed. Her head was throbbing. She tried to open her eyes, but the light was too bright. Gritting her teeth, and gripping the sheets in her hand, she forced her eyes open all the way.

Instead of finding herself lying on the floor of her apartment surrounded by Angels and Devils, she found herself in a cool and clean hospital room. Confused, she struggled to sit up and fumbled for the button to hail the nurse into her room. Within seconds, a bubbly redhead in emerald green scrubs opened the door, grinning.

"Finally, you're awake. I'll get your doctor."

"Wait." She grimaced at her voice and cleared her throat. "What happened to me?"

The nurse considered for a moment, then thought better of it. "I think it's best to let your doctor fill you in. I'm new, and I wasn't here when you came in. I'll just page Dr. Winslow. I think he's in the ER today."

Dr. Winslow? Griffin sat up a little straighter. The doctor she'd been treated by several times in the past was named Dr. Winslow. If it was the same doctor, then it was too much to be coincidence. Either he was a demon, or another unlucky human that God had placed in the mess she found herself in.

Within five minutes, Dr. Allen Winslow was entering the hospital room, a stethoscope hanging around his neck, chart in his hand. He closed the door and crossed to the bed. "Welcome back to the world of the living. Do you remember much about what happened?"

Griffin regarded him warily before deciding the blunt approach was going to be the best bet. At least if he was a demon, she would get it out the way immediately. "That depends."

"On what?"

"Whether you're a demon or not."

Allen was taken off guard but he sat down in the chair and shrugged off his lab coat, lifting his sleeve to reveal a tattoo on his bicep. "That's a protection symbol. It protects me from demonic possession. I'm not a demon. But now I want to know how you know about demons."

"Because one named Alaria tried to kill me. She's been haunting me my whole life. I'm the Chosen."

Allen's face went devoid of all color at that moment. "No. It's not possible."

"I said the same thing when the priest told me. But it's true. Or at least, Alaria and Gabriel seem to be pretty convinced it's true, anyway."

"You've seen Gabriel? The Archangel?"

"Only once, really. Michael saved my life when Alaria sent the Hell hounds after me." Griffin paused and cleared her throat again. "How do you know about all this?"

"My family is made up of Warriors. We've been fighting demons for as long as anyone can remember. It's just what my family does. Except for my wife and I. I preferred to heal people rather than hunt them down." He leaned forward in his chair and put his elbows on his knees. "You're sure? About being Chosen? The world is really getting ready to end?"

"They tell me I'm the only one who can save it. I was ready to let Alaria take me to Hell. My parents died, then my grandparents, then I was raped, there were drugs, boys, my foster parents abused me, he tried to force himself on me and I killed him. I was a prostitute to pay for the bills I raked up from going through chemotherapy and radiation for leukemia. And then there was the baby. I got pregnant after the rape. Didn't find out until twenty weeks. I delivered a boy and gave him up for adoption. Alaria kept offering to take me to Hell and make me a ruler. I was on the verge of taking her up on it when Gabriel came to me. He told me that I was special, and gave me a key to a safety deposit box with enough money in it to pay my bills and let me stop turning tricks. He told me to look for a priest who knew biblical philosophy. It took months, but I found him, and he told me what I am."

"When do you turn thirty?"

"January first. I was born at the stroke of midnight. I'm twenty-nine."

"It's February now. That means we have ten and a half months. That's a long time to hide you from demons, but I think it can be done. They can't find you unless you're asleep. That's how they get to you. They zoom in on your subconscious and use it to access your memories and extrapolate where you're located. A demon familiar with Earth could find anyone down to the country in a matter of minutes and could have an exact location in a night. I know how to block them out and keep them from getting to you. I'll get the herbs that I need to set up a ring of protection. It's important that you don't sleep unless you're inside one."

"Will that keep me safe?"

"Safer. It will keep them from being able to find you quickly. They'll still find you eventually, but they'll have to use up some of their strength to be present on Earth for long periods of time to search. I'm sure Brax will want to take you to get the protection tattoos. They'll keep you safer yet."

"Brax? You mean you aren't going to keep me safe? I thought you were a Warrior?"

"I haven't fought in years, Griffin. I'm out of practice, and I'm getting too old to even try. Braxton is my son. He's the best Warrior that I've ever met. He was born to do this. I tried to keep my children away from this life, but they both have it in their blood. They couldn't help it. I'll call him, and he will keep you safe. There's no one else alive that could do a better job at keeping you safe from the forces of Hell."

"You're sure? I don't want to go with someone just to end up dead in a week."

"Brax is the one person that I am the most sure of. Don't worry. He'll keep you alive."

Griffin chuckled then and shook her head. "You mean he'll keep me alive until I have to kill myself."

"I'll go call him and then start to gather the things that we need to keep you safe. I know it's going to be difficult, but try not to go to sleep right now, no matter how sleepy you are. If you do, they'll be able to find you, and that's the last thing that we want."

Alaria paced, her heels clicking on the black obsidian floor and her temper fuming. That little human bitch! She'd dared to not only turn down her offer, but had effectively eliminated any chance she had at winning the Choosing. She'd known that the odds had been stacked against her, that she had her work cut out for her, but she'd really thought she'd had Griffin right where she wanted her.

She'd used her events too early; that was all. A strategic mistake. She would make the most of it. If she couldn't win, she would at least make sure that they didn't lose. Alaria would kill the human and begin the Apocalypse. It wasn't as good as ruling Earth for a thousand millennia, but it would have to do. It was her only chance to have some revenge against God for what He had done to her.

"I tried to tell Him that this was a mistake."

Alaria whirled at the voice behind her. "Beelzebub. What are you doing here?"

Beelzebub, a slick man in a gray pin striped suit with a black silk tie and shiny leather shoes, smiled dangerously and sat down in one of the thrones that sat at one side of the room. "I came to help you."

"No offense, but I think I can handle this all on my own."

"Oh, then I was mistaken when I was told that you involved Michael in a pissing contest over a HUMAN!!"

Alaria managed not to wince, but just barely. That was always the problem with Beelzebub. He was hard to read. You never knew if he was mad or not. And this time, she'd gotten it completely wrong. He was absolutely furious. "The Chosen, Beelzebub. Not a random human. Any normal human wouldn't be worth the trouble. She refused to Choose us. I have to kill her."

"No, you don't. You still have two events left, don't you?"

"Yes. I saved them in case I would need them after the Veil was lifted."

"And need them you shall. We are going to use it to lure her to us and force her to Choose us."

"And how do you propose we do that? There is nothing that we can do to her that she won't see for a ploy to change her mind. And frankly, anything we do to her is simply that. A ploy to get her on our side. It won't work."

"It will if we can find something that she loves so much she would be willing to Choose as we saw fit in order to save. A husband perhaps? A child?"

And just like that, a light flipped on in Alaria's mind. "A child. I forced her to have a son after the rape I made. A boy. Given up for adoption. That's all I know about him."

"A mother's love runs deep. Even a mother who gave her child up. I would be willing to wager that having him held hostage might change her mind."

"Finding him could be problematic. I didn't anticipate needing him, so I haven't kept track of him. I don't even know where she was when she birthed the little whelp. It could have been anywhere at all on that damned planet."

"It won't be nearly so problematic if we bring in Lilith."

"No. I am not dealing with that blonde bitch. She's nothing but a giant pain in my ass."

"She is also at the right hand of our Lord. I suggest you show respect."

"For Hell's sake, Beelzebub, you've been at his right hand for millennia. Lilith has been walking the Earth. She is not affiliated with Hell."

"That does not change the fact that were she to return for more than a short visit, then I would have your seat, and you would be out in the cold. That is why you don't want her involved, Alaria."

"Whether that is true or not is of no importance. Lilith is more of a liability than a help. And the last thing I want is for her to completely take over. We have time here, Beelzebub. We don't want to make our move too early. The earlier we move, the more time they have to counter—to fight back. If we're going to do anything, we want it to be right at the end. Close enough to the end that they don't have time to react. They'll just have to do what we say."

Beelzebub considered that for a long moment. "Perhaps you're right. We'll wait a little while. But I want you to be looking for her. I'm going to go above and see if I can find out some information. There's a Warrior Lilith tells me could be a problem, and I want to try and deal with him now as opposed to later. If we're going to have a chance at this we don't want any more unnecessary complications. This has become complicated enough as it is without any more human interference." He walked across the chamber and pushed open the heavy black doors. "This is it, Alaria. Any more fuck-ups on your end, and that's the end of it. I want you to find that child."

Chapter Thirteen

February 15th, 2029 - Russia

BRAXTON HAD just fallen asleep when his cell phone began insistently vibrating on the nightstand next to him. It had been several days since he'd gotten more than a few moments of sleep, and he was relishing the few hours that he had finally managed to steal for himself while waiting for supplies to take back to the village.

Annoyed and concerned, he rolled over and snatched up the offending device, flipping it open and holding it to his ear in one smooth motion. "Someone had best be dying for you to be calling me at three in the morning."

"Brax, it's Dad."

That got his attention. His father never called while he was on a job unless it was something important. Immediately panicked, Braxton sat up and turned on the bedside lamp. "Mom? Sam?"

"Both fine. But there is something going on here—something I think could be very big."

"What is it?"

"I can't tell you over the phone. I don't think it's safe. But I need you to come home as soon as you can. I've got a job bigger than any you've ever done."

"I'm in the middle of a job now, Dad. I can't just leave. I've got a team over here."

"How long will it take you?"

"Hopefully only a day or two more. We've been here for a week. Look, I'll arrange to swing through after I'm done, but that's the best that I can do. Can you handle it until I get there, or do I need to call someone to come in now?"

Allen considered that for a long moment. "No. I think this is best kept in the family. I don't want anyone else to know about it until we're ready."

"What's it about?"

"I can't say, Braxton. You know the rules. They're your rules as much as mine. No discussing sensitive information on the phone. You can't see me—I can't see you. Anyone could be listening."

Braxton sighed, knowing his father was right. "Okay. Just stay safe until I get there. I'll call you when I land. Tell Mom and Sam hi and I love them."

"Will do. Be careful, son. And come home safe."

"Don't worry about me. I got this."

Then, as he always did, Braxton hung up before his father could respond. Concerned about his father, he settled back into the pillows and stared at the ceiling. What in the world was important enough that his father would be calling him home in the middle of a job? His father was smart, and if he thought that there was something going on that he couldn't handle, he would have let Braxton call in an associate.

He'd met plenty of people throughout his years as a Warrior that were good and that could be trusted, and there were a couple that he would trust with his parents. One of whom was his sister. Samantha may have gotten married to a real estate billionaire five years earlier, but she was still a Warrior at heart, and she was still the first person Braxton turned to when he came up against something he didn't think that he could handle on his own. She was tiny, at five-foot-three inches and one-ten soaking wet, but he had seen her take down men more than twice her size without breaking a sweat. His sister was a firecracker.

Which made him wonder why his father hadn't simply called Samantha when'd he'd needed supernatural help. She was more than capable of handling anything that could possibly have come up, and more importantly, she lived in California. That was much closer than Russia. It had to be something their father didn't want Samantha to know about, and that made Braxton nervous. Generally speaking, they were a very close family.

Deciding to put it off until he could finish his current mission, Braxton rolled over and closed his eyes, determined to grab some rest before his alarm went off. He had long ago trained his body to go to sleep on command as he so rarely had the opportunity to sleep a whole night, and he felt himself drift off. He tumbled off that edge and fell through a sea of inky black.

Suddenly, he stood in a room, Gabriel right next to him. He looked around slowly and discovered that they were in a small but clean apartment. He glanced to the Angel, who shook his head and gestured toward the center of the room where a woman with flowing black hair stood facing off with an Angel dressed all in black. Between them, crawling desperately toward the Angel, was a woman, her face bloody and her flesh ripped and jagged from the fangs of Hell hounds. He easily recognized those wounds; he had seen them before.

"What's going on?"

Gabriel looked at him sharply. "Shut up. If they discover that we are here, you will be killed. This is something you need to see."

Understanding that he needed to be quiet, Braxton turned to watch the faceoff between Angel and Devil.

"I warned Gabriel that he was too lenient with you. This is unacceptable."

"Michael, so nice of you to join us for the festivities. Please, step aside and let me finish what I came here to do."

"That's not going to happen, Alaria. I won't let you kill her."

Braxton took a step forward, but Gabriel tossed out his arm and stopped him. "Do not interfere. Watch. If she discovers your presence, she'll kill you."

"What is this? What the hell is going on?"

Gabriel glared at him. "If you shut up and watch, you'll soon know."

The woman called Alaria spoke again in a singsong voice. "But you hate humans. You used to find them insignificant and unimportant."

"This one is different. Generally, men are good for nothing other than mild amusement. I've never seen why my Father found it necessary to make them, but He did, and it is my job to protect them."

"You're the Angel of War, Michael! You love a little bloodshed."

Braxton jumped when one of the Hell hounds brushed his leg as it stalked around the room. His heart pounded against his ribcage, and he held his breath until his chest burned. The beast sniffed the air suspiciously, but continued moving. Gabriel chuckled next to him.

"Hell hounds are stupid creatures. They smell something, but they can't discern what. Alaria, the Devil there, is so preoccupied she wouldn't notice if you were over here dancing." He shook his head in mild amusement. "I'm amazed she isn't questioning why Michael is here instead of me."

"Why aren't you handling this, if you're supposed to be?"

"Because it is more important to this that you are here. And without me here with you, I could not have made sure you would be adequately protected from detection. Even still, too much movement and conversation will alert one of them."

Michael was speaking again, and Braxton turned his attention to the other Angel. "Wars can be Godly. And while it is true that as a rule I enjoy watching humans destroy each other, I do not encourage it when I am not ordered to do so. Wars effect change. If God feels something needs to change and does not want to interfere with free will, I am sent to plant the seeds of war. But this war, it is between us, Alaria. It does not involve the humans. You will not kill her."

"It's one human. One insignificant life. And she's important to me. You would enjoy the Apocalypse. Lots of wars then. Step aside and let me start it. Then you'll never have to deal with humans again."

"I'll enjoy the Apocalypse when God is ready for it. After a thousand millennia of angelic rule. I'm sure there will be plenty of wars between now and then."

"There's no guarantee the world will end after the rule."

"And there's nothing saying that it won't. Or maybe we'll do this again. Wouldn't that be fun?" Michael shrugged his shoulders. "It's of no concern. Go away, Alaria. I'll not let you have her."

"You would take on the legions of Hell over one human? I'm willing to go to battle over this, Michael. Can you say the same?"

Michael looked up to the ceiling, and it became transparent. Braxton took in an audible breath and his eyes flitted between the writhing mass of Angels that circled the apartment and Gabriel, who was standing beside him calmly.

"What the hell is this? Why are they fighting over one woman?" Braxton's voice was a whisper, the urgency and fear he felt dripping from his words.

"I never come unprepared. When Gabriel came to me tonight and told me that you had taken her to Hell, I knew you had something planned. To borrow a human phrase, I called in the troops." Michael glanced to the side and nodded. "Right on time, Gabriel. Alaria was just telling us that we were about to battle Hell again."

Braxton looked around nervously, trying to determine if either the Angel or Devil knew that he was there. Neither were looking at him, and the Hell hounds were still circling. Gabriel laid a hand on his shoulder reassuringly.

"Michael is my brother. He can always sense me. He's known I was here since the first moment. I've used my powers to shield you from both of them. Your presence hasn't been detected."

"Can't he hear you, though?"

"No. I can have private conversations."

Alaria sneered. "This is not over, Michael. The Veil is off, and I'll have her yet."

"You're welcome to try. But I promise you, Alaria, if you kill her, this will cease to be between Devils and Angels."

"You wouldn't dare involve them. This is none of their concern."

"It will be if you break the rules. They agreed to the terms, and you were charged with carrying it out. If you don't abide by the rules, I'll see to it that you are chained to the bottom of your own pit for the rest of eternity. I promise you, you will never see the surface of the lake again."

"You're welcome to try."

There was a noise like the pages of a book turning and the room filled with demons. Braxton paled as he looked around the room for a weapon. Almost at the exact same moment, Michael reached behind his back and pulled his sword from its sheath. Gabriel shook his head in warning.

"Do not move. Do not speak. If even one of them senses you, we'll have a battle on our hands."

Michael was speaking again. "If you want a battle, Devil, then a battle you will get. But you are outnumbered a thousand to one."

"I'll take out some of your troops."

"I'll take out all of yours."

After a moment, Alaria took a step back. "Very well. We'll fight another day then." She looked at the woman on the floor, barely conscious and writhing in pain. "Enjoy your reprieve. The next time I find you, you won't be so lucky."

Alaria disappeared with a loud bang, and slowly, the demons surrounding the apartment also dissipated. Once they were all gone, Michael turned to Gabriel. "I'm going to go take precautions to prevent this from escalating onto Earth. I'd suggest you take care of that human."

Gabriel waited until Michael had disappeared before speaking. "I cannot tell you what you just witnessed or I would be impermissibly interfering with God's plan. But since you have been blessed with the gift to see some important events, I felt that you should be able to witness the most incredible of them all. I don't know if this will occur during your lifetime, or if it will occur a hundred years in either direction. Human time has no meaning for me. All I can say is that I have a feeling you're important. I don't yet know how, but I wanted to show you this, just in case it does ever happen during your lifespan."

"What do I need to do?"

"Keep your ears open. Pay great attention. All I can tell you is that something very important is happening. Anything past that and I could get in trouble for disclosing or I don't have an inclination to tell you." Gabriel held out his hand, and a soft yellow light emanated from it. "You must go now. I've called for your hospital services, and they will be here shortly. I must stay here to make sure that she does not die before they arrive. Do you remember how I taught you to leave one of these dreams?"

"Yeah, I got it."

"Then go, but do not tell anyone of what you have seen this night. If the wrong creature finds out, you will become as hunted as she."

Ten seconds later, Braxton woke shaking and covered in sweat, his hands clenched in the sheets. With only a moment's hesitation, he rolled out of bed and pulled on his clothes. There was definitely no sleeping now. Supernatural visits, even angelic ones, tended to make him loathe going to sleep.

Braxton hefted his bag off of the conveyor belt at the Philadelphia airport, his eyes gritty from little sleep and his muscles cramped from trying to get that sleep on a plane ride that had been several hours too long. A dark bruise covered one cheekbone, and the line of stitches above his eyebrow itched like crazy. Breathing was uncomfortable due to broken ribs, and one ankle was black and blue. It had been a rough month.

It had started out with a call about werewolves. Braxton always regarded reports of mythical creatures with a healthy dose of skepticism, but had discovered that, more often than not, something was going on, whether it was a ghoul or a prankster. When the Vatican had told him there was a pack of werewolves preying on a small village in northern Russia, he had expected to be doing the job of a good game warden and eliminating a pack of real wolves.

Truthfully, it had ended up being something in between. Not a werewolf, and not a real wolf. It had been a witch hypnotizing men who had shunned her and making them literally eat each other until there was only one left. Then she had cooked him and served him up at a community dinner. Killing her had not been easy, as she had continually conjured new horrors for him to contend with. In the end, it had required a team of seven Warriors to take her down, and they'd lost two. It had taken nearly a whole month to complete the assignment and the amount deposited into his bank account just didn't seem quite worth the cost. He'd rarely had such troublesome assignments.

He wanted nothing more than to go to the apartment he kept in Philadelphia for his short jaunts. He passed through to restock on supplies and visit his parents a couple times a year. Instead of crashing, he gave the taxi driver the address of the hospital where his father worked so that he could find out what was going on. He was asleep in the back seat before the car turned the first corner and didn't wake up until the cabbie smacked his shoulder and demanded to be paid.

Sleepy, grouchy and in pain, he limped into the hospital and went straight for the first nurse's station. She looked up from the computer screen, gave him a quick once over, and pointed.

"The Emergency Room is down that hall. Take a left, then an immediate right, go to the end of that hallway and turn left again."

"I'm not here for the ER. My father is an attending here. Dr. Allen Winslow. I'd like you to page him, please."

"You're Braxton Winslow?"

"Yes, ma'am." He leaned against the desk and smiled as winningly as one could with bruises and stitches. "The prodigal son has returned."

"He's in with a patient right now. Why don't I take you down to his office and you can wait for him there."

"That sounds wonderful. What is it my father does now, anyway?"

"Well, he was head of the ER for a few years. Still does a few shifts down there a month, but he primarily works in the ICU now." The nurse led him to a door and used a key card to open it. "Here you go. Just have a seat, and I'll see that Dr. Winslow knows you're here."

Braxton let the door swing shut behind the nurse and turned on the light. Almost like it was second nature, he began going over the office, checking for salt lines at the windows. He opened the desk drawers one by one, for no reason other than curiosity. He saw the bags of herbs to protect against various supernatural creatures, found a gun with silver bullets under the desk and a shotgun loaded with rock salt under the bookshelf. Satisfied, he sat down in the desk chair, woke up the computer and began playing a game of solitaire. He was on his fifth game by the time his father opened the door and walked in.

"About time. I've been here nearly an hour."

Allen looked at his son and shook his head. "That's the life of a doctor. You should know that by now." He leaned over the desk, grabbed Braxton's face and lifted it. "What the hell happened to you?"

"Witch. Nasty bitch. Cost me two men."

"They tend to do that. She was powerful, then?"

"Strongest one I've ever killed."

"The face the worst of it?"

"Couple busted ribs and a banged up ankle. Nothing I haven't had before. You want to tell me what the hell is going on here? I haven't ever had so many messages from you. The way it sounded, the world could be ending."

"It is."

Nothing his father could have said could have taken him off guard more than that. Braxton carefully leaned forward in the chair and met his father's gaze. "I think I'm going deaf. Because I could have sworn you just said the world is ending."

Allen collapsed into the chair on the other side of the desk. "I have a woman upstairs in a room that is afraid to go to sleep because Alaria haunts her dreams. She was torn apart by Hell hounds, and there is no medical reason why she is still alive."

"So, she sold her soul."

"Add to that a rape, cancer, her parents being killed, her adoptive parents getting shredded by the hounds, an abusive foster father, prostitution, drug addiction and routine visits from our least favorite Devil. Come on, Braxton. What does that sound like?"

"It sounds like the Chosen."

"It is. She's been visited by Gabriel, and Michael kept Alaria from killing her. The Veil has been punctured."

"And she's here?"

"She's here. Came in two months ago. She was in a coma for six weeks and had to have nine surgeries to fix her leg correctly, skin grafts from the burns and a couple plastic surgeries to fix the damage the hounds did to her face and chest. She just woke up two weeks ago. She's still got two or three weeks left of treatment in the hospital, but then she'll be released.

I've got her surrounded by salt, which we have to replace every time house-keeping goes through, and I've given her a protection bag to put under her pillow to keep the demons out. But I can't handle this, Braxton, and she has to stay alive until New Year's. If she doesn't, the world will end."

"I don't need to be reminded what the Chosen does, Dad. I know the story. But I'm a hunter, a Warrior. I'm not in the business of hiding from Devils. I kill them. I don't know how to do this."

"You're the only one who stands a chance at keeping her safe. You're the best Warrior I've ever seen. You were born to be a Warrior, Brax. I tried to stop you, I tried to stop Sam, but you both had a calling. You need to do this. There's no one else."

Braxton sighed and pushed himself to his feet. "All right. Take me to her. We have a lot of work to do."

Griffin was asleep. For the first time in almost two days, she felt secure enough to nod off. She'd spent the last hour putting salt over the windows and on top of the door sill and placing various herbs around her room that Dr. Winslow swore would keep her safe. She had refreshed the bag in her nightstand, put another under her mattress, and stitched a third into her pillow so that it couldn't be dislodged while she slept.

Housekeeping was gone for the day and the nurses were busy with other patients. She finally had a chance to rest. She had slipped her hand into the pillowcase to rest against the burlap of the herb bag and allowed herself to slip off to sleep. After what seemed like only a few minutes, the door opened and someone turned on the light.

Blinking rapidly, Griffin sat up, relaxing when she saw Allen. Behind him was another man. The stranger was taller, she guessed about six-foot-three, and was more than a little worse for wear. He wore a shabby leather jacket and snug jeans with scuffed black boots. His hair was dirty blond and a little too long, hanging into one eye. There was scruff on his face, and if she had to guess, she would say it had been the better part of a week since his chin had seen a razor. The skin around one eye was puffy and purple, and a neat line of black stitches bisected one eyebrow. He walked with a slight limp, and she saw several nicks on his knuckles. This was a man who knew how to handle himself.

"Griffin, I'd like you to meet Braxton, my son. He's just arrived from Russia. He's the one who's going to keep you safe for the next few months."

Before Griffin could summon the words to greet the strange man, he stepped forward and stared at her with hard silvery-gray eyes. "It's you. All these years I thought you were a dream or a trick. But you're real."

Griffin blinked several times as she fumbled for what to say. Finally, she shifted in the bed and cleared her throat. "Do I know you?"

Braxton laughed. "No, you don't know me." He looked at his father. "I've seen her in my dreams. I always thought they were dreams until the last one. Gabriel came to me and told me that I was important to the Choosing. Even then, I didn't believe that it would happen in my lifetime." He sighed deeply. "Maybe it's more that I didn't want to believe it."

Griffin offered a smile. "Guess this is meant to be then, hmm?"

Allen looked between his son and the slight blonde in the hospital bed. "It would seem there are forces bigger than us at play here." He crossed the room and dropped heavily into the chair next to the bed. "Well, let's figure out what to do, shall we?"

Chapter Fourteen

March 15th, 2029 - Philadelphia, Pennsylvania
"Do you hate me?"

Braxton glanced up in mild surprise when Griffin suddenly spoke after nearly two hours of silence. He'd been spending most of his time camped out in her hospital room, making sure that she was kept safe while she healed from the hounds and went through the last surgeries to repair the damage that they had done. Confused at her abrupt question, he closed the book he had been reading, deliberately placed it on the night stand and leaned forward until his forearms were braced on his thighs.

"Now, why would you think that I hate you?"

"Because you've sat there for two weeks and you've barely said a word to me. When you do talk, it's one word answers. I'm not an idiot, Braxton. I know you don't like me."

"It's not that I don't like you. I don't know you. And I don't want to get to know you. What you're mistaking for dislike or hate is simple indifference. I'm here to keep you alive until January. Not to coddle you and be your friend."

"That means you have to ignore me for the next eight and a half months?"

"Griffin, you're going to die. One way or the other, you will be dead in eight and a half months. What point is there in getting friendly, getting attached, and then having to watch you commit suicide? The best thing for both of us is to remain professional and indifferent. It does neither of us any good to form attachments this close to your death date."

"That's all I am to you? I'm the Chosen, not a person? I don't get to have feelings or friends? I'm a job. Just some simple job that you have to do for the next year."

"Don't take offense to it, Griffin. It's nothing personal. I think you're a perfectly nice person when it comes down to it. I just don't want to make attachments that can't possibly be permanent. I'll get you to the Choosing, and then that's it. Nothing more, nothing less. And that is just something that you are going to have to live with."

Griffin studied him for a long moment, trying to figure out why he was behaving the way that he was. Finally, she sighed and picked up her book again. "I think I'd like for you to leave now, if you don't mind."

Taken slightly aback, Braxton blinked several times to clear his head. "Excuse me?"

"I don't think I was unclear. I would like for you to leave. I'm not interested in being ignored for nine months. I am still a human being, and I am going to behave like one. If you don't want to, that's fine. I'll take care of myself until this thing happens."

Braxton had to laugh. "You think you're going to take care of yourself? You think you have the knowledge to hide yourself from Devils and demons? Not to mention all the Devil worshippers and witches who would love to see this thing go their way?"

"I've spent the last few years reading up on it. I know about anti-possession charms. I know what demonic possession is supposed to look like. Your father has shown me the combination of herbs to keep them out and keep me safe while I sleep. I know what a Devil's trap is and have diagrams on how to make one."

"All of that is fine and dandy, and it'll come in handy if we ever get separated for one reason or another. But you don't know half of what you think you do. You know what it's supposed to look like, but did you know that if a strong demon gets into a body it can access memories and live as the person indefinitely? Or that Devils can wiggle into dead bodies for a period of time if they want to? Hell, a Devil doesn't need to wear a skin suit. They can take the form of whatever it is that they want and be so real that no one would know the difference until they wanted you to. They have powers that I don't know about, Griffin, so I don't think that you know nearly everything you think you do. Odds are we're going to come up against things I've never seen. But I'm equipped with knowledge and supplies to deal with almost anything."

"Except for me. You won't deal with me. I'm just an annoyance that has to be ignored until you can hand me the knife and say 'Here honey, nice knowin' you.'"

Unwilling to coddle her or minimize the situation, Braxton nodded sharply and went back to reading. "Yeah, I think that's about right. The sooner you get used to it, the more pleasant these next few months can be."

Furious and unreasonably hurt, Griffin slammed her book shut and launched it at him. Braxton ducked and the book barely skimmed the top of his head as it sailed into the wall. Barely hiding his grin, he stood, fetched the book, and returned it to her. Once he had sat back down in the chair across the room, he cleared his throat to get her attention.

"Nice arm. I might be able to work with you yet."

Griffin slowly transferred herself from the side of the hospital bed and into the wheelchair the orderly had brought for her. Finally, she was getting out of the hospital. Braxton had made arrangements for them to stay at a cabin owned by his sister and brother-in-law, and he had left two days earlier to get everything set up. She'd gotten word from Allen only a couple hours before that Braxton was ready and would be waiting for her at the Boulder airport.

She was going to have to be on her own for a few hours. Allen was driving her to the airport, but then she would be on the flight for several hours including a short layover in St. Louis. It was a terrifying thought, going on her own with all of Hell on the lookout for her.

Griffin was scared and nervous. She didn't know what to expect from her trip or from the next several months. She knew that she was going to be primarily with Braxton and that she would rarely be allowed out of the place that he had deemed safe for her, if ever. She anticipated that they would be moving fairly often to keep the demons off of their trail, and she expected that he would never speak to her more than was absolutely necessary.

Making use of all the contacts Braxton had made over the years, they'd gotten her a new driver's license, passport, and other identifying documents. For all intents and purposes, Griffin Javensen had disappeared off of the face of the Earth. In a few months it would be true, so what did it matter? It wasn't as if she was going to need the small apartment full of knick-knacks and the clothes that she had so painstakingly picked out and bought. It was no small loss to her to have to give up all of those things, but she knew that she had no choice about the matter—her destiny had been decided long before her birth, and there was very little that she could do about it. She did what she had to do. She went along with it, because if she didn't, there was no way she would make it to the Choosing.

The airplane was stifling, even though it was a large craft. Griffin's seat seemed to push in around her, not letting her breathe quite right as she struggled to stay awake. Even though she had been medically cleared for release, it seemed as if she were still much more tired than normal, and there was no way to surround herself with the necessary herbs for protection in the middle of an airplane. She'd have probably been met by security guards at the gate if she had even tried.

She sat, her back ramrod straight in the seat, her mind racing at thought of the months she had ahead of her. She knew enough to know that her life was already over. She would be a prisoner in whatever safe house Braxton had readied for her for that particular night, and she would be completely at his mercy. It was something that she would have to put up with because he was the only one who could keep her safe from the Devils that pursued her. Even if he was the world's largest jackass.

He was also right. Griffin didn't have a clue what possession actually looked like, she didn't know the spells for a decent exorcism, and she had no idea of the protections that they could need over the next months. She was determined to learn. If she would accomplish anything in her last months, it would be that she would go out knowing that she could handle literally any situation that came her way. No matter how hard.

Luckily, the flight landed right on time, and she was able to make her way toward the front of the plane with little problems. She had barely made it off the escalator and into baggage claim when Braxton's arm shot through the crowd and his hand fastened around her wrist, dragging her as fast as she could move toward the nearest exit. He didn't so much as glance at her the entire way and ignored her sputtering protests until she was safely closed up inside the cab of the truck and he was pulling away from the curb.

"My flight was great, thanks for asking. No, they didn't serve an in-flight tray, so I'd love something to eat. Your Dad says hi, and by the way, you're an insufferable asshole."

Mildly amused, Braxton slid his gaze sideways to her for a moment. "The flight was on time, so I assumed it went as planned. It wasn't a transcontinental flight so there would be no food, which we have at the cabin I'm taking you to. I talked to my father after you got on board to make sure you'd gotten off the ground in one piece, and yes, I'm an insufferable asshole. Anything else you need to cover, or can we go home?"

"Home is about two thousand miles in the other direction. You want to go there, I'm more than willing to go. I'll even take you with me." Griffin smiled at him almost saccharinely as he pulled into traffic, and Braxton rolled his eyes, knowing in his gut that the next few months were going to be some of the hardest of his entire life. Mainly because he was beginning to think that Griffin was determined to make them exactly that—hard and miserable.

"You could make this easy, you know."

"You could, too. Until you stop insisting on treating me like some object that needs to be protected and not interacted with, I'm going to be as difficult as humanly possible."

Sighing, Braxton did the only logical thing. He changed the subject. "Once I get you settled, I need to take you in to town and get you the protection tattoos. Each symbol protects you from something different so there's no way you can be possessed or influenced. You'll be able to see the true form of a demon rather than the skin suit they're wearing."

"Tattoos? How many of them?"

"Thirteen—and don't freak out. I'm not having you get anything that I don't already have. The artist I'll take you to is good. She's actually the one who did mine ten years ago. They can be small, and I was figuring you'd get them across your back."

"I don't even get to pick where they go? Great. Anything else you want to decide for me? What I eat, when I sleep, who I fuck?"

"I already planned on making those decisions, but the fact that you realize it makes things easier. You can take a nap when we get to the house. Hopefully you're like a two-year-old and just cranky because you haven't been sleeping."

"I'm cranky because of you."

"Well, then, you'd best get over the attitude, because those things aren't going to change until you're dead. The sooner you realize that, the easier these last few months are going to be."

An hour later, Griffin stood in the room she'd been given at Braxton's brother-in-law's chalet. It was a sprawling cabin, done in rustic wood tones and leather that screamed quiet money without the overwhelming presence of fur and stuffed carcasses. There was a wall composed of nothing but windows, a sleek modern kitchen, and four bedrooms and bathrooms.

The bedroom Braxton had given her was warm and cozy, with a four poster King-sized bed covered in a thick quilt and luxurious sheets. There was a roughhewn dresser and wardrobe for clothes and a matching chest at the bottom of the bed that contained additional linens. There was a desk and chair against one wall, and an overstuffed leather chair and TV opposite it.

The bathroom that connected to the bedroom was a lesson in luxury: light marble floors, a soaking tub big enough for ten people, and a walk-in shower with full body jets. There was an array of perfumes and lotions, along with soaps in every shape and scent imaginable. There were huge, fluffy towels neatly stacked next to the tub, and there was even a fireplace—one of the two-sided ones so that it would heat the bedroom and bath at the same time.

Griffin had never felt so out of place in her life. She was afraid to touch anything, let alone use anything. It was by far the most expensive house she had ever been in. She would bet one night's rent in a place like this would be two months' worth in her small apartment. She was going to get to live there for months. The thought was both thrilling and terrifying.

She sat her one duffel bag on the bed and began unpacking her meager belongings. Two pairs of jeans, three bras, five t-shirts, half a dozen pairs of panties and four pairs of socks. It was what Braxton had brought her at the hospital several days earlier, and they were all the wrong size, though she wasn't going to complain.

When she opened the dresser drawer to put her clothes away, she found piles of underwear and bras, all with the tags still attached. Confused, she opened the next drawer down and found socks, stockings and more lingerie. Interest piqued, she did a quick search of all the drawers and the wardrobe, then perched on the edge of the bed, perplexed.

There were stacks of new jeans, t-shirts, blouses, sweaters, slacks, a couple of skirts and some dresses. There were even shoes. Boots, heels, serviceable tennis shoes, and a sturdy pair of snow boots. There was a wool coat, a thick down-filled coat and several zip-up sweatshirts. A whole wardrobe, all of it with the tags on.

Standing, she padded down the hall in her bare feet, knocked lightly on Braxton's door, and then pushed the door open. She froze, her eyes widening with shock.

He was standing in the middle of the room, stripped down to a pair of black boxers. His skin was darkly tanned, even in the winter, and his chest was rippled with muscles. Not gym muscles, but muscles earned from long days of hard, physical work.

His shoulders were broad, and he wore his scars well. There was a jagged one across his abdomen, a round hole that screamed bullet just below his rib cage, and several other scars over his chest and back. This was a true Warrior. Griffin was unable to either stop staring at him or remember why in God's name she had entered his room in the first place.

"Are you going to stand there all day, or are you going to tell me what you want so that I can get my shower?"

Shaking her head, Griffin tried desperately to remember. "The room that you put me in-"

"Yeah, what about it? Not big enough for the princess?"

"It's bigger than my whole apartment, Braxton. And gorgeous. I didn't come here to complain."

"Okay, you love the room. Why the hell are you here then?"

"There's stuff in it. All the drawers are full. I just wondered if there was someplace that I could put my stuff, or if I needed to go to another room."

"Neither. Sam had some things sent over for you. Apparently she had Dad look at the sizes in the clothes you were wearing when you came into the hospital and she went shopping. My sister loves to shop, and she loves to spend Finn's money. It's her favorite pastime."

"I can't accept all of that stuff."

"Sure you can, or else you'll have to run around naked. There are perfectly good clothes down the hall. Be grateful and take them. I left Sam's number by the phone downstairs if you want to call and thank her. I think she wants to talk to you anyway."

Resigned, Griffin nodded. "I'll go call her then."

"Good idea." Braxton stalked across the room, backing her up until she was just on the other side of the door. "I'm going to get a shower, then I'll be down for dinner. We'll take turns cooking, and tonight is your turn."

Her mouth open, Griffin watched in stunned silence as the door swung shut in her face. Irritated, she turned on her heel and bounded down the stairs, snatching up the phone with one hand and the small list of numbers with the other. Taking a deep breath to calm herself, lest she be rude to the woman whose house she was staying in, she began to dial.

"Hello?"

"Is this Samantha Winslow?"

"This is Sam Fisher, but it used to be Winslow. Can I help you?"

"My name is Griffin Javensen. Braxton gave me your number. I wanted to call and thank you for everything at the cabin."

"Oh! It's you! I've been wanting to talk to you. No problem about the stuff. It was fun. There are a couple different sizes of pants there. I don't know about you, but I swear I have to have three different sets of jeans depending on how big my butt is from one day to the next. And in the winter, I live in the baggy ones. If you need anything else, just let Brax know, and don't let him bully you."

"I don't think he knows how to be anything but a bully."

Griffin was shocked with what had slipped out of her mouth, but Sam laughed richly. "Oh, he can be, that's for damn sure. Spent most of his life bullying me. But he's a good guy deep down, and he'll settle once he gets to know you a little. He just takes the job too seriously. Just have a little patience with him. Braxton is a tough man, but when push comes to shove, there is no one better to have in your corner."

"I'll take your word on that."

"Is he being that bad? What's he doing?"

Immediately uncomfortable, Griffin shook her head, forgetting momentarily that Sam could not see the motion through the phone line. "I'd rather not get into it if it's all the same to you. He's your brother, he's taking care of things here, and any personal issues I have with him are small in comparison."

"Just because he's taking care of things doesn't give him a right to be a jackass. And yes, he is my brother, which puts me in the incredibly beneficial position of being one of three people on this whole planet who can get away with yelling at Braxton. Griffin, you're in a hard spot right now, and I know it seems like life can't get any worse. I won't lie to you and tell you these next months are going to be easy. You'd know I was lying, and so would I. But there is no reason that you have to be miserable either. So what's he doing?"

Taking a deep breath, Griffin fought a short battle over what to say. "It's not a big deal. He's just standoffish. Doesn't want to talk to me. He says I'm the Chosen, a job, and he'll treat me as a job, not a person. I don't like feeling like that's all I am."

"Well, of course you don't. That's not all you are. That's what you are, not who you are. Put him on the phone."

"I'd rather not, if it's all the same to you. I don't want to piss him off more."

"You won't. I will. And when I'm done, things will be better."

"He's in the shower right now. Should I just have him call you?"

"Is he really in the shower, or do you just not want to make him mad?"

"Both."

Sam laughed again, and Griffin couldn't help but like her. "Okay then. Tell him I need to talk to him and that I'll know if he's avoiding me. And don't let him push you around, Griffin. It's your life. You should be able to live it the way you want to. I know doing everything you used to is impossible now, but you can have some normalcy. You deserve it."

"Thanks. And thanks again for the clothes. It was very nice of you."

"Don't even think about it. We'll talk again soon."

"Okay."

Once they had hung up, Griffin headed for the kitchen, wondering what she was going to do about dinner. Principle told her not to make anything for Braxton because of the way he was acting, but she didn't want to make things worse. She was still debating her situation when she opened the door of the fridge and stared at the contents. Her stomach was telling her she was hungry, but she wasn't sure if her nerves would let her eat.

Finally, sighing deeply, she dragged out an armful of vegetables and a pack of chicken. A quick scour of the cabinets told her that Braxton had not thought to get any canned soup, so she was stuck making it, as she had originally feared. That was okay—she liked to cook, and chicken noodle soup was one of her specialties.

Rolling up her sleeves, she selected a knife and set about boning the chicken breasts. Once that was done, she set the bones boiling to make a broth and diced up the chicken to sauté. She chopped carrots and celery and set them aside, and she diced garlic and onions to go in as well. By the time she heard Braxton's footsteps on the stairs, she had strained the broth and added the vegetables so that they could cook. She was scraping pieces of chicken into the soup pot when he rounded the corner.

"What are you doing?"

"Making dinner. What does it look like I'm doing?"

"You actually listened."

Griffin tried not to smile and turned back to the stove so that he wouldn't see the corners of her mouth turn up. "I'm hungry. Had you bought something that comes in a can, I wouldn't be making enough for us both. But if I'm going to make soup, I'm making enough to have left-overs. It's always better warmed up the next day."

"Works for me. It smells good. Just yell when it's ready."

Incredulous, Griffin whirled around to face him with a wooden spoon clutched tightly in one hand. "Excuse me? You expect me to stay in here, make your food, and then just call you when it's ready? You want to eat, you can damn well help me make it."

"I think you've got it under control. But if you'd rather I cook soup than go outside and get wood for fires tonight, I'd much rather stir. Your choice."

Deflated, Griffin chose not to answer. Instead, she began studiously shelling peas to go into the fragrant broth bubbling on the stove top. Chuckling, Braxton pulled on a heavy coat, fished gloves out of his pockets, and headed outside. It was going to be an interesting nine months.

Chapter Fifteen

April 22nd, 2029 - Boulder, Colorado
GRIFFIN SLOWLY slid her shirt off her shoulders, wincing at the pain even small movement caused. It had been a week and a half since Braxton had taken her to get the thirteen tattoos across her back, and they were still incredibly painful. She had been trying to care for them the best she could, but the simple fact was that she couldn't reach.

She craned her neck to see her back in the mirror and made a face at the angry, raised symbols. They were infected—that was obvious even to her. There wasn't a damn thing she could do about it, save pouring hydrogen peroxide over her shoulders.

Considering the option, she fished around under the sink and found a bottle of rubbing alcohol. It would sting like hell, but it would disinfect the tattoos and help with the infection. A couple days of that and she should be good as new.

Satisfied with her plan, she reached around her back to unhook her bra and shimmied out of her jeans and panties so as to not damage the clothing. She grabbed a white towel off the shower hook and spread it out to soak up any rubbing alcohol that made it to the floor. Then, with a deep breath, she laid the bottle against one shoulder and poured.

The pain was instant and intense. She sucked in a breath and let out a yell she didn't know had been building up. It burned and felt like she was boiling her skin off. Her vision clouded with red temporarily, and she gripped the sink to keep her balance.

Braxton burst through the door, splintering the frame from the force of ramming his shoulder into it. She screamed and whirled, giving him a complete view of her entirely naked body as she grabbed for a towel to cover up with.

"What the fuck is going on? You screamed."

"I yelled, and you could knock!" She hastily wrapped the towel around herself and put her hands on her hips. "Obviously I'm not being murdered."

"You screamed. That generally means something is going on that shouldn't. I came running up here to rescue you, and you're pissed off. You're a real piece of work, lady."

Griffin took a deep breath and forced herself to get her nerves under control. "Okay, you're right. I'm sorry. I was trying to clean the tattoos, and the rubbing alcohol hurt. It surprised me, and I yelled. Now, could you please leave?"

His temper cooling, Braxton cocked one of his eyebrows. "You think I've never seen a naked woman before?" His eyes traveled over her slowly, purposely making her more uncomfortable. "Not bad. I've seen better, though."

Still struggling with her temper, Griffin managed a tight smile that betrayed the fury simmering just beneath it. "Get out. Unless you want me to claw out your eyes, you will get out right this second."

Braxton threw up his hands in mock surrender. "Hey, no worries. When you're done, come downstairs and I'll take care of your back. I can reach it much better than you can."

Twenty minutes later, her hair falling down her back in damp ropes, clad in thick socks, jeans and a light pink camisole, Griffin padded down the stairs. She checked the kitchen, and when she didn't find Braxton there, she continued through the cabin into the living room. He was sitting on the edge of the couch, laying out an array of things. She glanced over the selection and saw soap, a wash cloth, a tube of ointment, tissues, and a bowl of water that was still slightly steaming.

"Looks like someone isn't all jackass after all."

"Don't get your hopes up. Can't have you dying of sepsis right now. That would defeat the whole purpose. Come sit down and let me take care of those." He patted the cushion next to him and tore the wrapper off the bar of soap. "You should have told me they were getting infected. I'd have cleaned them before this."

Griffin sat gingerly, turning her back to him and pulling her hair around her shoulder so that it wouldn't impede him. "I didn't realize how bad they were getting. I've never had a tattoo before, and she told me to expect some redness and scabbing."

"These are really infected." Immediately consumed with his task, Braxton dampened one corner of the cloth and dabbed water onto her back. It was warm and pleasant, though it did hurt when he brushed against the tattoos. He dipped the soap in the water, then began slowly rubbing the bar over her back in a circular motion.

"I'm surprised you aren't scrubbing my skin off."

"Can't risk damaging the clarity of the symbols. They don't work unless they're perfect. Hold still."

He laid the cloth over her back and began slowly moving it back and forth, gently scrubbing. She felt the scabs starting to break loose, and some of the tightness that had been plaguing her for a week began to ease. His fingers brushed against her shoulders, and she involuntarily shivered at the sensation of skin-to-skin contact. It had been a very long time since anyone but a doctor had touched her.

Braxton watched the chill bumps appear on her skin and couldn't help but smile a little. She was trying to be unaffected by him, but he suspected it wasn't working as well as she hoped. He opened the tube of iodine gel and squirted some out onto his fingers. He absently brushed a couple stray locks of hair out of his way and noticed her involuntary shiver.

"This is going to sting a little, but it'll keep the infection out."

Griffin nodded and gritted her teeth in anticipation. She sucked in a breath when the ointment hit her raw skin and made a small noise in the back of her throat. And then, for reasons unbeknownst to either of them, Braxton leaned forward and blew gently on the area, his breath cooling the sting and raising more chill bumps on her skin. Her eyes alight with confusion, Griffin turned her head to meet Braxton's gaze over her shoulder.

"What are you doing?"

Braxton shook his head. "I don't have the foggiest idea." He took the cloth he'd used to wash her back and used it to wipe the ointment off of his fingertips. Then he slowly let them glide across her skin, trailing over her back and up her shoulder blade until he could take her chin in his hand. His other palm on the small of her back, he used gentle pressure to get her to turn until she was facing him, their faces inches apart.

"Brax—"

"Shh. I don't hate you, Griffin. You've haunted my dreams since I was a little boy. I saw you when your grandparents were killed. I saw you when you were raped. I was there when you were torn to shreds. And each time, I was helpless to go to you, helpless to make it stop. I can't let myself get attached to you because this is going to be hard enough. I think I've been preparing for this my whole life, and I just didn't know it until a few weeks ago. I know I'm an asshole, I know I'm harsh, but I have to be that way, or else I'm afraid come New Year's, I'm not going to be able to help you do what you have to do."

Going strictly on impulse, Griffin lifted one hand and laid her fingertips on his face. She traced the curve of his jaw, the arch of his cheekbones, the softness that was his mouth. Then she slid her hand around to the back of his neck, her fingers barely brushing his hair. Neither had noticed when it happened, but one of his hands had slid up her thigh to rest lightly on her hip.

She shifted forward, rising up, causing his hand to slide around her body to her ass. She pressed a chaste kiss to his cheek. "I don't want to die. But I know I have to. I don't want to make things harder on anyone, but I can't spend nine months without any human contact. You're strong, Braxton. You'll be able to help me. If you weren't strong enough, the Angels never would have chosen you. In a sense, this is as much your task as it is mine, and the only way we're going to get through this is if we work together."

He didn't respond to her reasoning. Instead, he skimmed his hand up her body, tangled it in her still damp hair and jerked her forward, clamping his mouth on hers. He knew, in one moment, with one kiss, that he was lost. There would be no going back.

Griffin came alive with his kiss, wrapping her arms around his neck, her mouth fervent on his. She tasted dark, like sin and rich chocolate; he was spicy and all man. Her breasts were crushed against his chest and his hard arms banded her to him, aligning their bodies from shoulder to pelvis. They were so close that his body heat seeped into her, warming that place inside that had been cold for so long.

"I want you." Braxton tore his mouth away and rained kisses on her neck, igniting fires wherever his mouth touched. "Will you let me have you?"

"It's a bad idea. You have no idea what I've done."

"I don't care. I think if I don't have you I might explode. I know what you've been through. What you had to do. It's part of the Choosing, Griffin. You were forced into it."

"I haven't had sex since my last trick."

Braxton grinned and slid one hand under her shirt to roll a hardened nipple between his fingers. "Say the word and you'll be having sex very soon." He nipped her lip sharply, sending a thrill down her spine. "Do you want me?"

Her head fell back under his ministrations, a groan gurgling in her throat. "Yes."

He took the opportunity to kiss her throat, trailing his tongue down her skin. "Will you let me have you?"

"Yes."

In what seemed like the time span of a heartbeat, Braxton lifted Griffin into his arms and headed for the stairs. She had known he was strong—had felt the ridges of his muscles under her hands—but she had never dreamed that he would be able to lift and carry her as if she weighed no more than a small child. She wrapped her arms around his neck for extra security and burrowed her face into his neck, trying to calm the butterflies swirling in her stomach.

It had been years since Griffin had let a man enter her body. Not once since the night of the last client had she let anyone put their hands on her. She hadn't wanted to. She had rarely enjoyed sex when she was having it several times a week. Even then, it had been at most mild enjoyment that left her feeling unreasonably dissatisfied when the act was over.

Something about Braxton made her want to give it another try. He was big and strong, and she felt safe wrapped in his arms. He could hurt her if he wanted to; he could force her to do whatever he wanted, but instead he had left the decision completely up to her, without pushing her in one direction. Just giving her the option to say no had made her want to say yes.

He cleared the last step and swiftly took her into his bedroom. His room was done in blues and tans and smelled like his cologne and faintly of the potpourri that Samantha had left all over the house. The bed was made from roughhewn wood and was covered with a thick navy blue comforter. He gently laid her down, and it was like he had set her on a cloud.

His body covered hers, pressing her into the mattress, his mouth seeking and finding hers. She felt a twinge of pain as her raw skin rubbed against the soft sheets, but even that couldn't withstand the onslaught of pleasure from his kiss. She lifted her chin to meet his demanding kiss, taking his tongue into her mouth and swirling her own with it. His hands found the bottom of her camisole, and he slowly pulled it over her head, his fingers searing her skin wherever they touched. When he tossed the tank aside and his hands took full possession of her breasts, her back arched in a primal response and a low groan rolled out of her throat.

Braxton flicked his thumbs across her nipples, and Griffin felt a tightening in her belly and a slow heat between her legs, a sensation she had never before felt. He met her eyes for a long moment, gray locking onto blue, and then he dipped his head and took the tip of one breast into his mouth.

The pleasure was so exquisite that she couldn't stop her hands from going to his head, holding him to her. She moaned softly, arching her body into his touch. He stroked the tightly beaded nipple with his tongue, lightly sucking. One of his hands slid down her body and dipped beneath the waistband of her pants, and his fingers skimmed over the entrance to her body. When he found her already damp, he groaned and lifted his head from her breasts.

Shifting off of her, he grasped the waist of her pants and pulled them off in one smooth movement, tossing them onto the floor. Seconds later, he was peeling her panties down her legs and sending them to join the rest of her clothes. With a wicked grin on his face, he used his head to nudge her thighs apart. He pressed a kiss to the inner part of her thigh and slid his hands up to grip her hips, holding her still. Then, he licked her.

Griffin's whole body came off the bed, so intense was the bolt of pleasure that shot through her. His tongue was wet and hot on her, and her body reacted to it by becoming wetter and hotter. He chuckled at her reaction, then continued his task, parting her with his tongue and stroking her slowly and gently. His hands gently rubbed her skin and pulled her toward his mouth to give him greater access.

She writhed on the bed under his ministrations, an unfamiliar ball of pleasure gathering deep within her. She felt her body straining for something, seeking release, but she wasn't quite sure how to get there. Griffin suddenly realized that her hands were buried in Braxton's hair, and she had no idea how they had gotten there. He didn't seem to mind, so she left them there, arching her pelvis up into him, her body aching for what he was providing, for what she had never before felt.

Suddenly, he stopped and pulled away. He slid back up her body, kissing her belly, her breasts, and then her throat. Confused, she lifted her gaze to his, her eyes blurred with pleasure and confusion. He chuckled softly and kissed her forehead.

"I don't want you to orgasm until I'm inside of you. I want to feel you when you do, feel you tighten around my dick and know that I did that to you. I want you to know that I'm going to do it again."

Griffin had no idea what to say to that, so she decided not to say anything at all. Instead, she grabbed the bottom of his shirt and yanked it over his head, splaying her hands on his chest. She reveled in the feel of his muscles beneath her fingers before reaching for his belt. With several practiced motions, she had the belt off and his pants undone, and was slipping her hands inside his boxers, cupping his thick length in her hands.

Braxton's eyes crossed when her small hands closed around him. He was already rock hard, and feeling her silky skin sliding over him was almost too much to bear. He closed his eyes, concentrating on not exploding in her hand and growled when she circled him with two fingers and slid them up and down quickly.

"Stop."

"Don't try to tell me you don't like it."

"Liking it is exactly the problem. I want to get inside of you."

Braxton stood and finished removing his pants and boxers and kicked them aside. Griffin couldn't take her eyes off of his body. Once he was completely naked, he eased onto the bed next to her, but instead of lying on top of her, he stretched out beside her, propping his head up on his hand and looking at her.

"This is your last chance to back out, Griffin."

Griffin lifted one hand to lay it on his face. "If I wanted to back out, I'd have done it by now. I'm not exactly a blushing virgin here."

"Regardless, once I'm inside you, there's no stopping. I want you to be sure."

"I'm sure."

"Griffin, you know this doesn't mean—"

"Don't. It's sex, and we both want it. We'll enjoy it. I'm not trying to turn it into anything that it isn't. So long as you don't go back to pretending I don't exist, I'll be fine. No explanation needed."

Braxton wasn't completely satisfied with her answer, but he decided it was something that would have to be further discussed at another time. When they were naked in bed and he was hard was not the right time or place to have an in depth discussion. He'd wanted her to be aware that he wasn't offering her any sort of relationship or commitment; she had accepted his condition, and it was time to move on.

He leaned over her and reached for the bedside table. After a minute of fumbling, he withdrew a shiny foil packet. With a practiced move, he tore open the condom wrapper and slid it on, unrolling the thin film of latex over his erection.

He slowly took her mouth, kissing her deeply and running one hand down the side of her body, skimming over her ribs, her hip, and the gentle curve of her thigh. Her arms slid around him, pulling gently until his hips were anchored against hers. He used one knee to part her legs and settled himself against her, centimeters away from the hot, slippery slide into her body.

He probed her with the tip of his penis, and she gasped at the contact, digging her fingers into his shoulders. He was long, and he was thick—it had been years since she had had sex. Just taking the head into her body made her feel filled to the brim and stretched to her limits. He slowly pushed himself into her, forcing her body to accommodate, stretching and filling her. Finally, he was fully inside of her, her wetness surrounding him, her heat seeping into his pores. He went completely still, his willpower plainly evidenced through the strain on his face.

"You okay?"

Griffin couldn't help the giggle that escaped her lips as she wiggled, trying to abate the remnants of pain from his entrance. "It's been a while." She groaned when he pushed even deeper and felt a strange sensation begin to build deep in her belly. "God, you feel good."

Braxton grinned as he began to move—heavy, slow thrusts that took him almost all the way back out before pushing inside her to the hilt. "You sound surprised."

"I am. Believe it or not, I never really enjoyed sex all that much. It was what I could offer, and it was what I did to survive."

His kiss silenced her, his mouth firm and warm moving on hers. His hands found hers, lifted them over her head and held both her wrists so that her body was completely exposed to his gaze, his touch, his kiss. Griffin, who had always made sure that she was the one in charge, that no man ever dominated her, found herself strangely turned on by the subtle sense of helplessness. She trusted Braxton not to hurt her or push her too far.

He stroked into her over and over again, torturing them both with the building tension and driving her to a frenzied state that she had never before experienced. She lost track of time, the room spun away, and she was left with Braxton's face, with his body inside of hers, and the ever increasing burn deep within.

He bent and nipped her collarbone sharply with his teeth and then soothed the spot with his tongue. He shifted down her body to leisurely lick her nipples, pulling one into his mouth to suck on it, using his tongue to tease the tightly beaded point while he did so.

She pulled her arms free and dug her nails into his back. Her body arched and her hips pushed against him, forcing him deeper. She hitched her thighs around his hips to hold him tighter to her. He released her nipple only to lave attention on the other one, and his hand slid between their bodies, his fingers finding that place that sent shockwaves through her. Skillfully, he used his thumb to stroke her into frenzy, and then with one flick of his fingers, he sent her flying.

Griffin shattered into a million pieces. Her body caught on fire and she flew apart, only to be snapped back together by the greatest pleasure she had ever felt in her whole life. She didn't hear her own scream as she came, didn't notice her fingernails digging into Braxton's back, and was barely aware of the spasms of her own body.

He didn't let her come back down. He kept stroking her, kept fucking her, deeper and harder, driving her back up the crest of orgasm before her body stopped trembling from the first one. His name was a sob on her lips and her moans drove him wild. Just as he felt her body tense and explode with climax, he let his own sweep him away, pounding mercilessly into her body and emptying himself within her with the most intense orgasm he had ever experienced.

Braxton shifted and settled Griffin more comfortably against his side, her body lying pressed against his and her head on his shoulder so that he could easily kiss her if he had a desire to do so. She let one of her hands drift over his chest, drawing nonsense symbols with her fingertips. It had been more than an hour since they had finished making love, and neither one of them had said anything.

Lazily, he lifted her chin and kissed her. Her hand stilled on his chest; she lifted it to his face, his two day stubble scratching her fingertips pleasantly. He felt a familiar desire begin in his belly and reluctantly lifted his mouth from hers. It wasn't the time to slip back inside her as he wanted to. As much as he would rather nudge her underneath him and have her again, they needed to talk.

"How do you feel?"

Griffin couldn't help grinning at his question. She slid her hand down his arm, twining their fingers. "I don't think I've ever felt better. I never dreamed it could actually be like that."

"You'd never had an orgasm."

Ignoring the urge to bury her face in his shoulder and blush, Griffin shook her head. "No, it would appear that I had not."

"But you used to do this."

"I know I did. I hated it. I rarely got any enjoyment out of it, and even then, it just ended up with me being frustrated at the end. What I did, I did to survive—not because I wanted to and not because I enjoyed it. I had to pay for cancer treatments, and as awful as it sounds, most of the time, I was too weak to do anything other than lay on my back. I was so desperate and so depressed, that I started using drugs. It was so easy to get into it. My supplier would give me a hit for a blow job. I started when I was nineteen. It lasted three years."

Braxton felt his heart squeeze at the pain laced through her voice. No one deserved the life that she'd been forced to live. She hadn't had a choice; misery had been forced on her. She'd been born to suffer. And still, she could lie in his arms and talk about her experiences—not with bitterness, not with anger, but with simple resignation. She had stopped even believing that it could get any better.

"It'll be better now."

Griffin raised onto her elbows and rolled so that she was lying across his chest, her brows lifted in mild amusement. "Better? It's not going to get better, Braxton. I'm going to die. You're going to have to watch me kill myself. This—what we just did? That was probably the best moment of my entire life. An hour where I didn't think about what was coming next, where I just let myself float away on what felt good. This is going to be hard. They're going to come after us, and the odds are good that neither one of us will survive, along with any other human who dares to get in the way."

Swiftly, and before Griffin could react, Braxton rolled her beneath him. He ripped open another condom, sheathed himself, and stroked into her in one smooth movement. She gasped at his sudden entrance, her muscles automatically pulsing around him. He pushed deeper, lowering his mouth to her ear. "Stop it. Stop thinking about it. We're safe for right now. I'll keep you safe. And you're right. You'll die, and I probably will too. So if these are the last few months that we're going to be alive, we're going to enjoy them."

"Braxton—"

"Shut up. Do you know how good you feel? How wet you are, how hot and tight around my cock? You make me want to explode the second I get inside you. But I don't want to because then I won't be making love to you anymore. You're velvety and slick, and tight as a fist. I could fuck you for days."

His words—his low, raunchy voice—turned her on to the point that she was teetering on the edge the moment he started thrusting. And he accomplished his goal. By the time he collapsed on top of her, hot and sweaty and thoroughly sated, she'd forgotten all about her task and was merely wondering when he would have the energy to do it all over again.

Chapter Sixteen

April 29th, 2029 · Boulder, Colorado

GRIFFIN TOSSED and turned. There was pale moonlight spilling in through the curtains, and the only sound was Braxton's even breathing. She turned her head and idly watched his chest rise and fall as he slept. Even in sleep he looked powerful. He was sprawled across the mattress, one arm stretched out to the side and wedged underneath her pillow. The blanket was draped over his waist, and his feet touched the footboard.

Over the past week, she'd learned every inch of his body. She knew what he liked, and he had learned to play her like a fiddle. Of course, their predicament required training in addition to sex. Braxton had taught her some basic self-defense and other protection spells and how to make potions that she might need. They spent their nights tangled up in one another, pretending for just one more day that nothing could intrude on the cocoon they had built around the cabin and their days preparing for the moment when something would.

They both knew it would end. Something would happen and they would have to leave. The Devils would find them eventually, or Braxton would decide they needed to move to avoid being found. Griffin dreaded that day. Not because she didn't want to leave the cabin, but because she was afraid that he would end what was between them. It was dangerous, and they both knew that, but it was so easy to pretend they were safe when they were inside the cabin.

A slight noise made her jump, and she rolled over quickly, her heart pounding in her chest. A man had materialized in the bedroom, dressed all in black with fearsome red wings folded against his sides. The sight of the wings calmed her racing heart, and she took two deep breaths before speaking, her voice a whisper.

"You were there the night I was attacked. You saved me."

The man nodded, his eyes glowing embers in the dark. "My name is

Michael, and I am an Angel of the Lord. Dress and come with me. There is something that you need to see."

Griffin felt no fear toward the Angel. She slid from the bed and tip-toed from the room, heading down the hall to her bedroom to put on something other than one of Braxton's t-shirts. She heard the Angel follow her, though he waited outside the door while she pulled on jeans, tennis shoes and a sweater.

"Where are you taking me? Braxton will have a heart attack if he wakes up and I'm not here."

Michael smiled in amusement. "Has Gabriel taught you nothing about Angels and time? You'll be back within the span of a single heartbeat from now. The Warrior will not wake. As for where I am taking you, I need for you to understand more about the Devil and Angel you so often inter-act with. There is more to them than meets the eye, and much more than either would ever have you know. Unlike my brother, I am not bound by the rules of the Choosing. Where we are going, you must be quiet. You may ask me questions, but do not move from the spot in which you are placed. I am taking you to the past, and even a singular step could imper-missibly interfere with time moving forward. Do you understand?"

Griffin nodded. "I understand."

Before she could blink, they were standing in a clearing. Trees stood taller than any she had ever seen, and vines ran between them in a complex pattern. The grass beneath her feet was mossy and springy, and she could hear the rustlings of birds and animals deeper within the forest.

"Where are we?"

"I don't know what you would call it in present day. This is a very rudimentary Earth, before the time of Adam. What you are about to wit-ness is something that has ramifications reaching even beyond the time in which you live."

"But I thought God made the whole Earth in less than a week?"

Michael chuckled. "Your understanding of time is amusing. What is a day to God could be millions of years to you. This would have been in the second or third day of your Bible. I don't remember precisely which."

Griffin gaped at him. "You haven't read the Bible?"

"Do you have any comprehension how many versions of that blasted book have existed since I was created? I don't have the inclination to read them all." He laid a hand on her shoulder and pointed with the other. "Watch this."

Gabriel and Alaria appeared in the clearing. Alaria was wearing a sleek white pantsuit, her black hair long and flowing. Her wings were liquid gold, seeming to be made from metal rather than feathers. As soon as they appeared, Alaria seized Gabriel and pulled him into a hug.

"I've been so worried about you." She laid her head on his shoulder. "It's been days since we spoke. I couldn't help myself, I had to summon you here. I know that it's looked down upon to go backward in time, but before Adam was the only time I could think of that was safe for us to see one another."

Gabriel turned his head from side to side, looking around the clearing. "It hasn't been safe to see you. These are uncertain times, Alaria. Lucifer's forces grow stronger every day. Lilith is leading raids against Heaven. The loss of life has been astounding. Father is not going to hold off on an all-out war for much longer." He seized her by the shoulders. "It is time to come home and fight. We need you."

"I don't want to fight."

"The fate that befalls those who refuse to choose will not be a good one, regardless of who wins."

"Gabe, I want to Fall. I want to be human. You know that." Alaria paced, her expression one of anxiety and ire. "You convinced me to go to Father and ask him to allow me to go to Earth. He refused me."

Gabriel's face crumpled with grief. "I thought surely he would see your strife and allow you what you desire." He straightened. "It's of no concern now. All the more reason to come home. Think of what will happen to humanity should Lucifer and his troops overthrow the throne. You love walking amongst them. Fight for them. Fight with me, side by side." He laid his hand on her face. "That is how it should be. You and I, next to one another, fighting for our home. Please, Alaria, come home."

Griffin's hand had gone to her mouth. She looked up at Michael with a mixture of confusion and curiosity. "What am I seeing?"

"This is why Alaria and Gabriel hate one another. I won't tell you their story. It isn't mine to tell. But this affects you insomuch as they both have a part in your life. You need to understand some of the motivations behind what they do. My brother has spent millennia trying to forget what you are seeing. This is his greatest misstep as an Angel."

"What is?"

Michael gestured back to the two Angels. "Watch."

Alaria was crying. "Gabe, please! Come with me! Lucifer has sworn to me that he'll make me human if I fight with him. With you we would be unbeatable. You can help me! All you have to do is come with me!"

Gabriel stepped back from Alaria, and Griffin was shocked by the disgust that registered in his face. "You brought me here to attempt to convince me to betray my Father? The One who created us? You owe your very existence to Him, Alaria. And yet you ask me to betray Him?"

"What about how He betrayed me?" Alaria sobbed. "I don't want to do this without you." She took a step toward him and gripped his hands in both of hers. "This isn't about the war. It isn't about ruling Heaven. I don't want to. I want to be human. I want to have children and grow old. I want to love a man. I want to feel everything they can feel. I want to know what it's like to have free will. Don't you want that?"

Gabriel shook his head vehemently, and it seemed to Griffin that he was trying to convince himself as much as he was trying to convince Alaria. "I want to go home and fight to preserve what has been made for us. We have so much more than they do. We get to sit at the feet of our Creator and feel His love. We can speak to Him and look upon His face. Is that really something you would want to give up for a chance at human love?"

Alaria's voice was a whisper. "In a heartbeat. I want a heartbeat. I want to live, never knowing what day might be my last. I want to enjoy the time I have, to make the most of it." She laid both her hands on Gabriel's face. "We could have a life together. We could experience humanity like we've done everything else. Together."

Griffin looked at Michael. "What is she saying?"

Michael shook his head. "Let her tell you, child."

Alaria grabbed Gabriel and pulled him to her, kissing him. She wrapped her arms around his neck and pressed her body against him. For an instant, Gabriel seemed to soften in her embrace, and Griffin would have sworn she saw his arms tighten for an instant, trying to pull Alaria closer. After a mere five seconds, Gabriel shoved Alaria back. She hit the ground hard and skidded several feet. Gabriel wiped his mouth.

"What in the name of all things Holy do you think you're doing?"

Alaria didn't even try to get up. She looked up at him with eyes so sad that Griffin's heart shattered in her chest out of sympathy. "I wanted to make you see what it could be."

"What you did is an abomination unto our Father! It is strictly forbidden!"

Alaria did get up then. "It's what I feel! Can you tell me, honestly, that you don't feel anything?"

Gabriel's eyes hardened into stone. His face smoothed into a cold mask, and he shook his head definitively. "I was your friend. You have sullied everything that I held dear." He stepped back. "Don't come to me again, Alaria. I don't want to see you even once more."

Gabriel disappeared, and Alaria crumbled to her knees, her hands covering her face, sobs shaking her whole body. Griffin let out a low whistle. "That was cold."

Michael chuckled. "To you, perhaps. Angels are not meant to have romantic relationships." He made a noise in his throat. "There have been several—shall we say—failings among my brethren. Admittedly, even I have not been immune to the temptations of activities less than Godly. But Gabriel always toed the line. My brother is someone to whom we all looked for guidance. He was an example to us. For him to waver, even as slightly as he did, has been something he has never completely recovered from. To be faced with what Alaria has become, well, that has only deepened his guilt. He blames himself for her." He nodded back toward Alaria. "Watch this next part and we shall go."

A man appeared, also in a white suit. His wings were inky black, and white-blond hair streamed down his back in a cascade of waves. His eyes were blood red. Alaria looked up.

"Lucifer."

Lucifer held out a hand. "You asked me for the opportunity to convince Gabriel. I allowed that because I knew that you needed to try. Can you see now that he is not going to join you in your quest for humanity?" He pulled Alaria to her feet and into an embrace. "My child, I can feel your pain. Let me take it from you."

Alaria wiped her eyes. "How could you do that?"

"I can see how your heart hurts. He has betrayed you and returned to God. He will take up arms against you and slay those of us who do not wish to be ruled. I am the most powerful Angel in Heaven. I can take your pain away if you will surrender to me."

Alaria cried harder. "I don't want to hurt. I want it to stop!"

Lucifer laid a hand on her forehead and a white light glowed around her. An apparition rose out of her and hovered several inches above the ground. Once it had formed completely, Griffin could see that it was Alaria and gasped audibly as she clapped her hand over her mouth. When Lucifer clenched his hand and a sword appeared, Griffin shook her head, tears welling in her eyes. He slashed once, and the apparition shattered into a million pieces. Alaria, still clad in her white suit, screamed as her wings retracted into her body. Her white suit changed to black and red leather, and a whip appeared in her hands. She looked around, confusion transitioning into the cold stare that Griffin had seen from her many times. Alaria turned to Lucifer and smiled.

"Let's go."

Griffin shuddered. "What did he do?"

Michael sighed. "He took from her the Angelic equivalent of a soul. We don't have souls in the same vein as humans, but we do have our Grace. It is what makes us an Angel. He took it from her and made her into what she is now." He took her hand. "That is all that you needed to see. I'm going to send you back now."

"Can I ask one more question?"

"Make it a quick one."

"What's with the wings? No two sets are the same."

Michael laughed. "Only Archangels have wings. We are the elite amongst the Angels. Each of us was given a different color. I never cared to ask why. There are only twenty Archangels. Or, there were. Seven Fell. Lucifer, Abbadon, Abalam, Beelzebub, Lilith, Azazel and Alaria." He smiled at her. "Any more questions?"

Griffin didn't think about the words before they tumbled off her tongue and through her lips. "Which Angel were you involved with?"

Michael's lips quirked into a semi-smile. "Couldn't help yourself, could you?" When she shook her head sheepishly, he chuckled. "That's not something I enjoy rehashing. Let's leave it at, she and I no longer have any contact with one another. Gabriel and I both know the sting—literally and physically—of our Father's disappointment." His smile faded back into a neutral expression. "Are you ready to go back now?"

Griffin nodded. "Yes."

"Close your eyes." When she did as told, Michael touched a finger to her forehead.

Griffin opened her eyes and found herself standing in the hallway of the cabin, clad only in the t-shirt that she'd had on before she'd dressed. She could hear Braxton's phone ringing in the other room and dashed back into it. She'd made it through the door before he sat up, and she then fished the phone out of his pants pocket for him.

She dropped onto the bed, her mind reeling from what she had seen.

She didn't even know how to begin to make sense of it. She was still in a daze when Braxton flipped the phone closed and turned to her.

"Go get packed. You're going to Sam and Finn's. There's a problem I have to take care of."

Not sure how to explain what she'd seen and heard to Braxton, Griffin nodded and stood before walking down the hall to her room to pack.

Chapter Seventeen

April 30th, 2029 - Purgatory

THE MAN LAY on the slab of stone; his wrists and ankles shackled with chains that led to the stone floor, holding him in his dark prison. The ceiling featured drawings, pentagrams, and other ancient symbols, creating the most powerful Devil's trap that had ever been formed. Below the table lay another trap. The very walls of the cave were decorated with symbols, curses, and spells designed to keep the man inside forever.

He had been there for millennia, since the Fall from Grace. He had been cast aside from both Heaven and Hell, destined to live eternity with no contact with anyone and with no ability to escape his fate unless the ones who had placed him there saw fit to release him. Azazel had begun to doubt that would ever happen and had accepted his fate. Until Beelzebub appeared in the chamber entrance.

"Come to torture me some more?"

Beelzebub strode into the room, unperturbed by the traps. "No, I've come to make you a proposition."

"I'm not interested."

"I think you will be. Do this for me, Azazel, and you'll walk the Earth freely."

"I don't believe Michael would like that idea."

"I don't answer to Michael. He and I put you in here, and only one of us can let you out. I've come to do so. Provided, of course, that you accept my terms."

"You have no guarantee that I won't just run as soon as you set me free. You're not strong enough on your own to force me back in here."

"I know. And I intend to address that concern in due course." He snapped his fingers and then sank onto the throne that appeared behind him, crossing one leg over the other and folding his hands on top of them. "Now, are you ready to listen to my terms, or should I just leave you to your punishment?"

"Get on with it."

"Excellent." Beelzebub smiled saccharinely and brushed imaginary lint from his silk suit. "The time of the Choosing is upon us. The Chosen has been born and the Veil has already been lifted. There are but seven human months before the Choosing shall take place. Alaria has failed in bringing the Chosen to our side through her events. A Warrior is protecting her, and the only recourse we have is to kill her. The End is much preferable to a thousand millennia of angelic rule. I've already convinced Lilith to assist us."

"Lilith is one of the strongest. You're the right hand of Satan. Why in the world do you need my help?"

"Because you have a particular set of skills. Skills I am interested in putting to use. I don't think it's any secret that you are hated among the legions of Hell and the hosts of Heaven. Playing one side against the other was not the smartest choice you made. However, your wings have been clipped, and you have been cast to us, so I assume your loyalties do not lie with Him."

"So, you want me to get her? The Chosen. You want me to find her and kill her."

"I want you to find her and convince her to die. It's your specialty, isn't it? Controlling the mind of your adversaries? Unless my memory fails me, you managed to manipulate even Devils and Angels in the Battle."

"I can do it. I'm just not sure why I would want to."

"If she dies by your hand, I guarantee you full freedom and a spot among the leadership in Hell. Alaria's left-hand seat is open, and Lilith wants no part of it. But should you fail—or should you betray me—I'm going to need a guarantee of my own."

"What do you want?"

Beelzebub snapped his fingers once more, and a piece of parchment appeared in one hand, a pen in the other. "I'm going to need a contract. The standard. I'm sure you're aware of the terms. Should you fail, you surrender your abilities and you will be chained to the bottom of the pit."

Azazel barely thought about it. "Anything is better than this. Give me the pen."

Pleased, Beelzebub released one of Azazel's hands and offered the pen, which was readily accepted. He watched carefully as blood poured from Azazel and through the pen and onto the contract. Once it was signed, the contract burst into flames and disappeared. The process complete, Beelzebub set about breaking the other three shackles and traps that contained Azazel.

Azazel waited impatiently as the stronger Devil worked, and leaped out of the circle the second it was broken. He started to stride toward the door, but Beelzebub's hand gripped his arm tightly. "Not yet. We're going home for a while, brother. We need to speak with Lilith and Alaria. We're going to wipe out the Warriors and the Chosen in one act. We need to be perfectly coordinated."

Azazel glared at the Devil. He stretched his arms over his head lazily and flexed his muscles. "Being locked down here for so long has made me bored and horny. I'd rather go have some fun before getting to work if you don't mind."

Beelzebub shook his head sternly. "You will have plenty of time to play with this wretched human once we find her. Work first."

"You've always been such a wet blanket, Bub. Lighten up a little. You know I'll find her. If you weren't completely sure of it, you'd never have let me loose."

Annoyed, Beelzebub muttered as he disappeared. "Damn straight."

Alaria paced the chamber impatiently, her heels clicking on the black tile. Beelzebub had hailed her to the chamber for an important meeting, then dared to keep her waiting. It was almost as if he either did not realize, or did not care, that there were precious few human months left before they would lose the Choosing. By calling her away from her systematic search of Earth, he was making it very difficult for her to locate and neutralize Griffin.

"Settle down, sweetheart. He'll get here when he gets here."

Alaria whirled and found herself facing Lilith. Lilith was the strongest Devil in existence; some even wagered she was stronger than Lucifer himself. She had averted being cast into Hell and was free to walk the Earth while the rest of them had to labor for centuries to claw their way out. Some still hadn't managed the feat. Lilith was notoriously fond of humans—of feeding on them, possessing them, engaging in sex with them, and controlling them. No one was sure how she avoided being cast out, though rumors had always swirled that Michael hadn't been able to cast her out, both because Lilith was stronger than he was, and because they had been partners for millennia.

Lilith had inhabited a form that was breathtakingly beautiful—she had long blonde curls, big blue eyes, striking cheekbones, a lush mouth, and a perfectly sculpted nose. Her breasts were high and large, her waist nipped in, and her hips flared in a way that would have any man panting. She had taken centuries choosing the right form, and once she had, she had guarded it as a mother would a child. Thinking about it, Alaria couldn't remember a time when Lilith hadn't been wearing that particular skin suit.

"Lilith. What an unpleasant surprise. What's lured you down to rub elbows with the rest of us?"

Lilith looked over her shoulder at Alaria and smiled sweetly. "You'd be wise to mind your tongue and show some respect, lest I rip it out of your head. Beelzebub asked me to meet with him here. I nearly didn't, but showing you up was just too big a temptation. You've been spending entirely too much time on my turf, Alaria."

"Earth is not only your domain. The rest of us play there, too."

"Not you. You've never played there. You bring your victims here in their dreams. But then again, you didn't want to give up your wings. Must have a soft spot for humans." She snorted. "Why have you not traded in your Angel form for something that won't remind you of up there? Goodness, if Lucifer thought about it, he would be highly suspicious of you still wearing your original form."

"Don't presume to think you know anything about me. I wanted nothing to do with Heaven." Alaria circled with the other Devil, their tones neutral, but eyes hot. "I'm not nearly the only one that didn't play dress up with humans. Lucifer and Beelzebub both have their original forms. Come to think of it, you're the only one of the Archangels that traded."

Lilith ignored that bit. "If memory serves, you didn't want anything to do with Hell, either. Your loyalties were always muddled, but we put up with it because of your talents. So long as you used them to help us, we were willing to tolerate some......eccentricities. Now, I think I may have to talk to Lucifer about what to do with you. You had one chance to prove yourself, and you've been bested by a little human girl."

"I'm fighting for your side, Lilith. I'd remind you not to forget that. And I was given the Choosing, not you. So, for once, you're in my domain, and I'm the one calling the shots. I'm the only one with any power over this."

Beelzebub chuckled as he entered the room. "Not exactly, Alaria, my love. Hello, Lilith. Glad you could make it."

Lilith smiled as she glided over to kiss the other Devil. "Always, for you. Now, care to fill us girls in on why we're all here?" She shifted her gaze sideways to the handsome man with chin length black hair dressed in a beat-up leather jacket, jeans and biker boots. "Does someone care to explain why in Lucifer's name Azazel is not still chained to a fucking rock?"

Azazel grinned, pushed off the wall, and strode into the chamber. "Seems you three have royally fucked things up and you need my help to get this Choosing underway. So, Beelzebub came and got me to clean up your mess to keep the world from going Godly."

Alaria crossed her arms and glared at him. "I need no help from the likes of you. You're a traitor to your own kind."

He laughed and threw an arm around Alaria. "Then it looks like we're two of a kind, doesn't it, love? Poor Lil, she'll never know the thrill of playing both sides."

Alaria shrugged off his arm and glared at him with eyes that glowed deep red. "I have never done anything close to what you did. Yes, I fought for my own reasons, but when the hammer came down, I was cast here with all the rest of you. I fought against the Angels and on the side of Lucifer. I never betrayed any of my brethren, and I have spent millennia wreaking havoc upon the human race." She stalked to one of the thrones and draped herself across it carelessly. "Now, if you don't mind, let's get this pow-wow over with so that I can get back to work. In case you haven't noticed, time is running out rather quickly."

Beelzebub glanced to the other two, who took the hint and sat, Lilith settling regally into one throne and Azazel collapsing haphazardly into another. "As Alaria said, time is running out. We have seven human months to find the Chosen and either convince her to Choose us or kill her. After consulting several witches and Seers, the odds of forcing her to Choose with her son are slim. It's highly probable that she would allow him to die."

Alaria sighed. "So, that leaves killing her, which is what I was afraid of."

"We'll keep the son as a backup plan. Lilith has managed to locate him. Nice, for a human. He should beg quite convincingly. We also have a Warrior issue. The legions report that after the hounds failed to kill her the night the Veil was lifted, a Warrior was called to her side. They have fled, and the minions lost all trace of them both. However, Ariander has told us there's a high possibility that we know the name of the Warrior protecting her."

"Ariander? He was thrown back into the pit a decade ago."

"He was thrown into the pit by a human woman—a Warrior from one of the oldest lines on Earth. It's a long, convoluted story, and it's hard to tell how much is true and how much is him wanting to get out of that lake again, but he swears he was inhabiting the body of a Warrior, the father-in-law of this woman, and that the son of this woman is a Seer who had a vision about the coming of the Chosen. He suspects that this Warrior has a role in the Choosing."

Lilith sat up a little straighter, her eyes bright. "I wouldn't put it past Him to install a safety device. Someone to protect her during the final year in case we tried to kill her. It's devious. Just like Him. We should have known they wouldn't respect the rules."

Beelzebub nodded, his expression serious. "I thought the same thing, Lilith. I have a plan, one that hopefully has already been set into motion. The body Ariander inhabited was Robert Winslow, a Warrior that was a constant pain in the ass while he was alive. His grandson's name is Braxton Winslow, a Warrior who moonlights for the Vatican and is a much bigger pain than Robert ever dreamed of being. He's strong, and he's smart. Though he's a human, he is not an adversary that should be underestimated. His body count is high. Some of our demons seem to be quite afraid of him, actually."

"If he's with her, he's shielding her from any of our location attempts. It's a fair guess she's protected by those damn skin ink symbols they like to carve into themselves." Alaria stood to pace, her mind reeling. "We need to find out where they are, and that's going to mean going to Earth to do it. We're not going to be able to find them any other way."

Azazel lifted a hand, calling their attention. "Did you forget about me, love? That's kind of my specialty. I may not be able to get you an address, but if I can get a sense of her, I can find her, and I can control her. Suicide sounds nice, doesn't it?"

Beelzebub cleared his throat. "Lilith and I are going to handle the Warrior. If Ariander's account is correct, and I think it mostly is, I've located a friend of this Braxton Winslow and sent a group of very new demons to inhabit a whole town. The Warriors are stuck, and who better to call than the best Warrior on Earth? If everything went as planned, Braxton should be on his way to the village now, leaving the Chosen with his sister, who by her own rights is a hell of a witch, but nowhere near the Warrior her brother is. Azazel and Alaria, you two are going to deal with her. I want her dead. I don't care how you do it. Be prepared for angelic interference. But the longer Azazel can stay in her head, the more familiar you can get with her surroundings, and the closer we can get to her. If we can find her, we can kill her. The Angels won't dare interfere too greatly. They won't risk losing this. We've already lost. An enemy with nothing to lose is the most powerful because they have everything to gain. That enemy is us. We all need to remember that."

Lilith smiled. "Goody. I get to go play with a Warrior. Can I fuck him before I kill him?"

Always indulgent with the powerful Devil, Beelzebub nodded slightly. "You can do anything you want to him, so long as he ends up dead. Shall we go?"

Once they had disappeared, Alaria looked at Azazel, distrust plainly evident in her eyes. "I don't like this."

"Doesn't seem you get much of a choice in the matter. You fucked up, and I have to fix it. So, let's get this done, and we never have to look at each other again."

Begrudgingly, Alaria nodded. "Okay. Come to the scrying pool. I'll show you everything I know about her and her whereabouts." She sighed, knowing what would come next. "I hate being forced to do things like humans."

Chapter Eighteen

April 30th, 2029 - Los Angeles, California

GRIFFIN WAS nearly in tears. She'd gotten on the plane with no issues in Colorado. Of course, Braxton had also had a ticket, so he'd gone through security with her, walked her to her gate and watched her get on the plane. There had been no opportunity for anything to go badly. Once she was in the air, however, things had gone from uneventful to terrible.

Halfway to Los Angeles, the plane's engine had begun acting up, and they'd been forced to land in Oregon. The airport there was incredibly small, and there had been a sixteen hour layover before she'd been able to get another flight out. That had even been a three-stop flight, with layovers in Dallas, Tucson and then finally, LA.

By the time the plane touched down and she was able to gather her bag and head to the baggage claim, she had been up for nearly forty-eight hours, and she was so tired she could barely keep her eyes open. There had been no way to draw a salt circle on the planes or at the airports, so she had not dared to so much as close her eyes.

Now that she was in LA, she'd gotten a voicemail informing her that Sam wasn't going to be there to pick her up. Instead, Finn was supposed to get her. Braxton had given her a picture of Sam to know who to look for, but she had no clue what Finn looked like, or how she was supposed to know that he was the right person.

Not knowing what else to do, she dialed Braxton's number as she waited for her suitcase to come down. After six rings, it went to voicemail. Annoyed, she simply hung up rather than leaving a message. It wasn't like the odds were good that he would call her back before she found Finn anyway.

Finally, after what seemed an eternity, she saw her suitcase and stepped forward to claim it. Once the suitcase was balanced on the wheels, she headed for the escalator and took it to the upper level, where people waited for those who had just come off of flights. She glanced around, hoping someone would stick out to her.

Halfway through the throng of people, a tall, handsome man in a flawlessly cut suit caught her eye. He looked completely out of place amongst the crowd of harried mothers and impatient lovers. He exuded power in the way that he walked, and he scanned the people coming up from the baggage claim with a practiced, almost disinterested eye. When he found her, however, he lifted his hand slightly, signaling her, and began working his way over.

"Griffin Javensen, I presume?"

Griffin regarded him with a healthy dose of skepticism. "That depends entirely upon who you are."

"Finn Fisher. Nice to meet you. I believe my wife was supposed to come and get you. You'll have to excuse her absence, but she's come down with a touch of the stomach flu."

"I'm not sure I should go with you. If you're Finn, then you know about me, and you know I have to be very careful."

"Of course. Did Braxton send you with any Holy Water?"

Nodding, she reached into the front pocket of her carryon and pulled out a small bottle. "Great idea. Drink it."

Willingly, Finn took the bottle and took a deep gulp. When he didn't begin to steam or boil, Griffin was convinced that he was not possessed. She studied him for another moment, then sighed and got out her phone. She tried once more to reach Braxton, and when he didn't answer, she left a detailed message about the man standing in front of her, just in case he turned out to be someone that she wasn't supposed to go with and he had to come rescue her.

"Okay, let me see your driver's license."

Finn smiled obligingly and pulled his wallet from the pocket of his slacks. She studied the license for a long moment, then handed it back and picked up her carryon. She'd done everything she could to make sure that he was who he said he was, and if he wasn't, well, Braxton would come and save her. After all, saving her was his job.

"Satisfied?"

"No, but I can't think of anything else to do to make myself satisfied, so let's get going. I'm tired, I'm hungry, and I'm cranky."

Finn took the larger suitcase from her and smoothly tucked her arm through his, leading her into the parking lot. Once they were outside, he guided her to a sleek black limo parked just beyond the doors and held open the door for her. Still slightly apprehensive, she slid into the back seat and spent several moments making sure all the windows worked—and that she could open the other door if she needed to.

"You've definitely been around Braxton." Finn slid in next to her and tapped on the divider between the back and the front seat. "Brian, would you take us home, please? Call ahead and have the cook put together something for Ms. Javensen. And have Samantha get her bed ready. She's had a rough flight."

Griffin cocked one eyebrow. "I thought it was Sam? Brax said she can't stand being called by her full name."

"She can't. She's had to adjust to it since we got married. It's a little more formal, and with the social circles we're forced to travel in, being known as Sam isn't particularly feasible. Though if you called her Samantha, I'd be willing to bet she'd smack you."

"She seems like the type."

Finn watched in mild amusement as Griffin fought to keep her eyes open. There were dark smudges under her eyes from not nearly enough sleep. Her hair was tangled and messily piled on top of her head, her clothes were wrinkled from spending too much time in airports, and her hands were trembling, a sign that it had been far too long since she'd eaten anything substantial. She was not a healthy woman. He sighed inwardly, mentally cursing Braxton. If they were going to get her through to the Choosing, they needed to be taking better care of her physically. She was worn down and wasting away.

Griffin hadn't ever seen a house quite like the one where Finn and Sam lived. It was an old house, turned white by years of exposure to sea salt, and it perched on a cliff, overlooking a private strip of beach and the bluest ocean she had ever seen. A stairway led down a sloping hill onto the white sand. The interior was tastefully done in dark woods and bright colors, making it feel homey instead of expensive, which it undoubtedly was.

The lady of the house was an interesting mixture of comfort and luxury. Sam had bounded down the stairs the second she'd heard the door open, a fireball of red hair and bright green eyes betraying her intelligence. She had a neat, compact body that was several inches shorter than Griffin's and was clad in cut-off shorts and what surely had to be one of her husband's t-shirts. She sported a glittering diamond on her wedding finger, another around her neck, and what looked to be real emeralds in her ears.

Sam launched herself at Griffin as soon as she skidded to a stop in the foyer, locking her arms around the older woman in a bone crushing hug. "Oh, I am so glad you're here. I know it sucks that Braxton had to leave, but I'm glad we get to meet you! Come on, the cook has food made. It's just soup and sandwiches, but they're delicious. And as soon as you're done, up to bed. You look like you haven't slept in a week."

Griffin found herself following Sam without a fight, grateful that there was someone else responsible for making the decisions for once. "Thanks for letting me stay here. I know it's asking a lot from you with what's going on. Finn said you weren't feeling well?"

"Don't think anything of it. I'm a Warrior, Griffin. Finn knew what that meant when he married me. This is part of my job. And besides, I've seen far too little excitement lately." She shook her head. "Just a touch of the stomach flu. I'm feeling better now, thanks."

"I got the feeling Brax didn't leave you much of a choice."

Sam pushed Griffin into a chair and sat a bowl of soup in front of her. "Ham or turkey?"

"Turkey, please."

"Brax, huh? You two seem to have gotten over your difficulties."

Griffin took several bites while she thought about how to answer the unspoken question. "We came to an understanding."

"The naked tango will do that sometimes."

Griffin choked on the bite of bread and meat, coughing and gasping until Sam got up and poured a glass of water, ice clinking cheerfully against the crystal. Gratefully, Griffin gulped water, forcing the food down her throat. "What in hell gave you that idea?"

"The two of you, alone up there for a month, both of you gorgeous people? If something didn't happen, the both of you are idiots." She leaned forward on her elbows. "So, tell me, are you an idiot?"

Griffin pondered for another moment and found herself liking Sam entirely too much. Finally, she sighed. "I've been called many things, but never has anyone thought I'm an idiot."

"Good. Glad to hear it. Braxton can be an ass sometimes, but he's normally good with women. When you told me how he was acting, I figured there was something going on there that I didn't know about. Sexual tension can turn the mildest mannered man into a jackass. And Braxton has never been known as mild mannered."

"Mild mannered is not the phrase I would use to describe him. I think he's a good man. If I'd known about the dreams, I wouldn't have pushed him so hard when he first started taking care of me."

"What dreams?"

"He said he had dreams about me while he was growing up. That he saw me through most of my events and he'd had to stand by and watch while a little girl went through all those things, unable to help, not knowing why he had to see them—just somehow knowing they were real, and never being able to make them stop."

Sam tapped her fingers on the table. "He never told me about that. Now I'm gonna have to kill him."

Instantly worried, Griffin pushed her bowl back. "I thought you would have known. I shouldn't have said anything."

"Yes, you should have. If Braxton was always supposed to take part in this, things make much more sense. Like how you always ended up at Dad's hospital. How he was always your doctor. I'd been wondering about the connection, but now it seems like it was Braxton that was destined to find you, not my Dad."

"I just don't want to make things harder on him when I die."

Sam looked at Griffin hard. "Be realistic. With what you and Braxton have to do, it will be a miracle if he survives. He knows that, I know that, we all know that he probably won't survive. It's the job. So, if he has to die for this thing—if you have to die for this thing—better that you got to be happy together for a few months before it happens." She stood and briskly cleared the dishes. "Enough of this talk for right now. We've got plenty of time. Let's get you upstairs and into bed. I'll wake you in a couple hours."

Sam was like a mother hen, taking Griffin into a room, efficiently unpacking the suitcase she'd brought and laying out a pair of pajamas. She showed Griffin the salt lines on each of the windows and watched with approval as Griffin checked the pillows for the herb bundles. Then, she insisted on cleaning the tattoos that were still healing across Griffin's back. Once all of that was accomplished, she left, promising to return before dinner.

Griffin slowly pulled on the pajamas Sam had set out, peeled back the blankets, and shimmied between them. She checked her phone one more time to make sure she hadn't missed a call from Braxton and then, seeing that she hadn't, closed her eyes. She fell into sleep like a stone fell in water and woke up in a bright white room with a white couch and chair.

Gabriel was there, dressed all in white, the requisite pitcher of iced tea sitting on the coffee table, one glass filled with ice next to it. She didn't even bother to question him. She simply sat and waited until the glass was filled and in her hand.

"I thought my tattoos protected me."

"Griffin, little can protect you from the two that were assigned the Choosing."

"What am I doing here?"

"It is getting close to the time of the Choosing. I am here to begin instructing you on what must happen the day of your thirtieth birthday."

"I have to kill myself."

"That is true, you do. However, it is not that simple. The Choosing can take place anywhere, but there has been a place prepared for you, near the place your Catholics call the Vatican, which will hold the demons at bay for seven days. It was made with the intention of allowing you to safely complete your task should you choose Heaven. I cannot tell you the exact location, but should you find it, you will immediately know that you are in the correct place."

"So, the week before I get to chill out in some secret place that will keep demons out?"

"You must not take this lightly. They will try to get in, they will try to lure you out, and they may try to burn it to the ground. There is nothing they will not do to get to you in the final days. If they know that they are going to lose, they will kill you to keep that from happening. You're hunted now, Griffin. Even as we speak, demons the world over are looking for you. It is imperative that you stay alert and pay attention to all of your surroundings."

Griffin held up her hands in mock surrender, her patience with any other-worldly being wearing very thin. "Okay, okay. I'm alert. Is that all?"

"No. In addition to requiring your life in exchange for the Choosing, you are required to use a sanctified knife." He extended his hand and gave her a white handkerchief. Inside was a silver dagger, the handle engraved with many complex symbols. The blade was straight, and one quick touch told her it was razor sharp.

"What's this for?"

"This knife is special. It was dipped in the blood of the Son. Using this to sacrifice yourself will eliminate most of the pain. It cannot take away all of the pain, but it will make death much more comfortable. There is no knife on Earth more powerful than this one, but it can only be used once. It will kill anything you use it on, including Angels and Devils. It has never been touched by any hand other than that of God and now, the Chosen. It is His gift to you for the Choosing. Should anyone else touch it, the charms will be broken, and it will be nothing more than a normal knife. Keep it close, Griffin, and do not let it leave your side. Should you lose it, any blade will do, so long as it is blessed and cleansed by Holy Water."

"Is there anything I need to do during the Choosing?"

"Yes, but you will know the words when it is time. This is all I can tell you today. Are you ready to return to your body?"

"No. I have questions."

Gabriel smiled indulgently. "I know you do, child, and I would like to be able to answer them, but there is little that I can tell you without breaking the rules."

"Alaria. Tell me what Alaria is doing."

Griffin watched the Angel fight an intense personal battle, trying to decide what he could and could not tell her. Finally, he sighed. "There is much about Alaria that you do not know. Much about her that could come to light in the coming months. It will be interesting to see what she does. She's interested in self-preservation, not in the Choosing itself. Higher ranking Devils have interfered with her role in this. I do not have the ability to tell you who, or what they are doing, but I will warn you to be especially vigilant. There are Devils that know much more about Earth and human nature than Alaria, those with powers that those symbols on your back will not affect."

Without another word and without giving her a chance to ask the hundred questions racing through her mind, Gabriel waved his hand and Griffin woke up to Sam shaking her shoulder gently, a sympathetic smile on her pretty face. She chuckled when Griffin struggled to sit up and perched on the edge of the bed to pat Griffin's leg.

"Sorry to wake you, but you were out for three hours. I want you to be able to sleep tonight, so I figured I'd wake you for dinner."

Griffin lifted her hand and found the white handkerchief with the knife in it. She turned on the bedside lamp and turned it over several times before looking at Sam. "Gabriel came to see me. He gave me this."

Sam gingerly took the handkerchief, laying it and the knife on the nightstand so that she could see it better. "This is Aramaic. Some powerful shit."

"He said no one but me can touch it. I'm supposed to use it to kill myself. Apparently it will make it hurt less."

"How thoughtful of them." Sam's voice dripped with sarcasm, and she carefully wrapped the knife up. "I suppose it's the least they can do if they're making you commit suicide."

"Is there somewhere safe I can put it until we leave here?"

"Yeah. I have a safe room downstairs. Devil's traps, salt in the walls, no windows—it's completely demon and Devil proof."

Griffin climbed out of bed and briefly considered staying in her pajamas before swiftly changing back into jeans; she opted not to brush her hair, instead tying it back in a ponytail. "Okay, I'm up. Let's get this done before I climb right back in bed and don't get up until tomorrow."

Chapter Nineteen

May 27th, 2029 - Los Angeles, California
Sam sighed deeply, her voice betraying the stress she was under. "Brax, you need to come back."

Braxton shook his head, the cup of coffee at his elbow long ago gone cold. "I can't. This possession is so much more than I expected it to be. The whole town is possessed. I've called in every Warrior I know, and we're still barely making a dent. It's been all we can do to keep them from getting out. I can't leave until this is done, and even if I wanted to get out, the odds of me making it past the city limits is small. We're losing Warriors left and right. I have to end this, Sam."

"There are more important things than one town, Braxton Michael Winslow, and one of those things is the Choosing. She's been here a month. It's only going to be safe for so long. We should have moved her already."

"So, move her. You and Finn have houses all over the world. Take her to one of them. I'll be back as soon as I can, but there's nothing I can do right now. Nothing's happened, has it?"

"I'm pregnant."

Braxton choked on the gulp of cold coffee he'd just taken and coughed several times. "What?"

"I'm pregnant. Eleven weeks. I just found out a week ago."

"Congratulations?"

Sam couldn't help the giggle. "Congratulations should never be a question. I'm thrilled. I want kids. But it puts things in a new light, Brax. I can't be running from demons when I'm eight months pregnant. It'll slow me down. Finn and I have been considering termination."

"What? Why? You just said you were thrilled!"

"I am. We are. We've wanted a baby for a while, but if you're going to be gone indefinitely, I need to be able to do your job. I can't keep her safe with a beach ball strapped to my belly. We always knew we could be asked to sacrifice anything for our job. I don't want to do it, but I don't know if I have much of a choice. We can have another baby."

"Don't. I'll be there as soon as I can. If you didn't want it, it would be different, but you're the one who keeps saying we can't forget to live, even though this is the year of the Choosing. How long until you can't run anymore?"

"I'll start showing in another nine weeks or so. By the third trimester, I won't be able to do anything. September or so."

"I can't imagine that I won't be back by then. Just give me some time to get this wrapped up, and don't do anything rash. We've got some time to play with. Have you told Griffin?"

"No, not yet. I didn't want her to feel guilty if I did terminate. She'd blame herself, and Lord knows she's got enough on her shoulders as it is without this added to it. No matter what, the Choosing has to come first."

"Well, don't do anything yet. Give me a few more weeks." Braxton glanced over his shoulder as he heard yelling from outside the house where he and the other Warriors had been holed up. "I've got to go, Sam—something's going on. I'm turning my phone off, but I'll try to check it when I can."

"Be careful, Braxton. Don't get yourself killed. I can't do this without you."

"I'll do my best. Love you. And congratulations."

"Love you, too. Go kick some demon ass."

Sam closed her phone slowly, laying her head on the table. Finn looked up from his book, his eyes sympathetic. "No luck?"

"They're getting slammed. Massive possession. He can't make a dent in it. It's going to be a while."

"You didn't tell him about Griffin."

"There's nothing he can do from there, and there's no sense in making him worry unnecessarily."

"Samantha, she's wasting away. At this rate, she'll starve to death before the Choosing."

"I know, Finn. She's been having nightmares, and they're making her sick to her stomach. Poor girl tries, but it's like she's being haunted. I don't know how they're getting through the protections. We're going to have to move her, and sooner rather than later."

"I can have the Austin property ready by this weekend."

"Do it. Maybe a geographic change will give us enough time for her to get her strength back."

"Has she realized the nightmares are demonic?"

"She hasn't said anything, but I'm sure she suspects. She keeps seeing the Choosing. Seeing her death. Seeing them kill her in various disgusting ways. I wouldn't be able to eat either if I continually saw myself getting ripped apart every time I closed my eyes."

Griffin turned off the water, stepped out of the shower, and wrapped a towel around her body. She glanced in the mirror disinterestedly, not caring to see her gaunt face. For nearly three weeks she'd been haunted by nightmares.

Gripping the counter when the room spun dangerously, she didn't even notice when the towel slipped down to pool on the floor. Dizzy, she tried to walk to the bed to lay down but pitched forward when the room lurched. She let out a thin cry when her head struck the corner of the dresser, and she sank to the floor unconscious, a trickle of blood trailing down her face from the small gash.

She walked on the beach; the moon shone above her head, the stars brightly illuminating the waves rolling lazily in toward shore. There was a man sitting on a table cloth, a picnic basket next to him. As she approached, he rose to greet her, kissing her cheek and offering her a glass of champagne.

They drank and smiled until her head was spinning, and then he kissed her. His lips were intoxicating, drugging her, making her crave what he had to offer. When he stood and offered a hand, she didn't hesitate in taking it. He led her to the edge of the water and they shed clothes as they walked until they were naked and her eyes could feast on his magnificent body.

His hair was black as midnight and hung around her face in curls that begged her to bury her hands in them. His face was sharp lines and soft curves, an interesting combination of classically handsome and dangerously rakish. He lifted her into his arms and carried her into the icy water, which was a welcome relief against her hot skin.

They kissed, and their limbs tangled in the gently rolling waves. His fingers trailed over her body, his mouth found her breast, and she was lost. Her legs came up to wrap around his waist; his erection probed the entrance to her body and then slid easily inside her. Her head fell back, her hair dipping into the water, her fingers gripping his shoulders

The waves increased in intensity. The sky went dark with clouds and rain. The dream man glared at her through red eyes, and his lovemaking became violent. He slammed into her body, his hands bruising her delicate skin, his teeth drawing blood, which he greedily fed on. Griffin screamed, struggling to tear away from him but was unable to break his hold.

He growled as he came, the veins in his neck standing out, the hot stream searing her inside to the point that tears sprang in her eyes. He threw her ruthlessly into the waves, laughing maniacally at her pain and fear.to

"And this is how the Chosen dies. Remember, bitch, I have done what Alaria could not."

Griffin's eyes flew open, the dream ending, and she found herself in the ocean, the waves crashing around her madly. Rain pelted her, and she fought to the surface over and over as the sea became stronger and stronger. She struggled toward shore, her lungs burning with exertion.

Each wave forced her under for longer and made it harder for her to come back up until finally, she went so deep that the water became peaceful. She writhed, trying to figure out which way was up, salt burning her eyes, unable to tell which way to swim. She sliced through the water, desperately seeking the surface so that she could take a breath.

She couldn't struggle anymore. Her lungs were on fire, her limbs went limp, and all the fight seeped out of her. She felt blackness closing in around her, and she wondered briefly if drowning hurt.

The water lit up with a bright white light, and a hand closed over her wrist, dragging her through the water, wrenching her above the surface and tossing her unceremoniously onto the sand. She coughed, water gurgling out of her lungs. Tears and salt water stung her eyes and the sand was rough against her naked skin.

Griffin rolled onto her back, looking up at her rescuer, and found Gabriel standing over her, his wings magnificently spread behind him. He glared down at her, his face reflecting his displeasure.

"I warned you, human. There are Devils that you cannot protect yourself from. Had I not been watching, you would be dead."

Griffin coughed, rolling onto her side and curling her arms around her body. Darkness closed in on her again. Gabriel reached down, gripped her chin in his hand and forced her to meet his gaze as best she could.

"Heed this, Griffin. I can see your thoughts. If I ever think that you are going to Choose them, I swear upon the name of my Father that I will kill you myself."

"You're an Angel. You can't kill a human."

"Oh, I can. And I would kill you in one supremely insignificant human heartbeat. I will lay down the life of every Angel in Heaven to protect you until the Choosing. But if you aren't strong enough to do this, I will keep you from Choosing them."

With that, Gabriel disappeared, and Griffin hit the sand heavily, breath still wheezing out of her lungs. She shivered from cold as the rain pelted her naked body. She shifted her eyes toward the house and saw Sam and Finn running down the beach, Sam armed with what appeared to be a shotgun. Satisfied that she wasn't going to have to lie on the sand and die, she gave in to the cool black that had been flickering at the edges of her vision and sank into nothingness.

Sam paced the foyer, her bare feet soundless on the tile. Her hair hung down her back in wet ropes, and she'd done nothing more than pull on the closest clothes she had seen, which ended up being a pair of her sweatpants and one of Finn's dress shirts.

She'd been woken up by the alarm going off and had spent fifteen minutes checking the house over before realizing that Griffin wasn't in her room. The balcony door had been wide open, and she'd immediately feared the worst. That fear had come alive when she'd seen a burst of white light on the beach and caught a glimpse of Griffin writhing in the sand.

She and Finn had raced across the beach and found Griffin unconscious and naked, her body bruised and trembling from cold. Finn had stripped off his shirt and wrapped Griffin in it, and they had gone back to the house as quickly as possible, Sam racing for the phone to call her father.

Griffin had come around enough to give them a brief rundown, and Finn had arranged for a plane to be waiting for Allen and Miranda at the airport. They were less than an hour away. Finn had had to leave for work, but Sam had not stopped pacing since they'd gotten back to the house. Her mind wouldn't let her stop; it was too busy racing with possibilities.

She'd personally examined Griffin's tattoos. They were perfect. The salt lines were unbroken. She'd checked them twice. The Devil's traps in each room were outlined in liquid silver—the most powerful traps known to humankind. Everything about the house was completely secure. Which meant the Devil that had gotten to Griffin was one that they'd never come up against before.

The only Devils she knew that were powerful enough to get through Devil's traps were Lilith and Beelzebub. It hadn't been Lilith; she was positive of that. Lilith's style involved as much blood and gore as possible. She enjoyed torturing her victims before killing them. She had never in recorded history taken the form of a man.

Sam was nearly equally sure they weren't dealing with Beelzebub. Though Beelzebub was technically strong enough to sidestep protections, he was slick. Had it been him, they'd have found Griffin dead in her bed with nothing amiss. He was known for quick, clean deaths. Rape wasn't his style.

That didn't eradicate the issue of how the Devil had found Griffin. The dream protections could keep Lilith and Beelzebub out. It couldn't keep Alaria out, but Alaria wasn't strong enough to hurt Griffin from within a dream. Had it just been luring Griffin into the sea, she'd have favored Alaria for it. Alaria's talents with the human mind were renowned throughout Hell. She was a master dream manipulator.

Which meant it was someone else. Someone stronger than the other three in that particular area. Someone who could move past the traps and protections undetected, who could visit Griffin's dreams, take control of them, and use them to harm her physically. There was only one possibility, and just thinking about it made Sam's blood run cold.

Azazel.

If Lucifer was desperate enough to free Azazel, the odds of them surviving the rest of the year had just gotten a lot worse. Azazel was a loose cannon. He was unpredictable, dangerous, and ruthless. He'd been confined after the Battle for playing both sides. Neither Heaven nor Hell trusted him, and that scared her.

Sam stiffened when she heard footsteps outside and jerked the door open, shotgun leaning against the wall, easily within reach should she need it. What she found on the other side, however, was not a herd of demons as she had half-feared, but her parents.

Miranda, still beautiful at fifty-eight, stepped forward and enveloped her daughter in a giant hug, surrounding her with comfort and the faint scent of her perfume. Sam breathed in deeply, allowing herself ten seconds to revel in her mother's embrace before pulling loose and turning to Allen.

"She's upstairs. I gave her something to make her sleep, but she needs a physical exam. We're not sure if she was physically raped or just mentally. She's bruised all over. I don't know what to think."

Allen nodded, shrugged out of his jacket, and started up the stairs. "I'll do what I can, but without a hospital..."

"That's not an option, Dad."

"It's not ideal, but we've protected her in a hospital before."

"Not from Azazel, we haven't."

That was enough to have Miranda clapping a hand over her mouth and Allen stopping halfway up the staircase. He slowly turned. "Impossible."

"There's no one else that could have done what happened here last night. He's the only one who could find her and manipulate her."

"Lilith—"

"Can't get past the tattoos to find her. Griffin is hidden from Lilith and Beelzebub."

"Then Alaria—"

"Could find her, yes. But only in her dreams. It wasn't manipulation. He took control of her dream and used it to hurt her. Alaria can't do that. He was here. He touched her. There're bruises all over her."

"Allen—"

Allen's eyes shifted to his wife. "It's okay, Miranda. Now that we know he's out, we can take steps to protect ourselves. It changes nothing."

Griffin woke when Allen entered her room. She struggled to sit up, her whole body screaming from the pain of moving. Allen crossed the room, set his medical bag down, and perched on the bed. She reached out, and he took her into his arms as he'd done before, holding her while she cried.

When she was done, she pulled back, dashing tears from her face with the back of her hand. "You need to examine me now, right?"

"It'll be different from last time. I need to see if it was physical or mental and treat any damage. Other than that, there's not much I can do. Not like we can have a Devil arrested for what he did."

"I thought I was safe. I thought they couldn't get to me through the protections."

Allen sighed, pulled on white latex gloves, and withdrew a rape kit from his bag. "So did we. The only thing Sam can come up with is that the Devil that did this is one that we haven't dealt with before, one that isn't bound by the typical rules. I need you to take off your clothes and lay back."

Humiliated, Griffin stood, shimmied out of her pajama bottoms and underwear, and sat on the edge of the bed, pulling the sheet over her body. "What does Braxton think?"

Allen patted the mattress to show her where to put her feet, picked up the kit, and opened it. "We haven't told him about this yet. There's nothing he can do from where he is, and he can't leave until the possession is taken care of. Sam and I decided that concerning him with this at this point is an unnecessary risk. He can't be distracted when he's on the job." Allen sighed. "I know you wish we could. Believe me, so do we. But I know my son, and the last thing we need is for him to get reckless while he's on a job. We need him to come back alive."

Griffin jumped when he touched her, wincing at the bolt of pain. Tears silently streamed down her cheeks. She was embarrassed, humiliated, and in pain. "I want him to come back."

"We all do, sweetheart."

The exam was over quickly, and Allen left the room to let her wash and dress. Griffin spent the five minutes she had alone trying to compose herself. By the time Sam, Allen, and a woman she had never met entered the room, she'd gotten the tears under control. Sam was immediately at her side, guiding her to sit down, sitting next to her on the side of the bed and holding her hand tightly, a physical sign of support. Allen leaned against the wall, and the strange woman settled elegantly in the chair across the room.

"Griffin, this is my mother, Miranda. Mom, Griffin Javensen."

Griffin managed a tight smile. "Nice to meet you, ma'am."

"Please, it's Miranda. I'm sorry we had to meet under such circumstances, but when Sam called Allen last night, I wanted to come with him. I thought perhaps I could be of some help, having grown up with Warriors." She smiled softly, the expression a thin cover for the anxiety they were all feeling. "Allen, don't make the poor girl wait any longer. Tell her what you found out."

Allen cleared his throat uncomfortably. "Griffin, there was evidence of physical trauma. Bruising and slight tearing indicate extremely forceful sexual intercourse, which is indicative of a rape, unless you've engaged in incredibly rough sex in the past twenty-four hours."

Griffin shook her head. "No."

"I didn't think so. The more troubling aspect, however, is the internal damage. It seems that you were burned internally. Can you think of anything that would explain that?"

Griffin's eyes widened slightly, and she nodded. "When he—when it had an orgasm, I felt—it burned. Seared me. It was awful."

Sam gripped Griffin's hand tighter, offering support. "It's okay. None of this is your fault. There's nothing you could have done to prevent it." She turned to her father. "Dad, what does this all mean?"

Allen considered how to respond for a moment. "I'm going to administer the morning after pill, and the drugs necessary to prevent you from contracting any sort of human disease, though I doubt pregnancy or infection are concerns here. There has never been any hint of a Devil impregnating a human in recorded history, and there is no reason to think that he would want to do something like that here when his obvious goal was to kill you. The sex, the rape, it was just to make your death humiliating, to punish you for not Choosing them. The burns are fairly serious, but they should heal on their own with some time. Antibiotics will keep you from developing an infection from the injuries. Other than that, physically, you'll be fine in a couple weeks."

Griffin nodded, taking it all in. "So, what happens now?"

Sam stood. "Now, we pack. We can't stay here. He found you here, and it's only a matter of time before they have our address. Since he came to you through your dream, when the dream ended, he would have had to leave when you woke. But he's gotten a good look at the place, and it won't take much to get the location. We need to be as far away from this house as possible when they get here."

Griffin struggled to her feet, wincing at the shock of pain that went through her at the movement. She looked past Allen and Miranda, her face drawn with worry and pain as she moved across the room to the dresser where she'd put all her clothes. "I'll pack a bag and be ready in an hour."

Chapter Twenty

June 15th, 2029 - Romania

BRAXTON SAT at a table in a tiny, hole-in-the-wall bar in a village in Romania, a bottle of whisky at his elbow and an empty glass in front of him. Desperate to drown the pain, he poured another shot and tossed it back carelessly.

They were all dead—every Warrior that had been called in to help with the possession. They were all dead. It was his fault. He'd made the call, he'd left them alone, and the demons had killed them all.

They'd been there for weeks, making little headway, losing a Warrior for every demon they took down. They'd been pushed back into one house, fighting to survive, running out of food; clean water had become an issue. The demons had cut the electric, and they were slowly getting picked off, and desperately outnumbered. No one had been willing to say it, but they'd all accepted the fact that leaving Romania alive had become increasingly unlikely with every day that passed.

Braxton had known they were running out of time. He'd recognized the signs that the members of the team were losing hope; that they were simply waiting to die. They'd had very little fight left, some none at all. He'd come up with a plan—one that was reckless, and more than a little dangerous, but one that would give them an opportunity to escape. In that position, almost certain death was a better alternative than completely certain death.

He'd organized short raids outside to find out where the demons were holing up. Once he'd made that determination, he'd been able to construct a plan to get away from them. He had thought it would only put him in danger and would give everyone else the best chance they had at escaping. He had made a fatal miscalculation. If he'd paid more attention, if he'd taken a little more time to think, he'd have seen it.

A barn sat a couple hundred yards from the house, and Braxton knew that there was a truck inside. He'd loaded a backpack and duffel bag with bottles of Holy Water and bombs he'd made to spray rock salt. His plan had been to sneak into the demonic headquarters, use salt and spray-painted traps to keep them inside, and then detonate the bombs. It wouldn't kill them, but it would likely be enough to force them from their hosts, buying enough time to escape. While Braxton was distracting them, the others would get in the truck and head for the nearest non-possessed town to hide. It was risky, dangerous, and had the potential to get him killed, but it would take out a good portion of the demons so that the other Warriors could come in and finish them off once they'd had a chance to regroup and rearm themselves.

He'd gone up to the attic, removed a vent to the roof, and slithered out as silently as possible. Slowly, he'd moved across the roof, constantly sweeping the area for demonic activity. He wasn't disillusioned enough to think they would leave the house unguarded, so he had a knife in his boot in case he came in contact with a demon between their safe house and the demon headquarters.

Braxton had slipped across the roof, sliding his arm through the loops on the duffel bag so that it wouldn't fall when he jumped to the ground. Then, taking a look around to make sure that there was no one near him, he'd taken a deep breath and dropped lithely to the ground. Sticking to the inside of the forest line, he had crept toward the village.

There. A demon. Silently placing the backpack and duffel bag on the ground, he'd withdrawn the knife from his boot. Moving quickly, he'd slipped behind the demon, yanked its head back with one hand, and slashed its throat with the other. When the stream of black and red matter poured from its mouth, Braxton darted back into the trees and retrieved his supplies.

Half an hour later, he had finished the salt line around the demon headquarters and was crouching in the shadows preparing his bombs. When he'd heard the explosion, he'd immediately scrapped all plans and raced back to the house, terrified at what he would find.

The house had been reduced to little more than a pile of smoldering ashes and small flames. He'd dug through the ruins for hours, trying to find some trace of a survivor. What he'd found were remains—the bodies of his friends, their skin boiling and peeling away from their bones.

It was all his fault. Braxton poured yet another drink and tossed it back, the burning in his throat a welcome distraction from the pain and grief that had been overwhelming him since that day.

He glanced at his phone when it rang, saw that it was his sister, and debated whether or not to answer. After a brief struggle, he decided he couldn't continue to ignore her and opened the phone, pressing it to his ear.

"Winslow."

"Brax, it's Sam."

"I know who it is."

"We need you to come home. Now."

Unused to the terror in his sister's voice, Braxton straightened. "What's wrong? Has something happened?"

"Azazel is free."

"That's impossible."

"I thought the same thing, but he lured Griffin out into the ocean and he raped her. She's burned inside, she's scared to sleep, and to be honest, I can't tell her it's going to be okay. Mom's done all she can to protect the house, but there's not a whole hell of a lot that we can do to keep Azazel out once he's decided to get in."

"You're sure it wasn't Alaria? Lilith? Beelzebub?"

"We're sure. The way it was done, the strength to get in, it wasn't a dream manipulation, Brax. Believe me, I've been through all the options in my head, and I cannot come up with anyone else that it could possibly be. I've been looking for another explanation, and there just isn't one."

"I'll be there as soon as I can, but it's still going to be a few weeks."

"Braxton, you're in a bar. I can hear the jukebox and the crowd in the background. And if you're in a bar, then the job is done. So, get your ass on a plane and get back here and do your job."

"The job is done because they're all dead."

"That's generally the point of doing a job. Killing the creepy crawly."

"Not the demons. The Warriors. They're all dead. All but me."

"That's terrible, but I cannot focus on that right now. We've moved Griffin to another house, trying to get them off our trail, and it seems to be working at the moment, but there's only so time I can keep them out. I'm fourteen weeks along now, and I'm starting to show a little. Another ten weeks and I won't be able to do the job at all, Brax. I'm getting bigger every day, and this baby is taking my energy. I'm doing my best, but there is only so much that I can do."

"Is she still having the dreams?"

Sam sighed deeply. "Not right now. Not since we moved her."

"Then move her again when they start."

"If they figure out who we are, they'll know all the properties, and we won't be safe no matter which house I take her to."

"Have they figured it out?"

"Not that I know of. Not yet."

"Then don't borrow trouble, Sam. I'll be there when I can, but I have to get my head on straight. I'm in no shape to take care of her right now. She's safer with you than she is with me."

"This is your job! You're the one who was picked to take her through this! You're the one sleeping with her, and you're the one that she wants here. She's giving up her life to save the world, Braxton, and it is the least you can do to get here and do your fucking job."

"You're a Warrior. You can take care of her as easily as I can. And I just watched fifty people give up their lives to save the world. Having to die doesn't make her any more fucking special than any of those people. Just because she knows the day she's gonna bite the dust doesn't mean she's worth more."

Sam sighed deeply, shaking her head. "If you actually believe that, big brother, you're not the man I thought you were. I'll do this as long as I can, but you keep in mind that it's not just me you're risking. It's our parents, my husband, my child. And I'll lay it all down for this, to do the job you're supposed to be doing. Get your head on, Brax, and come home."

Braxton didn't even bother responding, just snapped the phone shut and dropped it onto the table, pouring another drink and draining the glass. Setting the glass on the table, the cup sliding across the wood, he saw her—a childlike blonde in a pink dress, looking painfully out of place in the dive bar. Her curves would make a normal man weep and her breasts strained against the fabric of her dress, drawing the eye of every man inside the building. She had ringlets that fell to her shoulders and her eyes were so blue they were nearly purple.

She scanned the crowd disinterestedly, then her eyes settled on Braxton and she smiled, her tongue flicking out over full lips. She sauntered over to him, her hips swaying seductively as she walked, her eyes never leaving his. In that moment, Braxton made a decision.

"Looking for something?"

The woman placed her hands on her hips when he spoke and looked at him with mild interest. "What're you offering?"

Surprised when she spoke with a light Midwestern accent, Braxton gestured for her to sit and grinned when she slid into the booth across from him. "How about we start with a drink?"

The woman reached out, snagged his glass and drained it, her throat working as she slowly swallowed. "There. I've had a drink, and you've had a few. Have you had too many?"

"Too many for what?"

"If I have to tell you, darling, I'm doing something wrong."

Braxton chuckled and opened his hands, palms up, on the table. "Can't recall the last time I got picked up in a bar. Normally, it's the other way around.'

"I'm a woman who knows what she wants." She giggled. "I fly back to Vermont tomorrow, classes start on Monday, and I haven't gotten to have any fun in this God-forsaken country." She pouted prettily. "Think you can help me have a little fun?"

Braxton let his eyes wander over her. "How old are you?"

"Twenty-two."

"Are you sure?"

She giggled again, reached into her purse and fished out her wallet, flipping it open to show him the driver's license inside. "See?"

Braxton stood and took her by the elbow. "Well, Sarah, I'm Braxton. And I have a room next door at the hotel."

"Funny, I was hoping to get a room at the hotel next door."

"Plenty of room in mine."

"Perfect."

Braxton led the woman out of the bar with a hand on her hip. He guided her across the parking lot, marveling at how gracefully she moved in the six-inch stiletto heels. He pulled out his wallet, removing his key card. She began kissing his neck as he fumbled to get the key in the slot; he groaned and bodily lifted her through the door when it opened with a small snick.

They didn't waste time on foreplay. Both knew what they were there for, and neither was interested in waiting to get to it. He tugged her dress over her head, groaning in appreciation when he found her completely bare underneath it. Her small hands worked his belt easily; he heard the brief hiss of a zipper, and then his pants were around his ankles.

Shoes flew as he backed her toward the bed, and he kicked his pants off, cursing when one leg tangled around his ankle. Laughing, he shrugged and pushed her onto the bed, sliding on top of her, the fabric not quite shaken free.

Braxton fumbled for his wallet, found it near the bed on the floor, and withdrew a foil wrapper. He sheathed himself, used his hand to nudge her thighs apart, and shoved into her. Her back arched off the bed, her legs wrapped around his waist, and her arms gripped him tight as he thrust.

Over the next hours, Braxton buried himself in the strange woman time and again. He let her ride him, he put her on her knees, and she used her mouth on him until he thought he would die. He took her against the wall, in the shower, and on the floor. He wasn't gentle, he didn't romance her, he merely fucked her. He used her to bury the memories of the deaths of his friends, of Griffin, of the Choosing, of everything he wanted to forget.

In the dark predawn moments, all of it came rushing back at him. The woman stood, gloriously naked, and looked at him hungrily. Then, in a moment, everything changed. Her eyes went from blue to red, and before Braxton could make a move for the gun under the mattress, she snapped her fingers and he found himself tied to the head and foot boards.

He struggled briefly, just because his nature wouldn't let him do otherwise, then glared up at her. "Who are you?"

"If you have to ask, I am doing something wrong. I had assumed my reputation would precede me."

"Lilith."

She smiled evilly. "In the flesh. Well, you know all about my flesh, don't you?"

"Did you have to fuck me beforehand?"

"You enjoyed it. Don't even try to tell me that you didn't. And I enjoyed it as well. Your stamina is quite good for a human. A Devil will do whatever you want in bed, so there's never any worry about turning me off." She pulled on her dress and smoothed it over her curves. "Now, let's get to business, shall we?"

"What business would that be?"

Lilith crossed the room and opened the door, allowing a man dressed in a navy blue silk suit to enter. Beelzebub surveyed the situation with little more than mild interest. He waved a hand, and Braxton found himself wearing boxers and a t-shirt.

"I should have known you'd have to engage in that barbaric activity before we could get this done."

Lilith shrugged carelessly. "I enjoy that barbaric activity, and you've known that for a very long time." She smiled, perched on the bottom of the bed and ran her finger up the sole of Braxton's foot. "He's quite good at it."

"I'm not interested in his sexual prowess. I'm interested in the human girl."

"Ahh yes, the Chosen. What's her human name? Griffin?" Lilith pretended to ponder for a moment, and then giggled almost childishly. "It doesn't matter. I want to know where you've hidden her."

"Can't find out yourself?"

Beelzebub crossed his arms and lifted one eyebrow. "You're well aware of how good at this you are, Warrior. But now we've—to borrow a human phrase—got you by the balls. So, why don't you make this easier on everyone involved and just spill what you know? We're going to kill you either way. If you tell, I'll do it, and you'll feel no pain. Make this difficult, and I'll leave you here with Lilith. We both know that she can toy with someone for weeks before she kills them."

Braxton felt his stomach clench at the thought of being alone with the Devil until she tired of playing with him. He also knew that Beelzebub was right. He was good at his job. Without him telling them, they were unlikely to find Griffin, and even if they did find her, they would still have Sam and Finn to deal with. Regardless of the torture he would be subjecting himself to, he knew that doing so would, at the very least, delay the Devils from finding Griffin and give Sam more time to prepare for the Choosing.

"Well, as fun as it would be to let you have your way with me, Beelzebub, I'm much more fond of women than I am of men, so I think I'll take my chances with the pretty blonde."

Chapter Twenty-One

August 1st, 2029 - Austin, Texas

GRIFFIN JERKED out of a sound sleep with a feeling that something was horribly wrong. She slipped from bed, and when her feet hit the wood floors in her bedroom, she was sucked into a vision. She saw the demons racing toward the house in their human forms, their eyes blood red. She saw Alaria, the man from the beach she now knew was Azazel, and the blonde Devil she assumed was Lilith.

When the vision ended, Griffin raced for the dresser, pulled on the first clothes she found, and reached under the bed to drag out the already-packed bag she kept there. She took the time to slide the zipper and make sure the knife was still present. After reassuring herself, she pulled on tennis shoes by the door and raced down the hall to the room Sam and Finn shared.

She opened the door, flipped on the light without announcing herself, and offered an apologetic shrug when Finn and Sam sat up groggy and confused. Sam took stock of the situation quickly, her eyes scanning Griffin's attire and the bag in her hand.

"What is it?"

"They're on their way. We don't have long. We need to move."

Sam was on her feet in a heartbeat, reaching under the bed for a gun and tossing it to Griffin. Finn pulled on slacks over his boxers, dug a handgun out of his drawer, and checked the clip before tucking it into his waistband.

"How many? How long?"

"Three. Alaria, Azazel and Lilith. Not long. Maybe five minutes."

Sam and Finn exchanged a worried look, then Sam lifted one shoulder in a sign of helplessness. "Nothing we can do but not be here in five minutes then. Let's move." She tossed a duffel bag to Griffin. "Put those in the car in the garage. We'll meet you there."

Finn shook his head. "Go with her, Sam. I've got this. I'll do a quick sweep to set the charges and meet you there."

Knowing there wasn't time to argue, Sam nodded, put one hand on Griffin's back, and propelled her down the stairs. "If they're coming, we need to keep them from following us. There are Devil's traps under all the floors, outlined in liquid silver. They'll likely get stuck, or at least Alaria will. The other two may be able to get past them, but it'll cause them pain. The walls are filled with salt which will hurt them all, so we're setting charges to blow the house up. It'll spray salt and Holy Water, which will hopefully keep them off our asses long enough to get somewhere safe."

Griffin nodded sharply as she yanked open the door to the garage, snagged the keys from the hook on the wall and popped the trunk to toss in the two duffel bags. Sam reached into the trunk, withdrew a twelve gauge shotgun, and expertly loaded it with shells.

"I want you to wait here. The car is a safe point. Devil's traps on the roof and the undercarriage, and the frame is laced with salt. They can't get to you there. If I'm not back in five minutes, I want you to drive, and, unless you need gas, don't stop until you get to my dad. And whatever you do, don't sleep."

Griffin nodded, rounded the car, slid into the driver's seat and jammed the key into the ignition. Sam waited a few seconds to make sure Griffin was settled and then opened the door to slip back into the kitchen. What she found was Finn standing in the middle of the room, and Lilith two feet away from him.

"Nice of you to join us, Warrior. We've been waiting for you, haven't we, Finn?"

Finn looked to Sam. "Run. Go now."

Lilith shook her head. "Now, that's not a good idea. How is it, Samantha, that someone like you inspires such loyalty from men? I've been torturing your brother for two months, and he hasn't told me anything."

While the words sent a knife through Sam's heart, she made sure to keep her face expressionless. "Braxton is a tough cookie. Finn is my husband. Someone like you couldn't possibly understand what the bond is between husband and wife." She turned slightly, acknowledging the appearance of the second Devil, Azazel, who entered the room. "So, it's true. Someone let you loose."

Azazel smiled charmingly. "Someone did. It's so nice to be out and to be a part of something like this—to get to kill someone so important." He rolled his eyes. "Well, let's just say there's not been a better time to be a Devil, love."

Lilith clucked her tongue. "Let's get back to this whole marriage issue." She cocked her head to the side in curiosity. "Now, I'm not a human and never have been. I've been walking the Earth for more years than you can comprehend. From what I understand, marriage is all about the human heart—about being connected to each other." She looked at Finn and smiled. "Do I have that right?"

Knowing the route they were on was not good, Finn nodded hesitantly. "That's a good way to describe it."

Lilith nodded. "That's what I thought."

Without a sound, without looking like she even moved, Lilith plunged her hand into Finn's chest and ripped it back, his heart beating in her bloody hand. Sam heard the scream that filled the room, but it was several seconds before she realized that it was her own.

Lilith turned, her eyes glowing red as Finn fell to the ground. She looked at the heart, warm and soft in her hand, and then lifted her gaze to Sam. Without a word, she tossed the organ to the Warrior. Sam didn't catch it. It hit her on the chest, leaving a bloody print where it touched the fabric of her shirt. With one smooth motion, Sam lifted the gun she still held in her hands and fired, the slug hitting Lilith directly in the face.

Azazel moved to charge Sam just as Griffin ran through the door and fired the gun Sam had given her several times, shattering the bones in his face and sending the body crumpling to the ground. The rounds had been laced with rock salt and Holy Water. The combination sent the Devil back to Hell, where he would be forced to find a new host body.

Sam hit her knees next to Finn and lifted his head into her lap. She leaned down and braced her forehead against his. "I love you. I'm sorry this happened to you, and I will always love you." She whispered the words, her lips barely above his. "I'll kill them, Finn—I swear to you I will."

Griffin stood back as she watched the heartbreaking scene, but heard the tell-tale beeping of the alarm Finn had carried in his pocket telling her that the charges were about to go off. She ran to Sam and gripped her shoulders.

"We have to go. The house is going to blow up."

Sam looked up, tears running down her face. She shook her head to clear it, and Griffin saw her eyes sharpen. "Okay. Get the salt out of the pantry. I need to make sure they can't possess him." She turned her head back to her husband, and her fingers struggled to remove the wedding ring from his finger.

Griffin ran to the pantry and opened the door. She grabbed the box of salt from the shelf and nearly dropped it when she closed the door and found Alaria standing there. She started to scream, but the Devil clamped a hand over her mouth.

"I'm not here to hurt you. They left me back on the hill because they thought they didn't need help. I need you to find out about me, Griffin. You'll never believe it if I tell you everything on my own, so find the answers. Find the one who knows about me. And when you're ready to make a deal, I'll find you. I can help you get through this."

Alaria removed her hand and Griffin coughed to clear her throat. "Why?"

"Because you can give me something no one else can. I'm not offering to help out of the goodness of my heart. You can do something for me, and in return, I'll make sure you make it to your birthday alive. Now, get out of here before you blow yourselves up."

Griffin didn't stop to question. She ran to Sam and started dumping the salt on Finn's body. She grabbed Sam's arm and helped heave the pregnant woman to her feet. "We have to go now."

Sam nodded, her mind already compartmentalizing the grief and focusing on the task at hand. "We have ninety seconds to be out of range before this place goes up." She burst into the garage, went to the driver's side, and slid behind the wheel. Griffin had barely gotten in the passenger seat before Sam slammed the car into gear.

Griffin was silent for a while and then looked at Sam as the sun started to break over the horizon. "What do we do now?"

Sam glanced over at Griffin and managed a tight smile. "We survive." She made a turn onto a highway and hit the accelerator. "We'll ditch this car soon. We've got several places throughout the country with cars outfitted for this kind of work. I'll pick up some cash, too. No paper trail. If they found us, they know my name, and we're not safe in public. And they've got Braxton, so we have to consider ourselves the only ones in this now. I don't know if he's alive or dead, but he can't help us, at least not right now, either way."

Griffin wanted to ask about Braxton, but she figured that the grief was still too strong for Sam to focus on her brother, too. "Where do we go?"

"I don't know yet. We'll bounce around a lot. We can't stay any one place for very long." She sighed and looked at Griffin for a long moment. "And I need to schedule an abortion."

"What? Why?"

"I was hoping Braxton would come back and take over. I can't protect you as well as I need to be able to with a beach ball around my waist. I'm at nineteen weeks, which means I'm getting close to the point of not being legally able to terminate."

"I thought you wanted the baby."

"I do. But there are more important things than my ability to procreate." Sam managed to hold the tears back. "I can always have another one. If I get you killed because I'm hugely pregnant and slow, then there is no do-over."

Griffin nodded but didn't say anything, her mind racing for a solution. They rode in silence for the rest of the day. Neither spoke when Sam pulled over and transferred their stuff into another car—a beat-up Ford with Florida plates and a small arsenal in the trunk. Griffin didn't even flinch when the car they'd been using was set with charges or when she saw the explosion in the rear view mirror as she took her turn behind the wheel.

Finally, after taking many random exits, traveling in odd routes, and making only the stops that were needed, Sam pointed to a motel on the side of the highway. Griffin obligingly pulled into the parking lot and waited in the car while Sam checked in. Fifteen minutes later, they were settled in a room with two beds, a small television, a dingy bathroom, and one worn-out dresser.

"Not the Hilton, but it's good enough for one night." Sam dragged out a bag of supplies and set about safeguarding the room with herbs and salt, dashing Holy Water around every door and window. "I'm going to go to the diner across the street to grab burgers. Wait here."

While Sam was gone, Griffin worked on putting her plan into place. She dashed out to the car, loaded down one duffel bag with half the weapons and supplies, then stowed it under the sink in the bathroom, hoping against hope that Sam didn't find it. She added one change of clothes and her fake ID to the bag and was lying on one of the beds, flipping through channels when Sam returned with a bag of greasy fast food.

They ate in silence, barely acknowledging one other. By the time the remnants of dinner were in the trash, the clock was moving steadily toward midnight, and both women were yawning, emotionally and physically drained. Sam had gotten a quick shower at the truck stop where they'd exchanged cars, but Griffin had opted out, already working on her plan.

When Sam pulled back the covers and slid beneath them, Griffin stood, stretching. "I think I'm going to run a bath. The tub looks nasty, but if I scrub it out, it should be good for a long soak."

Sam looked over her shoulder at the other woman and nodded. "Good idea. You'll need it. There's no telling the next time we'll be in a place to do this again."

Griffin offered a small smile. "We'll figure it out." She sat on the edge of Sam's bed. "I'm sorry about Finn. He was really wonderful."

Sam teared up a little but fought it back. "He was a wonderful husband and person. He would want me to finish this." She reached out from under the blanket and patted Griffin's hand. "Enjoy your bath. We'll talk tomorrow. It's still too new for me to process right now. I need some time." Sam waited until Griffin was at the door then sat up a bit. "Don't stay in there too long."

Griffin chuckled. "Just until the water gets cold."

She shut the door softly and spent several minutes clattering around. She started and stopped the water to feign washing out the tub, flushed the toilet, ran the sink for a moment, then finally turned on the water and let the tub fill, going so far as to use her hand to splash a little so if Sam was awake she would think Griffin had gotten in the water.

That done, Griffin went into stealth mode. She withdrew the bag she'd stashed and carefully lowered the lid on the toilet and stood on it, drawing from years of sneaking out of foster homes to get her out the window undetected. She wrapped a towel around the handle to damper any squeaking and silently thanked God when it went up with little fuss. She leaned over, left the note she'd written to Sam on the sink, then carefully dropped the bag onto the ground and wiggled out the window after it, taking the time to lower the window behind her.

Having successfully gotten out of the room, she shouldered the bag and hurried across the street to the bar that was next to the diner. Looking as inconspicuous as she could, she ducked into the building and sidled up to the bar, one goal in mind. Ten minutes later, she darted out into the parking lot, a set of keys in hand that she'd lifted off a drunken lawyer. Without hesitation, she slid behind the wheel, started the engine of the black Cadillac, and pulled out onto the road.

Chapter Twenty-Two

August 6th, 2029 - Philadelphia, Pennsylvania

Griffin hadn't thought she'd ever see Father Dooley again. She'd tried to stay away from him after he'd found out what she was, thinking that he would be in danger if the Devils found him. When Alaria had spoken to her, curiosity had gotten the best of her, and she'd felt compelled to find out what the Devil was talking about.

She'd taken some risks and gone back to Philadelphia, where she'd chanced stopping by her bank for what money she had left, which was enough to get her through until December, and she had purchased a used Toyota that would be reliable enough for what she needed. After that, she only had one stop before she got back on the road, and that was to see the man who had started everything for her.

The church looked exactly the same as she remembered. Griffin stopped at the threshold, dipped her fingers into the Holy Water and drew the cross across her chest. Heels clicking on the stone floor, she made her way into the sanctuary, the gun a reassuring pressure against her spine.

"Hello?"

"One second!" Father Dooley called out from his chambers, and Griffin heard his chair scrape the floor, then a muffled swear as he stubbed his toe on the desk, trying to get his shoes on before coming out into the sanctuary. He stopped in his tracks when he saw Griffin. "Thank God. You're still alive."

"Sam called you?"

"Only a dozen times. I should call her and tell her you're here."

Griffin shook her head vehemently. "You can't. She's pregnant. She was going to abort the baby to take care of me. I can't let her do that."

Father Dooley, his eyes full of sympathy, drew Griffin into a hug. "Griffin, you need someone to help you get through this. You can't do it on your own. With them after you like they are..."

"I have it under control. She lost her husband because of me. I won't let her lose her child, too." Griffin pushed past him into his office and dropped down onto the couch. "I need your help."

"With what?"

"Alaria came to me. Said I needed to find out about her. That once I did, I would understand and that she could help keep me alive until my birthday. She seems to think I can do something for her, something she wants that no one else can do. And if I'll do it, she'll keep me alive until the Choosing."

"It's most likely a trap, Griffin."

"What could she be talking about?"

Dooley rose, went to his bookshelves, and withdrew a slender leather book. "There's a tale that's fluttered around from time to time that the Chosen, as a gift for doing this great service, gets to ask one thing of God. Some suggested that this was the way that they might get to continue living past the thirty years. Others surmised that it was a way to soften the blow, letting the person ask a favor for someone else. The theory is that God has bound Himself to do whatever is asked by the Chosen, so long as it does not affect free will. So, basically, after you die, there's a possibility that you might get a one shot deal to do something that no one else has ever been able to do. Demand something from God. And I'm betting that Alaria wants you to demand something for her."

"Is it true? Do I get that?"

"No one knows for sure. I don't think it's likely, but it's possible that it could be a reward for choosing Heaven. But there's no way to know for sure until after it happens."

"Is there anyone who is an expert on Alaria that I can talk to?"

Dooley sighed deeply. "No one that I know of that specializes in her in particular. But there is a priest in Australia who is an expert on Devils. If anyone would know about her, it would be Dean Masters. He's in Melbourne."

"I need to talk to him."

"The phone isn't safe. You know that."

"I'll go there then. Give me an address."

"That's not a good idea."

"I don't care. All I'll ask of you is that you not tell Sam where I am until she's past the point of viability. Two more weeks and she can't get an abortion legally. She'll regret it later if she does." Griffin wrung her hands, her desperation clear on her face. "I can't be responsible for more death. I can't take it."

"I can't make any promises. Samantha is a Warrior, and one nearly as talented as her brother. She'll be willing to do anything she can to get through this. There's not going to be much I can do to discourage her from that."

Griffin rose and held out a hand. "Thank you. For everything you've done. I know I've put you in danger by coming here."

"It's my job, Griffin. Any man of the cloth would be proud to stand between the Chosen and those that seek to stop her from what must be done. It's my honor and privilege to help you." He held her hand warmly and brought her in close for an embrace. "Go with God, child. There will be peace in the end and rewards greater than you can imagine. I know the path seems bleak and hard, but I promise you if you stay the course, you will not fail." He bent to scribble on a piece of paper. He stared at it for a long moment before handing it to her. "Here's the address."

Braxton lay in the hotel room bed, his body covered in shallow cuts and mottled with bruises. His throat was dry from dehydration and screaming, and his stomach had long ago ceased to rumble from hunger. The Devils had left him alone several hours earlier, and he had no idea when they would be back. He didn't doubt that they would be, since he was still alive; the only question was when.

He halfheartedly struggled against the bonds at his wrists, stopping when he made no progress other than the sturdy ropes biting into his flesh. He closed his eyes, half in defeat and half from exhaustion, and considered trying to sleep.

The room filled with a warm light, and with a small noise, Gabriel appeared, resplendent as always in his white suit with his blond hair slicked back into a neat ponytail. The Angel looked at him in mild annoyance.

"How you humans manage to consistently get yourselves into such messes is beyond my comprehension."

"Are you here to mock me or to help me?"

"I see no reason why I can't do both." Gabriel flicked his wrist and the binds fell, leaving Braxton's arms free. "There's been a complication."

Braxton sat up, cringing at the soreness in his muscles from inactivity. "What's happened?"

"Lilith killed your brother-in-law. They found Griffin in Samantha and Finn's care. He was an unfortunate casualty of the encounter. Griffin and Samantha escaped unharmed, but after your sister expressed her desire to end her pregnancy, Griffin snuck out in the middle of the night and ran. She's on her way to Australia to meet with a priest."

Braxton dug around on the floor for the clothes he'd been wearing the night he'd been captured and dragged them on despite the smell. "Looks like I'm going to Australia."

"You need to go home first, to convince your sister to maintain her pregnancy. Griffin is safe at the moment, and you have my word she will remain so, at least until you are able to get to her. I'll protect her personally. The child Samantha carries is important, not only to her, but also to God."

"You'll have to forgive me if what your boss wants doesn't trump my duty to Griffin."

"Oh, but it does. The survival of that child could affect the Choosing, Braxton. You must do as I've told you to do."

"How is it going to affect the Choosing?"

Gabriel sighed in mild annoyance. "That is not for you to know. Eventually, you'll learn that humans are not always privy to the same information as Angels. I am here to tell you what must be done, not why you must do it. The reasoning will be made clear to you at some point."

"How long do I have to get to Griffin in Australia?"

"Long enough. Don't be so concerned about time, human. If your time runs short, I'll come to you yet again."

Braxton pulled on his boots, found his wallet amongst the debris, and checked to make sure the cards were still in their proper places. "Any chance you'll get me to where I'm going, or am I on my own?"

Gabriel smiled as he began to disappear. "I already saved your ass, boy. I'd be grateful if I were you, not demanding."

Braxton sighed as the Angel disappeared. He set about packing any of his things that hadn't been destroyed by the Devils. Within five minutes, he was slipping out the door and sliding behind the wheel of the car that some unlucky bastard had left unlocked in the parking lot. He used his pocketknife to cut the wires under the dash and pressed them together until the engine roared to life. He twisted them to keep them together and put the car in gear.

Griffin sat across the table from Father Dean Masters, tapping her foot impatiently as the man searched through book after book, looking for information on Alaria. He was a younger priest, maybe in his early thirties, with mousy hair, thick black glasses, and a nervous smile. He was handsome enough, in his own way, but seemed much more at ease with books than he did with people.

"Now, why are you looking for information on Alaria? She's never mentioned in the canonical version of the Bible."

Griffin sighed. "Father Dooley gave me your name. I've always had an interest in this sort of thing, and he thought that you would be a good person to talk to. Especially since I'd already had a vacation to Melbourne planned. Happy coincidence."

The lie tasted bitter on her tongue, but Griffin was unwilling to put the man's life in danger because she had sought him out for her answers. The less he knew, the safer he would be.

"I don't remember the last time someone asked me about this particular demon. Though, I don't know why. She's very interesting."

Even though Griffin knew most of the story from her visit from Michael, she asked the obvious question. "Why is that?"

"Well, the story goes that she was one of the first to join with Lucifer when he took up arms against God. She didn't sign on for the typical reasons. Alaria was an Angel, like most of the high-powered demons were, and she particularly enjoyed being on Earth. The theory is that she joined with Lucifer because she thought that Angels should have free will like humans, specifically the choice to live on Earth as a human. She didn't want to overthrow Heaven. She wanted to be able to choose her own existence. Lucifer had promised her that when he won, he would make her human, so she joined with him. She was one of the fiercest warriors that their side had. In the end, she was cast into the pit with the rest of them."

"Why in the world did Lucifer give her the Choosing, then?"

"Alaria became one of the most vicious demons out there. She was enraged by being cast into the pit, and funneled that anger toward God and humans. Woman scorned and all that jazz. Lucifer wasn't about to waste that sort of anger." He paused. "Wait. How do you know about the Choosing? That's supposed to be a secret."

"I'm a researcher. I know a lot." Griffin brushed the lie aside with a flick of her hand. "That's not important. What do you know about her now?"

"Just that she's waiting for the birth. No one knows when it will happen, so don't even bother asking. Not that I would tell you if I did know, because I wouldn't."

Her heart beating hard against her ribs, Griffin asked the question she had wanted to ask from the very beginning. "Does she still want to be human?"

"Oh, I can't imagine that. She's a demon. She has no soul. Any remnants of angelic humanity that she had would have had would have been washed away centuries ago. No, she's just another angry demon." Masters stood, cleaning the lenses of his glasses with the untucked tail of his shirt. "Now, if that's all, I have a lot of work to do."

Griffin took the hint and stood as well, offering her hand, then drawing it back when the priest just brushed by her on the way back into his private chambers. She shook her head as she walked toward the door of the church, her mind automatically shifting to her current task, which was finding a safe place to stay while she was in Australia. What she'd hoped would be an information gathering mission had turned into little more than a complete waste of her time.

Chapter Twenty-Three

September 5th, 2029 - Melbourne, Australia
GRIFFIN WORKED for the rest of the day to prepare the house she'd rented under a false name. She salted every window and door, put herbs around the perimeter, and stitched protection bags into every pillow in the house. She spent the better part of a week hunting down weapons—tucking guns and knives into every hiding place that she could.

The knife she was to use in the Choosing, she kept on her at all times. She'd bought a piece of thick leather, sewn it into a pouch and strapped the pouch to the inside of her thigh. She only took it off to bathe. More than anything else, she could not afford to lose that knife.

She placed Devil's traps in every room, knowing that they wouldn't hold Lilith and Azazel but feeling better with them nonetheless. Boxes of salt went in every room, and she lined the doors and windows with glue, giving the salt something to stick to so that a gust of wind wouldn't take her protections flying. She installed security cameras and motion detectors, trying to think of anything and everything that would give her a few extra seconds to run should she be attacked there. She kept a bag of supplies in the trunk of her rented car, another under her bed, a third in the bushes outside the house, and a fourth buried half a mile from the house in case she had to flee with no time to grab anything.

In the back of her mind, she knew that she would not be able to stay there for long. That they would catch up with her. That she would have to run. But it was September. She only had three months left, and she desperately wanted to spend at least a portion of them as normally as she could. She wanted to forget what she was, what she had to do. She wanted to ignore the feeling of death growing inside her every day. She wanted to believe, even for one moment, that she might survive beyond her thirtieth birthday.

So Griffin did normal things. She went to the grocery store, cooked dinner, and went to a movie. She shopped for clothes and picked up trinkets at the market. When she came home and something just felt wrong, she found herself feeling in her satchel for the gun and vial of Holy Water she always kept on her just in case.

The hair on the back of her neck stood up, but she didn't have the feeling that what—or who—ever was in the house was one of the demons she was hiding from. She hadn't had any dreams warning her about them coming, so she quietly unlocked the door and slipped into the house, anticipating a burglar or an Angel. What she found was neither.

The light flipped on when she was no more than five feet inside the door. And there, sitting on her couch, his feet propped up on the footstool, idly flipping through a magazine, was Braxton. Griffin froze when she saw him, unsure of how he'd found her, where he'd been, what had happened, or how angry he was at her. When he lifted his eyes and she saw them burning hot, snapping with fury, she found herself putting her hand to her throat and rubbing, knowing the confrontation was going to be heated.

"Brax. What are you doing here?"

"Did you think I'd just let you run away and disappear? That you could sneak out on Sam in the middle of the night, and never even check in and we'd just what? Forget that you had ever existed? What kind of man do you think I am?"

Griffin felt her own anger bubble up at that. "The kind who put me on a plane to go to people I'd never met, with no clue what they looked like, and who disappeared for months. Who left me to be raped by Azazel, who never called to check, who abandoned his sister so that her husband had his heart ripped out of his chest by Lilith. You swore to me that you would keep me safe, but you couldn't keep your head on straight, and when things got a little complicated, you took off at the first opportunity. That's the kind of man I think you are, Braxton. The kind who doesn't give a fuck about anyone but himself, and who doesn't care what kind of collateral damage gets left behind. Because you did forget I ever existed for months. You forgot we all existed to go do a job."

Slowly, Braxton set the newspaper aside and rose to his feet. Even from fifteen feet away, Griffin could see the tension in his muscles as he moved. "There were lives at stake. I had no choice."

Griffin laughed, the sound bitter even to her own ears. "Braxton, even I have a choice. It may not be one worth making, but I have one. If I have a choice, then dammit, so did you! You chose to stay there, just like you chose to go. And we were the ones who paid the price for that. Not you!"

"I didn't pay a price? I watched fifty Warriors get boiled to death. Funny, I think that's a pretty high price. It wasn't like I was on vacation. I was doing a job, and then I was getting tortured by Lilith."

Griffin filed that tidbit away for later. "They'd have died without you. They'd have probably died quicker without you. They wouldn't have called you unless they were desperate, and we both know that you knew when you went there that at least some of them wouldn't be coming home. It's tragic. I hate it. You knew it when you went. And you know, somewhere you know, that it wasn't your fault. Even still, you stayed away for months! If you'd come straight back, none of this would have happened. You were so busy drowning your guilt in a bottle of bourbon that you let Finn die!"

Braxton advanced, backing her against the door she'd come in through. "This is not about me. This is not about what I did or did not do. They were my calls to make, and I made them. This is about you. You snuck out through a fucking window and disappeared off the face of the Earth. Sam had no idea if you were alive or dead, if the demons had gotten you, or if you'd killed yourself and just gotten it over with. Like it or not, Griffin, you have a job to do. You have to get to New Year's. We will get you there. Whether it's me, or it's Sam, that is not your call, and that is none of your concern. You want our help? That's the price. You stopped getting any say in what happens when they pierced that Veil."

Griffin's hand met Braxton's cheek before she could stop it and before he saw it coming. The sound was like a gunshot in the room, and instantly, Griffin looked shocked, her hand falling limply to her side, the ramifications of what she had done racing through her brain as she waited for him to respond. The response she got, however, was far from what she'd expected to get.

He grabbed her by the upper arms and yanked her against him. Griffin had time for one gasping breath before his mouth crashed down on hers. Braxton swept his hands down her body, gripping her by the hips to lift her up, pinning her against the wall and molding her curves to the harder planes of his body. Of their own accord, her hands went to his head, fingers threading through his hair, the heat of his mouth permeating down to the soles of her feet and radiating out into her fingertips.

Their breath meshed, and their tongues tangled wildly, almost violently, each of them battling for dominance. For the first time since Braxton had slipped out of bed that last night they'd spent together, Griffin felt life coursing through her veins, waking her up, making her feel alive, as if there was more to tomorrow than another step toward her death.

Her head fell back as his mouth ravaged her skin. His hands found the neckline of her t-shirt, and with one forceful jerk, he ripped it down the middle, dragging the pieces down her arms to fall forgotten to the floor. Her fingers, nimble and slim, slipped the buttons from the holes on his shirt, and she slid the garment off of him, the touch of her hands making his skin sizzle.

Griffin's feet hit the floor, and she began pushing him backward toward the couch, whispering nonsense between deep, seeking kisses, both busily removing the rest of their clothing. By the time Braxton's knees hit the couch, there was a trail of shoes, jeans and underwear from the door into her living room.

They tumbled onto the couch in a tangle of arms and legs. Their mouths wandered, trailing kisses over skin. He found her nipple with his tongue, and her back arched, a bolt of pleasure making her groan in appreciation. Crazy with desire, she shifted beneath him, lifting her hips, wrapping her thighs around him, and drawing him to her. He gripped her hips with his hands, shifting them, parting her thighs, and probing gently.

Griffin shook her head. "Condom."

Braxton swore and leaped off the couch. He fumbled for the duffel bag that still sat by the door. Clothes flew as he pawed through it. Triumphant, he yanked out a box of Trojans and spilled them all on the floor trying to pull out just one. He ripped it open with his teeth and rolled it on his bulging erection as he walked back to the couch. Without a word, he covered her body with his and anchored their hips together. When he found her wet, he entered her with a powerful thrust, joining their bodies, embedding himself in her heat to the hilt.

Their coupling was fast and rough. Neither had the patience or the desire for slow lovemaking. Instead, it was reassurance that they were both still alive, that despite what they'd each been through since they'd seen each other last, they still fit—the passion still sparked. Griffin wasn't so far gone that she couldn't still feel, that she couldn't still live. Relief coursed through them both along with the passion and the lust. They arched together, their bodies moving, clawing their way up the cliff of pleasure.

With a strangled cry, Griffin flung herself over it, her eyes closing tightly, her body arching, spasming, and clenching Braxton tightly. He stroked into her three more times before joining her, his body collapsing onto hers, her arms coming around him to hold him, their breath coming in short, shallow gasps, and their grips on each other tighter than necessary.

When their breathing had returned to normal, Braxton sat up, grabbing the blanket from the back of the couch to drape over their naked bodies. He lifted her legs into his lap and ran his hand over her calf familiarly, almost reverently.

"I didn't abandon you." He said it so softly she almost missed it.

Griffin chose not to say anything, sensing that he wasn't done.

"Those were my friends. I thought it was safe. Even when Sam called me and told me Azazel was out, I didn't think things would happen like they did. You're right. It is my fault that Finn is dead. By the time they let Azazel out, I was stuck. We were trapped and being picked off. I couldn't have left if I'd wanted to. I wanted to come back to relieve Sam. The last thing I wanted was for her to terminate her pregnancy. She and Finn wanted kids badly, and for it to happen when it did seems like a cruel twist.

"When she called to tell me about Azazel, I'd just lost every person I'd been working with. I'd snuck out of the house we were holed up in to try and distract the demons long enough for us to escape. It was dangerous and stupid, but we were desperate. If we'd stayed, we'd have all gotten killed eventually. There were more of them than I'd ever seen in a single place. I got almost to their headquarters when I heard the explosion. By the time I got back, they were all dead. For the rest of my life, I'll never forget the smell of their bodies burning. I tried to find them, but all I ever found was pieces."

Griffin reached out and laid her hand on top of his, offering him her strength. Tears welled in her eyes and she used her other hand to brush them away. Still, she remained silent, knowing Braxton well enough to be sure he needed to do the talking.

"I blamed myself. I was convinced that I could have stopped it if I'd gotten there sooner, if I'd done more, if I hadn't left. A thousand ways I was the reason they were dead. I was drinking myself into oblivion and couldn't even bring myself to think about coming back here and taking over. Griffin, you need to know I didn't stay away because I wanted to. I stayed away because I was in no shape to take care of you. I believed with all my heart that Sam and Finn would be able to handle it. I was afraid I would get you killed. I was grieving and guilty and feeling a lot of things I didn't want to let myself feel. I was no good for you. At least, I didn't think

I could be any good for you." Braxton sighed and pulled his hands from under hers. He ran his hands through his hair and sat up on the couch, putting distance between their bodies for the first time. "You're not going to like this next part."

Griffin smiled reassuringly. "Tell me, anyway."

"The last time I talked to Sam, after we got off the phone, a girl came over. Looking back, I should have seen it for what it was as soon as she stopped at my table. An American tourist, a young woman, and I wanted to bury it. I took her to my hotel. I won't get into the gory details, but I spent the night with her. By the next morning, it became quite clear that she wasn't who she'd told me she was. It was Lilith. She tied me to the bed, and Beelzebub came in. They tortured me, trying to get your location out of me. I knew Sam and Finn were moving you—I thought you'd be safe if I just kept my mouth shut. The longer they were distracted by me, the longer Sam and Finn had to hide you—to keep you safe. I don't know exactly how long I was there. Days, weeks, a couple of months—I really couldn't tell you if I tried. Eventually, I lost track of what I was telling them. My high school locker combination, the phone numbers of everyone in my cell phone, all the stories my mother told me to get me to go to sleep when I was little. I don't really know how long I was left alone before Gabriel came in. He cut me loose, told me where to find you, told me about Sam, and left in a snap."

Griffin grabbed his hands and squeezed them, her heart constricting at the thought of what he had gone through. He returned the squeeze absently, still wrapped up in his story.

"I went home and dragged my sister, basically kicking and screaming, from an abortion clinic. She was determined to terminate and find you to finish this. If I'd been thirty minutes later, it would have been over. Once she was done chewing my ass, she booted me out of her house with instructions to find you and bring you home. We've still got a few months left to get through, and no offense, Griffin, but you can't do it alone. Both because you don't know the ins and outs of this life and because I won't let you. I'm as in this as you are now, and I promise you, I won't leave again. From now until midnight on December thirty-first, it's you and me. I will keep you safe. I will keep you alive."

Griffin turned her head to look at him, her eyes troubled. "Are you sure?"

"I am positive." Braxton took her hand in both of his. "You are not alone, Griffin. You won't be alone for any of this from now on."

"Then I think there's something I need to tell you." She shifted uncomfortably. "Alaria came to me before I got here. The night that Finn died. She told me to find out about her, to find out why she did what she did when she was cast out."

"You can't trust a Devil. You know she's a liar."

Slowly, she nodded, biting her lip nervously. "I went to Father Dooley in Philadelphia. He told me about a priest here who specializes in Alaria. That's why I came here in the first place. I talked to him when I got here and he told me some things that surprised me."

Curious, Braxton sat up and rubbed his hands over his face, fighting off fatigue. "What did you find out?"

Griffin struggled to decide whether to tell him about the visit from Michael. Finally, she decided to stick to what the priest had told her. "She didn't join Lucifer because she wanted to overthrow God. According to the priest, she joined because she wanted free will. She wanted to choose to be human, to live as she saw fit instead of obeying every whim of God. Lucifer promised her that if he won, he would let her have the choice. He lied to her, and when he was defeated, God cast her out with the rest of them. It didn't matter why she fought, only that she had. She said I could do something for her that no one else can and that if I'd agree to her terms, she'd make sure I got to the Choosing in one piece."

"You believe her?"

"I didn't. Not until I talked to the priest. All I've ever heard about Alaria is that she's selfish. She wants what is best for herself. Beelzebub, Azazel and Lilith are all involved in this now. That puts her at the bottom of the food chain again. Now she sees a way out. Whatever it is she thinks I can do, it's obviously worth enough to her to risk the wrath of the other Devils."

"She wants to win more than she wants you to Choose Lucifer."

"That's my take on it. If that means switching sides in the middle of things to ensure that she gets what she wants, then that's what she'll do. I asked Gabriel about her when I got to your sister's house, and he told me that she's more interested in herself than the Choosing and that it would be interesting to see what she decided to do. That, added to what she said, and to what I found out from the priest makes me think that she's for real on this. For whatever reason, she thinks I have something she wants more than she wants for me to scream out Satan's name when I shove that knife in my chest."

Braxton mulled it over for a moment. "You're sure you can trust this priest?"

"No. But I'm sure I can trust Gabriel the Archangel. If anyone has a vested interest in me doing what I'm going to do in December, it's him. I think that if he thought Alaria was yanking my chain, he'd have come to me. Or he'd be here now. I know they watch. I can feel them sometimes. Both of them when I sleep. Gabriel when I'm awake. The fact that he hasn't come to tell me that it's a supremely bad idea tells me a lot."

"What do you want to do?"

"I want to find out what she wants. I want to know the price of her protection. Whatever she wants, it's going to be huge. Someone like her, she's not doing this out of the goodness of her heart. She's going to want something big from me. I need to know what it is, so that I can decide if the price is something I'm willing to pay."

Both looked when they heard a rustling in the corner and saw Alaria materialize, resplendent in her typical leather, her hair swirling around her face. "Well then, let's talk shop, shall we?"

Chapter Twenty-Four

BRAXTON, MORE uncomfortable than he could remember being in a long time, placed three steaming cups on the table. "I don't even know if you drink coffee, or drink at all, but here you go."

Alaria couldn't help the smile that bent the corners of her mouth, genuine humor softening the hard lines of her face, making her look close to human. "We can. Most prefer not to, but there are those of us that like human food and drink. Generally, I'm not one of them. But the gesture is appreciated."

"I was getting some for us anyway." He sat down next to Griffin, between her and the Devil, so that he could protect her were Alaria to try anything. The placement wasn't lost on either woman, and both respected it, albeit for very different reasons.

Griffin wrapped her hands around the mug and stared into the black liquid. "What's the deal? What do you think I can give you?"

"I don't *think* you can give me anything. I *know* you can give me what I want. I was there when God and Lucifer made their deal, when they arranged this party we're in the middle of. I know the details unlike anyone else. Aside from Gabriel, of course." She sighed in slight annoyance. "I know you're here, Angel, so you might as well stop lurking and join the conversation."

Moments later, Gabriel appeared in a cloud of soft white light. He brushed imaginary lint from his always pristine white suit and chose a seat across the table from Alaria. "I can't participate. You know that. I'm bound from disclosing any more information than I already have."

"That doesn't mean you can't assure her I'm not lying, and talk about it once it's out in the open. Bend the rules, Gabe. It's not the same as breaking them."

Braxton held up a hand. "Wait a second. You're an Angel. You're on the other side of this. Yet here you are sitting at a table with a Devil, discussing this over a cup of coffee like it's Sunday afternoon gossip. What the hell is going on here?"

Gabriel looked down. "I don't have a cup of coffee, actually. Though I would love one, if you have some milk and sugar." He shrugged when Braxton and Griffin both gaped at him. "We can taste. We can eat, sleep, and do anything that you do. Over time, I've developed an affinity for some human sustenance. It's not necessary, of course, but there's some psychological comfort in it for you, seeing us behave as you do."

Shaking his head, Braxton poured another cup and sat it in front of Gabriel. "One of you, please talk."

Alaria nodded. "I'll start. He can nod his head in agreement until it's all on the table so he doesn't break any of his precious rules. You already know this part of it, but I'll tell it to you anyway. In the beginning, when Lucifer took up arms against God, he came to me, asking me to join with him. I told him no that time. I wanted more, and I set out to get it. It was no secret in Heaven that I wasn't content. I loved being on Earth, walking with the humans. It'll burn Angel's here's ears," She waved her arm at Gabriel with a small smile, "But I even enjoyed taking human lovers. I liked to immerse myself in their culture, their religions, their families. As an Angel, we got far fewer choices. It was part of the price we paid for being in Heaven, for being the chosen ones who were allowed to gaze upon His face. It was a great honor and a great privilege, but one that I thought we should be able to choose to take or to reject. I always felt, deep inside, that I was meant to be more than a pawn—that I was meant to do more than serve. I asked Him to let me Fall. I wanted to go to Earth and never return." For a moment, Alaria's eyes grew wistful as she remembered. "I'll never forget that moment. God put his hand on my head, looked into my eyes, and told me I was more than they were, that I had a place next to Him for eternity, and that my place was there. He turned me down flat."

Gabriel huffed. "Being one of us is an honor no human can fathom. You were stupid to want anything else."

"That's your opinion. Not mine. It's not the point. After God told me no, I went to Gabriel and begged him to come with me. He refused, and left me broken. Lucifer came to me then, and made me a promise. He promised that if he won, if he triumphed over God and took over Heaven, that he would make me human. That he would send me to Earth to live a human life and forget I'd ever existed. I wanted those seventy or so years to do whatever I wanted. After that, I'd go where humans went. I'd live their afterlife, whatever that was. Before the split, everyone went to Paradise. There was no Hell, and Heaven was only for the Angels. The Battle changed everything. God knew why I was fighting. I didn't care about who ruled, or what happened. I wanted to be free. When the hammer came down and Lucifer was defeated, I got punished with the rest of them, just because I fought, with no care for the reason. I ended up in Hell with the rest of them. I won't lie—not this time at least. I learned to love it. Torturing people, eating their souls, and doing what Devils do the best. I did it all. I was good at it. I was bitter and angry, and most of all, I was hurt. That made me more dangerous than almost anyone else down there. When God and Lucifer met to decide what happened next, Lucifer took me with him. He wanted to take advantage of all of those emotions I had."

Gabriel cleared his throat. "I don't agree with her decision, with wanting to Fall. I certainly don't condone anything that she's done since. Nothing she's said thus far is untrue."

Griffin and Braxton exchanged a look. Braxton nodded slightly, accepting that working with Alaria was the right decision. Griffin spoke. "Why did you torture me? Why did you do all that you did?"

"I wanted to win. I wanted to prove that I was better at being evil than Gabriel was at being divine. My Father chained me in Hell! Left me to burn with all of them that wanted to overthrow Him. He knew why I'd done it, and He looked at me like the rest of them. Like I was no different than Lucifer and Beelzebub, like I was just like Lilith. I wasn't."

"That's where we disagree. You did the same as they did. You killed Angels and you joined with Lucifer. The reasons don't matter. You know that. You knew what the punishment would be, and you chose to follow."

Alaria sighed and took several deep breaths to get herself back under control. "We could argue over this for millennia and never agree on it. This is not the point. Griffin, when we all met to figure out how humanity was going to end, it was a very complicated process. Hell hadn't been contemplated; He hadn't planned for what happened. Humans were never meant to have an expiration date. They're like an ant colony for us—fun to watch and a never ending source of entertainment. Once there was Heaven and Hell, Lucifer wanted his cut of the souls. Pardon the pun, but the Devils' share, to use a phrase you both know. Once there were two places, it became another choice for humans to make with their infernal free will.

"They decided that every person ever born would have a chance to decide for themselves, when they were old enough to understand the brevity of the situation. Even we didn't want to torture babies and the mentally ill. If you couldn't understand, you automatically got a pass into Heaven. Commit suicide, straight to us. Die to save someone else, go directly to the pearly gates. Have a heart attack fucking your mistress, well, you're my piece of ass now. That wasn't good enough for Lucifer. He wanted a chance to get them all. God refused to let the entire human race be judged on the choices they make daily. He gave them free will, not expecting that Hell would ever exist, so He refused to damn them to us just because they chose not to follow Him right then. He wanted to give everyone the chance to choose Him up until their last breath. So, they compromised and came up with the Choosing. That way Lucifer gets his shot. Kind of. If you pick him, they get a million years to try and convince people to sin, without the counterbalance of Angels. Choose Heaven, get the opposite. Choose neither, or die before you get there, and there's an in-between. The Apocalypse. Fire and brimstone, the Anti-Christ, seven plagues, seven years of suffering, and the Final Judgment. Lucifer gets a short time to play, but everyone gets judged on their individual merits. It was a sort of compromise between the two.

"God didn't like just letting you suffer for thirty years without hope. He didn't like not being able to help you, to live in your heart the way He does in the heart of every other man, woman, and child. He decided to give you a gift. Not as incentive for Choosing Heaven, because that wouldn't be fair, and well, Lucifer has a goody bag set up for you as well, so it's pretty equal that way, too, but to show you after the end how much you did mean. He decided to let you do what no one has ever been able to do before. He allows you to demand of Him one thing. Whatever you want. The only thing you can't do is mess with free will. This is so big, He would even let you rescue someone from Hell if that's what you wanted. I want that favor. That's the price of my help. When you Choose, when God asks you what boon you would like for doing this great thing...I want you to demand my life."

Gabriel's coffee cup hit the table with a loud crack. "You can't be serious."

"As a heart attack. It's been millions of years, but what I want has not changed. I wanted to punish God for what He did, for sending me there. That's why Lucifer gave this to me. Beelzebub interfered, and I don't like that. The more they interfered, the more I thought, and the angrier I got." Alaria smiled sharply. "It's easy to let yourself forget things when it seems like there's no way out. I had to survive, and I learned to enjoy what I've done. I won't ever apologize for it. You're not Choosing Hell, and if you don't, I'm going to the pit. So, you see, I need you as much as you need me. I'll keep you alive and you keep me out of the pit. I want to be human. Or to go back."

"He'll never let you back in."

"Yes, He will. Because He can't tell her no." She laid her hands on the table, palms up. "That's the deal. I'll do whatever I need to do to keep you safe, and you give me your favor."

Gabriel shook his head. "This is absurd. To even suggest that God would let you into Heaven, to become an Angel again. You have gall, I'll give you that."

"I don't want my wings. I want a heart that beats. If He won't do that, I'll settle for the wings. I never wanted to be an Angel, but it's infinitely better than being a Devil that's going to end up chained to the bottom of the Lake of Fire. My existence as I know it is over. The only thing left to figure out is if it continues as a human, with a soul to be judged at the end like everyone else, or if it ends with me in that pit."

Griffin looked up, her eyes wide. "What happens if I say no?"

"Frankly, I keep trying to kill you. I'm not a person, Griffin. I'm a Devil. I'm not nice. I'm not your friend. We need each other. It is in my and your best interest to do this. If you say no, I have no reason to keep you alive."

Gabriel sighed in resignation. "Alaria is not bound by the same rules that I am. She was given much more freedom. Every human born is born with a soul created by God, which makes them more likely to end up in Heaven than in Hell. In order to make you a blank canvas, she was given a lot more leeway to interact with you, to strip you of that. I've been bound in what I can tell you, or show you, and what I can do. I can tell you this. I told you before that there were things about her that might come to light throughout this process. It seems that I was right, and for once, my confidence in her was not misplaced. Do it, Griffin."

Before she could even open her mouth to ask a single question, the Angel disappeared the same way he'd appeared. Griffin took several deep breaths and lifted her eyes to meet Alaria's gaze. "You two used to be friends?"

Alaria's eyes darkened with grief very briefly. "Once upon a time we were much more than friends." She shook her head briskly. "I'll want a contract, of course. If you renege on our deal, I'll own your soul. A contract for your soul is the only thing that can override your trip to Heaven when you Choose."

"Could I use my favor to come back to life?"

"Yes, you could. You can ask anything."

Braxton gripped Griffin's hand hard. "Then you have to do that. You have to choose to live."

Griffin leaned over and braced her head against Braxton's. "Can you guarantee me I'll still be alive on my birthday? One hundred percent, can you guarantee me that?"

Braxton sighed deeply. "You know I will do everything in my power to keep you alive. But no, I can't guarantee it for absolute sure. No one can."

Alaria shook her head. "That's where you're wrong. I can. I can get you through to the Choosing. You have to decide, Griffin. Is a guarantee that you'll make it, that you'll save the human race, worth your life? Or do you want to take your chances on not making it, not getting to ask for anything, and starting the End of Days? What's your choice?"

Griffin dashed away tears. "I don't have a choice. I'll do it."

Alaria, in a gesture more for show than for function, snapped her fingers. A piece of parchment and a pen appeared on the table. "Here's our agreement. Read it over."

Griffin read the paper and found it surprisingly simple. Alaria would guarantee her survival to the Choosing. In exchange, Griffin guaranteed to ask for Alaria's humanity as her one favor from God. If she didn't do so, Alaria got her soul. No fine print; no hidden terms. Just four lines explaining everything they had talked about. It was painfully, tragically simple.

"What do I need to do?"

"Take the pen and sign it."

Griffin picked up the pen and put it to the paper. There was a sharp pain, and she watched in awe as her blood flowed through the pen and out onto the paper. The pen signed her name on its own accord, her signature appearing perfectly on the paper. When it was done, the paper burst into flames and disappeared. She turned her hand over, looking for a cut, and was surprised when she didn't see anything.

"It doesn't leave a wound. The contract draws blood directly from the heart. It's the purest blood in the human body. This protects us both. If there's one thing folklore got right, it's that a Devil can't renege on a contract."

Braxton cleared the coffee cups, a not so subtle sign that the meeting was coming to a close. "What now? How exactly are you going to protect her?"

"I'm not. That is your job. What I am going to do is keep the Three Stooges off your trail. I'll lead them in other directions, plant false trails, and try to buy you some time. When it's time to finally run for the sacred place, then I'll join you. If need be, I'll fight. In the meantime, I'm going to do a bit of digging. It might take a while, because they are keeping a fairly close watch on me. I know that there are ways to extend the life of the protections around the place that Gabriel prepared." She rolled her eyes and chuckled. "I wonder if he really believes I don't know about that." She shook her head. "That's of no consequence. Simply, stay here. Stay under the radar, and don't do anything to draw attention. If they get close, I'll warn you beforehand. Pay attention to your dreams. That's the easiest way for me to get ahold of you."

Before either Griffin or Braxton could respond, Alaria was gone in a flash of flame and lightning. For several long minutes, neither of them moved and neither of them spoke. Finally, Braxton held out a hand.

"Let's go."

"Where?"

"Up to bed. It's late, and we're both tired."

"That's it? You don't have anything to say?"

"There's nothing to say, Griffin. We've done what we had to do. We both know the Choosing is the most important thing that there is, and we both owe a duty to get there to complete it. If that means giving up your chance to keep living, then that's what you have to do." He tugged her to her feet. "Tonight doesn't change anything. It just gives us a clearer path to the end. No one knew that you could ask before fifteen minutes ago, and the hope was over as soon as it was there. No use dwelling on it."

Chapter Twenty-Five

September 25th, 2029, Melbourne, Australia

It became obvious within a few days that Sam hadn't lied when she'd told Braxton that Griffin was slowly wasting away. She barely ate, spent most of her time walking on the beach, and barely took time to brush her hair or change out of her pajamas. The few times she'd let him put his hands on her, he had noticed how much more her ribs protruded through her skin.

All efforts he made to get her to eat were met with a blank stare, and he hadn't heard her laugh in days. Even her eyes were getting darker, sinking into her face and becoming dull, almost flat, as if she wasn't there at all.

Every morning, Braxton would carry a cup of coffee to the back deck and watch Griffin walk through the sand. Sometimes, she laid in the sun; other times she would splash in the water or throw a ball for the neighbor's dog that would race down to join her. A couple times she disappeared for hours, and just as he started to worry, she appeared with bags full of odds and ends from the market: a collar for her canine buddy, a shirt for Braxton, and a colorful scarf she mailed to Sam. Once, she'd even shown up with a horse, and had spent hours cooing to the large animal, riding up and down the beach, taking it into the water, leaning down over its neck and holding on, her hands tangled in its mane. Each day, the sight became even more heartbreaking.

Braxton had spent time trying to research what was happening to her, and to the best of his knowledge, it was a built-in safety feature. Her soul was literally loosening itself from her body. Her hold on reality, on humanity and mortality, was slipping. It was a measure meant to make what she had to do easier. The less human she felt, the easier it would be to let go, to let herself move on. To Braxton, that seemed almost as horrible as what she was being forced to do—to rob her of the last few months she had to ensure she would Choose. It was insult on top of injury.

Sighing deeply, he walked to the kitchen for another cup of coffee and headed down the narrow path leading from the house to the beach, briefly wishing he'd remembered a jacket for some protection against the cold breeze. Griffin sat on a blanket, a cream sweater hanging on her small frame, her sweatpant-clad-knees drawn up to her chest and her arms wrapped around them. Her hair was loose and blowing in the wind, tangling from the unforgiving fingers raking through it.

"You should come in, get something to eat." Braxton dropped easily next to her and handed her one of the mugs he carried. "I'll make you some toast."

"No, thanks. I'm not hungry." Griffin turned her head and offered him a weak smile. "You never come down here."

"Felt like getting out of the house a little." He tugged on the blanket and draped it around both of them, easily lifting her to sit between his legs so that he could wrap his arms around her in addition to the blanket. "We need to think about leaving. You've been here for six weeks. I've been here for more than three. It's only a matter of time before they find us, and it might be the best thing to have some distance on them. It'll take us a while to get off this island and back to somewhere safe."

Griffin shook her head. "We have time. I'd know if we didn't. I want to stay. I like it here."

"You know we can't stay forever."

"I know. A few more days won't hurt. We'd know if they were close." She leaned back into him, taking some comfort in the warmth of his body, wishing that it could completely thaw the chill that had seeped into her bones. "Everything seems far away when we're here. When we go home, back to the States, it's more real. It's where this started, where I went through all of those things. I don't want to have to face the end yet."

"You don't have to face it yet. What we have to face right now is survival. Nothing has changed from February till now. Don't think about the days, the hours, the weeks that you have left. Worry about today. We have to worry about being safe, as safe as possible each night when we lay down to go to sleep. I don't think that place is here. Escape is difficult, the airport is a long drive, and there's no other place to go. There's no other means of escape unless we sprout fins and swim."

Griffin turned her head and rubbed her nose on his throat, making him smile at the sweet gesture. "When it happens—when I have to do it, I don't want to be alone."

Braxton rubbed her arms briskly to get the blood flowing again. "Don't worry about that. I'm here with you every step of the way." He sighed as they watched the waves roll onto the sand. "I'm sorry, Griffin. So damn sorry that you have to do this."

"Better me than some mother of four from Tuscaloosa or something. There's no one I'm leaving behind. I don't have any family. My mother tried to cut me from her stomach, and my father carved them both to pieces. The only one who can guarantee that I get to Choose is the one who took them away from me, who took my grandparents, who arranged for me to lose my virginity by being raped. I have a seventeen-year-old son, Braxton. A son. I'm someone's mother. I never even held him. I was a whore. A drug addict."

"You know that was done because of this. That's not who you are, it's what happened to you. We both know if you would have gotten attached to that baby, she'd have made you have a miscarriage. You cannot blame yourself for this."

"I don't anymore. People get dealt bad hands every day. They overcome it. I didn't. Not until Gabriel came to me. Brax, I'm dying. A little at a time, day after day. I can feel it. It gets easier to imagine. Most days, when I'm down here, I just daydream. In my head, I can live a different life." She smiled and leaned back against him. "Would we be together, if I wasn't the Chosen?"

Braxton shook his head. "No. You'd be married with a house full of kids. You'd never even know that demons exist." He kissed her cheek. "I wish you'd never had to meet me, Griffin. I would gladly give you up in a heartbeat if it meant you got to die an old woman surrounded by her kids."

"And here I'm thankful that I got to be happy for a while, no matter how short." Griffin was silent for a while, contemplating. Finally, with a light in her eyes that he hadn't seen since before he'd left her with Sam and Finn, she turned and looked up at him. "Did you get the feeling that there was something going on between Gabriel and Alaria?"

Braxton considered that, thinking back to the night Griffin had signed the deal with the Devil. "Not now. But before? Yeah, I think there was something."

"Angels can fall in love?"

"I don't think it's that simple. Everything we know about them says that they're supposed to be better than humans. That they were made to sit up in Heaven with God and do nothing other than worship. They don't have nearly the free will that we do. Obviously they have some, but I don't get the feeling that romance would have been tolerated."

"I think I'd like them both better if they were together. Star crossed lovers and all, separated on different sides of a battle, desperately in love and fighting for what they believe, even though it's different." She laughed wryly. "That would make it too human, wouldn't it? Trying to describe what must be going on there."

Braxton chuckled, his breath warm on her neck. "It's a nice thought. I think I'd like them better that way, too. They're opposites, aren't they? Alaria is sin. Gabriel is literally a saint. Both of us would trust them more if we saw a little of the other in them."

"I think I trust Alaria more. Her motives are at least honest. She's looking out for herself, and she can't get what she wants if she betrays us. Gabriel is just following orders. He doesn't have an interest in this, and that makes me nervous."

"I think his interest is not getting punished. If there's one thing Christianity teaches us, it's that God doesn't tolerate failure well. He wiped out Earth, burned cities to the ground, cast out half His Angels. He has endless patience with most of us, but those He's chosen to lead? It's fail and die."

Griffin nodded, considering that. "Regardless, I can relate to the self-preservation thing Alaria has going on. I think I understand her. She was forced into this just as much as I was. In a different way, because of something she did, but she did a bad thing for the right reason. That has to count for something, doesn't it?"

"Your human insistence on understanding everything is a source of eternal amusement and annoyance."

Griffin and Braxton were on their feet in a heartbeat, Braxton shoving Griffin behind him before they were even really sure who it was that had appeared. When they saw Alaria, they relaxed slightly, and Griffin poked her head out, offering a slight smile."If it helps, we were saying good things."

"That doesn't matter. You need to get back to the house and get packing. Lilith and Azazel will be here in a matter of hours. Beelzebub has found a witch that can locate people anywhere in the world. It will take her some time to do it, but that time is not indefinite. I will deal with her, but it has to be close enough to the Choosing that we can safely leave to go to the site."

"I haven't had any dreams."

"Because you haven't been truly sleeping. In order for you to see, you have to rest. You've been dozing for only a few minutes at a time. It's not enough to make the connection onto the dream plane. I haven't even been able to reach you. I've taken a big risk coming here, but I couldn't let them surprise you. Get packed and ready to go." She waved them in front of her, looking around nervously. "How long do you need?"

Braxton, his smile from mere minutes earlier already replaced with a look of steely determination, opened the door to the house and let both women in. "Thirty minutes."

"I'll wait with you. If you hear me yell for you to run, you go. Do not ask questions, do not hesitate, you go."

"You said hours."

"It's a guess, Griffin. If the witch is better than anticipated, it could be in an instant. If they suspect me, they've followed me here and we're being watched. I don't sense anything, but I don't often visit Earth. I don't know precisely what to look for." She grabbed a duffel bag from the closet. "I'll take care of your clothes. Pack what you need."

Griffin went to the bathroom and began haphazardly throwing things into a bag. "Are you going to tell me what happened between you and Gabriel?"

"It's a long story. One that spans millennia."

"Cliffs notes version?"
 "We weren't lovers, if that's what you're hoping for. We were friends, companions. We walked together and talked. When we needed to, we watched over Earth together. Right before the Fall, I told him that my feelings for him were more human than they were Angelic. He returned them, but by then, we were on opposite sides of a very deep abyss. Neither of us could cross it even if we had wanted to. When the Battle ended, Gabriel was given the task of chaining me to Hell. It was a punishment for both of us. Me for my actions in the Battle, and Gabriel for feeling what he wasn't supposed to feel. We weren't allowed to have human emotion, and God made sure Gabe knew not to allow it to happen again."

"He doesn't sound very nice."

"God is wonderful and amazing and everything you think He should be. He is forgiveness and miracles and wonder. There is nothing He cannot do, other than interrupt free will, and nothing He will not forgive. There are times when He is as merciless as He can be merciful. He is jealous and sometimes bloodthirsty. Humans were modeled in His image, and Angels, in their true forms, are ugly and frightening. Everything you learn in Sunday school about repenting and Heaven and God hurting, it's all true. He is complicated and complex, but the one thing that is unwavering is His love. He knows what you can be and what you can do. For humans, He is everything you would ever want. He expects more of his soldiers. We're an army, there to do His bidding, and He punishes us as a human leader would. To disobey is unforgivable for us. Gabe is still trying to earn His forgiveness back."

"Can he?"

"If he gets you through this, I imagine that will do it. That was another part of his punishment. Doing this, and seeing what I had become. A constant reminder of what we once had." Alaria sighed and shook her head. "It's a wonderfully horrible life. You take the good with the bad and obey, or else. For the vast majority of them, it's all they could ever want."

"Why do you want to be human?"

Alaria considered that for a long minute while she packed Griffin's clothes. "Grass is always greener, I suppose. I want to know what all the fuss is about. I want to have choices, to eat and drink and sleep, and to feel my heart race when I run. Senses are dulled when you're angelic or demonic. You can't feel sensation as well. That's why you always find demons having sex or torturing. Those are some of the most powerful sensations out there, and we only get the watered down version. It was supposed to keep us from wanting the real thing, to make it less appealing. For me, it had the opposite effect. It made me want it more. I still want it."

"Do you have a soul?"

Alaria laughed. "Good God, no. None of us do, no matter which side of Heaven you're on. A soul is a completely human condition." She zipped up the bag efficiently and slung it over her shoulder. "Enough chatting. Let's get moving."

"I should hate you."

"You do hate me. It's just covered up with needing me. That's why you're trying to find something to like with this conversation. You want to believe that there's some good in me. That's very human of you."

Braxton came in from the kitchen, his phone to his ear and a gun in the waistband of his jeans. He looked at Griffin quizzically, the question in his eyes obvious. Ready to go?

She nodded slightly and picked up the bag Alaria had set down. He waited another minute before snapping his phone closed. "Tickets are booked. We just have to get to the airport."

"Where are we going?"

"Argentina, for now. I have friends throughout South America that will hide us for a few more weeks. We can travel up through Mexico and back into the States when we're ready. More places to hide in the jungle."

Alaria stiffened, her eyes going dark. She blurred to the window, cursing. "They're here. All three of them. It took less time than I had hoped." She shook her head when Braxton removed his gun from its place. "No. There's no fighting them—you know that." She swore again. "They had to find out what I'd done sooner or later, I suppose. Come here. I can transport you to where you need to go. I'm going to make several stops and drop you off randomly. Once you're there, run as fast as you can and get safe. They'll follow my trail."

"Will they kill you?"

The Devil smiled: a cold, violent smile that reminded them all of what she was capable of. "They'll have to find me first." She waited a breath for them to grab the bags and then gripped each one of them with one hand. "Hold on."

The sensation was like being ripped apart and snapped back together over and over. Only each time Alaria jerked them through space, there wasn't even time to breathe before she took them again. There was no stopping it, no recovering, nothing but intense agony. Whether the trip lasted for a second or an hour, there was no way to tell. They would surface for a brief moment, then be jerked back in. Each time, it took a heartbeat longer, until it became evident that transporting them through space was taking all of Alaria's strength.

Finally, they were deposited in the middle of a busy street in a dusty town, where Spanish rolled over them in rapid fire. Braxton was on his feet in an instant, dragging Griffin from the spot where they'd landed, shoving her down the street, into buildings, across cobblestone streets, and through alleys so narrow that they could only fit down them single-file. They hadn't spoken for the better part of an hour when Braxton tersely told her to wait in the shadows while he ducked into a store for supplies. When he emerged ten minutes later, three bags in his hands, he offered her a tight smile.

"I've been here before. We're in Peru. This is a bit further north than I wanted to start, but it'll do. There's a hotel that I always use this way. The woman who owns it is a very talented witch, and her protections will help shield us. Add our own protections on top of it, and we'll be safe for a bit. Long enough to recover from that trip and to make a plan."

Griffin nodded and pushed off of the wall she had been leaning against. "Alaria risked her life for us."

"Because she needs you to stay alive. Don't mistake this for her being like us, or her being your friend. She's not our friend. We're working with her because there is no other choice."

"Doesn't change the fact that she could die because she helped us. Kinda defeats the purpose of getting something from me if she's dead."

Braxton acknowledged the point with a nod and dragged her down yet another alley. "We need to get safe. We can argue about Alaria later." He led her through the streets, dodging people and vehicles until they came to a small hotel far from the hub of the city. Braxton spoke in rapid Spanish, exchanging money for a key with very little fanfare.

Griffin waited until they were in the threadbare room before speaking. "Do you know people everywhere?"

"Most places, anyway. Alaria isn't stupid. She's likely studied me, so she knows where my haunts are. She's nothing if not thorough. Let's just hope that the other three aren't as interested in me." He tossed the bags on the bed and began unpacking bundles of herbs and boxes of salt. Without a word, Griffin grabbed the salt and began lining the window and the door.

"How are we going to get home?"

Braxton looked up from sewing herbs into the pillows. "What do you mean?"

"We left all our stuff. No money. I don't even know how you bought all this stuff."

"Griffin, this is my job." He chuckled. "I'm used to this sort of thing. Having to run suddenly. I have contingencies in place all over the world to cover me if I need them. I'll have to go to a bank, but we'll be fine. The Vatican has a great expense account for stuff like this."

Griffin sighed and sat down. "The place Gabriel told me about where we'll be protected. It only lasts a week, so there's no way we can go there now. I know Alaria thinks that you can extend the life of the protections there, but how much more time can it possibly buy us?"

"I'm hoping we'll get a full month. That way we only have to get to Thanksgiving before we can go."

"That's only six weeks." Griffin fell back on the bed, the enormity of that finally hitting her. "Two and a half months and I'll be dead."

Braxton finished the protections and dropped down next to her. "Yeah, and it sucks. What you've been doing to yourself is even worse. You're acting as if you're already dead. You've been sitting on that beach, letting yourself slip away for weeks. You're not dead yet. We have to keep you safe, but that doesn't mean we can't try to help you. What do you want to do? What's on the bucket list?"

She couldn't help the smile that forced its way out. "I don't have one. I've spent my whole life trying to just get by. All of the stuff that she did to me, I was always just barely hanging on."

"Live a little now. We can travel the world the next few weeks. It's not a vacation, but we can go almost anywhere. You want to see Italy—we'll get on a plane. Always wanted to visit the Eiffel Tower? Well, France is nice in the fall." He gripped her face in his hands. "Today, with Alaria, running just now, it's the most life I've seen out of you since I got to Australia. Everyone dies. You're dying fifty years sooner than you should, and in a horrible way. I would do anything in my power to keep that from happening if I could. Watching you sacrifice yourself is going to be the hardest thing I have ever had to do. Dammit, Griffin, watching you commit suicide right in front of me before you have to is even worse."

Surprising them both, she leaned over and kissed him. For once, her mouth was hot and active instead of unresponsive as it had been. She pushed him back onto the bed, climbing on top of him and fusing her mouth to his. His hands slid up her back, tangling in her hair, and he rolled her beneath him so that he could press her body into the mattress. He let one hand drift down her body, brushing the curve of her breast. When her breath rushed out on a moan, he smiled.

There had been no time to change, so she still wore the baggy sweatshirt and sweatpants she'd had on when he'd walked down to see her on the beach. With one practiced movement, he stripped the shirt over her head and tossed it to the floor. He kissed the curve of her throat and the slope of her shoulder down to the gentle rise of her breast. When her back arched and her eyes drifted closed, he gave her what she wanted and took the tip into his mouth, sucking strongly, relishing the flavor of her skin, slightly salty from the sea air they'd been in, and warm from the Peruvian sun.

Braxton had taken Griffin to bed every time that she would allow it.

He always made love to her gently, worshipping her body, making sure that, at least for a few moments, she forgot everything except what he was capable of making her feel. This time, however, was markedly different.

Their coupling was urgent and frenzied. Clothing was tossed to the floor, hands wandered, and Griffin, for the first time, took a leading role, teasing him with her mouth and hands, giving back some of the pleasure that he had given to her. She leaned over the side of the bed and fished his wallet from the pocket of his jeans. She flipped it open and withdrew the single condom inside.

"We're gonna need to get more of these."

Braxton groaned as her little hands unrolled the latex over him. "Top of the to-do list."

Griffin chuckled and rose onto her knees. She slid on top of him, taking his hands and placing them on her hips, using one hand to guide him into her body. When she sank down, taking him in fully, they both groaned.

She rode him hard and fast, rocking her hips against his, driving them both to orgasm. Her back arched, offering her breasts to him. He devoured her skin, nipping with his teeth before soothing with his tongue. Her hair streamed down her back, her eyes closed in ecstasy. When she finally soared over the edge, her gasp was ragged and harsh. Her body clenched him tightly, yanking a strangled moan from his core as Braxton followed her into release.

Braxton only left briefly to obtain additional protection before returning to the hotel, and to Griffin. Every time they finished, it was almost as if he was pulling her back to him. They slept in short spurts, their bodies aching for one another.

He left once to bring back food, and they ate naked on the bed. Griffin laughed, teased, and was happier than he could remember seeing her. Thanking God for the brief reprieve from her oppressive fear and dejection, Braxton didn't give her a single opportunity to remember the obstacles facing them.

Finally, as the sky lightened from the sun coming up, they collapsed into an exhausted slumber. Griffin settled her head against the solid plane of Braxton's chest, the sound of his heartbeat lulling her to follow him into the cool black that was the sleep of the exhausted. She turned her head to press a kiss to his chest as her eyes drifted shut.

"I love you."

Chapter Twenty-Six

October 23rd, 2029 - Pennsylvania

Braxton looked over at Griffin as he drove, her head leaning uncomfortably against the window as she slept, a sweater wrapped around her bony shoulders. His brows creased with worry as he looked at her, an uneasy feeling in his gut telling him that their time together was about to end.

He'd spent a month taking her all over the world, showing her everything he could. They'd swum in the Caribbean, walked along the cliffs in Ireland, played blackjack in Las Vegas, and been to the top of the Eiffel Tower. At every new place, her face had lit up with wonder, and she had made a huge effort to be in the moment. Yet every day, he could tell a difference, he could see her slide further down the precipice that would eventually take her away.

It was never overt. The changes were subtle from day to day, but when he thought about her the first day compared to the last, it was glaring. She was eating less and throwing up a good portion of what she managed to choke down. She was sleeping more, dozing in the car almost as soon as they started driving, and becoming exhausted from almost any physical activity. Sex would drain her for hours, though she turned to him more and more in that way. The bones in her face were more pronounced and her clothes sagged off her hips as she lost weight. It was almost as if he was watching her be ravaged by some horrible disease, but the disease was time. As winter grew closer, she grew more listless, more tortured by the nightmares that told her what was coming.

One night she'd wake screaming from seeing herself burn—feeling the lake, the chains. The next, she was being torn apart by the Hell hounds. She experienced herself dying every night in unimaginable ways. He understood they were to prepare her for the Choosing, and that some were being sent by Beelzebub to try and drive her over the edge, knowing that if she gave in and killed herself, he would win. Every night when she woke screaming from feeling herself drive a knife through her own heart, or from one of the other countless visions, Braxton would gather her close, hold her, stroking her hair and murmuring words of comforting nonsense until she drifted back to sleep.

They never spent two nights in the same place. Braxton wasn't getting prophetic dreams like Griffin did, but he knew the signs of being pursued, and he knew the Devils were not far behind. They hadn't seen Alaria since she'd warned them in Australia, but she sent word through the dream plane of how things were shaping up. As far as they knew, she was still leading Lilith and Azazel on a goose chase through Hell, purgatory, and Earth, but Beelzebub was after them, and Braxton knew it wouldn't be long before they had to go to the Choosing place.

He'd started working his way toward Philadelphia. He'd sent a message to Sam, who was staying with their parents, and had her start developing protections on the house to shield them from detection. The charms on the Choosing place had to be strengthened to give them more than a week, and he knew he and Alaria would not be able to take Griffin with them when they went to work on the protections.

That meant leaving Griffin again, which was something he was loath to do but knew could not be avoided. Griffin had to be protected, and the Devils were getting too close for comfort. They had to get the monastery protected, and that would take powerful magic. They would be unable to keep something of that magnitude from attracting notice, and the only way to keep the Devils from realizing what was going on was to keep Griffin away. That meant leaving her, and even six months pregnant, Sam was the most capable Warrior he knew. She was the only one that he would even consider trusting with Griffin's life. Added to that, she was one of the few people that Griffin knew and likely one of two that she would trust enough to stay with.

He saw knowledge in her eyes when their route started moving back to the city where it had all started. A weariness that she had been fighting set in more firmly, giving her a haunted, tired look. With a little more than two months left to live, instead of drinking Mai-Tais on a tropical beach as Braxton had been hopeful she would be, she was running for her life from three of the most dangerous Devils that Hell had produced. Watching her waste away, going from the vibrant, fiery woman who had thrown a book at his head the first time they'd met, to a shell that was barely alive, was almost more than he could take.

The feelings had snuck up on him. He'd known for months that he cared for her; he wanted to get her through everything as comfortably and as painlessly as possible. The attraction had been almost instant, and even though he'd know it was a bad idea, he had been unable to resist. After finding her in Australia, things had changed even further. Despite the fact that Braxton knew beyond a doubt that he would, sooner rather than later, hold Griffin's lifeless body in his arms and bury her, he found himself falling in love with her.

Each time he turned his head and looked at her, his heart ached. For what should be, for what could have been had she been born even a minute sooner or later. It was too easy to picture her resplendent in a wedding gown, heavy with his child, holding their baby in her arms. Entirely too easy to picture her growing old, watching grandchildren with adoration and love. All the things she should have been able to do and was being robbed of simply by nature of her birth.

It would be all too easy to ask her to run away. To try and escape the Choosing, to cherish those few months she might have past her birthday. To damn the whole world and try to save her life. She, who was so selfless, so giving, so willing to sacrifice for a world that had given her only heartbreak and struggles.

"You're wearing your broody face."

Braxton was shaken from his thoughts by Griffin's voice. He spared her a smile, glancing at her out of the corner of his eye. "I thought you were asleep."

"I can't sleep twenty-four hours a day." She yawned and stretched, sitting up straighter in the seat next to him. "I'll never get that time back."

"Don't think about it."

"Brax." Griffin reached over and covered his hand with hers. "I have to think about it. I have to be ready for it. If I ignore it, it will only be harder. There's nothing to be done."

"You still shouldn't dwell on it. You need to enjoy the time that you have left."

Griffin looked sad for a moment, then smiled. "I am. As much as I can. I'm with you, which is more than I thought I'd get." She sighed. "It's like everything is going out of focus. I can see and feel, but it's like it's through a barrier. Nothing feels as good, food tastes bland, everything looks dull. It's good, I suppose, that it's like this. If it's all bland, I won't miss it as much, right?"

Braxton was at a loss. He shook his head. "Let's not talk about it right now. We still have a few weeks."

"You're taking me to Sam."

He noticed it wasn't a question and nodded. "I am. She's working on protections and spells to keep you shielded for a few weeks. I need to go to the Choosing Place and try to strengthen the charms. There's no way that we can keep ahead of them for another two months, so we need to get you safe."

"How long will you be gone?"

"Never for more than a few days. Alaria will be there full-time, working with the witches and spellcasters, but I don't want to leave you alone for long. I've spoken with Sam, and she's going to keep you with my parents for two weeks, and then bring you to Jerusalem. The faith and the religion there will make it uncomfortable to Devils and harder for them to find you, which works in our favor. It won't keep them out, but the natural protections and the spells she's going to put on it should keep you safe until we can move you into the monastery. I'll be close and I'll come check in every few days."

"Sam is still pregnant. I don't want her in any danger."

"She won't be. She's going home as soon as we can move you in. I will only be a couple hours away at all times. Alaria will be on standby to zip in if we need her to."

"You're trusting her an awful lot."

Braxton sighed. "I know. I still don't like it, but you're right. She's risking her life, her existence, on this. I know it's not out of the goodness of her heart, but I think I feel better about it being that way. I can trust that she's selfish and she wants her request. I wouldn't trust her if she was trying to sell us on her having a change of heart."

"I like her." Griffin shifted in her seat and took a drink of water. "I think she got screwed about like I am."

"You're nothing like her."

"Not now, but at first? I don't think she was that bad. She fought for her freedom, and she was punished for that. I think the way she is..." Griffin trailed off as she considered how to explain her train of though. "I think it's a product of all those centuries of knowing she's stuck. How do you survive in Hell if you don't do what they all do?"

"Griffin, she put you through twenty-nine years of hell. Abused, beaten, raped. The baby. All the things that you went through, she did."

"I know, but every time, she took me to Hell first and offered to let me stay. At first, I thought it was because she enjoyed me saying no, so she'd get to use her events. Now, I think she was hoping I'd do it so she wouldn't have to."

"Never underestimate the degree to which Alaria is evil." Gabriel materialized in the backseat with a slight pop, looking, as always, perfectly groomed in his pristine white suit. "She is working with us only because you can give her what she wants. She is not a good being, and she is not kind. She enjoyed every second of what she did to you, and if you step out of line, she will enjoy torturing you for the rest of eternity."

Griffin twisted in her seat to see the Angel. "You didn't come to talk about Alaria."

"No." He sighed and looked pained for a long moment. "I have tried to obey the rules to their letter. I have not interfered except to remedy a rule being broken by the Devils. The stakes are too high, and there are too many Devils involved for my association to remain so small. I will still be sending you the ceremony for the sacrifice inside the dream plane, but today I am here to speak to you, Braxton, about the protections on the Choosing Place."

Braxton looked in the rearview mirror, his eyes hard and intense. "You have my attention."

"I do not have the ability to extend the protections. Even if I did, I would not. They were put into place by God Himself, and that ability has not been bestowed on any of the legion of Heaven. However, while I generally find humans to be mildly annoying and rarely interesting, they are, if nothing else, resourceful. There are some that have managed, through a combination of faith, witchcraft, sheer determination and centuries of spell work, to gain a basic understanding of how the powers of God work and how to apply protections. Alaria is aware of some of them, but her knowledge is limited to only those that choose to use their abilities. There is one who is stronger than them all that Alaria does not know of."

"Will they help us?"

"I believe that she can be persuaded. Do not be fooled, Braxton. This woman is nearly as dangerous as the Devils, and has more power than any one human has ever before been able to harness. She has, thus far, chosen to abstain from using her abilities, but with her help and the prowess of the magicians Alaria is gathering, I have no doubt that you will be able to accomplish your goal."

"Where is she? Who is she?"

Gabriel smiled, and Braxton saw a hint of amusement in the expression. "I wish I had the time to take the luxury of being vague. I do so like watching you humans squirm and flail, trying to determine exactly what we mean. Fortunately for you, however, time is short, and it will take time to convince her to aid you. Her name is Dana Lewis, and she lives in a place called County Clare."

"Does she know we're coming for her?"

"No. She'll know before you get there, though."

"Is she human?" Griffin turned almost completely around in the seat to see him better, the question popping out before she could stop it.

"For the most part." Before either could ask any more questions, the Angel disappeared, leaving them alone again.

Sam, Miranda and Allen were waiting for them when Braxton turned the car into the driveway of their house in Philadelphia. Sam felt tears well in her eyes when she saw Griffin. Even brief weeks earlier, the woman had been full of life and fire, struggling against her fate, talking animatedly with the other woman about a myriad of topics. Even when Azazel had tried to drown her, she'd fought to recover, only giving up when her body gave out. Sneaking out of the hotel and shimmying out the window had shown nerves and determination. As she walked up the driveway, barely strong enough to shoulder her duffel bag, she was a whisper of the woman that Sam had met the first day after Finn had picked her up from the hospital.

When Griffin just walked past all of them without a word and went into the house, Sam looked to Braxton, her brows knit with concern. "What's happened to her?"

Before Braxton could answer, Alaria appeared. Allen automatically stepped in front of his wife and daughter, shielding them with his own body before remembering that Alaria was bound to help Griffin. Sam, who had not forgotten, shoved past her father in annoyance.

"What's happened to her?" Sam repeated her question in annoyance, her hands on her hips.

Alaria glanced into the house where Griffin was entering one of the guest bedrooms. "Exactly what is supposed to happen. It's a measure put into place to make things easier on her. It loosens her hold on humanity and makes the transition less frightening."

Miranda shook her head, her eyes sad. "That's horrible."

"It's necessary." Braxton hugged his mother and sister and shook his father's hand. "I've been watching her fade."

Alaria sighed. "It's normal. It was a—let's say—palliative measure put into place to lessen her suffering. God wanted to make things as comfortable on her as possible. This is so she won't feel so much grief and pain at the end."

Sam shook her head, a look of disbelief on her face. "You can't possibly think this is helping her! She's wasting away to nothing. At this rate, she'll starve to death before the end of the year. This is a slow torture." Her eyes welled with tears. "She is giving up everything to save this miserable excuse of a world, and they can't even let her enjoy her last few weeks! Instead, they have to be filled with running and blood and death. That's not just unfair, it's ungodly."

"You'll get no argument here." Alaria turned to Braxton, dismissing the conversation. "Go do what you need to do so we can get gone. The longer we stay here, the greater the chance of the other three finding me. I can disguise my tracks for a while, but it's not indefinite, and the sooner we're gone, the better off everyone is going to be."

Braxton nodded, his eyes drifting up the stairs. "I'll just go say goodbye to her and be back down." He couldn't help the small smile that passed over his mouth. "Try not to kill each other while I'm gone."

Alaria leaned against the wall disinterestedly. "I'll play nice, but make it snappy."

Braxton climbed the stairs two at a time, ducked into the room Griffin had taken, and closed the door gently behind him. She had already changed from jeans and a sweatshirt into pajamas and was lying on top of the blankets on the bed, staring at the ceiling. Without a word, he slid onto the mattress next to her, shifting her so that she was lying on her side with her head on his chest.

"I know you need to leave." Her voice was so small he had to strain to hear it. "Just please promise me that you'll come for me this time."

"I promise. In two weeks, Sam will bring you to Jerusalem. I'll see you every few days until we can move you into the monastery. You won't be alone."

"I'm not afraid to die." She sighed. "I was. I have been. I think about it all the time. About what it'll feel like, what happens after. I know where I'm going. I know death isn't it. That's better than a lot of people have it.

I think that's the scariest part, the wondering what happens after you die. I get to go to Heaven a hero."

"What scares you then?"

"Not being here. What's happening to me now. Feeling myself slipping away. I know what I have to do, and I'll do it. I don't struggle with that. There's no choice. I won't be responsible for the whole world going to Hell. The struggle is feeling myself die and knowing it's going to be like this for weeks yet."

"You heard us talking downstairs."

"None of you were whispering." She dashed tears from her cheeks. "I got robbed, and it sucks. I never had a normal life. I never got married, I never raised a child, I never got to do all the things that billions of people take for granted. I never got to do that because I was born to die. My only purpose on this Earth is to drive a knife into my heart and make one stupid fucking choice. No one knows what that feels like. I never understood the phrase "weight of the world" until this last year."

"There's nothing I can say to make you feel better about that. It's the truth, it's your life. I would think you would get at least some comfort out of knowing that without you, there would be no world. There would be no future for anyone."

"I don't care about the world." The words came out before Griffin knew they were there. "The world has done nothing but screw me over. I'm doing this for Sam, and your parents, and Father Dooley. Because I love them. Because the only people that have ever shown me any kindness are in this house. And dammit, Braxton, I'm going to shove that knife into my heart and scream for the Angels for you!"

"The entire drive the other day, all I could think about was asking you to run away with me. Just the two of us. We'd take off, say screw the Choosing and screw the world. We're going to go drink piña coladas and tan on a beach until the end of time. Then I remembered that even if we run away, you still have to die. I'll admit that a part of me thinks those extra few months might be worth it."

Her eyes showing life for the first time in days, Griffin rose onto her knees to face him, her hair swirling around her face. "Tell me. Just this once, before you go. Say the words. I want to hear them." Her fingers unbuttoned his shirt quickly, setting off little fires under his skin wherever they touched. "I want you to take me. I want you inside me, and I want you to tell me. If you only ever say it once, I want to hear the words. Make me forget, Brax. For ten minutes, make it go away."

Helpless to turn her down, Braxton rolled her onto her back, his broad hands gently sliding her pajama bottoms down her legs. When her hands impatiently went to his belt, he batted them away, taking care of the garment himself. Where he would have kissed and laved attention on her body, she was anxious, tugging him down onto her, wrapping her legs around him. Silently, he sheathed himself with a condom and parted her thighs with his knee. When he gently probed and found her warm and wet, he gave into her breathless demands and slid heavily into her.

"Say it."

"I love you." The words slipped out like he'd been saying them to her his entire life. He pressed his face to her neck, bracing himself on his forearms, their bodies pressed tightly together as he slowly, gently, rocked his hips, giving her friction exactly where she needed it.

"Again."

"I love you."

Griffin couldn't stop the tears, couldn't stop her demands to hear him say those three words over and over. And say them he did. With every stroke into her body, he said them again, until they were muffled against her mouth, tangling with her own words. Even as her body arched, pulsating with pleasure from her release, the tears broke free. Her arms held him tighter to her, her legs holding his hips tight to hers, not allowing him to break their connection.

He drove into her until the tears dried up, until they were replaced with breathy moans, and her hands went from clinging at him to her nails digging into his skin from ecstasy. When her hips moved with him and her body tightened once again, he let himself tumble over the edge with her, collapsing onto her, covered in sweat, and his chest heaving from the breaths he was forced to drag in.

They didn't speak, didn't need to. Everything they'd been forcing themselves not to say had been said. They lay in the dark, limbs entwined, until Griffin, exhausted and sleepy, drifted off. Braxton allowed himself five minutes past that, then gently slipped from the bed, pressing a kiss to her forehead before he pulled on his clothes and left.

Alaria was still downstairs, perched awkwardly on his mother's settee, a delicate teacup in her hands. His parents sat across from her, shoulder to shoulder on the couch, their faces drawn and tight. Sam, her belly bulging against her sweatshirt, perched on the couch arm, Miranda's hand placed protectively on her knee.

Alaria stood when she saw him descend the stairs, her raven hair falling down her back in a shimmering curtain. She sighed from boredom and walked to him. "Are you ready to go, or do you need more time for sex?"

Braxton scowled, his brows drawing together. "Let's get going."

With a sigh, Alaria reached for his hand, dragging him to her so that she could get the amount of contact needed to make transporting him as comfortable on them both as possible. With not even a backward look, she closed her eyes, and they disappeared with a loud crack.

Chapter Twenty-Seven

October 31st, 2029 - The Choosing Place

"THE WITCH IS working well. With any luck, we'll be able to move Griffin here by the end of next week. The charms are getting stronger. It's getting harder for me to get in." Alaria spoke before Braxton had made his presence known, and he was reminded of how powerful she really was. Her face was covered in sweat, exertion making her look exhausted.

They'd been working on the spells for two weeks. He had been gone for the last three days, spending that time getting Sam and Griffin set up in a small house in a nearby village so that they could be kept close. Alaria had worked harder than any of them. The witch they'd gotten had been a reluctant addition but was smart and talented, spinning webs of protections that Braxton had never even known about.

The longer they were there, the more uncomfortable Alaria became. They were trying to make it easier for her, but the results were modest at best. Instead of complaining, she would just disappear during the times the others were sleeping so that she could get a few hours of relief from the constant pain of being inside the monastery. The manner in which she was dealing with it gave Braxton a grudging amount of respect for the Devil, and the longer they were together, working side by side, the more he found himself initiating conversation. He still had no misconceptions about her motives, but what he'd told Griffin had been the truth. He could trust someone who was only in it for herself.

"Are you going to be able to stay here once we're done? Or is it going to be too much?"

"I'll find a way. I won't have a choice. Once we're done, I'm either stuck in or I'm stuck out. Better for everyone, including me, if I'm stuck in. It's as much a protection for me as it is for Griffin."

"Is there a way we can make it easier on you?"

Alaria shrugged. "Not a clue. I've done everything I know to do, but I'd say if there's any additional relief to be had, it's going to come from Gabe."

Braxton dropped the brush he was using to paint symbols on the walls into the bucket of red paint and sank to the floor to take a break. "What do you think the odds of that happening are?"

"Probably about as likely as Lilith transforming herself into a fluffy pink poodle."

They both laughed at the image, and Braxton leaned his head against the wall as Alaria dropped to the floor next to him. Since arriving at the monastery, he had found himself becoming more comfortable with the Devil. She worked hard, mostly kept her mouth shut, and had, so far, given him no indication that she was being anything but honest with them about her motives.

"Can I ask you something?"

Alaria shrugged. "Go for it. I won't promise to answer, but you can ask."

"You and Gabriel. What happened there?"

She considered for a long moment, obviously debating about how much, if anything, to tell him. Finally, she sighed. "Humans don't know much about Angels. They think what the Bible says is all that there is to it, when really, that's just the tip of the iceberg. We don't just watch over humans, intervening when He tells us to. We get to soar the heavens, every star, every planet, any moment in time. Gabe and I—we were friends. Griffin wanted to make it into something romantic, but it wasn't. Michael and Lilith, that's a different story, but not Gabe and I.

"We did everything together. Flip sides of the same coin. We studied philosophy and religion. We went anywhere in the universe that we wanted with nothing more than a thought. I liked it on Earth—the decisions you got to make that you thought so little of. What to eat, what to wear, who to fuck. Amazing decisions that most people never even think about. I began to spend more and more time amongst humans, and that's where the rift really started. Gabe's always been loyal to a fault, and he saw me enjoying human things as less than Godly."

Alaria took a deep breath and ran her hands over her face, her forehead creased from the pain of remembering long ago hurts. Braxton sat silently, sensing how painful it was for her to recount the experiences.

"Eventually, I heard rumblings of discontent with Lucifer and Lilith. Rumors that they were planning a coup—that they were going to challenge for the leadership of Heaven. I went to Gabe, and I was torn. He convinced me to give Father a chance. So I did. I went to His feet, begged for the choice, and received nothing more than a pat on the head. I begged Gabe to side with me, to cross over. Lucifer was promising us freedom. The freedom to choose. We could Fall to Earth, be together. I don't know if I was falling in love with him, or if I was so desperate to feel human emotion that I fabricated it, but my feelings for him were human. I loved him. He returned the feelings. By then, the war was picking up steam and his allegiance was unwavering. I begged and pleaded and struggled. It was sad and pathetic and completely real. We cried and fought, yelled and screamed, each trying to bring the other over. We were both convinced our side would win and terrified about what would happen to the other one. Eventually, I had to choose a side. I chose Lucifer, and the hope for life on Earth. Gabe stood with our Father."

Pausing again, Alaria reached for Braxton's bottle of water, drinking deeply to cool her burning throat. Unwanted tears prickled her throat and she laughed bitterly as she screwed the lid back into place. Braxton took the bottle without a word and drained it, uncomfortable with the direction the conversation had taken.

"We both fought brutally. We shed blood, and we took our brethren's lives. It was horrible and poignant at the same time. Nothing will ever be like it again. At the end, when it was over, when those of us left stood on the battlefield and saw God strike Lucifer into the pit, they treated me like all the others. He made Gabe personally take me down to Hell and chain me there. It was his punishment for his feelings for me. Those who stood with God were revered and rewarded. Those who stood with Lucifer were cast down into Hell without a backward glance. Those who refused to choose, well, that's the really ironic part. They were cast to Earth. They got to live my dream, and Gabe and I were assigned to the Choosing. Centuries of having to deal with one another while knowing that the precipice between us was so great that not even an act of God could change it." She sighed again and laughed, the sound just a little bitter. "So, there you have it. My sob story."

Braxton turned his head to look at her, a flicker of sympathy stirring. "I wish I wouldn't have asked."

"Too much sad stuff lately?"

"Nah. It's not that." He chuckled. "I still think you're an evil bitch. But now I know why you're an evil bitch, and it makes me feel bad for you. That's not a feeling I like in regard to a Devil."

"Most Devils are one-dimensional. They wanted to rule Heaven. There are a few like me, who had their own reasons and picked the wrong side. I'll tell you what I told Griffin when she asked me about this. Make no mistake. Even the ones who didn't want to take over, who got caught in the cross fire, who were lured in by promises and desires, they're as evil as Lucifer. We all learned to survive and to thrive down there. The longer we're down there, the more evil we become."

"You still want to be human."

"I'm a conundrum." She smiled. "I never forgot what it's like. Lucifer is a cold, sneaky bastard. He'll turn on his own just as quickly as he will a human. I don't want to serve a master. I want autonomy. I just want to be me, whoever that is. To live and die like you get to."

"Being human isn't all that great. You don't know what I would give to have my feelings dulled right now." He sighed deeply. "What I have to watch Griffin do, what I have to help her do...it's unfathomable to me. I have to help her die."

Uncharacteristically empathetic, Alaria shook her head. "No. What you have to do isn't help her die. What you have to do is give her the strength to die. I've seen the two of you together. She depends on you for strength. When she sees that you're strong, she sets her shoulders, grits her teeth, and knows she has to do it. If she sees you waver, she wavers. Far be it for me to tell you how to handle her, but I would seriously consider not talking about running away with her anymore." She smiled when he stiffened. "I don't mean it from my end. She would go if you asked. She would know her soul was mine, and she would do it anyway because she loves you that much."

"You see a lot for a Devil."

Alaria smiled. "Don't read anything into it. I see a lot because I have hundreds of thousands of years of experience watching humans and knowing how they tick. You've always seen me for what I am, and I don't want you turning into Griffin on me and trying to assign me some sob story."

Braxton chuckled. "You must be a beast at poker."

The mood lightened; she patted his knee and heaved herself to her feet. "You have no idea." She bent and picked up a paintbrush. "We should get back to work. There's a lot of space left to put these symbols on, and we only have the witch for a few more days before I have to zap her home."

"Are you going to be able to get back in once the protections are in place?"

"I hope so, but if not, you'll have to take her, and I'll be stuck here until everything is over."

Braxton went back to work, drawing the symbols on the wall in chalk before painting over the outline. After several minutes of working silently, he sighed and dropped the brush back into the half empty bucket. "Can I ask you one more question?"

"I already told you my story, so please don't ask anything else about me."

"Not about you. About me."

Her curiosity piqued, the Devil shrugged. "Go ahead then."

"Do I really feel what I think I feel?"

Alaria felt a wave of sympathy, a feeling she had rarely experienced since the Fall. "You think God is making you feel like you're in love with Griffin." It wasn't a question.

"I know He can't make me, but we both know there are ways around that."

"If I had to guess, they've probably interfered, but it really doesn't matter. Knowing isn't going to make the feelings go away, it isn't going to make this less hard, and it won't make losing her any easier. Whether the feelings initiated within you, or because of some sort of Angelic interference, they're real."

"Can't you tell?"

Alaria laughed. "It's not like that. I can't look inside you and see if the Angels have messed around in the same way I can see where your soul is headed. It's not like there's a scent on you or something."

"What could they do?"

"Braxton, I know that your experiences have been with creatures like me. You're used to seeing the supernatural as evil. For the most part you're right. Angels aren't the same. They don't play by the same rules. Demons and Devils, they'll manipulate you overtly. They'll make deals or slit your throat or convince you that ten years is a lifetime. Angels are a bit more under the radar. They set up a situation, put you in a particular place, and based on who you are, they know basically how you'll react. For you, I can see just by looking at you, before you ever say a word, that you're the type who would give your life to save almost anyone. What does God do? He puts you in a position where you watch a girl be raped and then where you see her nearly torn to shreds by the Hounds. He puts you where you can look but can't touch. By the time you met Griffin, you already felt protective. You were already struggling to compartmentalize her into a job. She was human to you, and she's not hard to look at, either. You take a man who is feeling protective and overbearing, and a woman struggling against her fate and desperate for some human interaction, and you put them together with no one else for months. It was a recipe for a romance. I don't doubt for a second that they knew that would happen or that it had a very good chance of happening."

"So, they're not real then."

Alaria sighed in frustration. "That's not what I said. You love her. You're in love with her. She's crazy in love with you. Anyone with eyes can see that. Did you come to that on your own? I don't know. I don't know if you would feel the same way were she just some girl off the street that you met at a concert. In the end, you feel what you feel, and whether or not those feelings started completely from within you or with some manipulation from up above, I don't know. I don't think that the answer matters."

Braxton didn't answer; he didn't need to. He picked his paint brush back up and returned to work, his mind racing with questions. Alaria didn't push him to answer, and he wasn't sure if that was because she didn't care, didn't want to know, or didn't want to make him talk when he wasn't comfortable.

He had often told Griffin that the worst thing they could do was to forget what Alaria was. Standing there, working shoulder to shoulder, her long hair tied back in a braid and her red and black leather traded in for jeans, boots and a sweater, it would be easy for him to forget. She didn't look like a Devil. She just looked like a woman, and while he knew that made her even more dangerous, he still struggled to maintain his guard.

"She's a complicated woman."

Braxton shook his head, the room spinning from the speed at which he'd been snatched out of the monastery. Gabriel was sitting in a white arm chair, one leg crossed lazily over the other, his blond hair as perfectly coiffed as always. Braxton looked around and took in the cheerfully crackling fire, the white couch, the coffee table with a pitcher of iced tea and lemon slices, and two glasses, already full.

"What am I doing here?"

"I typically only bring Griffin here. This is a place I use to talk to humans when I don't want anyone else to be able to see or hear. We're completely secure here. No one other than you and I will know what is said inside this room."

Braxton sat down slowly, his brow furrowed. "It sounds like you have something pretty important to say."

"There's a lot happening that you do not yet know about. A lot that you must be prepared for. You've been asking a lot of questions."

"Eavesdropping isn't nice."

"Neither is asking a Devil something you should be asking an Angel. If you have questions about my involvement, you are better off to leave her out of this."

"Alaria didn't say anything. She doesn't know and told me as much. Since you're here, I will ask you." Braxton's eyes were flat and hard in his deceptively friendly face. "Have you made me fall in love with Griffin?"

"Yes." Gabriel took a drink of the tea and gently sat the glass back down. "Just as Alaria told you we could. You have been important to this since you were four years old. You are the best Warrior that walks the Earth and the one and only human who could be entrusted with the task of getting Griffin to the Choosing alive. The task that you have in front of you is the single greatest responsibility that has been given to a human since Mary. We had to take steps to ensure that you would do everything in your power to get her there alive. Regardless of your arguments, all humans dig deeper and try harder to protect the people that they love." He shrugged. "Given the option, I would do it again a hundred times."

"When you saw me in that hospital, and again when I was seventeen, you told me that you had no idea what part I played. Even when you took me to see her, you told me you didn't know."

"I didn't. Once Griffin was in your care, it became obvious to me. Hormones are easily manipulated, and the two of you did the rest from there. Alaria was right about one other thing. The origin of this does not matter. Your feelings are no less real because of the manner in which they began. More importantly, you cannot question them because you will need the strength those feelings give you to proceed."

"This isn't about making me feel better or offering some reassurance. This is because you need me to continue to play along."

"I don't care about you one way or the other. To me, you're a pest, a bug to watch in an aquarium for the second in which you are alive. To me, your lifespan is a heartbeat. I do not care about you. I do not care about Griffin or Alaria or any one of the human beings that walk on this Earth. I care about pleasing my Father, and to do that, I have to get Griffin through the Choosing. In order for her to do what she needs to do, your emotions are a boon. We cannot interfere with free will. You did not do one single thing that you did not want to do, or decide to do, on your own.

Now, I suggest you move on."

"If this was as insignificant as you're trying to tell me it is, you wouldn't have brought me here to talk about it. Why am I here, Gabriel?"

Gabriel smiled and folded his hands on his knee. "You're rather sharp for a human. The time for the Choosing is drawing nearer, and the Devils seeking Griffin are getting closer. They've been working quickly to find her, and they're eliminating most places very rapidly. Azazel is wily, and he is smart. Griffin will not be safe outside of this place for long. You need to bring her there as soon as is possible."

"We have to finish the protections. If we don't, we'll be out of time before the end of the year. It's not ideal, but it's what we have to work with, and there's nothing I can do to make it go faster."

"Sleep less and paint longer. I've just come up with two things you can do." Gabriel stood, his patience wearing thin. "There's something brewing, Braxton. Something important, and something big. I suspect that Lucifer is up to something. A plan B, if you will, in case the Choosing does not go his way. A way to circumvent the rules. I don't yet know what it is that's going on, and I won't unless Father wishes for me to, but you need to be more careful than you have been. The closer the Choosing is, the more danger you're in. You'll need Warriors, and you'll need weapons. There will be a battle for her. They will not let you go peacefully, and they will try to slaughter you all. Call in your troops. Get as many as you can as fast as you can. You will spill blood over this, and all we can hope is to have enough troops on the ground that we can buy you enough time to get to midnight."

"I thought the Angels would help."

"Michael will lead our troops. He is preparing for a battle. Do not concern yourself with our readiness. We have more to concern ourselves with than this alone. We will be there." Gabriel lifted his hand to send Braxton back.

"Wait. Before I go, I need you to do something for me. You're asking me to do a lot, and I'll do it gladly, but I need something in return."

Amused, Gabriel turned up his hands. "What is it?"

"I need you to make that monastery comfortable for Alaria. She's in a lot of pain from the protections, and there's nothing more that we can do to help her. She's no good to us if she's writhing on the floor from pain."

Gabriel considered that for a long minute, then gave a short nod. "So be it."

Chapter Twenty-Eight

November 30th, 2029 - The Choosing Place

THERE WEREN'T any birds. Griffin was struck by that as she looked out the window of the monastery. A fire crackled cheerily in the fireplace, but she was focused on the cold—the chill of the glass panes as she laid her palm on the window and the stone floor under her bare feet. A layer of frost coated everything outside, making the trees shine white in the dim light from the rising sun.

Even in late fall, there should still have been animals. Squirrels, birds, rabbits. Something should have been rustling in the forest. It was dead silent. That told her that they were coming. Her time was running out, and it would not be long before they would be under siege. She knew that deep in her bones—in every cell of her being. Nothing would stop them from coming, and her time was now measured in days instead of weeks or months. Thirty-two days. Seven hundred and sixty-eight hours. Forty-six thousand and eighty minutes. It seemed like a lot of minutes. Griffin wrapped her arms around her middle, tears clouding her vision. It wasn't enough time.

The pain was intense, rippling through her until she could feel it in her fingers and toes. Her throat closed and her stomach knotted until she couldn't breathe. Trying to snap herself out of it, she concentrated on what she could feel: the cold chill beneath her feet, the softness of Braxton's sweater on her skin, the window on her forehead as she laid her head against it. Slowly, in excruciatingly small increments, her ability to breathe returned. She made herself straighten, wipe the tears from her cheeks, and turn her back on the window.

It would be so easy to sink into it; to dwell on her reality. She was dying. In forty-six thousand and seventy-two minutes she would drive a knife into her heart, and she would die. It would be too easy to not think of anything else. To think about how her bones jutted out, how her skin was paper thin, how her eyes were sunken into her head, and how her hair was like straw as her body wasted away. Walking up the stairs took her breath, and food tasted like cardboard.

Intellectually, she knew that there was nothing she could do to stop it. She was programmed to shut down in anticipation of the Choosing. It was some built-in safety feature ensuring that she would do what she was supposed to do. She was going to die either way. The choice she really got to make was whether or not she was going to take the rest of the human race with her, and that was not something she was willing to do.

Shoulders set, Griffin pushed off the wall and forced herself to leave her room. She shivered as she entered the hallway and the colder air enveloped her. Holding onto the railing, she descended the stairs slowly, swearing under her breath as her heart began racing from exhaustion halfway down. By the time she got to the bottom of the stairs, her breath came in fast gulps, and she was too tired to even imagine going back up them. If her degradation continued, by the time her birthday arrived, she wouldn't even be able to walk.

She spent a minute catching her breath, then trudged through the maze-like monastery until she found Braxton and Alaria, their heads bent over a spell book at the large dining room table. When she cleared her throat, they both looked up, and the pity that flashed in both sets of eyes was almost too much to bear.

"I got tired of sitting on my bed."

Braxton shook off the pity and jumped up to pull out a chair for her. "Do you want something to eat? There's plenty of stuff in the kitchen. Sam went to the grocery store and stocked up before she went home. It's enough to feed an army for the next month."

Even though her stomach clenched with nausea at the mere mention of food, Griffin nodded. "I'm starving."

Forty-five minutes later, when Braxton was holding her hair back from her face as she threw up every bite she had managed to force down, she felt herself starting to get angry. Tears scalded her eyes as she threw up, and she crumpled to the floor, weak from the heaving. Braxton eased out from behind her and went to the sink to wet a washcloth. When he handed it to her, she angrily threw it against the wall, a sob wrenching its way out of her chest.

"I don't want to be like this! I want to enjoy the next month, Braxton. I want to eat a pound of chocolate a day, make snow angels, decorate a

Christmas tree, and bake too many pies. This is my last chance. My last Christmas, my last month, my last everything. And I can't even keep anything down. It's not fair!"

"No, it isn't. There's not one damn thing about this that's fair, but it's what we've got to deal with. All you can do is keep trying."

Griffin drew her knees up against her chest and leaned back against the bathtub. "I'm never going to get married. I'm never going to hold a baby in my arms and know that love. I'm never going to get to watch my children grow, to have grandchildren, to get old. I've accepted that. My son will never know me—never even know who I am. I made peace with that a long time ago. Hell, I'll be thirty and he'll be graduating high school. Keeping him would have damned him to the same existence that I've had. I did right by him in giving him up. He's not mine. Never was. I always thought I'd get another shot at it. I always thought I'd get my day, in the big white dress, to drink and dance and make love to my husband. I thought we'd have wild, crazy honeymoon sex, and I'd give him lots of babies." She sighed. "Now, I just want to be able to keep down dinner. I want to walk down the stairs without feeling like I'm going to pass out."

They both turned when they heard a rustling, and Braxton sighed when he saw Gabriel appear. "What do you want?"

Gabriel lifted one eyebrow in mild amusement. "Is my presence unwelcome?"

Griffin laughed bitterly. "You rarely bring good news."

"This time I do. Your, shall we say, problems, have not gone unnoticed. I've been given authority to temporarily stop your winding-down process."

"My winding-down process? You mean how my body is shutting down to make sure I'm willing to Choose?" Griffin forced herself to stand up. "At least have the nerve to say it like it is. You're killing me. Slowly and painfully. You're killing me." She shoved the Angel as hard as she could. "Call it what you want, say what you want, but my birthday is just the icing on the cake. I'm already dead! You killed me the second I was born!" She shoved past him. "Answer me this, Gabriel. Do you enjoy having my blood on your hands? Do you enjoy sitting in your perfect white room, drinking iced tea, and watching me suffer? I am dying! My life is over! And you have the unbelievable gall to come in here and act like you're doing me a favor? Spare me the theatrics. You're doing this because you're afraid I won't survive till my birthday if you don't. We've all thought it. I'll die of starvation and dehydration well before I turn thirty. Don't act like you're doing me a favor. You've not done one goddamn thing because of me. It's all about what is going to make it easiest on you!"

Braxton cleared his throat as Griffin disappeared up the stairs. "Well, she told you, didn't she?"

"Your input is completely unnecessary." Gabriel brushed imaginary lint from his shoulder. "Given the emotional tumult she's going through, I'll let this slide. Her appetite and fortitude should return shortly." He turned to leave, then stopped and sighed. "She's not exactly right. I don't enjoy this. My duty has been to protect and to guide. It is not my choice to lead her to her death. But I promise you, she will know peace."

"How long do we have before the fight starts?"

"Two weeks, give or take. You'll want to get your soldiers here. The Devils are using things that you will not want to deal with. Call in every soul that you can."

"I'll get them here as soon as possible, but I need you to do one thing for me."

"I don't often do favors for humans and this is the second time you've asked for one recently."

"Keep my sister safe. She won't go home. I know her. She's skulking around somewhere close, waiting until it's too late to send her away, and she'll show back up. I won't see her baby die. Griffin is already dead, and I might as well be. The odds of me getting out of here in one piece are slim to none. I'm fine with that. This is the life that I chose, but Sam has something else to live for. Keep them safe."

Gabriel nodded. "Consider it done."

Braxton offered a tight smile, then turned to follow Griffin up the stairs. He heard the slight rustling that told him Gabriel was gone a moment later. He opened the door to Griffin's room slowly, stepped inside, and found her staring out the window, her socks tossed on the floor and her hands pressed against the cold glass.

"What are you doing?"

Griffin turned to look at him. "I like the feel of it. Temperature and texture make me feel more grounded. Cold, hot, rough—anything. When I feel myself slipping away, I touch something, and if I really, really concentrate on what it feels like, I can bring myself back, at least for a while."

"Gabriel says it should get better now. You'll be able to eat without throwing up, and you'll have more energy."

Griffin turned. "Did you mean it when you told me you love me? Or were you just saying it because it was what I needed to hear?"

At that moment, everything Alaria had told him snapped into focus, and it became crystal clear that the Devil was right. It didn't matter whether or not he questioned his feelings. It didn't even matter if they were truly real. All that mattered was that Griffin was sure. That she knew she was loved, and that she found the strength in that to get her through the unspeakable horrors she would have to go through. In that moment, he made a decision, put all of his doubts aside, and gave her what she needed.

"I meant it. I mean it."

"I know this is selfish, and I know it's stupid, and I know I'm dead in a month, and what I should be doing is letting you go and pushing you away to make it easier. Because in the end, I get to die, and I'm not stuck grieving me. You and Sam, you don't get that lucky. I'm not selfless. I want this, and I want you, and dammit, I can't stop wanting it. Will you say 'fuck it' with me?" She took a great big breath, her eyes shining with hope and tears. "Will you marry me? Give me my one day? Will you do that for me?"

Braxton crossed the room, took Griffin in his arms, and hugged her close. He knew it was what she needed. He knew it was what would get her through. Though he questioned whether the flood of emotion that made his heart pound, his gut clench, and his eyes fill was genuine or pressed upon him by some unseen force, he couldn't deny the intense reaction he had to her words. He couldn't fight back the wave of desire to do exactly what she asked of him. Instead of trying to make sense of it, he let it carry him away, trusting his instincts that doing what she asked would be doing what she needed, and that it would make her stronger and help her live to see the Choosing.

"Yes."

Chapter Twenty-Nine

December 2nd, 2029 - The Choosing Place
Alaria paced in her bedroom impatiently. Twenty-nine days and counting, and the humans wanted to put on a wedding! Instead of focusing on preparation and defense, they were worrying over wine and music. And it was her fault.

She'd told Braxton to concentrate on Griffin, to make sure that she felt strong and that she would be able to do what they needed her to do. Alaria hadn't anticipated that would require marrying the woman. She most certainly hadn't anticipated that it would require she be involved in the damn festivities.

Her mind made up that the wedding was a supremely bad idea, Alaria yanked open the door and stalked down the hall toward Griffin's room, knowing that if she was going to stop the damn thing, it was going to be through Griffin. After all, she'd ruined any chance of talking sense into Braxton with her own words.

Heels clicking on the stone floor, her long legs ate up the short distance, and in a dozen steps, she had reached Griffin's door. She reached for the doorknob, paused momentarily to debate over knocking, then swore at herself for even considering it. She was allowing too much humanity to seep through. She needed to remember what she was—and that was not someone who knocked on doors

She pulled the door open and stopped. Griffin was standing in the bathroom, wearing only her bra and underwear, trying to do her hair in the mirror. Even though Alaria had seen and caused unimaginable pain, the sight nearly broke her un-beating heart.

Griffin's blonde hair hung limp and stringy, having lost its luster from months of malnutrition. Her spine jutted out through her skin, and her hipbones sharply protruded. Her mouth was set in a determined line, and her hands shook as she tried to make the curling iron do what she wanted it to do.

Battling herself, her very nature, and the glimmer of humanity that was trying to burst free, Alaria wavered, going back and forth between doing what she'd come to do and just leaving. Finally, muttering under her breath and completely pissed off at herself, she closed the door and walked across the room, leaning against the entrance to the bathroom.

"I can help."

Griffin turned, her hand going to her throat with a gasp. "My God, you scared me. How long have you been standing there?"

"Just a couple minutes." She pushed off the wall. "Do you want help or not?"

Griffin shrugged. "There's only an hour left, and there's not much to be done with me. My hair is helpless."

Unwanted sympathy stirring, Alaria walked to the vanity. "I can do whatever you want me to. How to you want your hair to look?"

"If it's up I look so bony, so I was trying to get the beach-y, wavy, curly thing going that everyone on television makes look so easy."

Alaria smiled. "Sit." She waited until Griffin had perched on the bed and grinned at the blonde. "Watch and learn."

When Alaria snapped her fingers and Griffin's hair was suddenly in perfect waves flowing down her back and over her shoulders, shiny and thick, Griffin gasped. "How did you do that?"

"Magic. We all have certain powers, certain energy. It's not exactly like a witch, since we're already supernatural, but Angels and Devils can do things like this just by wanting to. It's how Gabe has that infernal white room and the never ending pitcher of tea, and it's how I conjure weapons at the drop of a hat. We all use it differently, but we can do little tricks like this. It's just learning to manipulate energy and materials."

"Well, it's amazing." Griffin looked at Alaria sheepishly. "Is there any way you could do that little trick with a dress?"

Alaria couldn't help the smile that forced her lips to curve. "Yeah. I can do that with a dress. Stand up."

Alaria closed her eyes, wind whipping up around them. She concentrated on the energy in the air, in molding and changing it to do what she wanted it to do. She pictured the fabric, the draping, the decorations; she even began spinning a spider-web-thin lace veil. Griffin gasped, her throat clogged with tears, and Alaria opened her eyes, taking in the satin dress. There were rhinestone straps that tied around Griffin's neck and trailed down her back, a slit in front that revealed jeweled high heels, and a veil that flowed down her back and swept out behind her.

"Not bad if I do say so myself." Alaria smiled. "I think you're all set. I'll go see if your groom is ready."

Griffin reached out and grabbed the Devil in a hug. Not expecting the embrace, nor sure what to do about it, Alaria patted her back awkwardly. Griffin stepped back, tears shining in her eyes. "Thank you. I know you don't think this is a good idea. I know it's not a good idea, but I just want it so bad. I don't want to die never having experienced this. If it's just one damn day, I want it. It's selfish and it's cruel to Braxton because he's the one who's going to have to live without me. He's the one who has to live with these choices, not me. I can't help it. I love him. I want this. I want it so much that nothing I do to try and convince myself to call this thing off works. I've tried. I lay awake all night last night trying to work up the courage to tell him this is a bad idea. I couldn't do it. Nothing could convince me to wake him up and tell him we're not doing this.

"Thank you for not laughing at me and not telling me all the ways that this is the stupidest thing that I've ever done and for giving me this dress and making me pretty and being here in general. I know what you are, and what you did, and believe me, it's hard for me to look at you and not hate you for what you put me through. I know now that you did it because of what was done to you. You were made to be this way; it's not something that you chose and I'm glad that you're making other choices now. You're a good person, Alaria. If you weren't, you'd have killed me a thousand times by now and won your way back in with Lucifer, but you haven't. I trust you, and I like you. I didn't want to, but I do."

"You're babbling." Alaria offered a tense smile. "It's okay. Enjoy the day. There'll be plenty of work to do tomorrow to make up for the time off." She strode to the door and opened it. "I'll go let Braxton know you're ready."

She shut the door and leaned against it, her mind racing. She'd done not one thing she'd gone in there to do. Instead of stopping the God-forsaken wedding, she'd helped Griffin turn herself into a bride! What was she thinking?

"Perhaps not all of your soul has eroded after all."

Alaria turned her head and sighed. "Hello, Gabe. What brings you here this afternoon?"

"I love a good wedding, and this one should be rather interesting, what with all the Warriors present and the most notorious Devil of all in attendance. I wouldn't miss it for the world."

"I'd escape while I still could if I were you. If you stick around, you might get roped into performing the damn ceremony."

Gabriel pondered that idea briefly. "That's a fabulous idea. I'm glad you thought of it."

Alaria shook her head in disgust. "Angels." She started walking down the hall. "Please tell me you didn't come here just for the festivities."

"No, I didn't. I came to speak to you outside of the range of prying human ears. I can't drag you into my room, but I can take you there if you go willingly. Will you join me for a few moments?"

Alaria studied him for a long moment. Not once since the Fall had he invited her into the chamber he maintained. Slowly, she nodded. "Sure. Let's go."

Within the time it took to blink, they were standing in the white room with the couches and the pitcher of iced tea. She sat when he gestured toward one of the two sofas, crossing one leg over the other, and folding her hands on top of her knee.

"What's going on?"

"We have a problem. It's come to my attention that Lucifer has developed an alternate plan. One that we didn't anticipate, and one that we can't stop."

"I don't know anything about it. What's he doing?"

"He is gathering supernatural creatures. Witches, warlocks, wizards, anyone or anything that he can find that has any measure of magic and worships him. They are weaving a spell to open the gates to Hell regardless of the Choosing."

Alaria whistled slowly. "That certainly complicates things. What do you intend to do?"

"Michael is gathering a squad to try and deal with it. The problem is that most of these witches are human. Our Father will not allow us to simply kill humans. This is the choice they are making, and He will let them see the consequences of it if they manage to succeed."

"That's some serious mojo to pry open the gates. No one has ever managed it before."

"No one has ever seriously tried, because both sides were relying on the Choosing to be the definitive thing. We all thought we would win, and they all thought they would. No one expected any other outcomes. Lucifer knows he's losing, and he's desperate to circumvent it. They're developing another plan to try and deal with the loss of the Choosing. If they manage it, there will be no way to stop this war from spilling onto Earth."

Alaria nodded. "I'll be public enemy number one."

"You will be cloaked. They won't be able to find you, and you'll have Braxton, who will do everything he can to keep you safe. I've known you since the beginning of time. You're very resourceful, but yes, if they are able to get out, it's likely that you will be hunted. Humanity may not survive. They will be faced with the things of nightmares: demons, Devils, witches, werewolves, and vampires. All the things they make their infernally annoying movies about will be their reality. The loss of life will be astounding."

"Is there anything to be done to head them off?"

"Nothing that is not being done already, but we can't interfere with free will. We can't make them stop. We can only try and stop them from succeeding by reinforcing the gates and strengthening the protections."

"What about Griffin?"

"This makes it even more important that she Choose on her birthday. If she were to fail to do so, it would weaken the gates because it would allow freer access for demons to move between Hell and Earth."

"Well, damn. This keeps getting better and better." Alaria sighed. "There's nothing that's led me to believe that she doesn't intend to go through with it. I think she will. Braxton is making it easier on her. I'm more interested in what is going to happen if they do get the gates opened."

"Angels will be dispatched to Earth to round up the Devils and demons and put them back. There will be massive loss of life and an almost inevitable collapse of human society. It will be very difficult to live through." Gabriel sighed deeply and looked pained, the expression on his face clearly illustrating the fierce internal battle he fought. "I'm telling you this because you still have time to reconsider. You can have Griffin ask to let you come back. You could help us. We could work together again, like before."

Caught off guard, Alaria sat back and stared at Gabriel, studying the face that she had known for so long. Finally, after a long moment, she stood and crossed the room until she was only inches from him. "Gabe, I can't. I was trapped as an Angel. I didn't want it. I still don't. I loved being there with you, which is why I wanted you to come with me so badly. All these years of being a Devil, of being in Hell, it hasn't changed what I want.

I want to be human. I want those choices. I want that life. I want the sweet urgency of never knowing how much time you have left and of trying to cram so much into so little time." She reached out and took his hands. "I loved you, Gabe. In some amazing Angel-human way. Some tiny part of me that hasn't been eroded since the Fall still does. I'll admit there's a little bit of me that yearns to get my wings back and return with you, but the majority of me still wants what I wanted back then— which is to be one of them. I don't know if I'll like it. Hell, I may be begging for you to take me back with you inside a human year, but I want to know what it's like. I can't give that up. It's the only thing that's kept me somewhat sane all this time."

Gabriel nodded. "Okay." He squeezed her fingers once and stepped back. "If you ever change your mind, I'll do my best to help you." He smiled, a rare occurrence even when they were both Angels. "Ready to go back?"

"Yeah. Let's go to a wedding."

Braxton paced nervously, muttering under his breath. He wore black slacks and a button-up shirt with the sleeves rolled up to the elbow. What was he thinking? A wedding was just going to make it worse. Being forced to watch Griffin die was bad enough, but being forced to help his wife die? That was more than any man should be asked to do.

"You're right. It is. It's not fair that we're asking, and no one would blame you if you backed out."

Braxton looked up and saw Gabriel standing in the doorway. "What are you, a mind-reader?"

Gabriel shrugged. "Don't think so loud if you don't want people hearing the thoughts. It's not exactly difficult to hear you."

"She needs this, so I'm doing it. I don't even know if what I'm feeling is real, but it doesn't matter. The only thing that matters is that she has the strength to get through this. Anything else is just acceptable collateral damage."

"Yes. And you're going to have to remember that shortly. Griffin surviving is the only thing that matters, and no one else can take priority." Gabriel sighed. "You're going to be asked to do horrific things in the next weeks. Time is drawing short, and the Devils are desperate. Azazel and Lilith are trying to figure out how to get into the monastery. Within the next three days, you will find yourselves under attack."

"The charms should hold. There's no way they can get through."

"That will not stop them from trying." Gabriel offered a smile. "That is for another day. Nothing will happen today. Today, you will sacrifice your heart for her. It is not a sacrifice that goes unnoticed, though it will be one in a long line of sacrifices that you will make. I came here not to talk of unpleasant things but of the marriage that is to be forged here this afternoon. I know this is not my normal way of things, but I'm here to offer my services."

Taken aback, Braxton took several seconds to consider. "What do you mean, your services?"

"Anything you need. I can conjure a cake in a heartbeat. I can provide music or those silly human decorations and flowers. Angels have nearly unlimited domain over such things. What do you desire?"

Braxton laughed. "Whatever Griffin wants. She's the bride. It's her day."

"If she's like the other human females that I've had opportunity to observe, then the answer to my question is everything." Gabriel nodded. "I can do that. It will be ready for you in a moment or two. Have you someone to perform the ceremony?"

"I was just going to ask one of the guys that came in. It's not like I can call a preacher here."

"Is there anyone Griffin would like?"

Braxton mulled that over for several seconds before nodding. "Father Dooley, from back home. He's special to her. He helped her find out who she is."

"Brad Dooley is a good man." Gabriel opened the door. "I'll return with him shortly. I suggest you take your place at the altar. From my understanding of human time, this is supposed to begin in fifteen minutes."

Alaria stood in the back of the chapel portion of the monastery, taking in all the work the Angel had done. Lights and candles twinkled, flowers lined the aisle, and sunlight poured through the stained glass. Music was playing from somewhere, though she didn't see a pianist. Shaking her head, she turned to watch Griffin walk down the aisle toward Braxton, as beautiful as she could be in the white dress. Braxton looked like he was caught somewhere between awe at seeing her and terror at the prospect of marrying her.

The priest from Philadelphia stood at the end of the aisle, holding a Bible, tears shining in his eyes. Griffin clutched a bouquet of pink roses, and her heart pounded so loudly it was a minor miracle none of the humans heard it. Finally, Griffin reached Braxton and he took her hands, squeezing her fingers to offer reassurance.

"Friends and family, we find ourselves gathered here today to celebrate the union of Braxton Winslow and Griffin Javensen. They have come together, in the most unlikely of ways, and seek to join themselves in marriage in the eyes of God." Dooley took a breath to choke back the tears. "I've had short notice to do this and these aren't the most traditional of circumstances, so I'm going to go a bit off-script here. Marriage is a holy sacrament. It's meant for two people who wish to spend their lives together and who seek the blessing of the Creator. The situation that you two have found yourselves in is, at best, fantastical and, at worst, tragic. To find love in that—to come together and marry—even for this short a time, is the very definition of a miracle.

"Griffin, when I met you for the first time, you were scared and hurt. You were seeking meaning, a reason for the horrors that life showed you. The reason is that you are Chosen. Chosen to do this great service at the cost of a great sacrifice. Now, you stand before me, a woman who has accepted and embraced her duty and who has made the most out of a short life. You are more than this, and the world is a better place for having had you in it. You are more than the things that you've been through, and you have touched the lives of others. Griffin, you will never be forgotten, and you will always be loved.

"Braxton, I've known you for a long time. You're the greatest Warrior that's ever lived. You've dedicated your life to making Earth a safer place for everyone. When Griffin came to me and I realized who she is, there was no hesitation before giving her your name. By some twist of fate, you've been chosen as much as she has—to protect her, to guide her and to keep her safe. Somehow, you've managed to let yourself step outside of that role, to feel what you've never felt before, and to let yourself love. There is never any bad from loving. Devoting yourself to another does not make you weak, it makes you stronger. Without loving her so unconditionally, you could not have brought her through this as you have.

"Fate has not been kind, but today we put that aside and we celebrate the beautiful love that has been borne of fate. With everything that you've had to go through, you still found one another and allowed yourselves to be vulnerable, to feel, and to love. What most people take a lifetime to realize, you two have seen in a year. Never have I seen a love so great and so strong. There is no shame in today being bittersweet, as we remember where you've come from and know where you're going." He paused and looked between the couple. Griffin had tears running down her cheeks, though Braxton was still holding strong. "Know that today is your day, and in the presence of Angels, and the sight of God, it is my honor and privilege to unite the two of you. This is the most holy of weddings, the most blessed ceremony which I have had the pleasure of attending or officiating.

"So, without further ado, I ask you both: do you promise to love one another, fully and without holding back, until death parts you? Do you promise to trust one another, to listen, and to forsake all others? Do you promise to hold each other deep within your hearts, leaving room for no other until death parts you? Braxton?"

Voice steady, Braxton nodded and spoke. "I do."

"Griffin?"

Much wobblier, Griffin cleared her throat before speaking. "I do."

Father Dooley smiled. "Are there rings?"

When Griffin and Braxton both shook their heads, Gabriel snapped his fingers and a pair of rings appeared in Father Dooley's hand. Looking shocked, but taking it in stride, he chuckled. "The surprises never stop when there's an Angel in the room." He handed the smaller band to Braxton. "Place this ring on the third finger of her left hand." When Braxton did as he was told, Father Dooley offered the other to Griffin. "The same thing, please." He waited a beat. "The rings signify the lifelong promise that this man and woman have sworn to. It is an outward symbol of their dedication to each other, a declaration to the world that they have joined in front of God and that their lives are forever as one. What God hath joined together, let no man put asunder."

He laid his hands over theirs. "I'll borrow from the words of our Lord. In first Corinthians, God says 'If I give all I possess to the poor and give over my body to hardship that I may boast, but do not have love, I gain nothing....It does not dishonor others, it is not self-seeking, it is not easily angered, it keeps no record of wrongs. Love does not delight in evil, but rejoices in the truth.It always protects, always trusts, always hopes, always perseveres.Love never fails. And now these three remain: faith, hope and love. But the greatest of these is love.'" He dashed tears from his cheeks.

"In the name of the Father, the Son, and the Holy Spirit, with the authority vested in me by the Roman Catholic Church, I now pronounce you husband and wife. You may kiss your bride."

Braxton curved one arm around Griffin's waist and brought her flush against his body. A jubilant smile on his face, he dipped her back until she was balanced on one foot and clinging to his shoulders. He captured her mouth in an enthusiastic kiss that stole her breath and weakened her knees. He righted her as quickly as he'd lowered her, and turned to face the crowd of Warriors. They clapped and cheered, though he noticed the smiles didn't reach their eyes. His gaze settled on Sam, who cradled her bulging stomach with both hands and allowed her tears to stream down her cheeks unchecked. She smiled sadly and waved as they passed her.

Griffin smiled at Braxton and squealed when he swept her into his arms and carried her up the aisle. She flung her arms around his neck and laughed, the sound echoing through the chapel. Braxton thought briefly that he'd never seen her look happier. The look on her face and the sound of her laughter made it all worth it. Every sacrifice he'd made, every one he would still have to make—they were a small price to pay for making the end of Griffin's life even a tiny bit happier.

Chapter Thirty

December 15th, 2029 - The Choosing Place

GRIFFIN SPENT most mornings looking out the window, searching the woods for any sign of life. A bird, a snake, anything that would tell her that her instincts were wrong. Every morning, there was nothing. So after a while, she would resign herself to yet another day of being afraid, and go downstairs to eat. At least she was keeping food down since Gabriel had given her a reprieve from the wasting away. She'd managed to put on a few pounds, filling out her gaunt frame slightly.

It was snowing. Big flakes falling from the sky, piling on top of one another, coating the ground and the road and covering the cars. The snow was coming down so thickly now that it was almost impossible to see.

Griffin had always loved the snow and could vaguely remember sitting on her grandmother's lap, watching the flakes drift down, amped with excitement that she would get to go outside with her grandfather and play in it as soon as he got home. Even throughout her time in foster care, she'd always loved the first snowfall.

Mind made up, she left the window and crossed the room, her clothes hitting the floor. She pulled on jeans instead of her sweat pants and donned a thick grey sweater and wool socks. She hopped on one foot to tug on her boot before switching and yanking on the other. Rifling through her closet, she realized she didn't have a coat, then saw Braxton's hanging up by the door. Feeling more relaxed than she had in months, she grabbed the coat and dashed down the stairs, swinging around to hurry through the kitchen and out the back door.

The cold air was fresh and crisp on her face, and she curled her toes inside her boots, enjoying the feel. She tipped her head back and let the snowflakes settle on her skin, melting from her body heat. After a moment of enjoying the snow, she spread her arms out and fell backward.

The impact jarred her, but the snow cushioned the fall. Feeling like a child, she moved her arms and legs, reveling in the simple joy of making a snow angel. When she'd sufficiently cleared the snow around her, she simply lay there, staring up at the dreary gray sky, watching the snow drift down. She let the tears take her.

"How long has she been out there?"

Alaria looked over her shoulder at Braxton. "Only about fifteen minutes. I've been keeping an eye on her."

"She's making snow angels."

"Brilliant deduction, Sherlock." Alaria laughed. "There's no harm in her playing in the snow for a while. This might be her last chance to do it. Nothing's going to happen to her there in the yard with us right here. It's not like she's by herself. There're a hundred Warriors in this building, and at last count, one vampire."

Braxton dropped a pile of books on the table and joined Alaria at the sliding glass doors. "Gage got here?"

"Yeah, and speaking of, how in the hell do you know one of the oldest vampires still living? I didn't think that the Vatican believed in those sorts of creatures."

"I'm not the Vatican. In my experience, most of the monsters kids are scared of exist in one form or another. Vampires happen to be one of the few cases where myth got it more right than wrong. Gage is a good person to have in your corner. All that money and all that experience—there's nothing he can't do." Braxton shook his head. "Though owing him a favor is not something that anyone should do." He sighed. "Hopefully it isn't too painful when he calls this one in, 'cause this is a big-ass favor."

Alaria made a noise in her throat, her attention caught by a flash of movement outside the door. She reached for the handle, trying to focus on what was going on and pulled it open. "What in the hell is that?"

Braxton followed her out onto the porch, acknowledging Griffin climbing to her feet with an absent wave. "It's a person. They're across the line, so it has to be human." He took a few steps. "It's okay, Alaria, it's just a kid." He waved and went to the edge of the deck. "Can I help you?"

The child, maybe twelve or thirteen, looked up at him with eyes alarmingly blank. Before all the pieces could click together for Braxton, the boy drew a gun and fired, the bullet striking Braxton in the shoulder. He hit the ground with a shout, and his eyes widened in fear as he saw many more people walking through the woods. The puzzle pieces fell into place, and he yelled to Alaria.

"Familiars! They're Familiars!" He scrambled to his feet and saw Alaria grab Griffin and disappear with her inside. Before he could get to the door to get to his gun, a man blurred through the door and across the lawn. Without a word—without hesitation—he grabbed the boy and broke his neck, baring his fangs and snarling.

Braxton grabbed his gun off the table and spared a glance to where Alaria was standing with Griffin. "Make sure she's safe and then get back out here. There are a hundred of them, at least. Get every Warrior you see."

"Most are off-site, but I'll round up who I can." She grabbed Griffin's arm. "Come with me."

Griffin nearly fell when Alaria jerked her arm and dragged her down the hall, panic making her strides faster than normal. "What's going on?"

Alaria cast a glance over her shoulder to make sure they weren't being followed. "Familiars are humans who are being controlled by other creatures. Witches, vampires, demons. It's mind control. They don't know what they're doing, but they're human, so our protections won't keep them out. There are only two ways to stop it. Kill them, or kill the creature controlling them. With that many, it's at least twenty demons doing it. Going after that many is a suicide mission." She opened a door and looked inside quickly to make sure the room was clear. "They're hoping Braxton values human life to the extent that he'll risk going after the demons. That is not a good idea." She snapped her fingers and handed Griffin the gun that appeared in her hand. "Shoot anything that comes in that door that isn't me or Braxton. Stay here, do not move, and scream if anyone gets in." She snapped again and then tucked an extra clip into Griffin's waistband. "Do not hesitate to fire, Griffin. They'll tear you to pieces if they get to you. There's no saving them."

Griffin nodded. "Go."

Alaria didn't hesitate. She turned on her heel and disappeared, reappearing with a crack outside. Gage, a tall man with coal black hair and clear silver eyes, ripped through the mob of Familiars. Blood stained the snow as he used his fangs as much as his hands to dispatch the threats. She took one moment to appreciate his ruthlessness before rushing into the mass.

Braxton charged into the fray, his hands steady on the butt of the gun, blood running down his arm from the angry-looking bullet wound. He felt his heart clench each time that he pulled the trigger, but he knew that there was no other option. Familiars would continue to fight until either they died or the person they were after did.

Gage tossed two bodies aside, his eyes glowing red. He glanced back at Braxton and cursed. "Get inside and guard Griffin. There aren't enough Warriors in this building to deal with this. They could be coming in the front. We've got the ones back here." He strode over, his gaze going to the wound. "I can take care of that."

Braxton looked over at his shoulder and briefly considered the offer. Vampire blood, when ingested in small quantities, had healing properties. The only danger was that, were he to die with it in his system, he would come back. "Thanks, but I'll pass. You sure you can handle this?"

Gage glanced at the mob of Familiars swarming in through the gate with a look that held no more interest than a fly would have. "Braxton, I'm thirteen hundred years old. Get the hell out of my way and go take care of your wife."

Alaria whirled, tossing a body as she did so. "Third floor. Sixth door on the right."

Braxton nodded, turned, and ran back into the monastery. He leaped up the stairs and swung around the corner to jog down the hallway that would lead him to Griffin.

Griffin paced the room anxiously, the gun Alaria had given her heavy and awkward in her hand. She toyed with the safety, pushing it on, then off, then on again. The hair on the back of her neck stood up straight as she heard movement in the hallway, and her heart jumped into her throat when she heard the door next to her hit the wall as it was kicked open. Heart pounding, she thumbed the safety off and wrapped both hands around the gun.

When she clearly heard several pairs of feet, she closed her eyes and sent up a quick prayer that Gabriel was close and would come to help. When she opened her eyes and there was no Angel in the room, her throat closed from fear. For all the times that she'd had encounters with demons, she'd only ever faced Alaria alone and Azazel only in a dream. Even when she was at her most frightening, she'd never believed Alaria would actually kill her. The Familiars were mindless shells of the people they had once been. She didn't doubt Alaria had told her the truth when she said they would tear her to pieces.

The first crash on the door made her jump, and the gun hit the floor as she clapped both hands to her mouth to muffle the scream that tried to wrestle its way out of her throat. Panicking, she dropped to her knees and fumbled with the gun, backing into a corner with it clutched to her chest. Her knuckles turned white from the intensity of her grip on the weapon. The second crash brought tears to her eyes, and the third crash splintered the door.

She saw a mass of hands trying to break the door open, and she forced herself to stand, sliding up the wall and trying to make herself invisible. Slowly, she took a deep breath and pulled the slide on the gun to load a bullet into the chamber. She checked to make sure her extra clip was still in the waistband of her jeans and silently thanked Alaria for making sure she was armed before leaving her there.

She screamed when the door broke and raised the gun. There were at least fifteen, none of them more than twenty years old, all of them charging toward her with eyes that were cloudy gray and looked so blank and empty Griffin knew it would haunt her for the rest of her life. As the first one forced its way past the broken door frame, she gritted her teeth and pulled the trigger. The recoil from the weapon was a surprise, and her head slammed against the wall.

The bullet hit home, and the boy dropped to the floor, blood and bits of bone splattering the mob behind him. They didn't even look at him; they just kept coming. Tears streaming down her face, Griffin screamed and kept firing. One by one, the Familiars hit the floor, some with two or three bullet holes in them. When she ran out of bullets, it took two empty clicks before she realized she was out, and she fumbled to release the empty clip. She dropped the full clip on the ground and had to fall to her hands and knees to get it. By the time she snapped the new clip in, they were nearly on top of her. Griffin had never known true panic until that moment.

She fired again, and a girl, who was no more than two feet away from her, fell—her arms outstretched, trying to reach Griffin. The next one, a boy about seventeen, clawed at Griffin's arms, scratching her, and she struggled to break free. She pressed the barrel of the gun against his chest and pulled the trigger. She gasped when blood splattered her face, and she shoved the body backward into the crowd of Familiars still coming at her.

Her back hit the wall, and she fought them off, punching and kicking, shooting when she could get free enough of them to manage the trigger. She was fighting from instinct, with no thought to it, and she'd buried four bullets into the wall before she realized there were no more.

Sobbing, covered in blood—some of it hers, most of it not—she sank to the floor, her hands shaking so severely that she couldn't maintain her grip on the gun. She heard a voice out in the hall, yelling for her, and she vaguely recognized it as Braxton's. She lifted her head, trying to blink blood and sweat from her eyes, and cleared her throat. Her vocal chords were so raw from the screaming that it took her three tries before she could form any words.

"In here."

Braxton swung into the room, fear on his face. He took in the situation quickly, his gaze moving over the bodies on the floor and settling on Griffin. He saw the blood on her face and clothes, the deep furrows in her arms and the bruises already purpling on her cheek and chest. He dropped to his knees next to her and grabbed her by the shoulders.

"Are you okay? How badly are you hurt?"

Still dazed, Griffin shook her head. "I don't know. I don't think I'm hurt bad. Just my arms, I think. I don't know. There were so many. They just kept coming. I kept shooting, and shooting, and shooting, and there were always more." She looked up at him, eyes wide and filled with confusion. "What happened? Where did they come from? Who were they?"

Braxton tucked her hair behind her ears. "Let's go get you cleaned up." He stood, scooped her into his arms, and stepped over the bodies to leave the room. He cradled her against his chest and descended the stairs carefully. When he turned into the kitchen, he saw Gage, Alaria and all ten of the Warriors that had been present dragging the bodies into a pile. They would be burned, but there was no need for Griffin to see it.

Alaria saw them a moment before Gage did, and came inside. She smelled of the smoke from the fire that would burn the remains. She assessed the situation with a cool look and lifted her eyebrows. "What happened? I locked her up."

"They got in through another entrance. There're about fifteen bodies upstairs that need to be dealt with. I don't think she's hurt badly, but she's pretty traumatized. I need to get everyone back here. We need more manpower if something like this happens again. Obviously they're not going to wait until New Year's Eve to start with the attacks."

"I'll take her and clean her up."

Braxton nodded and shifted Griffin's slight weight to Alaria, who wrapped one arm around Griffin's waist, using the other to hold Griffin's arm across her shoulders. He stared at them for several seconds before speaking. "I appreciate it. I know I should be doing this, but—"

Alaria shook her head adamantly and tightened her grip on Griffin to keep the other woman from sliding. "No. You should be taking steps to make sure she's safe moving forward. Not a single one of your Warriors is going to listen if either Gage or I call and tell them to come home. They'll think we've killed you both and that we're trying to get them to come in and be slaughtered. I can handle hosing her off."

Braxton looked back and forth between the phone and Griffin several times, then nodded. "When she comes back to herself, let her know I'll be up as soon as I can."

Alaria nodded, then half-carried Griffin down the hall toward the bathroom. Efficiently, she stripped the other woman's clothes off, sat her in the bathtub, and turned on the water. Griffin wrapped her arms around her knees and rocked back and forth, blinking rapidly as Alaria poured water over her head. Alaria sighed as she began to clean the deep scratches on Griffin's arms and battered down the flickers of sympathy that stirred within her. It was going to be a long two weeks.

Chapter Thirty-One

December 30th, 2029 - The Choosing Place

THEY'D BEEN under attack for six days. Witches, demons, Familiars and more supernatural creatures than Griffin had ever known existed were sieging against the monastery walls. She now knew what werewolves looked like, had been forced to kill a shapeshifter, and had seen glowing red eyes in the dark as vampires prowled around the perimeter.

Braxton had been preoccupied with what he did best—killing demons. He had stationed an armed guard with Griffin at all times, and she was being kept away from all doors and windows. After the attack, he had shut down. He had shifted into Warrior mode and had begun organizing those who had flown in to help. There were armed patrols, snipers on the roof and guards at every door. No one was allowed inside without being extensively searched.

Griffin was a prisoner. She was never alone, not even when she bathed and slept. The knife that Gabriel had given her remained strapped to her thigh, and she carried Holy Water and a gun on her person at all times. The monastery had been instantly transformed from a safe haven into a war zone the second the first Familiar had attacked.

Every time she closed her eyes, she saw them. The wide, unseeing eyes, the choppy movements. It was worse than any zombie movie she'd ever seen. There was no reaction when bullets hit them, and they wouldn't stop coming until they were either out of blood or their brain was damaged. Images of the children she'd been forced to kill haunted her, wresting her from sleep with screams that pierced through the silence of the night.

It had been over a week since Braxton had lain down with her. He came to check on her several times a day but left her in the hands of other Warriors most of the time. She knew, on a logical level, that it was easier for him to deal with the situation when he had things to do. If he stopped to look at her, to spend time with her, it would hit him that there were fewer than thirty-six hours left, and that was too much to bear.

Every time she saw a clock, Griffin felt her heart tighten in her chest. It was a combination of nerves, terror, anxiety, and nausea. Her heart would race, her palms would sweat, and she would get dizzy, as everything she'd never gotten to do flooded her mind. As her birthday grew closer, she wished more and more fervently that she could just run away and leave the whole thing for someone else to deal with.

Deep down, she knew that she was incapable of doing that. She was committed, and there was nothing that would keep her from Choosing. As much as the thought of dying terrified her, she knew that what she was doing was much more important than any human desires that she had. She trudged on, gritting her teeth against the nausea and battling down the terror that bubbled up within her every time she happened to pass a clock.

Finally, as midnight approached and New Year's Eve ruthlessly marched toward her, she slipped from bed, draping her robe around her shoulders and crossing the room. Her guard jumped when she opened the door, then smiled at her sympathetically. He was young, maybe twenty-five, and still wet behind the ears. He'd never had to kill a demon, but he was dedicated to their fight. It broke her heart that she knew he would likely only live to see the sun rise one more time. .

"I'm going to Braxton."

"Ma'am, he's in with Alaria and Gabriel. They're strategizing for tomorrow. The Devils are launching more aggressive attacks against the protections, and our witches don't know how much longer they'll hold. I don't know if now is a good time."

Griffin smiled reassuringly. "I'm going to die tomorrow. I want to spend my last night on Earth with my husband. There's not a Devil or Angel that exists that is going to take that away from me. Either you take me to him right now, or I start screaming at the top of my lungs until I either get his attention, or you have to knock me out to shut me up. Let's be honest, hmm? Braxton is going to be much angrier if you hurt me. Either way, it doesn't end well for you. I think you should just start walking in whatever direction he happens to be and spare us both the drama."

Swallowing hard, the boy nodded. "Right this way."

Griffin patted his shoulder as she followed him. "Good choice."

They wound their way through the monastery quickly, the boy insisting on making her duck to crawl beneath all the windows, even though they had all been covered with wood. Finally, after ten minutes, the man knocked on a door and jumped about three feet when Braxton yelled for him to enter. Griffin stepped in front of him, nudging him out of the way to walk into the room.

"Griffin. Where's your guard?" Braxton stood, concern knitting his brow. "You know better than to leave your room alone."

"He's right there in the hall. He walked me down here, just like a good little puppet." She closed the door and leaned against it. "Are the protections holding?"

"For now, but their time is limited. The witches are becoming very strained from holding them."

"Are they going to break within the next eight to ten hours?"

Gabriel pondered that for a long moment while Alaria and Braxton exchanged a glance, communicating without words. Finally, the Angel broke the silence. "I believe we have approximately twenty-one human hours before they breach our defenses. That will require us to fend them off for three hours and fifteen human minutes."

"There's nothing that we can do to stop it?"

Braxton shook his head. "We've done everything we can. They're going to get in. It's inevitable at this point."

"Then I want you to come with me. I want to get some sleep, and I want you to sleep with me."

"Griffin, I can't leave. We're so close, and there's so much to do—"

"Go." Alaria sighed. "Gabe and I can handle this. Go take a few hours."

"I'd really rather stay here and manage this to make sure that everything goes the way that it should."

Gabriel stood. "I assure you that your operation is safe in my hands. No one has a more vested interest in this going well than the four of us. I can promise you that everything will be precisely where you left it in a few of your hours. This may be the last chance that you have to spend any time at all with Griffin. I would encourage you to say your goodbyes."

Braxton looked between the two and knew he was outnumbered. He nodded and rose. "Six hours. I'll be back in six hours."

Griffin held out her hand and smiled when Braxton took it. Silently, they left the room and ascended the stairs to her bedroom. Alaria waited until Gabriel had pulled the door shut before speaking.

"I kinda feel bad for them."

Gabriel strode back to the table, the firelight dancing off his face. "Her reward awaits her in Heaven."

"What about his?" She sat on top of the papers they'd been poring over to effectively end the work they'd been doing. "Braxton is giving up just as much as Griffin. He probably won't make it through tomorrow."

Briefly, Gabriel looked pained. "It is not my intention to see him die. I can't control the outcome of tomorrow, but I've no knowledge of him needing to perish."

"Then he'll be left to pine after Griffin and suffer here on Earth."

Frustrated, Gabriel tossed up his hands. "What do you want from me? You complain that he'll die, and then you bitch that he'll live!"

Taken aback by the language, Alaria held her hands palms-up in a gesture of peace. "Where did you learn to talk like that?"

Flustered and embarrassed, Gabriel flushed red and mumbled. "I do pay attention to the vernacular."

Alaria laughed and slid off the table. She sauntered to the fire to stand next to the Angel. "I've seen more of you in the last two weeks than in the last two millennia. It's nice working together again."

Gabriel snorted in a way so undignified Alaria had to bite her cheek to keep from laughing. "We could have been working together this entire time. It was your choices that kept us apart."

Her voice soft, Alaria spoke. "How long are you going to keep punishing me for that?"

"It isn't my place to punish you. I was only following orders."

She shook her head. "I don't mean what Father made you do. I'm not talking about casting me out. I'm talking about *you* forgiving me. I don't want His forgiveness. It doesn't matter to me. Yours does."

Gabriel stared stonily into the fire. Alaria had almost given up on getting an answer when his voice filled the room. "I forgave you a long time ago. I understood why you wanted humanity. I was close to taking it, too, just because it was so important to you. I never wanted anything other than your happiness. If Father had given you what you wanted, I'd have gone with you. I couldn't take up arms against Heaven. It went against every fiber in me. I couldn't make that sacrifice."

"I know." She crossed her arms and glanced at him quickly before turning back to stare into the flickering flames. "Where do we go from here?"

"I don't know." He studied the side of her face. "There's more of you left than I thought there was. It changes things." He sighed deeply. "I'm worried about what will become of you if Lucifer succeeds in opening the gates."

"I'll be fine." Her eyes were sad. "I always am."

"I'll answer if you call for me. If you get into trouble, yell for me." He offered her a slight smile. "I'll protect you as much as I can."

Alaria staunchly ignored the stirrings in her belly. Instead, she concentrated on the red and orange colors dancing in the fireplace. "I've missed you, Gabe." The words came out before she could control them, and she instantly regretted them. Gabriel was silent for several moments, and she was beginning to think he hadn't heard her when his shoulders dropped and he smiled sadly.

"I've missed you, too." He waited a beat before continuing. Alaria knew him well enough to know the pause was time for him to decide how much more to say. "There is something I want to speak of, but I need your word it does not leave this room and that it will never be spoken of again."

Without hesitating, Alaria nodded. "You have it."

"When you took me back in time before the Battle began, you expressed your feelings through a human reaction."

Alaria bit back a smile. "I kissed you." She struggled to maintain a straight face when he glared at her. "Sorry. This is a big deal for you. Please, continue."

"I want to know why. I didn't allow you a chance to explain yourself then, and I cannot help but entertain the notion that, had I stayed and not judged you so harshly, that perhaps you'd have chosen a different path."

Alaria nodded to make sure he knew she was listening. It took her nearly ten seconds to decide what she wanted to say. "I wanted to make you see how I felt."

"Explain it to me now." He looked at her, his eyes filled with guilt and kindness. "I'm listening to you now."

"I wanted humanity. I wanted everything they have that we don't. More than anything, I wanted to experience it with you. We'd been companions for so long I couldn't imagine living without you. The more I thought about living without you around, the more I developed human feelings. By the time I brought you to me that day, I was desperate to make you see how I felt and convinced you felt the same. I wanted to see if you and I could make a human existence together."

Gabriel's voice was little more than a whisper. "I treated you badly. I was cruel to you, and it was unnecessary. This is hard for me, even when so much time has passed. When you—did what you did, it made me feel emotions I am not proud of. I felt...certain stirrings."

Alaria bit the inside of her cheek to keep from smiling and reached out to place her palm against his face. "There's no shame in feeling, Gabe. That's one of the biggest reasons I wanted humanity. I wanted to have no guilt for feeling what I feel."

"I want to make it right, Alaria. I betrayed your trust by my actions." He covered her hand with his own. "If you become human, there can be no future for us. I'll have to watch you grow old and die."

Alaria closed her eyes. She pulled her hand out from beneath his. When he reached out and cupped her face, she leaned into his touch. "For one minute, Gabriel, could you please just chill out and let the moment happen?" She opened her eyes and locked her gaze onto his. "We might not survive tomorrow. It's more likely than not that we'll both be dead before the dawn of the next year. For one minute, on the night before we're likely going to die, just let it happen."

Gabriel cleared his throat. "What, precisely, are you proposing?"

Alaria laughed. "This."

Her mouth was soft and firm at the same time. She linked her arms around his neck and pulled him closer to her. She angled her body until it was pressed solidly against his. When he didn't move, she giggled and reached down to grab his hands in hers. She placed one on each of her hips and brushed her nose against his.

"It's a kiss, Gabe. It's not evil, or an abomination."

Gabriel blushed for the second time in the millennia Alaria had known him. "I've, uh, never done this before. Well, the once you kissed me, but..."

Alaria laughed again. "That so doesn't count." She slipped her arms around his neck again. When she pressed her mouth to his again, his hands tightened on her hips but he didn't respond. Amused, she pulled back and smiled up at him.

"You could try kissing me back, y'know."

Gabriel couldn't help the smile that fluttered across his face. "I'll try."

Alaria kissed him again, her mouth hungry and hot. Gabriel gasped from the onslaught, and she took immediate advantage of the opening to flick her tongue against his. Of their own accord, his hands travelled from her hips to tangle in her hair and his mouth moved against hers, hesitant and unsure. She groaned from the contact and arched her body against his feverishly. She unbuttoned his jacket and shoved it down his arms, then ripped open his shirt and sprawled her hands on his chest, growling deep in her throat at the feel of hot, smooth skin under her palms.

The contact was unlike anything Gabe had ever felt. When she covered his hand with one of her own and moved it to her breast, he was helpless to stop her. Then, somehow his hand was under her shirt and her flesh filled his palm. Her nipple pressed into his hand, slightly rough and hard, and a bolt of sensation ricocheted through him. Her mouth was still on his, and there was a tightness in his gut that he'd never experienced.

Somehow, they'd crossed the room, and he was pinning her against the wall before he could realize what he was doing. His other hand left her hair and slid down the side of her body to her thigh. He applied pressure and she lifted her leg to wrap it around his hip. Before he knew what he was doing, he had ripped her shirt over her head and tossed it onto the floor.

Alaria pushed his head down so that his mouth was against her neck. When his teeth nipped at the tendons there, she nearly purred. Her foot dropped back to the floor and her hands went to his waistband. With practiced movements, she shoved his slacks down his legs and wrapped her hands around his hard, thick penis. Gabriel growled and jumped from the unfamiliar contact, and Alaria wondered briefly if he had even ever touched himself.

She unfastened her own pants and stepped out of them. Wearing only her heels, she pushed him backward, their mouths fused together. There was no time for foreplay and romance. She shoved him down onto the table and stood between his legs. She bent slightly and licked his erection from base to tip, purring in satisfaction when it jumped and Gabriel groaned loudly. Desperate to feel him inside her, she climbed on top of him, held his erection in one hand, positioned herself over him, and sank down, enveloping his flesh with her own. The sensation, one Gabriel had never felt, was too much. He drove his hips up, surging into her. His fingers bruised her hips from gripping so tightly. She pistoned her hips against his, then lifted herself up and sank back down.

In the span of a breath, Gabriel flipped her over and pinned her to the table, his big body dwarfing hers. He grabbed her thighs and pulled her leg around his hips. Going on instinct, he drove into her, his thrusts hard and fast. Her fingers bit into his shoulders and she thrashed on the table. His other hand grabbed her chin and held her head still so he could clamp his mouth on hers. She felt the tremors in his muscles that signaled climax and rolled her hips against his to increase her own pleasure.

He tightened within her, on the verge of orgasm, and she jerked her hips rapidly to give herself the pressure she needed, exploding around him. He lunged up and roared as his first orgasm swept him away.

Alaria knew it would happen before Gabriel did. She laid on the table, still naked and covered in sweat when he stirred next to her. His blond hair was a mess, his body sweaty and gloriously naked. He sat up and looked down at her, the expression in his eyes one of terror, confusion, and guilt.

"It's okay."

Gabriel sprang to his feet and raced across the room to grab his pants. "It's not okay. What have I done? What have we done? God in Heaven, what have I done?"

Alaria climbed to her feet and crossed the room to him. She reached out and took the fabric from him. "We did what we have both wanted to do for the last ten million years. There is no shame in this."

"I'll be punished." Gabriel shoved her shirt at her. "We should cover ourselves."

Alaria tossed it back onto the floor. "I'm not ashamed. I'm not ashamed of you, or me, or being naked, or of anything we just did." She pinned a hard gaze on him. "Are you ashamed of me, Gabe?" She wrapped her arms around his neck and pressed her flesh against his. "Or are you feeling guilty because you enjoyed it?"

He averted his eyes from hers. "This should never have happened."

Alaria smirked. "This should have happened long ago." She reached between their bodies and took him in her hand, sliding her fingers up and down his erection. When he hardened and lengthened, she smiled. "Shut it off, Gabe. For one damned night, shut it off and let me have you."

Though he knew it was a mistake—knew they would both pay for what they had done—he was helpless to resist her. He stooped, lifted her in his arms, and carried her back to the table.

Griffin led Braxton into her room with a determined step. Somehow at peace, she stood in front of him, her fingers steady as she unbuttoned his shirt and sent it drifting to the floor.

"Take off your shoes."

Braxton bent to obey her, kicking off his boots and pulling off the socks. His throat clogged with emotion as he looked into her face for what he knew was going to be one of the last times. Once he straightened, she undid his belt, then unbuttoned and unzipped his jeans, sending them to the floor as well. Silently, he stepped out of them. Her hand slid down his arm, and she twined her fingers with his.

"Come lie down with me."

Still silent, Braxton followed her to the bed and slid under the covers with her. He lay flat on his back, one arm curled underneath his head, the other stretched out to pillow hers. She curled into his side, laying her head in the crook of his shoulder, and wrapping one arm around his waist. After several minutes of silence, Braxton cleared his throat.

"I don't know what to say here, Griffin. I don't know if I should say anything."

"I don't think there are any rules. No instruction manual." She propped her head up on her hand. "No one has ever done this before. We're just playing it by ear."

"What do you want to do?"

Griffin laughed. "Travel the world, have babies, and grow old. Seeing as I'm going to die tomorrow, I'll settle for spending the night with my husband."

Absentmindedly, he ran his fingers through her hair. "This all feels so surreal. Like we're going to get through tomorrow and someone is going to tell us that it's all been a joke."

"It's not a joke, Brax." She laid her hand on his face. "This is our last night. This is my last night."

"How are you so calm? When I think about it, I want to punch something, yell—do something! You just talk about it like you're discussing whether or not to go to the grocery store tomorrow."

"I've made peace with it." She stared up at the ceiling. "All of this, it's like a dream. It's like I'm watching it happen to myself through some sort of a camera lens, like a movie. I know it's real, that I'm actually going to die tomorrow, and I'm not sure if it's some sort of feature built into this whole thing or if it's just me, but I'm not scared, at least not right now. Tomorrow is the day I do what I was born to do, and I think my soul knows that. I've been careening toward this since my first breath, since my first heartbeat."

Braxton pressed a kiss to her forehead. "I don't want to let you go."

"You have to. We both know you would find it in you to stab me your-self if you thought I wouldn't do it."

He chose not to respond to that, partially because it was true, but mostly because he was ashamed that it was. "I wish we could make tonight special for you, or tomorrow. But with everything going on—"

"I know." She laid her finger over his mouth to shush him. "You don't have to apologize. We're being attacked. Warriors have given their lives to get me here. I'm not about to jeopardize that, to make it worth nothing, so that we can have a candlelit dinner. The odds of any of them making it out of here alive tomorrow are slim to none. I will not let that be for noth-ing."

He gathered her close, relishing the feel of her hair against his face; the feel of her skin under his hands. "I will never forget you." He kissed her fervently. "I will always love you. You've shown me what love is this past year. I didn't want to feel it—tried not to—but every time I looked at you, I fell deeper. You are the strongest, kindest, most amazing person that I have ever had the honor of meeting. I want you to know, if you never have known anything else, that this world is a better place because of your life, and I am a better man because of you."

"I want you to be happy, Braxton. Being with me, that is so selfless. It's helped me get through this, and I honestly don't know if I'd have the strength to do this without you here. But me letting this happen? That was selfish. I know that it's no good for you, and I've let it happen anyway, be-cause I wanted it and because I love you. I want you to know that it's okay to move on—that it's okay to be happy." She braced her forehead against his, tears slipping down her cheeks. "I need you to promise me something."

"Anything."

"Don't waste a second of your life mourning me."

"Griffin—"

"No. Don't argue. Promise me. I want you to have the life that you deserve, that we should have gotten to have. I want you to find someone and marry her, and have lots of babies, and coach softball, and intimidate poor, unsuspecting teenage boys who come to take your daughter on a date. I want you to walk her down the aisle, and hold your grandchildren. I want you to grow old with someone special next to you, holding your hand. I want you to watch your grandchildren grow up, and I want you to die an old man, at home in his bed, with a good woman next to you. I want you to get everything I won't. You have to promise me, to swear on all that is good and holy, that you will not let this be the end for you." She framed his face with her hands. "I need that, Braxton. I need to know that you'll be okay. That you'll move on. I need you to promise me."

His heart shattering into a thousand pieces, tears trying to force their way out of him, Braxton nodded. His voice was harsh and strained as he spoke. "I promise."

Chapter Thirty-Two

December 31st, 2029. 10:23 P.M. - The Choosing Place
Ninety-seven minutes. Griffin paced her bedroom like a caged animal, her eyes barely leaving the clock. She could hear the din of the Warriors on the lower level and the chanting of their witches, trying with everything they had to keep the protections intact. Outside, she could also hear the demons and their witches, with different chants. Even from three stories up and a hundred yards away, she could feel the power rolling off of them.

Desperate to know what was going on, she glanced to the window, contemplating the plywood that had been put over it to keep anything out. She peered at it, considering which angle was the best. Finally, she shrugged and wiggled her fingers underneath it and pried it from the window. What she saw outside was enough to freeze the blood in her veins.

There was a writhing mass of black that she knew was an army of demons in their true form. Hell hounds, the slavering beasts that had haunted her childhood, paced anxiously. A wizened old man held a cane with a chunk of crystal on top of it, his arms outstretched, chanting, while the sky swirled and turned red with the magic. A circle of witches held hands and worked spells, channeling their magic into the warlock. In front, taking it all in, were the three Devils.

They were going to get in. She knew that instantly and unequivocally. The casual stance that the three took told her that was true. There was no way they would have been merely standing, waiting, looking as if they were having a nice chat about the weather if they weren't sure they would get inside. She backed away from the window slowly, suddenly scared that they could see her.

"It won't be long."

Griffin squealed and jumped, relaxing when she saw Alaria. "You scared the hell out of me!"

"Sorry." Alaria somehow looked anything but. "I came to check on you before this whole thing gets started. There's not long left. Having cold feet?"

"No." Griffin sat on the foot of the bed. "I feel calm. Today is my day. This is why I was born. Somehow I don't feel anything other than ready. I thought I'd be a crying, blotchy mess, curled up in a ball in the corner. Instead, I feel energized, calm and content."

"That's how you're supposed to feel. Your soul knows why it was created, and it knows it's almost time to be set free." Alaria glanced over her shoulder. "There are four armed Warriors outside the door. They'll protect you from anything trying to get in. Whatever you do, stay in this room. You can do the Choosing right here if it gets to be midnight and neither Braxton nor I have come to get you."

"I thought I was supposed to do it in the church?"

"That would be better. It's where it's supposed to take place, and the natural protections in the sanctuary offer some defense from the others. It's not safe for you to go wandering around by yourself, though, and I don't think that God is going to care if you're in this room or that one. If push comes to shove, I need to know that you're going to be able to do this, possibly by yourself, at midnight. Can you do that?"

Griffin nodded. "I don't see as I've ever had much of a choice. I'll do what needs to be done."

Alaria looked as if she wanted to say something, then shook her head, her eyes going dark. She dashed to the window and peered out of it, swearing under her breath as she took in the situation. Then, with absolute calm and a look on her face so stony that Griffin thought briefly she would need an anvil to crack it, she smiled. "They're in. It's party time." She strode across the room, picked up the bag she'd brought in with her, and tossed it to Griffin. "Salt the door when I leave. Spray the traps over every inch of this room and herb every crack and corner—anything that could buy you a second if you have to run. If you get into trouble, yell for me. I'll hear you no matter where I am in this damn cavernous monstrosity."

Griffin opened her mouth to respond, but Alaria was gone before she could even make a sound. Stunned, she did the only thing she could think to do. She crossed to the window to see what was happening.

Beelzebub felt the give in the protections the moment that it happened.

He smiled and smoothed the nonexistent wrinkles from the shoulder of his expensive Italian suit. He turned his head to the left to study Azazel, bare-chested and clad in nothing other than leather pants and boots, then to the right, where Lilith wore a flowing white Grecian gown, her blonde locks cascading down her shoulders in perfectly arranged curls. He knew they had felt it as well, but both were waiting for him to make the first move.

"Brother, you find the Chosen and kill her. Do not let anything else distract you from that task. Sister, you find Gabriel and carve his wings from his back. I want the Angel to die for this. No one—" he raised his voice to include the rest of his soldiers. "No one is to touch Alaria. That traitorous bitch is mine. It is my hands that will rip off her head." He smiled sharply and bared his teeth. "My children, tonight we bathe in Warrior blood! The protections are down, and the Chosen is inside those walls, guarded by an army of Warriors. There will be a great prize for the one who brings me the head of Braxton Winslow." He lifted his arms. "Go dine!" When he lowered his arms, he placed one hand on the shoulder of each of the other two Devils.

Together, they stood for a minute, watching the demons rush the monastery. The inky black sky with the cold moonlight spilled over them, illuminating them so that they looked almost ethereal. The mass of demons and hounds crashed against the walls and the gate. Wood splintered, concrete crumbled, and they fought one another to cram in through the door.

"Let's make our Father proud." Beelzebub lowered his arms and buttoned his suit coat. "Show time."

Together, the three Devils walked through the doors to the monastery and into the fray of an already raging battle. There were humans, Angels, demons, vampires, witches, and werewolves; creatures on both sides, fighting viciously for what they believed in. As soon as the three Devils crossed the threshold, they split in different directions. Azazel disappeared to hunt down Griffin. Beelzebub went in search of Alaria, winding his way through the fight with grace and agility. Lilith had already forgotten her assignment, and focused in on someone much more interesting.

Michael stood in the middle of the battle, commanding his Angels, his magnificent red wings spread out behind him, a sword gripped in one of his hands. As demons charged him, he alternated between running them through with his sword and brushing them aside with his wings. When his eyes focused on Lilith, he smiled viciously, and she was reminded why he was the Angel of War.

They strode toward each other, and Lilith clenched her fist, her own sword appearing in her hand as she glided toward him on needle thin heels. Neither stopped until they were toe to toe. Michael was strong and solid in all black, with fearsome red wings, long black hair, and shocking blue eyes; Lilith was beautiful and feminine in layers of white, gauzy fabric with sparkling heels and shining green eyes.

"Hello, lover."

Michael gnashed his teeth. "This time, Lilith, I am going to personally drag your putrid ass to hell and chain you so deep into that pit that you will never again pollute this Earth with your disgusting presence."

"You couldn't do it the last time, Michael, and I'll be damned if you so much as try to do it again." She smiled saccharinely and brushed her hair off her shoulders. "I was supposed to carve off Gabriel's wings. After further consideration, I think Lucifer would prefer to be presented with yours."

The two circled for several long moments, studying one another, waiting for the perfect moment. Finally, with their muscles tense and their eyes fierce, their swords collided with a crash so loud it shook the entire monastery on its foundation.

Griffin jumped when she heard a crack that sounded like lightning striking inside the monastery. She rocked back and forth, her arms wrapped around her middle. Forty-three minutes. She stood, sat back down, huffed out a deep breath, and stood again. She was halfway to the window to peer out and see if she could tell what was going on when she stopped dead in her tracks.

The sound of whistling froze the blood in her veins. Heart pounding in her ears, she dashed to the door, pressed her eye to the peephole, and saw that all four guards were gone. She saw a man—tall, broad-shouldered, and shirtless—meandering down the hall in her direction, his lips pursed in an eerie whistle.

Azazel. She glanced around, desperate for a plan. She knew there was no way she could fight off a Devil, especially that particular one, for—she glanced at the clock—forty-one minutes. Struggling against the urge to scream for help, she grabbed the bag Alaria had left, slung it over one shoulder and snuck into the bathroom, closing the door behind her as silently as possible, and then ducking into the other bedroom that was connected to it.

She crept to the door, which led into a different hallway, and eased it open it as slowly as she could, praying that it didn't squeak. Once it was open, she stuck her head out and looked both ways and saw Azazel disappearing around the corner that would take him directly to her door. It wouldn't be long before he realized she wasn't in there.

Holding her breath, she dashed down the hall in the other direction. As she ran, she looked to her left and saw the vampire, Gage, fighting off a crowd of Familiars, four of which she recognized as the Warriors that had been her guards. He was dispatching of them quickly, using fangs and his bare hands.

The stream of fire caught her off guard and sent her crashing to the ground, her back singed from the flames, her skin burning. A scream forced its way from her throat, and she scrambled backward, kicking her legs and trying to get her feet back under her. Azazel walked toward her slowly, his boots clicking on the stone floor.

Unbidden, she was swarmed with images of the night that he'd raped her. The burning, the pain, and the oppression of the ocean as she'd come back to consciousness; the moment when her lungs had given out and she'd realized that she was going to drown. She looked up at him, her terror plainly evident on her face.

"I thought they'd have you better guarded. Even the most enthusiastic Warrior can be easily controlled if his mind is not as strong as his body. Those four were pathetically easy to dispose of." He tipped his head to the side. "I've thirty-eight minutes to play with you before you have to be killed. Have you any idea how I should spend the time?"

"Go to hell." Griffin spat the words with hatred, her mind racing, trying to form a plan. Her fingers brushed against the bag, and she remembered the Holy Water inside. It wasn't a solution, but it might buy her enough time to run. If she could get to Gage she might stand a chance. He wasn't human, but he was old and strong. He wasn't an Angel, or Alaria, but at the moment, he was her only chance at remaining alive.

"Gladly. Just as soon as you're dead." Azazel reached out, plucked her off the ground, and held her up by her throat. "Beelzebub wants me to just kill you and get it over with." He lowered her slightly so that her toes were on the ground and she could breathe. "I think that's a waste of thirty-seven minutes."

Griffin saw Gage come around the corner and saw him take in the situation. She knew that if she was going to act, it had to be right then. She worked the cap off of the water bottle with her fingers and let it fall to the floor. When Azazel looked down at the slight noise, she brought her arm up and splashed Holy Water in his face.

Skin sizzled and steamed as the blessed liquid hit him. Azazel dropped her, and before she could even get her balance, Gage was between them, his fangs bared, eyes glowing red, one hand stretched out to keep her behind him, and his full attention focused on the Devil. Azazel wiped his eyes and growled.

"Now I'm going to rip your damn head off."

"You're going to have to get through me first." Gage nudged Griffin further behind him until her entire body was hidden behind his.

Azazel assessed the new threat with a casual glance. "A vampire? Don't you think you're fighting on the wrong side, son?"

"I think I know where my loyalties are."

"Lucifer is your father as much as mine. It's demon blood that runs in your veins. Have you really forgotten where it is you came from?"

Gage snarled. "I'll never forget that. As long as I live, I'll try to keep that from happening to anyone else. I've chosen my side. To get to her, you'll have to kill me."

"You're a vampire. You're not a demon, not a Devil, not an Angel. How is it that you think you stand a chance against me?"

Gabriel appeared with a blast of white light, resplendent in white, his wings spread out behind him. "He might not, but I certainly do." He shielded Gage and Griffin from the Devil. "Before this night is over, you will be re-chained to that rock. Heed my words, you will never be free. I will see you rot in that hole."

"Not if I kill you first."

Gabriel spared a glance to Gage. "Get her out of here. Get her somewhere safe and guard her with your life for the next thirty-five human minutes. Do not let her out of your sight, do you understand me?" He didn't wait for an answer before turning his attention back to Azazel. "Let's see how it ends up, shall we?"

Gage grabbed Griffin's hand and dragged her down the hall. She followed as quickly as she could, winding through the hallways and descending a set of stairs to the second floor. The scent of blood was pungent there, seeping up through the ceiling of the first floor as the sounds of the battle raging grew closer. She gasped in relief when he skidded to a stop and doubled over to catch her breath.

"They'll find us. One way or another, I'm going to fight to get through this." Griffin gasped, her arms braced on her knees and her hair hanging into her face.

Gage nodded. "I've realized that myself. The chapel is the safest place, but also the place that we want to go with as little time left as possible. I think our best bet is to keep moving." He studied her face. "If I say run, you run, and you don't stop until you're in that sanctuary. Then you do everything you know how to do to keep them out, and you put yourself in a salt circle. Do you understand?"

"I understand." She managed to straighten. "Should we leave the monastery? I can do this anywhere. It might be safer if we just run for the next half hour."

"There are demons all over the perimeter. We'd never get away unnoticed, and the last place I want to be with you in the last minutes is out in the open. Believe it or not, we're safer in here than out there." He took her arm and walked down the hall at a slower pace. He pressed her against the wall and peered around a corner, ducking back when he saw several demons walking down the hall. "Damn."

"What?"

"Demons, half a dozen. Garden variety, but still a pain in the ass." He went quiet and listened for a moment. "There are Familiars coming up behind us. We have to move, and quickly. Do you have a weapon?"

Griffin removed a gun from the backpack and showed it to him. "Alaria left me this."

"It'll work. Don't be afraid to use it."

Together, they crept down the hall, then ran across it, trying to avoid the demons. They weren't successful, and one saw Griffin duck through a door. The shouts behind them and the sound of many pairs of feet struck fear through both of them. Gage swore and pushed Griffin ahead of him. One glance over his shoulder told him the situation was dire.

"Remember what I told you about running?"

"Yeah, why?"

"Do it! Run!" Gage shoved her hard and sent her flying down the hallway. He stopped, turned, and charged into the mass of demons and Familiars, his fangs fully extended and his roar echoing through the entire floor. Griffin didn't stop to watch the horror she knew would be unfolding.

Instead, she swung down the stairs and ran as fast as she could.

As part of the preparation for the Choosing, Griffin had been forced to spend hours upon hours studying floor plans of the monastery and memorizing different routes. She knew every inch of the cavernous, castle-like building. When she ran, leaving Gage to fight off the Familiars and demons, she knew the only way to get to the sanctuary was to cross the ground level, which would require her to pass through the mass of fighting Warriors and demons.

As she moved through the building, she kept her back toward the wall, gun in her hands, and found herself whispering prayers that she would manage to get there alive. She slipped into the narrow servants' staircase, grateful she was wearing tennis shoes that didn't make noise on the floor. The staircase dumped out into the kitchen, behind the pantry in a crumbling room that was once used for laundry but was now empty. She opened the creaky wooden door just enough to slip into the pantry and spent two minutes cramming the box of salt into her bag. Heart pounding, her lungs burning from a breath she hadn't realized she'd been holding, she left the pantry and dashed across the thankfully empty kitchen.

The kitchen led to a huge dining room and the entry, which was where demons and Warriors still clashed. The scent of blood was thick and sweet, and she saw bodies littering the floor. Ten feet from her, a Hell hound ripped a man apart, his eyes already glassy and dead. Lilith and Michael were engaged in what looked like a vicious sword fight, both of them bleeding. She saw Alaria, clad in her red and black leather, her hair flowing down her back, a whip in one hand, dagger in the other, working her way through a crowd of Familiars. Griffin was preparing to make a run for the Devil when she saw Beelzebub enter the room. From the look on his face, and the purpose with which he strode toward Alaria, she knew she had to wait.

Alaria turned and saw Beelzebub walking toward her. She smiled wickedly and sauntered in his direction, her heels clicking sharply, her whip—with the chain on the end—clinking against the stone floor with each step. She lifted her other hand and studied her fingers, forming a white hot fire ball with nothing more than a thought. Casually, with one flick of her wrist, she sent it at him. Beelzebub dodged, but it struck him in the shoulder, melting his suit and singing the skin beneath. Unconcerned, he brushed a hand over the wound and flicked off the ash.

"Your betrayal has not gone unnoticed, sister."

Alaria shrugged. "Better with them than you. Millions of years of service, and still the outcast? I decided it was time to move on."

"This was your chance to win favor with Lucifer. You've waited for this since the Fall. Just as we're about to get it, you betray us and join ranks with our greatest enemy?" He hissed. "Did you really think He was going to take you back? Give you a shiny new set of wings?"

"Something like that."

"Think He'd be brave enough to send Gabe down to Hell to fish you out of the pit?""

"I don't pretend to know what He would do. It's a moot point since you're not taking me back down there." She bared her teeth in an absolutely horrifying smile. "I've always liked Earth. Now that Michael is about to put Lilith back where she belongs, that frees up some real estate for yours truly."

"I wouldn't hold your breath." Beelzebub struck out with a lightning bolt, knocking Alaria back several steps.

Alaria regained her balance and raised her whip to lash out at him. "Then it's a good thing I don't breathe."

Griffin watched the exchange with bated breath. The Devils clashed violently with whips, swords, fire, and lightning. More than one demon was slaughtered just because they got too close to the fight. After several minutes, the loud crash from Michael opening a hole in the floor distracted Alaria, and she looked over long enough to see the Angel grab Lilith by the throat and carry her into the hole, the stones miraculously coming back together once he was gone. The distraction gave Beelzebub the opening he needed. He swept her feet out from under her and put one foot on her chest. He leaned down, grabbed her by her hair, and wrenched her head back.

"I'm going to make you wish you were dead. You'll never get out of the lake, Alaria. We're going to take turns carving you into pieces, then put you back together and do it again." He gripped the dagger in his hand, prepared to drive it through her chest and kill the body she inhabited to send her essence back to Hell, where she would be trapped.

Before he could plunge the blade into her, Griffin raced out of the kitchen, the consecrated blade clutched in her hand. With a Warrior's cry, she flung herself onto Beelzebub's back and sank the blade to the hilt in his throat. Shock on his face, he threw her off, grabbed the knife, and pulled it out. The moment he saw what she'd used, fear flooded his eyes. The wound glowed, then turned black and spread, slowly encompassing his entire face, traveling down his arms. Light emanated from the knife, and with a deafening explosion, Beelzebub's essence was forced from his body and sucked down into the floor through the spot Michael had taken Lilith.

Griffin didn't even have time to take a breath before Alaria grabbed her and disappeared with a crack. They reappeared in the cellar. Alaria swore for a good thirty seconds before she was able to turn to Griffin. "How much time?"

Griffin looked at her watch and felt her heart clench with fear. "Twelve minutes."

"Good. That's not a lot. Lilith and Beelzebub should be stuck for at least that long. Have you seen Azazel?"

"Gabriel was fighting him."

"Gabe isn't a War Angel. He'll hold him off, but he doesn't stand a chance. Azazel is the most dangerous anyway. We need to get you to the sanctuary. That damn wizard they have is making things exceedingly difficult. He's making it hellacious to try and teleport. Just that one little pop drained me. It doesn't help that this place is crawling with demons and Familiars. I swear they brought a thousand of the damned things." She went silent and listened hard when she heard a noise at the top of the stairs. She ran up the stairs, taking them three at a time. She yanked the door open, grabbed Braxton, and jerked him down the stairs. "How did you know where we were?"

Braxton shook his head and took in Alaria and Griffin. "I didn't. I got away to go get her to take her to the sanctuary, and the door was kicked in. The guards are dead. Gabriel is nowhere to be found, and Gage is half dead from fighting off about fifty demons. We're dying fast. We have to get her there now and protect her the best we can. I'm trying to get everyone to fall back and guard the entrance to the chapel."

"I'll take care of that. You take her and get her to where she needs to be. I'll round up any survivors and meet you there in five minutes."

"There's only nine left, so five had better be enough time."

Alaria looked at Griffin, held out one hand, palm up, and a dagger appeared. "It's not as good, and you still have to bless it, but it'll do the job."

Braxton grabbed Griffin's hand and dragged her up the stairs. "What happened to your knife?"

"I used it to kill Beelzebub."

"I don't even want to know." He propelled her down the hall, into the kitchen, through the pantry, and back into the room she'd snuck into several minutes earlier. He grabbed the handle to an old creaky door and pulled it open, revealing the servants' tunnel that led into the priest's chambers at the sanctuary. They ran through it, racing both the clock and Azazel, who they both knew would not likely allow the Choosing to occur without at least one final appearance.

Braxton shoved through the door into the sanctuary and looked around quickly. Griffin followed him, sticking close, her heart pounding in her throat. As the door swung shut behind them and they stood to the side of the rows of pews, they both froze. Azazel was perched in a pew at the back of the sanctuary, one leg out in the aisle, the other on the pew. When he saw them, he clapped slowly, the sound echoing throughout the church.

"You almost made it. I'm impressed. Six minutes to go, and you're still breathing." He approached them slowly and lifted his eyebrows when Braxton swept Griffin behind him with one arm. "How sweet. It isn't going to make one bit of difference, but it's a nice token. You're a fine Warrior, Braxton, but it's over now. There's no one left. Gabriel's gone, Michael's preoccupied with Lilith, and Alaria is off trying to round up dead Warriors."

Braxton pulled Griffin tight against his back. "Get that knife blessed and get inside a salt circle. I'll hold him off as long as I can. Don't let anything you see or hear stop you, do you understand me?"

Griffin nodded, tears prickling her eyelids. "I understand."

Azazel cocked his head. "Saying your goodbyes? Or a last ditch plan?"

Braxton braced himself and let go of Griffin. "Go!"

As soon as the word left his mouth, Braxton charged the Devil, tackling him around the waist and carrying him to the floor. Griffin didn't wait to see what happened. She raced to the storage room and the vat of water with the rosary on the bottom. She plunged the knife into it, murmuring the prayer under her breath. Hand still dripping, she raced back into the sanctuary, snatched up her bag and dumped it, scrambling to get the box of salt. Just as Azazel sent Braxton soaring through a stained glass window, she got the circle drawn around her. Four minutes.

Braxton wasn't getting up. He moaned once, tried to force himself to his feet, then collapsed to the floor, unconscious, maybe dead. Griffin swallowed the scream of grief, the knife clutched in her wildly shaking hands, eyes glued to the clock. Three minutes. Too long. Azazel would surely be through the circle in less than that. When the door opened and Alaria came in, disheveled and bloody, but on her own two feet, Griffin could have sobbed with relief.

The Devil assessed the situation with cold observation: Braxton bleeding on the floor, Griffin crying in a protective circle, Azazel advancing on her, his intention evident on his face. She used her remaining energy to reappear in front of Griffin, directly between her and Azazel. When Azazel saw her, he swore.

"Don't you ever die?"

"Beelzebub isn't as good as he once was. He'll be a while fishing himself from the bottom of the lake and even longer trying to break the bonds of Hell again. He might even really be dead. That knife is supposed to kill whatever you stab."

Ninety seconds. Griffin couldn't help the scream when Azazel tackled Alaria, desperate to get to her, and they nearly landed on her feet. They would have if the protections hadn't tossed them both back, smashing them against the walls hard enough the cement crumbled and the whole room shifted. Sixty seconds. Her eyes on the clock, Griffin lifted the knife, looked at it, turning it over in her hands, and felt a warm calm wash over her. She let her eyes drift to Braxton and felt a pang at not knowing if he was dead or alive.

"I love you." The words were a whisper as she watched the second hand sweep around the clock. Ten, nine, eight—Azazel ran toward her, a roar rising from his chest—seven, six, five, four—the weakened protections only tossed him back three steps—three, two, one.

Midnight.

Hands shaking, heart racing, Griffin gripped the handle of the knife and looked up at the ceiling, the words filling her head and spilling from her lips. "After thirty years, the slate wiped clean, I stand here today, ready to claim my birthright. I accept my role as a voice for all the people, and I have made my choice. God in Heaven, Lucifer below, hear me! Today, I Choose." She held the knife out, both hands wrapped around the hilt, and with a gulping breath, she plunged it into her chest. Voice strangled, blood soaking her sweater, she finished. "I've paid the price for this privilege with my life, willfully given. As payment for my Choice, I demand the life of Alaria."

Griffin spread her arms and tipped her head back up. The pain faded away and all her senses dulled as cool blackness flowed over her. Slowly, she closed her eyes and let herself be carried away. As the last dredges of life seeped from her, she whispered her final words.

"Heaven take me home."

END

Enjoy this Sneak Preview of *Devil's Despair*,
Available Now!

Prologue

"That was a really scary story."

Amaya sat up in her bed, her curly hair frizzy from being asleep. She turned on the lamp and studied the man in the white suit that stood next to her window.

"Are Mommy and Daddy gone again?"

Gabriel smiled reassuringly. "I don't want you to worry. They're always back when you wake up, aren't they?"

"Most of the time," she agreed readily, tossing back the blankets to join him at the window. "Uncle Gabe, what do they do?"

"They keep people safe. Your parents are good people, and they have very important work that they have to do. Sometimes, that work takes them away from here and from you. When that happens, it's very important that they know you're safe, so they ask me to stay and watch over you." He laid a hand on her head. "One of these days you'll understand."

"I'm nine and five-sixths now, you know. I'm practically a grown up."

Amused, Gabriel chuckled. "Practically isn't actually, muppet. Back into bed now. I don't need your mother mad at me because you've had no sleep for school tomorrow."

"What they don't know won't hurt them."

"Yes, but if you're yawning through your lessons, they'll know, now won't they?"

Knowing when she was beaten, Amaya looked up at him with hopeful eyes. "Will you tell me another story at least? You always tell me a story when you watch me."

"Get into bed." He followed her to the bed and sat next to her, leaning against the wall with his legs stretched out in front of him. "What story would you like?"

"Did Griffin really die? In the last story, at the end, she died."

"Yes, she really died. She did a very important thing, and without her sacrifice, you would never have been born. She was a special woman, and we should always remember what she did."

"What happened after that?"

"A lot happened after that. Is that the story you want?"

"Will you tell me about how my parents got married? I don't even know their names. Just Mom and Dad. They say it's too dangerous."

Gabriel adjusted the blanket so that it covered Amaya's shoulders. "They're wise in that. These times are very uncertain, and your parents play a very important part. You'll know all you need to know when you're old enough to understand."

"Can you at least tell me how they met?"

He chuckled softly. "There is a lot that happened between the Choosing and when your parents were married. Don't you want to know that story first?"

Amaya huffed a sigh and crossed her arms over her chest. "Do I have much of a choice?"

"Not if you want a story."

"Then it'll have to do, won't it?"

Gabriel ruffled her hair. "Remind me again how you humans begin your stories? 'A long time ago, in a galaxy far, far away'—is that right?"

Despite herself, the child giggled. "Once upon a time."

"That's it. Once upon a time, several months before the Choosing, it became clear to Lucifer that he was going to lose. The Chosen was going to Choose Heaven, and the Angels would walk the Earth for a million years. Because Lucifer is not known for playing fair, he decided he needed to have a plan to find another way to get free from Hell. He convened his Devils, and his demons, and they all tried to come up with a way. Finally, Beelzebub figured it out. Do you have any idea what he figured out?"

"What?"

"Well, think about it. What's the one thing God can't interfere with?"

"Free will."

"Right. And who has free will?"

"People." Amaya scrunched her nose, thinking hard. Finally, she jumped in the bed with excitement. "He found a person that could let him out!"

"Very close. Remember, in Genesis, in the beginning, God created the Heavens and the Earth. He didn't create Hell until after the Battle. When He created Hell, He made it below Earth—far, far below so that no human could ever get there without being sent there. Now, I don't want you to think it's somewhere on Earth, or in Earth, because it's much more complex than that, but all you need to know is that to access Hell—to send people there and for demons to have access to Earth—there had to be a door. One door to let souls in after they die, and one door to let demons and Devils out. Lucifer was the only Devil that could never leave Hell. On each of these doors, God placed guards—magic protections that would keep Lucifer from leaving and that would control how many got out. In order to defeat the Choosing, Lucifer would need to find people who would, and who could, break them free."

"Why would anyone want to let him out?"

"Because they didn't know any better. Lucifer is very charming and very persuasive. Most people are easily swayed. Beelzebub spent ten years scouring the globe, finding every worshipper of Lucifer and rallying them. He found witches, warlocks, and creatures of Hell, like werewolves and vampires. Remember what they are?"

"People bitten by Hell hounds who die with the venom in their systems and those who die with demon blood in them."

"Exactly right. He found them all, or at least all of them that wanted Lucifer out, and he gathered them together. The ones that survived the Choosing—that weren't killed when it happened—came together and started working magic—spells, potions, sacrifices, and rituals. Powerful, dark magic that they pulled out of the bowels of Hell and manipulated into what they needed it to be. It took six months, but eventually, they cracked the locks, and demons poured out onto Earth. More than ever had before. Devils, too, and hounds. They broke the rules and found a way around the Choosing. God was enraged. He wanted to start the End of Days immediately. Some of the Angels, those who had been involved with the Choosing, who had seen what Griffin went through, what the cost of her Choice had been, begged God to reconsider and to allow them time to find a way to stop it. He gave them fifty human years."

"That's a long time!"

"Not to God. It's the blink of an eye. Do you know what they did?"

Amaya looked at him through dark eyes too wise for her years. "We both know you've never told me this one before."

Gabriel chuckled. "Very well. They brought together six very special people. Six people from across time, who were the best at what they could do. Together, they would have to close the door, and then they would have to cast the demons back into Hell. To do this, they would have to do several things. First, they would need to seal it shut by spilling upon it the blood of the first vampire, the one who first rose, a hybrid of demon and human. Then, they would need to seal it shut by killing the warlock who opened the Gate in the first place. Last, they would have to destroy the Gate to keep any demons from escaping back to Earth until the thousand millennia won by Heaven in the Choosing had elapsed."

"Who were the six?"

"Two were those who were termed the Lost. They should have fought for the other side, by nature of their very existence."

"Gage and Alaria."

"Very good. Then, there would be two fighters. One a Warrior, the other a Hunter by birthright, born to slay vampires. He would be strong and agile, with a touch of magic, and the ability to sense demon blood."

"Braxton. The Warrior is Braxton, isn't it?"

"Yes. Lastly, there would be two witches. One, a Healer, who could take into herself the pain of another and make them whole again. She would also be a direct descendant of the Chosen. The other was the most powerful witch who had ever lived. They would bring together Time—past, present and future. They would come together into one circle, without beginning and without end."

"How did they destroy the Gate?"

Gabriel smiled. "That's another story for another night. The first part of this story is a while before that. Tonight I'll tell you about how they stopped the purge and kept more demons from coming out of the Gates."

Amaya sighed. "Fine. You never tell me the story I want to hear. What happened after Griffin died?"

Gabriel stroked a hand over her hair. "I thought that was the story I'm getting ready to tell you."

"No, I mean right after. Did Alaria get her wish? Is she human? What happened to Braxton and Gage?"

"Can't you wait for that to be revealed in this story?"

Amaya shook her head so vehemently that her hair smacked her in the face. "No! That's part of the last story. I want you to tell me what happened right after the Choosing before you start something new."

"I think we might have time for that as well."

She grinned and wrapped her arms around his waist. "How does it start?"

"It starts as all good stories start. Once upon a time..."

About the Author

Sirena N. Robinson is an author who lives and works in the foothills of the Appalachian Mountains. When she is not helping her characters defeat unspeakable evil, she spends her days working as a drug and alcohol counselor and as a court-appointed attorney in the local Juvenile Court. A firm believer in wearing many hats, she spends many weekend traveling the country with her husband, daughter and Bengal cats attending cat shows. On off weekends, she can be found with the rest of her family at a hunttest or field trial helping shuttle dogs or holding down the fort at home, caring for the menagerie of dogs and cats living in her house.

Sirena writes in several genres, focusing primarily on novels with paranormal or supernatural elements. She has several other novels in various stages of planning, including a futuristic crime series. She writes both because she loves it and because she has no choice and is a self-proclaimed slave to her characters. She considers herself incredibly lucky to be the one chosen to tell their incredible stories. Keep in touch with Sirena via her blog at sirenanrobinson.blogspot.com or through her publisher Supposed Crimes, at supposedcrimes.com.

www.ingramcontent.com/pod-product-compliance
Lightning Source LLC
Chambersburg PA
CBHW070601170726
48291CB00003B/658